ISBN: 978-2-9596090-7-7
Printed on demand
Dépôt légal : April 2025

In accordance with the French Intellectual Property Code, any reproduction or copying intended for collective use is strictly prohibited. Any full or partial representation or reproduction, by any means whatsoever, without the author's or rightful holders' prior consent, is unlawful and constitutes an infringement under Articles L.335-2 and following of the Intellectual Property Code.

Copyright © 2025 Thierry Joubert

All rights reserved.

# ATHANOR

## "THE LEGEND OF THE THUNDER EAGLE"

Thierry Joubert

# INTRODUCTION

It has been a long time since I last set foot upon the soil of this world… a long time since a single voice rose up to the Land of the Ancestors…

Greetings to you, oh traveler of the spirit. I am Smérix, Celtic shaman of the Arvernian lands, in ancient Gaul. I am the humble teller of forgotten secrets unveiled by this tale—and through me, the author of this book, a modest scribe who may have once heard me, has transcribed this epic so that you might discover it.

The voice echoing within your mind as you read these words… is mine. And who knows? Perhaps through the weaving of our thoughts, these are the whispers of *She Who Has No Name, Who is All and In All…* the one who so loves to murmur the mysteries of life to those who choose to listen.

You who can hear me, try to open your mind, and let me speak to you from the Land of the Ancestors. Let me breathe this extraordinary tale into your heart, word by word…

This story, woven with myth and mystery, unfolded in

the year 652 B.C. At that time, mankind still walked hand in hand with nature, and the gods spoke to us through *Her*. We understood Her, loved Her, respected Her—sometimes even feared Her.

Let me tell you this, dear reader: we, the children of the Earth, have forgotten the songs of the trees and the murmur of rivers. We have severed the sacred threads that once bound us to our world, and to the invisible weave spun by the ancient spirits.

But perhaps, through this journey—one that shines with the virtues of resilience, the quest for meaning, and the power of destiny—you might recover a fragment of that forgotten bond.

Athanor and Anna, the souls at the heart of this tale, embody the depth of a love unwavering, a love that transcends trial and adversity.

Their bond dances upon the edge of the forces of light and shadow, revealing that the battles we wage within ourselves—echoed in us all—are never without purpose.

In truth, this is a journey where courage and will are tested, where each challenge met, each twist of fate endured, draws our heroes closer to the ultimate truth: that all suffering, all paths walked—strewn though they may be with unlikely encounters—hold meaning, hold reason.

So, sit yourself down. Let your imagination drift, and dive deep into this odyssey. Listen well, for the voices of the ancients speak to you through these pages, murmuring secrets of life, of death, and of rebirth.

Happy reading, dear friend—and hold these words close: **"All that is, all that surrounds us, has meaning. It is yours to uncover…"**

Perhaps by the end of this tale, those words will resonate

with you more than you ever thought they could…
That too, is yours to discover.

# CHAPTER 1

## *"The Prelude of Destinies"*

*Year 652 B.C., Arvernian Territory, Gaul.*

It was on one of those days etched forever into a man's memory that I, Smérix, humble Celtic shaman, became witness to the beginning of an extraordinary journey—one as harrowing as it was wondrous.

In those ancient times, we Celts had been rooted in the lands of Arverni for several generations, when fate unveiled itself in the lives of two young souls. It was long ago… so very long ago…

That evening, in the calm waning of the day, twilight approached, and a crimson sky stretched across the mountain peaks that sheltered our village.

High above, where the air grows thin and wild, the wind whispered the secrets of the gods, while the powerful beating of wings echoed overhead.

A majestic eagle soared through the clouds, gliding

slowly toward our valley.

It was a grand spectacle—a dance between the fading light of day and the threatening shadow of night.

To the left, the sun descended slowly toward the horizon, while to the right, a storm front crept forward, heavy and slow, streaked with lightning and grumbling with thunder.

The piercing cry of the raptor rang out as it neared a summit, wings unfurled in their full glory.

How many times had I watched that same sky, that same eagle, messenger of ancient omens?

To those who listen, nature speaks ceaselessly. We need only take the time to hear Her. Perhaps on that day, I should have paid closer heed to Her signs, the signals the gods sometimes grant us.

Atop the peak where the eagle flew, a figure sat perched on a stone ledge, legs crossed, forearms resting on his knees, his gaze lost in the distance.

It was Athanor, a fifteen-year-old Celt, balanced precariously on a rock, his dark wavy hair dancing with the wind.

A small scar ran through his left brow, and his deep blue eyes stared down at the valley with fierce intent.

He wore a cream linen tunic cinched with a leather belt adorned with Celtic patterns. His trousers matched in color, tightened at the ankles by leather straps. His bare feet touched the cold stone, grounding him deeply to the world around him.

Behind him, the golden eagle descended, solemn and proud. With its wings wide, it alighted gently upon a neighboring rock. Athanor turned to the bird, a smile lighting his face, before returning his attention to the oncoming storm.

He was not alone upon the heights that evening. Further down, hidden against the mountain's flank, a man with a commanding figure watched him unseen.

It was Alexix, a warrior in his forties, crouched behind a rock, one hand resting on it.

Bare-chested, his body bore the marks of battle—sinewed and scarred. He wore black linen braies, and his steel-blue eyes studied the boy and the eagle intently, while his wild, blond mane was tossed by the wind.

"Is it him?" came a voice behind him.

The voice belonged to Taranatos, a shorter, stocky man with light chestnut hair.

He approached with surprising agility for his frame. A brown tunic clothed him, and over it, he wore a thick woolen cloak, perfect for the chill of mountain nights. His sharp eyes gleamed with mischief. Without turning, Alexix nodded.

"Yes. That's him."

Taranatos grinned.

"I knew it! My flair never fails me!"

Alexix turned his head slightly, his gaze brimming with disdain.

"Has he ever told you about your smell? Your flair!"

Unfazed, he pushed deeper into the woods, followed closely by a barely offended Taranatos—likely used to such barbs from his companion.

The sharp wit and competitiveness of our warriors—yes, even under threat, humor and rivalry were ever their companions! It was our way, we Celts. Bold in jest, brave in life. Death held no terror for us. Why not laugh in its face?

Upon the summit, Athanor sat still beside the eagle when a shrill cry sliced the air. High above, another eagle circled, spiraling downward before landing softly on a nearby rock.

Now perched on either side of the boy, the two raptors beat their wings and called out with shrill cries. Athanor, clearly familiar with their presence, looked at them, smiling.

Far below, the storm still advanced, thunder growing louder with each passing moment, while opposite, the sun sank slowly beyond the horizon.

After a quiet moment shared with his companions, Athanor slowly reached out his hands toward them, as if to touch them.

He held the pose for several heartbeats—hair whipping in the wind, arms spread wide—then raised them to the heavens as if giving a signal.

The eagles took flight at once, leaving the boy behind. He rose, watching them soar, then began his descent from the mountain.

It was time to return. Day was giving way to night, and the thunder's distant murmurs drew ever closer.

\*\*\*

Later, in the valley, in a broad clearing near the edge of the forest, our village shimmered faintly in the night, lit by campfires and the soft glow escaping from wooden homes.

The valleys of Arverni… What a magical place! For our clan, come from the cold and bitter North, finding this land to settle was a blessing from the gods.

Perhaps they had guided us here without our knowing... No one shall ever say for sure. But in those blessed days—what would later be known as the seventh century before Christ—we lived in that enchanted land where nature flourished in all Her untamed glory.

Our valleys, cradled in the heart of ancient Gaul, were ringed by majestic mountains whose sharp peaks glistened like diamonds in winter's sunlight.

Dense forests teemed with proud stags and cautious wolves. Silvered waterfalls fed shimmering brooks, bringing life to the meadows below.

We Arverni, dwellers of these valleys, lived in harmony with our world. Our villages, built of wood and stone, nestled at the foot of the mountains.

That evening, bursts of laughter and conversation broke the quiet night as some villagers made their way to the local tavern.

Suddenly, a figure slipped between two houses. It was Anna, a fifteen-year-old girl—tall, slender, and feline in her grace.

Her long, wavy blonde hair cascaded over her shoulders. She wore a light white linen dress, drawn at the waist with a simple leather belt.

To ward off the cold, she had wrapped herself in a woolen cloak. Her finely laced leather sandals allowed her to move in silence—perfect for her nocturnal wanderings.

Keeping low, she passed swiftly beneath a window where light and voices escaped. Continuing noiselessly, she headed for the forest and vanished into the shadows.

Anna—beautiful and bold—embodied the free, untamed spirit of our people. Her resolve to follow her heart, even through the darkness of night, was proof enough.

She moved swiftly beneath the trees, pausing now and then to listen to the subtle murmurs of nature. At last, reaching a large boulder, she halted, scanning her surroundings with a sharp gaze. A flash of lightning revealed her almond-shaped sea-green eyes—just as someone leapt before her.

Athanor had sprung from the top of the boulder and, before she could cry out, placed his hand over her mouth.

Recognizing him, she calmed at once. Athanor, smiling, withdrew his hand and kissed her. Overjoyed to see him, Anna returned his smile and threw her arms around him.

"I knew you'd try to sneak up on me again."

"Gets harder every time," Athanor replied with a grin.

She stepped back to get a better look at him—then froze. Her brows drew tight, her face darkened with fear.

"What? What is it?" asked Athanor, puzzled.

Anna had no time to answer. A brutal blow from a club crashed down on Athanor's head. Garedix—a towering, one-eyed warrior—had lunged from the brush.

Twin brother to Alexix, he was broad and powerful, clad in black studded leather armor that covered his chest and shoulders. A matching leather loincloth reinforced with metal bands hung from his waist. His feet were protected by sturdy boots.

A brown leather patch covered the left eye he had lost, lending him a fearsome visage.

Terrified, Anna stepped back as Garedix approached. She had barely moved three paces when Alexix himself emerged and seized her by the arm. She struggled, but his grip was unyielding.

Weary of her thrashing, Alexix grabbed her firmly by the waist and hoisted her over his shoulder. Anna wriggled helplessly, to no avail. Garedix, meanwhile, lifted Athanor's limp body and did the same.

Without a word, the two men slipped away into the night, their shadows melting into the dark folds of the forest.

Thus were the threads of destiny spun—unpredictable and cruel—beneath the watchful eyes of the gods. These young souls, brave and innocent, were now entangled in a fate far greater than they could imagine.

That somber twilight brought more than just nightfall—it heralded trials yet to come, struggles and sacrifices awaiting them. And yet, within that darkness, there burned the flicker of hope, the light of love, the fierce and radiant spirit of youth.

The tale of Athanor and Anna had only just begun—under the silent, benevolent gaze of our Ancestors.

# CHAPTER 2

## *"The Awakening of the Soul"*

Later that night, we stood within a sacred clearing, hidden deep in the heart of the forest. Athanor and Anna stood before me, hand in hand, visibly unsettled by the solemnity of the moment.

I stood still, watching them with gravity. This moment—of the utmost importance to my people—I had awaited for many years, just as those who came before me had awaited theirs. For they, too, had borne the weight of this ancient task.

It was the most sacred of all rites within my calling as shaman—one that ensured peace and harmony for our clan, and prosperity for our beautiful valley. I showed nothing of it, but my heart was taut as a drawn bow. The choice of these two young souls was no trivial matter. It had to be right. The gods had chosen us to carry out their will, and error was not an option.

Without noticing, I nervously stroked my long white beard. Even then, time had marked my face. My wind-blown hair, pale and weathered like myself, cascaded over my shoulders.

My build betrayed a strength uncommon among men of my station. Even the simple, flowing gray tunic I wore did little to conceal it—perhaps due to the wide leather belt that cinched it a touch too tightly. Some said that my piercing gaze, often veiled beneath the shadow of my hood, lent me a mystical presence. In truth, that hood was more to protect me from the elements, and the light that stung my sensitive eyes.

Though my stature was broad and imposing, I strove always to remain humble and reverent toward the spirits and the old ways of my people. Some had long said I was too large and strong, that I did not fit the image of a true shaman.

Foolish prejudice… As if it were appearance that made a man what he is. In my humble opinion, it is our actions—our choices—that define us.

Forgive me, I digress… Let us return to our tale.

Behind me rose two towering menhirs, carved with ancient symbols, marking the entrance to a pathway lined with smaller standing stones, each set with flawless precision. This mystical path led to the sacred mountains, the most revered—and feared—place of our people: the domain of Alisanos, our mighty god of the mountain. The stones, weathered by the ages and etched with ancestral glyphs, looked as though they had stood since time began—placed, perhaps, by the gods themselves. Ferns and sacred plants grew at the base of the menhirs, adding life and green breath to this place of memory and mystery.

Standing guard at the threshold, my most loyal companions—Alexix, Taranatos, and Garedix—remained still as stone, like living statues. Taranatos, armed with a long, gleaming sword and a shield engraved with sacred motifs, stood with unshakable confidence. The twins, each holding a torch whose flames danced in the night, cast a mystical glow upon the scene. Garedix bore a long, sturdy spear, the symbol of his unwavering vigilance, while his brother Alexix, with a quiver full of arrows and a bow slung across his back, was poised to defend our cause with calm precision.

The two adolescents exchanged worried glances, heads bowed. Their hearts beat as one, amplifying the fear they felt before the ritual that awaited them.

"Step apart now, children," I said, breaking the silence. "Enter the small stone circles."

I pointed to two rings of stones, spaced a few paces apart.

"What's going on?" Athanor asked, voice tense. "Are we being sacrificed to the gods? Has Taranis grown angry with us?"

"Did we do something wrong?" Anna added, her voice anxious.

"Come now, little ones—don't speak such foolishness!" I replied kindly. "You've done nothing wrong. Quite the opposite. Now do as I say. Trust me. Go on, step into place!"

Their innocence, their fear—it was touching. They had no idea what they were destined for. Still casting each other uneasy looks, they obeyed at last, moving cautiously into the circles of stone.

Meanwhile, I turned toward my companions and drew a small leather pouch from my robe—filled with a sacred powder, glittering like stardust.

"Take the powder I gave you. Now we'll see if you've chosen wisely. Do as I do, and keep calm. Apply it to your eyelids, and then open your eyes slowly. Understood?"

The three men nodded in silence as I loosened the leather ties on my pouch. Tiny golden sparks spilled into the night air, dancing like fireflies. The warriors, mimicking me, opened their own pouches, though Taranatos made a skeptical grimace.

"Is this really necessary?" he muttered, squinting at the powder. "We're putting this stuff on our eyes?"

"Silence, Taranatos, and do as I say!" I snapped.

Ah, Taranatos—always the skeptic, always defiant…

The twins, for their part, closed their eyes and applied the powder without hesitation—still and obedient. They had always placed their trust in me, the humble voice of the gods' will. The powder crackled faintly, releasing tiny sparks as it touched their lids. Grudgingly, Taranatos followed suit. I did the same.

Meanwhile, Athanor and Anna looked on, confused and increasingly uneasy.

The warriors rubbed their eyelids with grimaces of discomfort as I slowly turned back to the two adolescents. They looked at me with wide, anxious eyes. I couldn't help but smile as I held their gaze, while my companions opened their eyes in turn.

The reactions came swiftly. The twins, stunned by the vision before them, instinctively raised their weapons and stepped back.

"By Taranis! They're demons!" Alexix exclaimed.

Taranatos stood frozen, mouth agape.

"They're burning, Smérix! They're burning!"

"They are not burning," I replied, radiant. "And they are not demons. They are the sacred Chosen Ones!"

These young souls, touched by the light of the gods, were far more than mere children. They were the future guardians of our people. I turned my eyes back to them—and what a sight it was…

They glowed with a soft, colored light: red for the boy, mauve for the girl. That light surrounded them, shielding them from the night that pressed in around us. Of course, they were unaware of it.

"What you see is their aura—the very essence of their life force, their spirit. Watch closely what happens next."

The twins slowly lowered their weapons.

"Step closer now, children. Take each other's hand. Do not be afraid."

"What's happening? What did we do?" cried Athanor.

"Do as I say. There is nothing to fear."

Hesitant, casting uncertain glances, they obeyed. Athanor stepped forward cautiously, his eyes full of worry, dreading what might come. At his side, Anna smiled gently and held out her hand, as if already sensing the wondrous magic about to unfold. As their hands met, and their auras intertwined, an explosion of light surged around them—intensifying, until their joined life forces burst into a towering violet flame that shot into the starry sky.

I stood there, awestruck—blinded by so much beauty. Once more, my companions flinched, stepping back with eyes wide in disbelief.

"You have just witnessed the union of two complementary souls," I proclaimed. "A rare and sacred occurrence! Few on this earth ever achieve such a bond. This—this is divine!"

Fate had bound these two together in a way few could understand. They were meant for greatness.

"Are they gods?" Taranatos asked, still dazed.

"No, they are not gods," I replied, sure and calm.

"You maybe shouldn't have hit the boy quite so hard, Garedix…" he muttered to his companion.

"You really think he would've come along willingly?" grunted Alexix through his teeth.

"True. That boy's a wild one—always up in his mountains," Taranatos added with a nod.

The two adolescents, hands clasped, looked at each other, still not fully understanding. I remained silent, observing them, savoring the moment.

"The love that binds you is deep, children," I said proudly. "Do not ever lose it. Only two souls united by such love can fulfill the sacred mission of the Guardians."

I paused, studying them carefully.

"Yes, you heard me right. You have been chosen to become the Guardians of the Sacred Mountains. The current guardians grow old, and the time is drawing near when they must leave the peaks. Then it shall be your turn to take up the mantle. We shall train you—teach you to move like the eagles that dwell in those divine heights!"

The responsibilities awaiting them were immense, yet their bond, their love, gave them the strength to carry it. I turned and pointed toward the majestic mountains rising above the trees.

"To be worthy of this task, you must show courage,

strength, loyalty, and faithfulness. These virtues will forge you into true Guardians. When your training is complete, you will be the fiercest warriors in all of Gaul! You will master the sword, the bow, and the spear—beyond even your masters standing here!"

The sky grew darker still. A fine rain had begun to fall, and lightning now carved streaks across the clouds. I continued speaking, circling the adolescents, gesturing to the warriors and their weapons.

"Garedix, Taranatos, and Alexix will teach you the art of war and the hunt. They'll show you how to ride better than any man alive. The day you surpass them in every skill, you will be ready. As for me, I will teach you how to strengthen your bond with nature—through medicine, through the stars, through knowledge lost to most of our kind. A shelter has been prepared for you in the forest. Your masters will lead you there."

The training would be harsh, but it was needed. They would learn not only to become warriors, but also protectors of our sacred heritage.

In the storm-churned sky above, the clouds twisted into the rough shape of a man's face—long-haired, bearded. The vision was unclear, but haunting.

"Taranis has chosen you. This is his sign!" I said, pointing skyward. "The peace of our people rests upon you. Nothing must befall the Eagles. The peace of the Sacred Mountains must not—must never—be disturbed!"

At that very moment, a thunderclap shattered the night. Rain began to pour harder, and the wind rose, casting shadows across our faces—mine and those of my companions—darkening us with a grim, ghostly hue. Fear flickered in the eyes of the adolescents, their faces still aglow with the light of their fused aura.

"No one but you must enter those peaks. Never... Now go forth, and let your destiny unfold!"

Those final words rang through the clearing like an echo from the future—a solemn reminder of the weight they now carried.

I turned and walked away, leaving the two young ones standing alone in the sacred glade. Panic overtook them as they watched me depart. The three warriors stepped forward, their faces lit by the flickering torches—shadows distorting their features, making them seem cruel, almost monstrous.

Slowly, they guided the adolescents toward the entrance between the great stones.

And so began the journey of these young souls—destined to become the protectors of our traditions, the guardians of our sacred peace.

A long road lay ahead of them, paved with trials, with ordeals and with danger.

They had no idea what awaited them.

... Neither did I.

# CHAPTER 3

## *"Trials of Body and Spirit"*

A few days later, in a clearing nestled deep within a dense forest, I sat upon a large stone. I was within a sacred circle roughly fifteen meters across, formed of flat stones carefully embedded into the earth. These stones, carved with ancient symbols, radiated a palpable energy, lending the place an atmosphere at once solemn and mystical.

Sunlight filtered through the trees, illuminating the carvings and revealing complex patterns that spoke of nature's forces and the spirits who watched over us.

Before me, Athanor and Anna sat cross-legged on the grass, watching me intently, their eyes alight with curiosity and reverence. I leaned on a staff etched with Celtic designs, lost in thought, feeling the weight of the centuries of wisdom I was about to share.

Ah, these young souls—so eager for knowledge, for illumination. The path toward understanding the world is a harsh one, but it is the only path for those fated to guard our sacred lands.

Athanor and Anna were the very image of hope—the living promise of continuity for our people. I looked upon them thoughtfully, already filled with an affection that would never cease to grow within me.

"To become a true Guardian, you must first come to understand the world around you. What is this world made of? What is your place among the elements that shape it?" I said, my gaze piercing. "The answers lie within you."

I stood, still leaning on my staff, cast a glance around us, then raised my eyes to the sky, where two royal eagles circled in majestic silence. Then I turned back to the adolescents.

"First, you must understand that the universe is but one. A single essence expressed in a thousand forms. But before you reach for that truth, you must begin with your bodies… For the understanding of the world begins with mastery of the self. Our bodies are temples—the vessels of the universal energy!"

As I spoke, visions began to unfold in my mind—images of their future training taking shape like mist on a pond…

\*\*\*

I saw Taranatos standing before the two youths in a wide forest clearing, ready to teach them the rudiments of combat. He leaned on a long sword planted firmly in the earth—a symbol of both his authority and his mastery. The two young ones, each equipped with a small round shield and a finely crafted wooden sword, examined their gear with a mix of awe and amusement.

Athanor swung his blade through the air, flourishing it

before Anna with youthful bravado. Taranatos shook his head disapprovingly, released his sword from the soil, and strode toward them with purpose. With a sharp gesture, he pushed Athanor away from Anna, making it clear that this was no game.

"We're not here to play, Athanor! You'll be parrying Anna's strikes. This is your first lesson! Remember—strength is nothing without skill and precision. Every move you make must have purpose. Only then will it be perfect."

Discipline and endurance—these are the foundations of true strength. Every strike, every block, every fall is a lesson.

He stepped up to Anna, took her wrists gently but firmly, and corrected her grip.

"Like this! Nice and firm—not too tight. You must keep your wrists supple!"

Retrieving his sword, Taranatos positioned himself beside her to demonstrate the proper stance and movements.

"Like this. Keep your footing solid, and strike this way!" he said, cutting through the air with a series of sharp, controlled motions before resuming his stance. Anna and Athanor watched, trying to remain serious as they mimicked him.

"Go on now! Athanor, block her strikes. Watch her movements closely—anticipate them. A fight is as much about defense as offense. You'll switch roles when I say so," he barked.

The two obeyed immediately, beginning their training under the watchful eye of their teacher.

My visions shifted to another day. The two youths were sprinting through the thick woods, with Alexix following close behind on horseback. Sweat beaded on their brows, their breath short, and yet they ran with bows on their backs and a fire in their eyes.

"Move it! You're slower than old men!" bellowed Alexix.

Athanor, exhausted and irritated, shot him a glare.

"We've been running for hours!" he snapped.

"We're almost there. Have some spine," Alexix replied curtly.

They pressed on through the underbrush until they reached a small clearing where several targets had been set up. Alexix brought his horse to a flawless stop and dismounted with ease. The adolescents collapsed to the ground, drained but still determined.

The clearing, bathed in the last golden rays of sun, opened into a wide space where the targets—shaped like human silhouettes—stood waiting to be pierced.

"On your feet! This isn't rest time! Start shooting! Miss a target and we're back to running!" barked Alexix.

Panting, Athanor shook his head, growling in frustration.

"Agh!" he groaned, pulling himself upright with renewed resolve.

He grabbed his bow and nocked an arrow. Anna got to her feet as well, struggling to catch her breath. Calmer now, she tried to breathe slowly while Athanor, jaw clenched, fought to stay composed. Anna picked up her bow, fully focused.

Without waiting, Athanor let his arrow fly—but rushed and off-target, it missed completely. Beside him, Anna drew her bowstring with care, taking her time to steady her breath. Athanor, frustrated, hurled his weapon to the ground.

"No! No! No!" he shouted.

Anna loosed her arrow, following its flight with her eyes. It struck the very edge of the target and wavered—but held. She jumped for joy, raising her bow to the sky while Athanor scowled in disappointment. Alexix smiled.

"I did it! I did it!" Anna cried, euphoric.

"You see, Athanor? Your anger serves no purpose. Just like your strength—if you don't master it, it'll undo you," said Alexix, still smiling.

Ah yes, self-control—that is the greatest of all powers. A calm and focused mind can achieve wonders that brute force alone could never reach.

"Speaking of running… Let's go again, Athanor! Anna, you stay here and keep practicing your aim," Alexix added, laughing heartily as he swung back onto his horse.

Disheartened, Athanor picked up his bow and began running once more.

"Sorry, my love! You should've followed my example!" Anna teased, laughing as Athanor and Alexix disappeared into the trees.

"Come on, boy! Put some fire in your legs! You learn by failing!" Alexix bellowed.

Anna watched them go, a soft sigh escaping her lips as she saw Athanor struggle. Then she turned back to the targets and resumed her training.

Thus passed the days, each bringing new challenges—pushing these young souls beyond their limits, compelling them to uncover their truest potential.

\*\*\*

Back in the sacred clearing with me—Smérix—the two adolescents listened closely, their eyes fixed on me as I rose to my feet and began pacing around them like some old sage whispering the secrets of the universe.

"All that exists—the grass beneath your feet, the tree you touch with your hand," I said, raising my arms to the sky, "the air you breathe, the mountains towering above us, the boundless sky, the wind, the rumbling thunder, and even the bird that soars in silent majesty…"

I paused, leaning toward the youths, gazing deep into their eyes, seeking the hidden truths within their souls.

"All of this is but a fragment of She-Who-Has-No-Name. Every part of the world around you is a piece of the language She uses to speak to us…"

The language of nature is subtle—and immensely complex. Every element, every creature is a letter in this sacred alphabet we must learn to decipher. And they would need to learn it, if they were to overcome what lay ahead.

I straightened up and returned to the stone where I often sat. The children, before me, were brimming with curiosity. They remained silent, attentive, drinking in every word as if they were nourishment. It moved me deeply, though I showed nothing.

"We, too, are part of Her," I continued, gently, with warmth. "Even the gods. But for us to exist as part of that great Whole, we must fulfill the tasks entrusted to us at birth. For we are born incomplete—unshaped—and we must become."

Seated once more, leaning on my staff, I went on:

"These trials we must endure through our destiny—they exist to shape us, to cleanse us of the stains clinging to our human souls, so often muddied with base emotions. In every life we are given, there is a path we must walk. Only by completing it can we be reborn—more pure, more divine, closer to the form we were always meant to reach. And until we purify ourselves—until we face and pass the trials placed on our path by She-Who-Has-No-Name—we are born again, over and over, to try once more."

I paused, glancing toward the two eagles that had just landed on the stones of the sacred circle. I smiled, then resumed.

In that very instant, a barbaric music rose—low drums beating, echoing in our chests. As if conjured by some enchantment, it began slowly, startling the children, who looked to each other in astonishment.

A soft breeze stirred the trees around us, turning the leaves to reveal their pale undersides, as though they too were unveiling their hidden face.

"Close your eyes, children… and place your hands upon the earth."

Enchanted by my voice, captivated by the strange new feeling washing over them, the two obeyed without a word. They had entered into harmony with the moment—with nature, and with the elements themselves. I could feel in them a rare and profound sensitivity—a gift, a deep ability to absorb the essence of all things around them.

"Do you hear it? Can you feel it—the music flowing into you from the spirits of our ancestors? Listen to nature! Feel her lament. Let her whisper to you the secrets of her heart!"

With my staff, I began to strike the ground to the rhythm of the drums, making the beat rise like thunder from the soil. I watched as Athanor's and Anna's chests rose and fell in time, their breathing attuned to the pulse of the forest, eyes closed in deep communion.

"When one has truly fulfilled their path, they may finally become what they were always meant to be. Then—and only then—they may join She-Who-Has-No-Name, who is all and in all."

As I spoke, visions filled my mind once again—of the two youths training with the sword, striking, blocking, falling, rising again and again.

"The strength and beauty of your love is proof that you have completed the cycle of your past lives," I continued, as I saw them practicing the spear with Alexix—flowing through precise movements like a warrior's dance.

The music grew louder, urging me to strike the earth harder with my staff.

"You must now complete the final trial—the one that will bring your cycle to an end, and allow you to become who you truly are! Remember this, children—only one truth remains: She-Who-Has-No-Name can take any form, for She is all things! There is nothing in this world that is not Her...!"

My visions grew more vivid. I saw the adolescents mounted on horseback, bows in hand, trying to strike targets while galloping. My staff, guided by the pounding rhythm, seemed to come alive. It rang, it thundered—faster, stronger, as though the earth itself were speaking through it. My voice trembled with fervor, rising beyond my will, powerful and solemn.

"All that surrounds you, all that lives, all that is… Me, you, and every man—we are nothing. We are Her! Through the tree, the mountain, the bird, the river—She speaks, She sings!"

Still on horseback in my vision, I watched them lance straw effigies, firing arrows in the hunt, creeping toward a stag that eventually bolted into the woods.

"The tears that fall from your eyes, for emotions we cannot always control... The love you feel for one another—this too is Her voice. Her language, spoken through you. My purpose is to teach you to understand this universal language! I will teach you to read a tree, a bird, the sky, the mystery of the stars that guide our steps... and so much more."

The wild music surged, louder and louder, as I beat the rhythm with renewed intensity. In trance, I saw them grow stronger—more agile, more graceful. The same scenes played again and again in my mind, years passing in a heartbeat, all to the rhythm of that sacred music—until they finally surpassed their masters with dazzling brilliance.

And then... silence.

The music stopped—abruptly.

My staff halted, planted firmly in the earth.

We remained still for a long moment, eyes closed, listening.

Listening to the breath of the wind in the trees...

To the heartbeat of nature still pulsing in our chests...

Thus, with every breath, every heartbeat, every moment of learning and becoming, they drew closer to their sacred calling.

The path was long still—but these young souls were ready.

Ready to embrace their destiny, guided by the love and wisdom that bound them.

# CHAPTER 4

## *"The Dawn of Darker Hours"*

*Plains of Scythia—Several Years Later*

The Scythian plains stretched as far as the eye could see—barren, silent, beneath an endless sky. One could almost feel the weight of history and of the ancestors in every breath of wind, carrying faint murmurs and the rare scent of earth and dry vegetation.

Two riders climbed slowly up a low hill, their gazes sweeping the landscape with stern vigilance. The dry, dusty air tickled their nostrils, while the scorching sun made the horizon shimmer like molten silver.

The younger of the two—a Scythian barely twenty— radiated a nervous energy. Of average height but athletic build, he bore the mark of these harsh lands, where winters bit with frost and summers blazed with merciless heat. His short black hair framed a pale face, weathered by sun and wind, with a ruggedness one could almost feel. His sharp green eyes scanned the surroundings ceaselessly, and a tribal tattoo wound around his left forearm—an indelible sign of his belonging.

The tattoos of the Scythians—often depicting beasts or intricate geometric forms—were badges of honor and status, each a tale of valor and loyalty. To those who knew how to read them, they spoke in stories.

He wore a supple leather tunic, reinforced with metal plates that moved fluidly with his body. A finely tooled leather belt held a sharp dagger and a quiver brimming with arrows. His thick woolen trousers were tied at the ankles with leather straps, and his sturdy boots were made for endless rides across this unforgiving land.

His mount, a strong chestnut horse, moved with a natural grace. Its gleaming coat stood out against the dusty plains, and its powerful muscles rippled beneath its skin. The animal's steady breath and the rhythmic beat of its hooves echoed in the hot air, while its brown eyes gleamed with loyalty and wit.

The young warrior advanced with visible unease, while his companion—some twenty years his elder—appeared tense, but composed.

"We've been searching for days. There's no water around here," the younger one muttered, his throat dry, lips cracked from the sun.

"Patience… To find water, one must first seek it. Sometimes it takes a while, sometimes not. It all depends on the gods. It has always been that way."

Taller and broader, the older man's face was marked with battle scars. His black hair was shaved at the sides, the top braided back, revealing a stern brow and sharp black eyes that missed nothing. Every breath of cool air on his skin was a blessing in this sweltering heat.

"Well, I think the gods are enjoying our little scavenger hunt a bit too much lately," grumbled the younger Scythian.

"Water is sacred! Vital! It must be earned, you ungrateful whelp!" snapped the elder, clearly irritated by the younger's complaints.

His voice was hard, resonating through the still air like the echo of their ancestors. He was a proud and courageous man, with a will of iron. His faith in the gods of his people was unshakable. He had to be a man of rank, for he wore thick leather armor adorned with tribal symbols and metal plating, offering maximum protection without hindering movement.

At his waist hung a sharp short sword and a small pouch of provisions. His reinforced leather boots were built to withstand the harshest terrain. His horse, a black stallion just as sturdy, moved with quiet confidence—a perfect match for its rider's resolve.

The steady rhythm of hooves, the low hum of insects, and the soft rustling of leaves from a nearby tree formed the symphony of that heavy day.

Then, suddenly… silence.

The breeze still blew—but it made no sound. The leaves no longer rustled. The insects flew in eerie stillness. Even the horses had fallen silent.

The young warrior glanced at the tree's unmoving leaves, confused. Just as he was about to lift his hands to his ears, his companion came to an abrupt halt and spoke in a deep, grave voice.

"Too quiet. It's as if the gods have abandoned this plain. Perhaps we've strayed too far from our lands."

At these words, the younger man flinched—then, pulling himself together, nodded stiffly. His forced scowl failed to hide the apprehension flickering in his eyes. He glanced about, beads of sweat forming on his brow, sending chills through the stifling heat.

The elder gave him a long, solemn look, then suddenly burst into a grin and clapped him hard on the back.

"I like it! Maybe the gods have a surprise waiting just beyond that hill! Come on, then!" he bellowed with a grin.

His voice rang out in the stillness—a bold echo, full of fire. Nudging his mount, he resumed the climb.

After a brief hesitation, the younger warrior followed.

At the hill's crest, the two men halted, gazing out over the vast steppe spreading endlessly before them. The horizon was undisturbed—except for a dark patch of earth, down in the flat plain, surrounded by the same arid hills from which they had come.

"There! Looks like a lake—come on, let's go!" cried the older warrior.

They galloped down the slope at full speed, the strange silence still reigning around them. Their mounts thundered across the flat terrain that stretched before them. The wind howled in their ears, and the rhythmic pounding of hooves echoed through the dry, hard earth. It was a strange sight indeed—two riders racing through the steppes, raising clouds of dust behind them, wrapped in relentless silence. Several kilometers still separated them from the dark patch ahead…

\*\*\*

Elsewhere in the region, in a dried-out canyon, a

towering figure trudged forward, dragging a massive sack filled with tools behind him. Shovels, picks, hammers, sledgehammers, chisels, and other instruments clinked and clanged against the uneven ground with every jolt.

The man was a force of nature. Bare-chested and barefoot, wearing only short linen trousers, his skin was a peculiar gray—cracked and dry, like the earth beneath his feet. His long, salt-and-pepper mane hung halfway down his muscular back.

His face was hidden from view, but his breathing— deep, raspy, almost a growl—filled the canyon. He hauled his load forward, his scarred body slick with sweat. The air reeked of earth and toil, a mix of dust and sweat heavy in the stillness.

The giant approached a crevice in the rock wall. Narrow, but just wide enough for him to squeeze through—though his enormous sack would not pass easily. Bending low, he heaved it up and forced it through the opening, shoving and compressing until it slid into the wider cavern beyond. With a grunt, he stretched his massive torso and slipped through into the depths of the stone.

Inside, he pulled the sack forward and approached a torch planted in the ground. Dropping his burden, he struck two pieces of flint and lit the torch. The sudden light crackled and filled the cave with a wavering glow.

The chamber was much larger than one might guess from outside. Crushed rock littered the ground. Jagged stalactites hung from the ceiling, casting long, toothlike shadows in the flickering light, as if ready to devour any intruder. The sharp scent of freshly broken stone mingled with the screeches of bats disturbed by the firelight. They fluttered in a frenzy above him, but the giant paid them no mind. He had work to do—and little concern for chaos.

Strangely, no matter how vivid my vision, his face remained hidden, as though he willed it so. The cavern didn't end there. Another crack, deeper and darker, stretched further into the bowels of the earth—a narrow path that led somewhere… far below. Ominous. Ancient. Bottomless.

\*\*\*

Back on the plain, the two Scythian riders neared the dark shape they had spotted from the hilltop. Near it stood a majestic oak—completely isolated in the middle of the desert, like a sentinel guarding some secret at its feet.

"Look at that—an old oak! That's a good sign!" the elder exclaimed.

As they drew closer, the truth became clear—it was not a lake, but the yawning mouth of a massive cave plunging deep underground.

The riders slowed, approaching the ominous void at a cautious pace, disappointment etched on their faces. The silence weighed heavily now, laden with some unspoken omen. Around them, swarms of insects filled the air—flying noiselessly before suddenly dropping, struck dead in mid-flight.

Then they saw it.

The blackness at their feet wasn't just the cave—it was a carpet of dead insects, thick and still, creating a morbid tapestry beneath their horses' hooves.

"Cursed gods! They're mocking us! I'm out! I don't like

this—not one bit!" the younger warrior cried, panic creeping into his voice.

"It's just a few dead bugs. That doesn't scare me," his companion replied with a grin. "There might be water down there—look at the size of that oak!"

Ah, that strange courage—so close to recklessness. But is that not the very essence of bravery? To face the unknown with an unshaken heart?

He nudged his mount forward toward the cave's entrance. But to his surprise, the sound of galloping hooves began to echo from deep within the vast opening. Hooves—distant but approaching—resounding louder with every beat, breaking the quiet air with rising dread.

***

In the canyon, the enormous man now wielded a giant hammer. With brute force, he began striking a massive rock dislodged from the cliff.

BAM! The impact echoed like thunder, the cave vibrating beneath the blow.

BAM! He struck again, rhythmically—powerful, resonant. The sound traveled down the cavern and into the deep abyss below.

BAM! BAM! BAM!

On the plain, bizarrely, the hammer's rhythmic blows seemed to fuse with the infernal clatter rising from the cave—hooves, groans, and a deep rumble shaking the earth.

BAM! BAM! BAM!

***

The Scythians' horses reared, agitated and spooked. The elder's steed lost control—kicking wildly—until a violent buck threw him to the ground. His horse bolted into the desert, terrified. The younger rider, panic overtaking him, backed his horse away from the gaping maw.

"They're demons! Death is coming! They're demons!" he screamed in terror.

Another resounding BAM cracked the air. The fallen warrior struggled to rise, his companion watching, trembling, as the cavern exploded with sound—hoofbeats, monstrous howls, and the relentless hammering of the colossus deep below.

"We have to run! We can't fight death!" the younger man shouted, turning to flee.

The older warrior's bold pride had vanished—replaced now by fear.

Bam! Bam! Bam! The rhythm of the blows grew faster. Shrill cries and pounding hooves thundered louder and louder.

Suddenly, a whirlwind burst from the cave's mouth, hurling insect corpses into the warrior, who drew his sword and tried to keep his footing. He spat out dead bugs in disgust and turned toward his fleeing companion.

Bam! Bam! Bam! Bam!

"Come back! Where are you going? Get back here, you coward!"

The shrieking howls, now deafening, mixed with the rising cacophony of a horde in motion—hoofbeats, boots, and the pounding of the colossus's hammer. At that same moment, a black cloud—dense, opaque, alive—began to swell and surround the warrior, who leaned back against the wind, struggling.

Darkness closed in. The swirling mass, the galloping, the screams—all engulfed him.

And then—suddenly—the pounding hooves and stomping boots stopped. A tense, breathless silence fell.

Now came the heavy breaths. The beat of wings.

\*\*\*

Back in the canyon's depths, the colossus struck one final blow—an earth-shattering BAM!—shattering the great stone beneath his hammer. Dust exploded into the cave, and the world went silent. The contrast with the chaos just moments before was staggering—thick, stifling silence.

\*\*\*

At the mouth of the underground cave, the wind died as suddenly as it had begun. Caught off guard, the Scythian warrior stumbled and fell to the ground, completely disoriented—lost in absolute darkness.

The cries, the noise, the terror had already been overwhelming. But now—for him—the silence was far more terrifying.

He gasped, trying to rise. His eyes, wide with dread, stared into the black void. He sensed the worst. Trembling, he turned to face the depths where deep, ragged breaths and the rustle of wings whispered in the dark.

He knew.

The end was near.

Frozen in fear, he let out a scream—a desperate, rage-filled cry—just as shrill screeches and guttural snarls erupted from the shadows, rushing toward him at full speed.

Far off, the young warrior who had fled jerked his reins and stopped, hearing the dreadful cry of his companion echo behind him. And then—he saw it.

A monstrous, living black mass emerged from the Earth's bowels—surging out of the cave, swallowing all light in its path. Only the solitary oak still stood, untouched, defiant.

"It's… it's… demons… the demons are coming…" he stammered, paralyzed with terror.

Sweat poured from his brow, his limbs shaking uncontrollably. Without hesitation, he kicked his horse into a frenzied gallop.

He rode without pause—driven by pure panic—fleeing the horror, as though distance alone could wipe away what he had witnessed.

Eventually, he reached the top of a distant hill—and at last, he saw them: a nomadic Scythian tribe, slowly moving through the arid steppe.

His people. His clan, perhaps.

Exhausted, his horse soaked with sweat, he charged down the slope, shouting with all his might.

"Demons! The demons are coming!"

What truly happened in those arid plains of Scythia?

Who was that strange colossus?

What was that black thing that emerged from the Earth's depths—and more importantly… what else might come from below?

At the time, I knew none of this.

I was far, far from imagining what was about to

unfold…

And so ended these events—omens of greater dangers still to come.

A reminder, too, that even the bravest can be swept away by the mysterious forces of the unknown.

The gods watch. The spirits whisper. And life, with its shadows and its light, continues to weave the threads of destiny.

# CHAPTER 5

## *"The Call of the Sacred Mountains"*

*Valley of the Arverni — A Few Weeks Later*

That day, under a sky of purest blue, a royal eagle soared majestically above the valley of our village. Its wings stretched wide, casting a commanding silhouette as it circled through the heavens. Beneath it lay our mountainous and wooded homeland, where a silvery river meandered gently down into the plain.

What a divine sight! It was as though Nature herself were painting a scene of peace and majesty.

After a moment, the eagle dove in a breathtaking descent, streaking toward the river with awe-inspiring precision, its talons poised to seize prey unseen to human eyes.

It was a true aerial ballet—a dance of instinct and grace, where each creature played its part in the harmony of the natural order. Just before reaching the water, the bird pulled up sharply and skimmed its surface, then soared toward the far bank. With the river behind it, it crossed a flowering field, where the grass rippled in the breeze and the bright blossoms offered bursts of color to the eagle's majestic flight.

Now it rose again, climbing toward a forest, gliding just above the treetops. The rustling of the leaves beneath its wings became a melody in the morning air. Ahead, a small clearing opened, and with its piercing gaze, the eagle spotted a target. Instantly, it dove again—this time toward a frightened rabbit darting for the woods. Just as it reached for the prey, the rabbit vanished into a thicket.

Empty-taloned, the eagle skimmed the bushes… and just beyond them, a narrow path appeared, upon which a dog was running.

Her mid-length coat shone black and glossy, her eyes a bright, expressive brown gleaming with curiosity. Her bushy tail wagged cheerfully behind her. The dog bounded through the fields and forests, her paws light as wind.

She climbed a bare hillside with easy energy, her medium frame and lively pace betraying a boundless vitality—and a loyalty unshakable to those she loved. Reaching the summit, she stopped to gaze down at our village, nestled beneath a majestic chain of mountains.

Our community, encircled by wooden palisades to ward off intruders, stretched across several hundred meters and was dotted with great trees offering welcome shade.

The houses, built in rounded or oval shapes, were constructed with wattle walls coated in daub, and their thatched roofs released gentle streams of white smoke into the sky. Sometimes, human skulls—remnants of defeated foes—adorned doorways as symbols of protection and formidable strength. Battle trophies, such as gem-inlaid shields or war tunics embroidered with heroic motifs, decorated other entrances, reminders of our warriors' glorious feats.

Around the homes, well-tended gardens bloomed with vegetables and medicinal herbs. We used ancient techniques to cultivate our lands and raise our animals, creating a balanced, prosperous ecosystem. This harmony was our strength—our way of giving thanks to the Earth for her generous gifts.

A main road, paved with carefully placed stones, ran through the village, leading to a wide central square, a place for gatherings and the village market.

At its heart stood a towering sacrificial pyre, carved in the shape of a giant wooden man, arms raised toward the heavens. The willing slaves—those who offered themselves to appease the gods—were placed within that wooden figure before the fire was lit.

The pyre was surrounded by rune-engraved stones and offerings—fruits, flowers, and jewels—lending the place an air both sacred and terrifying.

These sacrifices, grim though they were, were our way of speaking to the gods—of proving our devotion and reverence.

Let me reassure you, such acts were rare. Most of the time, only animals were offered… and even that, to us, was painful. For we believed that all life held equal value, no matter its form.

We, the elders of the village, always deliberated long and carefully before deciding upon such an act.

A sacrifice to the gods could never be taken lightly. It

had to be for a just cause, of the highest importance to our people's peace.

One does not beg the gods for every whim…

My lovely dog—yes, she's mine—trotted on through the path leading to the central square. The earth beneath her paws was dark and muddy, worn down by the constant passage of villagers. Smoke curled from the rooftops, signs of the life within—where women cooked, and artisans forged tools and weapons.

She bounded down the slope, entering the main path where a few villagers went about their daily tasks.

The men, tall and muscular, carried freshly cut wood, tended horses, hammered iron in glowing forges, worked the fertile fields, or repaired wagons for future expeditions.

Clad in tunics that reached their knees and tight-fitting trousers, many wore long or short swords at their belts—ever ready to defend their home. Their hair, long and blond—rarely dark—gave them a proud, commanding presence. Their strength and resolve were the backbone of our community. Their bravery… an example to all.

On their side, the Celtic women—beautiful and fierce—were busy tanning hides, sewing garments, or grinding grain, often surrounded by children playing joyfully nearby. They wore long tunics adorned with intricate embroidery and were generously bedecked with jewelry—bronze, bone, and sometimes amber.

The children, dressed much like their parents, often carried miniature wooden weapons and engaged in mock battles, learning the warrior's path from their earliest years.

Life in the village, shaped by daily labor and sacred ritual, reflected the harmony and resilience of our people.

This united, self-sufficient community—deeply

connected to its traditions and beliefs—embodied the resilient spirit and ancestral craft of the Celts.

We were a proud people, rooted in our past and steadfast in our identity. Each day was a celebration of our survival… and of our culture.

At last, my lovely girl burst into the village square and ran toward the three inseparables—Taranatos and the twins—who were walking and talking some fifty paces ahead.

Those three—I can still see them as boys, squabbling, running, sparring with wooden swords and makeshift shields. Even then, they were bound by a tie they themselves still do not understand.

Alexix had always been the anchor of their trio. Even as a child, he was the leader—the most composed, the one who made decisions.

Taranatos and Garedix were more like mischievous daredevils, constantly challenging one another, plunging into the most absurd adventures.

One such adventure, I remember, would have grave consequences for their friendship… but that tale, I'll save for another time.

Now then—where were we? Ah yes… our three friends were crossing the village square.

"So, your son wants to become a shaman?" Alexix asked in surprise.

Taranatos, visibly displeased, nodded as he walked, hands clasped behind his back.

"Yes! To me, of all people! The mightiest warrior in the whole village! Why can't he be more like me? A great warrior!"

"You? The mightiest warrior?" Alexix snorted. "More like the loudest braggart!"

"I'm still stronger and braver than you! And tall weeds like you—I chop them down with my sword in no time!"

"Oh really? I'd love to see you try! Right now, by all the gods! Go on then—draw your blade and chop me down!" Alexix barked, suddenly stopping to face him.

The two men glared at each other, faces twisted in mock fury.

Garedix, shaking his head with a grin, was clearly unfazed. He was used to their bickering—it was practically a ritual.

Around them, villagers passed by, smiling knowingly. They too were used to these two clowns. Such was village life—rivalries and camaraderie, each encounter a play in itself.

At that moment, my dog, running full speed, veered sharply and darted between the two men. She crossed paths with a poorly dressed, grimy man carrying a load of wood.

Startled, the man stumbled, staggered, then caught himself—muttering curses at the dog now prancing away.

Not watching where he was going, the man slammed straight into Taranatos, knocking him flat into the mud.

Laughter erupted. Alexix burst out laughing as he saw poor Taranatos, muddy and livid, rise slowly to his feet. His eyes burned with rage.

Still bent over, he gripped the hilt of his sword… and in a flash, lunged at the man, blade drawn to take his head.

Garedix reacted just in time, blocking the blow.

A hush fell over the square as the two men locked eyes. Taranatos was panting, humiliated fury clouding his mind.

Garedix shook his head slowly, staring at him with calm

but firm insistence.

No one laughed anymore. The silence grew heavy.

"Go on, slave," Alexix said coldly, turning to the panicked man. "Pick up your wood and move along."

The man didn't wait to be told twice. He gathered his bundle and hurried off.

Taranatos loved his friend, and he knew—deep down—that his reaction had been excessive.

The man hadn't deserved death. There was no honor in such a kill.

So he calmed himself and, not wishing to lose more face, sheathed his sword without a word and walked away, his stride stiff with wounded pride.

Alexix turned to the onlookers, who had clearly hoped for more of a show.

"That fool?" he said, pointing after the retreating man. "He's not even worthy of being sacrificed to the gods! And now we all know it! His death would serve no purpose!

Now get moving! The show's over!"

Ah yes... that's how we Celts were.

Joyful, brave, proud, loyal—always ready with a jest—but when our pride or honor was wounded, we could turn very violent.

After all, we Celts believed in the land of the Ancestors, and in rebirth. So death... wasn't really such a terrible thing.

Taranatos must've thought that if he'd sliced off that man's head, the poor wretch would've been more careful in his next life...

Meanwhile, my good little dog, blissfully unaware of the near-catastrophe she'd caused, had reached the entrance of my modest hut, where her well-earned bowl of water awaited her.

While she drank eagerly, the door opened and I stepped outside, my gaze fixed on the horizon—watching the protective mountains that ringed our sacred valley.

The years had etched deep lines into my face, silvered my hair further still… yet my mind remained sharp, ever seeking wisdom and knowledge with which to guide my people.

My dog stopped lapping and turned her head—drawing my attention to the path beyond the village.

A figure had just emerged from the bend in the trail, robed in grey… like me.

I frowned as I noticed two mounted warriors riding out of the woods behind the man. They trotted beside him for a moment, exchanged words, then spurred their horses forward and galloped toward me.

Bare-chested, their skin marked with tattoos, the warriors halted before me. With fluid grace, they dismounted and dropped to one knee in reverence.

At my signal, the one on the right raised his head. In his eyes—I saw it: determination… and loyalty.

"Is my vision failing me," I asked, narrowing my eyes, "or have I never seen this shaman before? Tell me—what is his name?"

"He says his name is Divinix, and that he comes from Greece. He made the journey just to meet you, Shaman."

"Greece? Well, well… Very well then. I'll wait for him inside. Bring him in when he arrives."

I cast a glance at Divinix, who stood waiting a short distance away, then returned to my hut.

Inside, the large round room welcomed me with

familiar warmth. I sat by the fire at the center of the space, contemplating the shelves lined with clay pots, bowls, cauldrons, and all manner of tools. Light streamed in through three small windows, and a doorway opened onto another chamber.

Then the entrance creaked open, and Divinix stepped inside, pausing on the threshold.

We inclined our heads in greeting.

"Be welcome, dear brother," I said warmly.

"Thank you. May I enter?"

"Of course! Come, come, sit beside me," I said, gesturing to a seat near mine.

"It is a great pleasure to meet the famed shaman who once set out to discover the secrets of Greek wisdom."

"You flatter me, Divinix," I chuckled. "I'm but a humble shaman with a curious mind."

He sat beside me, and I offered him a smile.

"Well then, pour the honey of your knowledge into these old ears of mine. What did you learn from the Greeks? What news do you bring? The Greeks! A fascinating people, so they say. Their culture is well advanced, is it not?"

"Yes, I must say, their knowledge in many domains is astounding. They are great builders—they craft homes and monuments by shaping stone. And their sense of trade... impressive! Like us, they study the stars. But unlike us, they preserve their knowledge, either painted on pottery or— more remarkably—through writing. That way, nothing is forgotten."

"Writing?" I asked, intrigued.

"It's a system of symbols and engravings that represent

words. They carve them onto flat stones. These form what they call texts. It's speech… captured in stone."

I scratched my beard, perplexed. Rising to my feet, I began pacing the room.

"Hmm… I have heard of such things. But to preserve all one's knowledge on stone—that seems like an invitation for strangers to steal it. Too dangerous, in my opinion. I am entirely against it!"

"Perhaps, for them, it is a way of leaving a mark on history."

"Or perhaps… they fear fading from memory," I replied grimly. "But we are Celts. Our people are strong. Our bond with nature and the Ancestors is strong. We will survive through time and age!"

Divinix nodded in silence.

Yes… back in those days, it was so. We passed on our knowledge only by word of mouth, and that made learning long and sacred.

Looking back now, I wonder…

Might it not have been wiser to share more freely what we knew, rather than guard it so jealously? Even now, as I pass on this tale through the hand of a scribe… Perhaps our ancient wisdom—our understanding of nature and its bonds—would be better preserved if we had dared speak louder…

"But tell me," I said at last, "to what do I owe the honor of your visit?"

He hesitated.

"Well… It concerns the Sacred Mountains, Smérix…"

I froze. My expression betrayed my alarm.

"Speak! What do you mean?"

Divinix searched for the right words.

"Well… it seems the guardians may be in grave danger."

"What? That is impossible!" I exclaimed.

"I'm not sure how to tell you this, but… it seems that strangers are on their way—intent on capturing a creature that dwells in the Sacred Mountains.

You, better than anyone, know the consequences such a sacrilege could bring…"

Agitated, I resumed my pacing.

"That would be more than grave! The gods would never forgive us! Their wrath would fall upon our people! We would be wiped from the earth!"

"I came as fast as I could to warn you," added Divinix, earnestly.

I stopped in my tracks, troubled.

"But why? Why would these strangers want to capture such a creature? For what purpose? It makes no sense! Who told you of this threat?"

"I can't explain now. It's far too long a story. But trust me—we must act quickly. Time is short. The strangers… are already on their way."

With firm resolve, I strode toward the door.

"Then I hope I am wrong to trust you! That this is nothing but tale and shadow!

But I cannot risk it. Let's warn the chieftain—at once!"

Divinix rose and followed me. I flung open the door and stepped outside.

A few minutes later, in the village square, nearly every able man stood ready, well-armed and holding torches, awaiting our word to depart.

At their head stood Chief Aridix—a robust figure with long, flame-red hair, carefully braided to fall across his shoulders, enhancing his already imposing presence.

His face, weathered by time and war, bore a deep scar that cut across his left eye—a living testament to his experience and valor.

By great fortune, his eye had been spared the day he had rushed to save Garedix from disaster.

A grim day, that one—a turning point in Athanor's fate.

You see, it was during a retaliatory raid, triggered by one of Garedix and Taranatos's reckless misadventures, that Athanor's father fell in battle.

Athanor was left an orphan that day—a mere babe. His mother had died giving him life.

Forgive me. So many memories rise like mist from the earth, and sometimes I wander in them.

Now is not the time for such tales… We'll return to it later.

As I was saying, Aridix—our chief—commanded respect by his very presence. He embodied the authority and strength of our people.

He held the reins of his nervous mount—a black stallion with sharp, gleaming eyes—firmly in his grasp, ready to ride toward the Sacred Mountains.

Behind him stood Taranatos, Alexix, and his twin, Garedix, all prepared and armed. The villagers, worried, watched in silence.

Once mounted, I approached Divinix and turned to the chief, who seemed hesitant.

"Night will fall soon, Aridix," I said. "We must go!"

"Are you certain, Smérix?" he asked. "To set foot in those mountains… it's sacrilege. And…"

"No, Aridix," I interrupted sharply. "I am certain of nothing.

But if what my brother here says is true… doing nothing would be far worse."

Doubt gripped me as well. Never had we broken that law. Never.

I turned my gaze to Divinix, hoping to find answers in his eyes—some sign, some divine confirmation to calm my spirit.

But he merely nodded solemnly, which only deepened my unease.

Yet what choice did we have?

Reluctantly, I followed my instinct. I spurred my mount forward, toward the village gate. My people trusted me—and without hesitation, they followed. Aridix took the lead.

As we plunged into the forest, the flickering torches cast pale light on the path, their glow dancing on the trunks and branches around us.

The sound of hooves echoed through the trees, mingled with the murmur of wind and the crackling of twigs underfoot.

The air was thick with tension.

Every man knew: this night could decide the fate of our village.

The heavy silence was broken only by the distant cries of nocturnal beasts and the soft whispers of warriors trading words of comfort or strategy.

And so, guided by the wavering light of fire, we rode into the unknown—ready to face whatever might rise against us, for the sake of our sacred lands and our sacred guardians.

The gods were watching.

And with every heartbeat, the voices of our ancestors

echoed within us, reminding us that our struggle was righteous… and noble.

# CHAPTER 6
*"The Assault of Shadows"*

Meanwhile, atop the Sacred Mountains, seated upon a rock that overlooked the valley of our village, Athanor and Anna—sacred guardians for ten years now—were watching the last golden gleams of the sun.

The wind brushed gently against their faces, while the shadows stretched slowly across the landscape, cloaking it in a tender twilight.

Above them, a royal eagle traced wide, majestic circles through the air. The sun's dying rays painted the sky in hues of gold and purple, a breathtaking canvas crafted by the hand of nature itself.

Athanor, now a man in the prime of his strength, stood proudly on the ridge. His long black hair was gathered at the sides into small braids, adorned with wooden beads and feathers—signs of his reverence for the Celtic ways. His sharp gaze, filled with wisdom, reflected the depth of his experience.

He wore a cream-colored linen tunic edged with Celtic motifs, leaving his muscular, tattooed arms exposed. A finely wrought dagger hung from his belt, and his braccae, of matching fabric, were tied at the calves with leather thongs, allowing him to move with ease. A dark cloak rested on his shoulders, fastened with a silver brooch shaped like a royal eagle.

Anna, beside him, wore a long linen dress woven with golden threads. Her blonde hair was braided with mountain flowers, a graceful touch to her serene figure. A silver torque encircled her neck, and bronze bracelets adorned her wrists. Her soft yet resolute eyes were fixed on the royal eagle, as if drawing strength and serenity from its majestic presence.

Their very presence here, in this sanctuary of the gods, was a living testament to the harmony between humankind and the natural world.

The eagle—faithful companion of the guardians—was circling ever closer. Neither Athanor nor Anna was surprised by its arrival. Their hands often met, a simple gesture that spoke of the unbreakable bond between them.

Together, they formed a perfect union, radiating a quiet wisdom and protective strength. Their love, palpable and strong, was a blessing to all who knew them.

"Do you think he'll make it?" Athanor asked, his brow furrowed in concern.

"He didn't look well."

"I don't know," Anna replied, her voice gentle, thoughtful. "When I left him, he was sleeping. Maybe he was just exhausted."

Athanor studied her face, then turned his eyes to the

eagle, which had now landed not far from them. The bird seemed agitated—its restless movements betraying a rare unease that piqued Athanor's curiosity.

"My friend seems troubled today," he said with a smile. "Maybe he's jealous."

"What I don't understand," he continued, "is why your mysterious bird came to our door in the first place?"

"You know the gods have their secrets. They must have their reasons." Anna hesitated, her voice dreamy. "What strikes me most is… his beauty. He's so stunning. Almost magical… unreal… He…"

She sighed, unable to find words that could truly express what she felt. Her eyes shimmered with emotion.

Athanor watched the eagle shifting on its perch, then lifting once more into flight.

"You see?" he said, looking at her with a teasing glint. "He's upset. You're a little too fascinated by our visitor. And to finish your sentence—he's beautiful, that's all!"

He grinned.

Anna turned to him with a smile of her own.

"Exactly. Now come on, let's go home. I'm starting to worry about him."

She rose and began walking toward a small hut visible further down the mountain's slope. The sun dipped behind the distant peaks, and the sky darkened rapidly.

Athanor stood and watched her for a moment. He noticed the leather strap holding her cloak in place across her back and smiled.

Quickening his pace, he reached out and tugged at it.

Anna, hearing his change of step, smiled as well.

With a swift motion, Athanor pulled at the strap,

causing her cloak to slip from her shoulders. She caught it before it could fall entirely, then turned with playful mischief in her eyes.

Around them, the night was drawing close.

"That cloak wraps you up like a cocoon," he murmured, his voice low. "Such a shame to hide a goddess's body beneath it. So many things my lips could whisper to it… if only it weren't hidden away."

Anna, slightly flushed, backed away as her lover stepped toward her. Just before he could catch her, she slipped aside and ran off laughing. Athanor, caught in his momentum, stumbled and fell heavily to the ground.

He scrambled up at once and gave chase.

"You have a task to complete first," she called, still laughing. "Maybe after that, I'll let you have your little conversation with my body!"

"Anna! Wait!" he shouted, still smiling.

Athanor slowed and began to walk again.

"All right, I get it. I'm the one gathering firewood."

He muttered as he went, picking up branches along the path.

They really are something, those two.

Their love is as strong as these sacred mountains.

They are an example for us all—a living reminder of the sacred values we hold dear.

Ah, if only all couples could live with such harmony… such mutual respect.

\*\*\*

At that very moment, my companions and I were making our way up the path to the Sacred Mountains, steep and treacherous beneath our horses' hooves.

Aridix rode beside me, followed closely by the warriors of the village. We urged our mounts forward, climbing with urgency.

We were breaking the law. None of us were permitted to enter this hallowed ground.

But the threat was too grave. If Divinix's words proved true, then the guardians—and our entire people—faced a peril far more dire than the mere profanation of a divine place.

Gradually, daylight faded, giving way to almost total darkness. I could feel my pulse pounding in my temples.

Stress and doubt consumed me.

Had I done enough as their mentor? Had they recognized the signs of approaching danger? Were they ready?

Had we prepared them well enough?

These questions haunted my spirit as we galloped onward.

Time was slipping through our fingers, and the path ahead was still long.

Two good hours of steep terrain and unknown obstacles separated us from the moment of truth.

It was unbearable.

What were we about to discover?

My whole body shivered at the thought.

\*\*\*

Further up the mountain, as the night swallowed the trail Anna walked, she spotted the soft, flickering glow of her hut.

The modest dwelling, built of wood and daub, clung to the hillside like a nest of warmth against the cold stone. A thick thatched roof shielded it from the mountain winds.

The walls, reinforced with stone, bore Celtic carvings etched with care—testaments to the lineage of those who dwelled within.

A thin plume of smoke rose from the stone chimney. Furs hung by the door, lending the home a rustic charm and comforting presence.

She had only a few hundred paces left before reaching the safety of her hearth.

But she did not see the shadows moving silently through the trees—stealthy figures cloaked in darkness, creeping toward the hut.

Still distant, veiled by foliage and night, they were little more than black shapes, accompanied by ominous sounds: the rustling of wings, muffled growls, the faint clink of metal.

Suddenly, the wind rose.

Leaves rustled and danced in startled bursts, the gusts thick with unseen warnings. The mountain itself seemed to shiver.

Anna paused, glancing up at the darkening sky, now rapidly filling with heavy clouds. The trees around her quivered. Her hair lifted in the wind.

She pulled her cloak close around her shoulders, shivering slightly.

*Athanor will be here soon with the firewood,* she thought, resuming her walk.

*A good fire will warm us both.*

***

Back on my horse, I pulled hard on the reins and came to a stop. A glimmer had just appeared high above—a flicker of light near the summit.

We were close.

"One more push! We're nearly there!" I called out.

At once, the troop pressed on, torches swaying in the darkness.

***

Meanwhile, along the narrow path leading home, Athanor walked alone, arms full of firewood. His eyes scanned the shadows, searching for his wife, whom he hadn't seen in a while.

He passed a large rock and spotted the glow of torches further down the mountainside—flickering lights, approaching quickly.

Riders.

Coming toward his home.

The smile vanished from his lips.

Tension gripped him. His eyes darted from the riders to the distant silhouette of their house—barely a kilometer away.

Abruptly, he dropped the bundle of wood and broke into a run.

***

Inside the hut, Anna lay on furs by the hearth, waiting.

The interior, warm and inviting, was lit by the soft flicker of a central fire.

Animal skins layered the floor, lending comfort to the

space.

The walls, made of timber and daub, were etched with Celtic runes. Shelves held jars of herbs and clay pots, and the air carried the sweet, spiced scent of dried plants mingled with wood smoke.

Simple wooden furniture—a low table and a few stools—stood around the fire.

Wicker baskets full of provisions, and kitchen tools carefully placed, reflected the humble rhythm of guardian life.

Suddenly, she heard rapid footsteps outside.

Smiling, she turned toward the door.

But the steps stopped—right at the threshold.

And then… silence.

Frowning, she sat up, listening intently.

Beside her, an iron sword rested against the wall. Slowly, she reached out and gripped the hilt.

A rustle of wings above made her glance upward.

Then, with a deafening crash, the door exploded into splinters.

A freezing gust tore into the hut, sweeping embers from the hearth and plunging the room into total darkness.

Shadows rushed in with it, and the silence that followed was heavier than any scream.

Before her eyes could adjust, a massive figure appeared in the gloom—cloaked, hooded, towering.

Anna leapt to her feet and raised her blade.

She could barely see her assailant, but something ancient in her soul stirred.

A cold, primal fear. And something deeper still—resolve.

"Let Taranis bear witness!" she cried. "You'll pay for this

sacrilege with your life, stranger!"

The figure gave no answer.

It stepped forward into the dark, its cloak rippling like a phantom's veil.

A blade rasped from its sheath with a cold, metallic hiss.

Two eyes ignited in the black—red as glowing embers, burning with inhuman fire.

\*\*\*

In the darkened night, Athanor—now running at full speed toward his home—heard his wife scream. His heart clenched with violent force. He was getting close.

"Anna!" he cried.

Through the shadows surrounding his home, he spotted dark figures moving. Drawing his sword, he charged with a warrior's roar, launching himself at the intruders. In the near-total darkness, blades met with fury, and the clash of steel echoed through the mountainside.

They were warriors—clad entirely in black, armed for death. Their leather cuirasses, reinforced with iron, caught the moonlight with a dull gleam. Their faces were hidden beneath dark hoods, revealing only cold, expressionless eyes.

Iron bracers covered their forearms, and their heavy boots struck the ground with the sound of judgment, their every step a promise of relentless force. The air stank of blood, of tanned leather and cold steel.

Each man bore at his side a cruel collection of short blades and daggers, ready to strike. But the fury of the Guardian was unmatched—he struck with pure fire. Two men fell beneath his blade, their cries swallowed by the din of battle.

Suddenly, a winged shadow dropped from above. A twisted creature, half-woman, half-bird—some infernal harpy born of the depths. Her black wings, raven-like and vast, beat the air with terrifying power, stirring whirlwinds of dust and dread. Her talons flashed in the night, and her eyes—yellow, feral, and gleaming—cut through the gloom with predatory menace. Feathers matted and stiff, tangled hair whirling, she stank of rot and death.

Faced with this abomination, Athanor did not falter. Even as the harpy shrieked and circled, he advanced, resolute and blazing with defiance.

Then, from the underbrush, two more warriors sprang forward. One lunged with a spear aimed at his chest. He managed to deflect the blow just in time, the point grazing his tunic—tearing cloth but sparing flesh. The heat of the near-strike seared his skin.

Spinning, he struck. His blade found its mark—clean, brutal—beheading the lancer in one swift arc.

He wheeled to face the next assailant as others began to surround him. From the house, screams echoed—Anna's voice, ragged with fury—and then a bestial growl unlike any human sound.

The battle within had begun.

"Anna!" Athanor howled, panic clawing at his chest.

Fuelled by desperation, he hacked and tore at the enemy ranks, trying to carve a path toward his home. But the winged horror descended, talons outstretched, slamming into him like a tempest. The impact knocked him off his feet. He crashed to the earth, the wind blasted from his lungs.

Even before he could draw breath, they were upon him. One sword plunged toward his neck, but he rolled aside—barely escaping death. The blade sank into the ground with a deadly thunk. He rose with a snarl, swinging wildly, his body screaming with effort, his heart with love and terror.

From the window of the hovel, he could see shadows flitting within—sharp wingbeats, crashing furniture, and flashes of steel.

\*\*\*

Inside, Anna fought for her life. She lashed out, her blade dancing, but her opponent—towering and monstrous—seemed impervious. With one brutal strike, he shattered her sword.

Then, a hand closed around her throat, lifting her from the floor with ease. In the firelight from outside, his silhouette emerged: vast, horned, and terrible. From beneath his hood, he growled like a beast.

"You fought well, little woman. But playtime is over."

"You'll die… Athanor will kill you… You can be sure of that," Anna managed to gasp, defiant even in his crushing grip.

The brute raised his sword and pointed it at her belly.

Anna stared him down, eyes blazing. She was Celt—death held no fear for her. Slowly, she closed her eyes and whispered, as the blade drove home:

"My love…"

\*\*\*

Outside the hut, Athanor fought like a man possessed.

His blade twisted shields and carved through iron and flesh. Blood poured from a deep gash along his arm and across his chest, yet he pressed forward, relentless. Another warrior fell at his feet, mortally struck. Without hesitation, Athanor stepped over the lifeless body, his face contorted by fury. He struck again, and again, his rage a wildfire no enemy could hope to contain.

From within the hut, no more sound came. Only silence… and then, a whisper—soft, sorrowful—brushed against his mind. It was Anna's voice… not heard, but felt.

"Anna!" Athanor cried out, a broken, desperate plea.

Surging through his attackers, he reached the threshold of their home—just as the second harpy burst forth, carrying something wrapped in a blanket.

He stopped.

In that fleeting second, he saw her clearly for the first time—her grotesque form, part-woman, part-raven, cloaked in feathers and darkness. The sight froze him. His blade, raised to strike, wavered.

The creature seized her chance. With a screech, she sprang into the air, her wings propelling her skyward, vanishing with her stolen burden into the black of night.

Stunned, Athanor stood motionless. His soul screamed, but his body would not follow. Around him, the remaining warriors slowly fell back, shielding their sister's escape.

From the distance came the thunder of hooves.

And in such moments of confusion and despair, is it not the nature of man to freeze before the face of horror? As though the mind, overwhelmed by the unthinkable, stalls—desperate to make sense of the impossible.

Fear… fear is a traitorous companion. It paralyzes. And yet, it is in these moments that the soul reveals its truest nature.

"Master! We must go!" one of the warriors called out.

But Athanor's spirit, though battered, had not broken. With a growl from deep within his chest, he charged again, hurling himself at those who blocked his path.

His determination, born of love and loss, was a flame in the storm. It reminded us that true bravery lies not in the absence of fear—but in the will to act in spite of it.

From the sky, the winged demon descended once more. Armed now with a heavy mace, she struck him from behind. The blow landed hard against his skull.

Athanor collapsed, blood streaming down his face, his thoughts swimming between waking and darkness.

And there—standing upon the threshold—appeared the horned figure.

A monstrous silhouette of muscle and shadow, covered in coarse, dark fur. Towering. Its face hidden beneath a heavy hood, only the tips of its horns and the glow of infernal red eyes could be seen.

And what is this beast, if not the embodiment of our own demons? The fears that gnaw at us, the towering doubts, the shrouded truths we cannot yet face.

Athanor, gasping, half-conscious, crawled toward his home. Toward Anna. Toward what he could no longer protect.

But the image of that horned shadow was already etched into his soul—an omen he would carry with him, long after this night of sorrow.

# CHAPTER 7
## *"The Circle of Hidden Truths"*

A deathly stillness hung over the Guardians' hut as we Celts approached, torches in hand, our horses snorting in the dark. Scattered across the earth, the bodies of the slain invaders bore silent witness to the fury of the sacred mountain's protector.

In the distance, thunder cracked—lightning slashed across the heavens. Above us, a mass of brooding clouds gathered fast, while the wind lashed at our torches, their flames flickering wildly, casting grotesque shadows across the scene.

How cruel the irony, that nature itself seemed to join in our mourning, painting the night with grief and fury. As if the storm shared in our sorrow—its winds carrying the sighs of the dead.

Dismounting, Divinix and I made our way toward the shattered doorway, while Chief Aridix barked orders, sending men to guard the perimeter.

Taranatos, already crouched near a trail of prints, was soon joined by Alexix, who followed the tracks of the fleeing enemy.

"Hey! I was the one who spotted them first!" Taranatos protested.

"Twelve men passed this way," Alexix replied flatly, crouching to inspect the ground.

"Thirteen," Taranatos corrected with smug precision, pointing into the woods. "They went that way, Chief."

Alexix shot him a sideways glance but said nothing. He stood and walked away in silence. As ever, the tension between those two simmered just beneath the surface—one day, I feared, that wound would have to be opened if it were ever to heal.

Standing before the hut, Divinix and I hesitated.

"What now, Shaman?" Aridix asked.

"We stay here," I answered solemnly. "The night is too dark now."

There are times when even the bravest must bow before the dark—an ancient truth we so often forget under the light of day.

Aridix turned to Taranatos.

"Take some men. Track them from a distance. Do not engage unless you must. Watch where they rest—and come back to report. Don't go throwing yourself to the wolves!"

With a cocky grin, Taranatos mounted his steed, flashing a mocking look at Alexix.

"Ah, blood's going to spill—and I'll be there for it. Not you!" he crowed, and galloped off, a group of riders at his back.

Alexix and Garedix dismounted and moved among the fallen, examining the bodies in silence. Divinix and I stepped back out from the hut, our faces heavy with grief. What had once been a sanctuary of life and sacred duty was now no more than a desecrated shell, echoing with sorrow.

"We were too late," I said at last, and my words hung in the wind like a curse. "The Guardians are no longer here."

The silence of the mountains, broken only by the whisper of flames and the breath of the wind, pressed in around us like a shroud. Their absence… it screamed louder than death itself.

\*\*\*

Higher up, perched on a rocky promontory above the valley, lay the Circle. Formed of ancient flat stones driven deep into the earth, it marked a sacred place known only to the Guardians. Each stone was flanked by a small, careful stack of firewood. Behind them loomed the entrance to a shadowed cave, its mouth aglow with the flicker of two torches. To the east, the pale face of the moon rose slowly over the peaks. To the west, stormclouds massed, black and heavy.

And there, staggering beneath the weight of grief and blood, came Athanor.

He bore Anna in his arms.

His steps faltered. His strength waned. But still he pressed on—one last effort. He crossed into the sacred circle and knelt. Gently, he laid her upon the stone floor.

She was alive.

But only just.

Her hands were slick with blood, clutching at her torn belly as though to hold in the life spilling from her. And still—still—her gaze found his, filled not with fear, but with infinite love.

Two golden eagles perched nearby, silent sentinels of the dying light. They watched without a cry, their eyes gleaming with the ancient wisdom of the skies. The thunder rumbled again, closer now, a promise of storm and ending.

The Guardians had fallen.

Kneeling before her, broken, Athanor took Anna into his arms.

She whispered. Barely audible.

"Help me… end this… my love…"

Tears streamed down his face as he rocked her gently.

"Yes… yes, my love… I will help you," he murmured, shattered.

With trembling hands, he stroked her hair, kissed her temple, pressed his brow to hers.

"I will find you again, wherever you go. Wherever you are—I will find you," he vowed, his voice cracking under the weight of a soul torn in half.

Those words—words weighted with eternal promise—rang out like a sacred vow.

Rising with effort, Athanor drew his sword and turned its point downward. His hand trembled, his eyes blurred with tears. Then, with a scream of agony and love entwined, he drove the blade into his wife's heart. Her final breath left her in silence, and night swallowed her cry.

Thus did love become release—an ultimate act of devotion, a farewell forged in steel and sorrow.

\*\*\*

Farther down the mountain, in front of the desecrated Guardians' hut, the Chief and his warriors stood near their horses, somber and silent. Divinix and I joined them just as Aridix pointed toward the heights.

"There! Look—someone lit a fire!"

I halted, eyes fixed on the glow rising above. A dark understanding settled upon me. I bowed my head, burdened by the weight of what I knew.

"Athanor is completing the rite," I said softly. "This is a terrible thing. I pray the Eagles are safe… or else the wrath of the Gods will fall upon us like thunder. And there will be nothing I can do to stop it."

In that moment, the vastness of the gods and the fragility of men crossed paths. I lifted my gaze once more to the distant flames, flickering like a soul returning to the stars.

"Anna is dead," I murmured. "Athanor is helping his wife cross into the Land of the Ancestors. The destiny of the Guardians was never ours to share…"

Divinix nodded slowly, his expression unreadable.

"Yes… they are bound to the Eagles," he said. "But how do you know it was the Guardian who died?"

"Her sword. Broken," I replied with a heavy heart. "It lay there, inside the hut."

Wearied and worn, I sank down upon a large rock, casting my eyes to Aridix.

"We will sleep here tonight," I declared, my voice thick with sorrow.

The Chief nodded, turning to his warriors.

"You heard the Shaman! Strip these cursed corpses from the sacred ground. And gather wood—we'll need fire tonight!"

At once, the men obeyed. Aridix and Divinix joined me near the fire, while others filtered in slowly—Alexix, Garedix, and more. All was silence. We shared it, knowing it was sacred.

A warrior fed the flames, and we watched as they danced and cracked, their tongues of light telling a story older than any of us. A story of life, of death, and of truths hidden beneath the soil of time.

Then Divinix broke the silence.

"The strangers… they weren't after the Eagles," he said. "They came for the Thunder-Bird."

I turned to him, stunned.

"The what?"

"I haven't yet told you how I knew they would come," he said.

"I believe the time for explanations has come," I answered, my patience long worn thin.

Divinix inhaled deeply. His voice was low, steady.

"First, I must speak of what I discovered during my journey to study the Greek world."

"Then speak plainly!" I urged, leaning forward.

He nodded. His eyes took on a deeper, darker gleam.

"For countless generations, the sacred mountains have been forbidden to all but the two Guardians. Is that not so?"

"Yes! And what of it?" I growled, narrowing my gaze.

"But do you know why?"

"Of course I do!" I snapped. "The Eagles are the chosen of Taranis! Our god of thunder and storm! He entrusted them to Alisanos—and Alisanos entrusted them to us! That is the sacred charge we carry!"

Divinix raised a hand in calm.

"Forgive me, Smérix. But you, and all who came before you… have only part of the truth."

His words struck me like a blade through the fog. A tremor ran through my chest.

"Beware, Divinix. Were you not a brother in the path, I would see you punished for such heresy. Speak—but be certain your truth can stand the fire of my wrath!"

Divinix met my eyes, unflinching.

"The answer lies in a very old Hellenic legend… The Legend of the Thunder-Bird."

He paused. The wind stirred the flames. All listened.

"It began long ago, in the age when the ancestors of your ancestors first came to dwell in these lands. Even then, the mountains of Alisanos were forbidden. Demons, it was said, haunted their peaks. But one day, as fate would have it, a young man… broke that law."

# CHAPTER 8
## *"The Secret of the Ancients"*

*Sacred Mountains, centuries ago…*

In the dense forest of the sacred mountains, the day stretched lazily on, sunlight trickling through the thick canopy of leaves. A young man, no older than twenty, crept forward with a half-drawn bow, a single arrow nocked and ready to fly. His face bore the marks of determination and focus, his features drawn tight with the effort. He was tracking prey. A doe had just passed behind a large boulder.

With a powerful, silent leap, he climbed the rock, hoping to surprise the creature from above—his movements fluid, controlled, honed by years of forest craft. In him, I saw the very essence of our ancestral instinct, the sacred dance of predator and prey, not born of malice, but of reverence.

Reaching the summit, the young hunter remained still, bow drawn tight, eyes sharp. The doe stood fifty paces away, drinking peacefully from a river whose crystalline waters shimmered with sunlight. Nearby, a waterfall—no less than twenty meters high—spilled its silver veil into a natural pool, adding its voice to the serene harmony of the grove. The young man paused, momentarily spellbound by the beauty before him, his eyes wide in silent awe.

"The Elders are fools... These sacred mountains... this is the land of the Gods," he whispered, his words dissolving into the murmur of the cascade.

Ah, how well I remember the stories of the Ancients... the old songs that claimed these lands were shaped by the gods' own hands. Every stone, every tree, they said, still bore the breath of the divine. These mountains belonged to Alisanos, lord of stone and summit, while these forests were the domain of Cernunnos, guardian of the wild. They were present—I felt it, deep within the vision unfolding before me—watchful, unseen, yet so near...

Though enthralled, the young man never lost sight of the doe. His arrow still aimed, his hands trembling with adrenaline. Drawing a silent breath, he whispered a prayer to the spirits of the forest.

"Guide my arrow, Cernunnos... Let it grant her a swift and gentle death," he murmured, lips barely moving, heart beating slow and still.

But then—ah!—a wonder descended.

From beyond the treetops, a creature unlike any known to man flew into his field of vision and landed beside the doe. It was a bird, some kin of the royal eagle, yet covered in feathers of gold and silver. Its head and neck were pure white, and a luminous aura shone faintly from its body, perhaps the sun's own light captured and reflected by its sacred plumage. The grace of its stance and the soft might it exuded stunned the young man. His arrow remained drawn, yet he could no longer move.

Even now, I feel that same breathless awe—the reverence for that celestial creature, whose presence bound sky and earth, messenger of the gods, bearer of signs and mysteries.

The young hunter, lost in the vision, did not see the eyes that watched him—emerald-green and unblinking—hidden deep within the undergrowth. A figure, cloaked in leaves and bark, merged perfectly with the forest, witnessing everything.

The bird, having sipped from the river, took flight again. As its wings beat the air, it left behind a shimmering trail—golden motes sparkling in the fading light of day.

"By all the gods… damn me if that bird was real!" the young man gasped.

His voice startled the doe. With a bound, she vanished into the forest. The hunter did not chase. Instead, he stood a moment longer, dazed, then turned and fled through the trees, the image of the radiant bird burning in his memory.

The glade fell silent once more. Only the rustling of leaves and the soft babble of the river remained. The hidden figure stirred.

Cernunnos stepped forth.

He, the forest's protector, bore the timeless marks of nature itself. His skin was sun-kissed, his face weathered and alive with the scent of moss and bark. His eyes, deep as emerald wells, glowed with wisdom and quiet strength. A wild beard, threaded with strands of moss, framed his strong jaw. From his temples rose antlers of a great stag, shrouded in lichen and leaves, blending him wholly into the world he guarded.

He approached the water's edge near the rock where the young hunter had crouched. Through a thinning in the canopy, he watched the divine bird soar into the sky, leaving behind its trail of golden dust.

Cernunnos sighed.

"Hrm… This bodes ill. Great unrest is brewing. Alisanos will not be pleased," he muttered into his beard, where no doubt beetles and spiders made their home.

No sooner had the words left his lips than a rumble of stone echoed behind him. He turned, slowly, deliberately.

"Ah. There you are," he said. "So… you saw everything, didn't you?"

the rock began to crack and shift, as if the mountain itself were awakening. Low rumblings echoed through the vale, and slowly, majestically, a figure emerged from the stone—peeling itself from the living rock.

It was Alisanos, the god of the mountain. His face was stern and immutable as the cliffs themselves, carved with angular, powerful lines. His skin bore the grey, granitic hue of high peaks, threaded with quartz and veins of glimmering crystal. His deep blue eyes shone with the wisdom of the heights and the storms. A mane of dark hair, braided with pebbles and mineral fragments, framed his daunting face. His thick beard, threaded with stone, proclaimed his eternal bond with the bones of the world.

Alisanos stepped forward, each of his strides shaking the earth, every step echoing like the heartbeat of the mountain. Before him stood Cernunnos, who met his gaze in solemn silence—between them flowed an ancient understanding, a mutual reverence beyond words.

"Yes, my friend," Alisanos finally spoke, his voice deep as the abyss, "That bird is not of our world. It holds too much power. And I fear we shall soon learn the reason for its coming."

The two gods stood for a while, watching the gleaming creature as it vanished into the distant sky. Then, each turned away and disappeared into the sacred silence of their domains, leaving the glade to its stillness.

\*\*\*

Farther down the slopes, the young hunter was tearing through the undergrowth, bounding over roots and rocks like a wild goat. He had lost his bow along the way, but did not slow. His chest heaved, his heart beat like a war drum. Below, nestled beside the river, the village of the Arverni awaited, unaware.

Ah! That frantic dash… it mirrored our eternal yearning—to touch the divine, to chase the miraculous, heedless of the dangers hidden in the sacred.

In the village, the day moved quietly, life flowing in its steady rhythm. But then, a voice rang out, wild and breathless.

"Come see! A magical bird! Up there! Come see!"

Villagers turned toward the sound. A boy was racing down the path, hair tousled, face flushed with excitement.

"There's a wondrous bird! I saw it! A creature of gold and silver wings! It leaves golden dust behind when it flies!"

A hush fell over the gathering. One figure stepped forward—an elder clad in grey, his long beard braided and adorned with beads, eyes as sharp as a hawk's.

"The sacred mountains… That's where it lives?" the boy gasped, wide-eyed.

One burly man scowled. "And what of demons? Did you see any?"

"No. No demons. Just the bird! The most beautiful thing I've ever seen!"

The druid's face darkened. "Sacrilege… What have you done? The sacred peaks must not be defiled!"

Then, from atop a red-cloaked horse, the chieftain spoke, his voice as cold and cutting as steel.

"If such a creature exists, it must be brought to me. I am your chief!"

His helm gleamed in the sun, his sword heavy at his hip, his cape catching the wind. He raised one gauntleted hand.

"Druid! Choose ten men. They shall go and capture the bird. If they fail… I will offer them to the gods."

A chill passed through the crowd. The druid muttered under his breath, heavy with dread, and pointed ten men from among the warriors without speaking. Then, without another word, he turned and walked away, the burden of prophecy heavy on his shoulders.

The chosen ten departed in silence, mounting their steeds, riding toward the forbidden heights. One of them stopped by the boy, leaning down from his saddle.

"No demons, eh?" he said darkly.

"No. None. I swear it," the boy replied, trembling.

The warrior studied him a moment longer, then added:

"If I return empty-handed… you'll pay."

Such are the ways of mortals… ever eager to chain the divine, to conquer what should only be revered. Their folly knows no bounds.

\*\*\*

Far above, perched on a lonely outcrop, the magical bird watched the world below. Its golden and silver plumage glistened in the sunlight. From this dizzying height, the human village seemed but a speck on the land, the figures of ten riders shrinking into the horizon.

The bird stirred, its wings stretching in a slow, regal gesture. And then, beside it, an old man materialized—tall, luminous, and wise. His hair and beard were white as snow, his tunic simple but finely adorned. He shimmered with a pale blue light, as if born of sky and memory. His eyes, piercing and serene, held the secrets of the stars.

He extended a gloved hand.

The bird tilted its head… and then, with infinite grace, it landed gently upon the outstretched palm. In that moment, a sacred bond passed between them, silent and eternal.

Beside the man, a woman appeared—an ethereal vision of grace. Her hair flowed like liquid night, framing a face of unmatched beauty. Her eyes, deep green, held the wisdom of the earth. Her robe, silver-threaded, billowed as if beneath water. Light clung to her in a shimmering halo.

She reached toward the bird, her fingers trembling with reverence, yet did not touch it—only brushed the air beside its feathers, her smile tender.

The man turned toward the abyss. His feet touched nothing, yet he stepped forward as if walking a forest path. With the bird perched upon him, he strode into the air, vanishing slowly into the sky, leaving behind a trail of radiant light.

And the goddess followed, gliding above the land, her presence both a farewell and a promise. Her silver trail lingered for a moment longer… before the heavens closed once more.

Thus, a new legend was born for our people.

A tale of wonder and warning.

A reminder that the sacred does not yield to the will of men.

# CHAPTER 9
## *"The Night of Revelations"*

Night had fallen over the hut of the mountain guardians, and silence reigned, broken only by the crackling of the fire. Around the campfire, Divinix had paused in his tale, leaving his audience suspended in breathless anticipation. I, Smérix, along with the others gathered there, kept my eyes fixed on Divinix, eager to hear the next part of the legend. Shadows danced across our faces, deepening the mysterious atmosphere of the tale.

"So? What happened next? Who were that man and woman who floated through the air?" I asked, my curiosity sharp as a blade.

"That man is a Greek god," replied Divinix. "His name is Zeus. He is, in a way, the king of all Greek gods. And the woman—she is Hera, his queen and companion."

"Zeus! I've heard of him," I exclaimed. "The Greeks say he rules the skies, the lightning and the thunder. Hmph!

Just like our mighty Taranis! Perhaps that is true in their lands… but here, he does not rule. Taranis would never allow it!"

Is it not fascinating how myths mirror each other across cultures, each people shaping their gods in the image of their fears and longings?

"Indeed," Divinix conceded. "But the legend says that Zeus, dazzled by the bird's beauty, fell under its spell and decided to keep it close. He gave the creature a choice: if it stayed with him, Zeus would grant it the powers of lightning and thunder, making it the Thunder Eagle… Otherwise, it was free to return to the sacred mountains—but it would then have to face Hades, Zeus's brother, who also coveted its company. In my opinion, the bird didn't take long to decide!"

Temptation and choice. The ancients knew well that every gift comes at a cost, often paid in freedom. What a paradox—to see a celestial being imprisoned by its own golden wings.

Aridix, ever skeptical, rose to his feet in agitation.

"That's all very pretty… the magical little bird and all that… but frankly, what does any of this have to do with us? There was no trouble until those foreigners came and wrecked everything! Why should we meddle in the affairs of a Greek god? Maybe I'm not the cleverest man here, but I fail to see the sense in this!"

Divinix looked at him with a faint, amused smile playing on his lips.

"I'm getting to that," he replied calmly. "Zeus cannot give the Thunder Eagle immortality because of his brother Hades. Even though he is the god of all Greek gods, such a decision cannot be made without the consent of the other gods. All he could do was extend his protégé's life as much as possible. But one day, when the end of that life nears, the Thunder Eagle must return to earth, to find a mate and pass on its legacy. No one was meant to know this. That's why Zeus took the form of Alisanos and ordered your ancestors to guard the sacred mountains, to protect the eagles who dwelled there… awaiting the return of the Thunder Eagle."

"And Alisanos allowed this?" Alexix scoffed. "Our god of the mountains is as strong as stone! No Greek god's going to order him around!"

Divinix kept smiling, clearly entertained by the warriors' reactions. I had to raise my voice.

"Enough! Let the man speak!" I cried.

It is vital to listen to every thread of a story—for only when woven together can we see the full tapestry of fate.

"I'm only telling you what I discovered in Greece," Divinix went on. "But admit it—this tale is troubling. And then I had a dream. In it, I was told the Thunder Eagle would soon return to earth… and that Hades, god of the Underworld, desired its power. That's all I know. But knowing your people's customs, I saw the connection immediately…"

His words shook us. A grim silence fell. A weight of unease settled in our chests.

"So we've been duped by some Greek god for generations?" I asked, my voice dark with disillusion.

"Not quite," Divinix replied. "In truth, you did well to serve loyally. Alisanos let it happen, for Zeus is powerful. He rules over the sky, the earth, and the seas—his brothers command them for him. Our gods are terrible indeed, but none match the might of the one who hurls bolts of lightning at all who defy him."

What irony, I thought, to serve an unknown god by the hand of another. But is this not the fate of many mortals—to follow paths laid out by unseen hands?

"What do we do now?" I asked. "Have they taken the creature?"

Without a word, Divinix pulled from his sleeve a feather—gold and silver. It shimmered in the firelight, and golden motes fell from it onto the ground. We all stared, dumbstruck by its wonder.

"I found this in the guardians' hut. It clearly belonged to the Thunder Eagle. The guardians must have found it wounded and tried to heal it. But the foreigners took it. You must go after them and bring it back—or Zeus's wrath will fall upon us!"

"If this god is so mighty," barked Alexix, "then why should we, Celts, be the ones to chase down these foreigners? I say we pursue them for vengeance—not for some Greek god!"

"Alexix is right," I added. "It would be wise to let their own god deal with it! We are Celts, not Greeks!"

At that very instant, a deafening roar shattered the air. A blinding bolt of lightning crashed down and split a massive boulder beside us in two. The thunder echoed long after the flash, a terrifying rumble that shook the hearts of even the bravest among us.

All of us rose to our feet, fear etched into our eyes, as we stared at the blackened sky. A heavy cloud mass loomed above our heads, pulsing with threat, as if it had a will of its own.

Thunder, the divine herald, reminds us of how small we

truly are before the forces of nature and the gods.

Divinix, however, did not seem surprised. After glancing briefly at the heavens, he lowered his gaze and raised an eyebrow, then cast a silent look over his frightened companions.

Some warriors, trembling with terror, curled up on the ground beneath their shields. The others, still standing, fared no better in dignity. The horses tethered to the trees nearby neighed and stamped nervously.

"I believe our task is not yet done," I declared. "We must find the Thunder Eagle and rescue it from these foreigners, must we not, Aridix?"

The chieftain did not hesitate.

"Yes, Smérix! That is exactly what we shall do!"

Finding a spark of pride amid his fear, Aridix turned to his men and bellowed:

"Stand up, you cowards! One thunderclap and you all fall to the ground, shaking like old hags!"

Ashamed, though still wary, the warriors straightened up. I sat down again, my gaze turning toward Divinix, who remained silent. Above us, the storm clouds began to drift away, to the great relief of the warriors, who slowly regained their composure.

Courageous hearts always find their place again—even after being struck low by fear. True bravery lies not in the absence of fear, but in rising after being felled by it.

"What do you think these strangers intend?" I asked. "Where do they come from?"

"Straight from the Underworld!" Divinix replied. "And that is where they're headed—with all the souls of their victims. They are bringing the Thunder Eagle to Hades."

"The Underworld?" I echoed, confused.

"It is the land of the dead, where the souls of the departed go. According to Greek legends, it lies far to the north of Thrace, in a land unknown. Hades rules over this subterranean kingdom, a place where monstrous creatures torment the damned for eternity."

"That place doesn't exist!" retorted Aridix, visibly shaken. "You know well that after death we join the land of our ancestors before returning through rebirth!"

"Apparently, the Greeks see it differently. Their gods are terrible, I warned you! You must stop these strangers before they succeed!"

"Tomorrow, I'll gather more warriors and horses," said Aridix. "As soon as my scouts return with news of their location and destination, we will hunt them down!"

"They won't return," said Divinix flatly. "They are already dead. You must leave at dawn for Thrace. I know a sailor who can take you to Greece. His name is Coleos of Samos. For a few gold pieces, he'd sail into the jaws of a kraken!"

I gave him a wary look.

"And what in the gods' names are gold pieces?"

Divinix pulled a small leather pouch from his belt.

"They are small, flat discs of gold, engraved—like this one."

He handed me a coin. The warriors' faces lit up with curiosity and wonder.

"They're used for trade," he explained. "Instead of exchanging a pelt for a sword, you give the number of gold coins the seller asks for. It's not that simple, of course—everything has a value limit…"

"All right, enough of that!" I interrupted, tired and

worn, my gaze turning toward the distant glow of the ritual flames.

Gold—that gleaming metal—will surely become the thread that binds worlds together, uniting those who possess it and enslaving those who desire it. How ironic, that men should be tied by cold metal, while so often ignoring the warm bonds of brotherhood and spirit.

"At dawn, I will speak to the Guardian."

The chieftain nodded solemnly and stood.

"He will come. His rage must be immense… That man alone is worth ten warriors. Tell him that Anna's death will be avenged a thousandfold. I, Aridix, swear it!"

He turned on his heel and walked away. We remained near the fire, a few warriors beside us, our eyes lost in thought…

The oath of vengeance—this burden of honor—binds the souls of the living to the spirits of the dead, transforming mourning into an eternal battle cry.

\*\*\*

Later that night, darkness cloaked the sacred mountain summit, a blackness so dense it felt almost solid, pierced only by flames that danced defiantly against the void.

On a rocky promontory at the cliff's edge, in the heart of that natural sanctuary, stood a funeral pyre, encircled by flat standing stones—markers of ancient rites. The wind whispered gently, carrying with it the murmurs of ancestral spirits.

Athanor sat cross-legged before the pyre, his body swaying to the rhythm of his labored breathing—each breath a struggle, each inhale an act of will. It seemed he communed with the essence of life and death itself.

Beside him, two majestic eagles perched on stones, shifting uneasily, their piercing eyes fixed on the fire, as if they too understood the solemnity of the moment. Their black feathers gleamed ominously in the firelight.

The sight was one of agony and implacable resolve. Athanor swayed, his mouth half open, his eyes heavy with grief and fury, staring into the devouring fire with a desperate intensity.

Pain—this merciless master—fashions within us an unshakable resolve. Each flame of the pyre reflected the turmoil within his soul.

Moonlight and firelight carved shadows across his ravaged face, drawing out every scar, every hollow. Blood and sweat mingled, tracing rivulets down his cheeks like inked runes of suffering. The wounds from his assailants still bled, darkening the ground beneath his right hand resting upon his knee—a symbol of his last act of defiance.

Every drop of blood, every scar, is a testament to humanity's endurance in the face of annihilation—a living proof of our ability to suffer and yet stand.

At the center of the circle, the body of his beloved wife burned atop the woodpile. Flames climbed high into the night sky—an unspoken, desperate prayer to the gods.

The crackling of burning wood mingled with the distant chants of the spirits, while the flames danced about her form, lifting her essence to the starry heavens. Athanor, helpless before the sight, watched in silence as each flame consumed a fragment of his heart.

As the fire consumed Anna's body, it carried with it the pieces of an eternal love—each spark a vow, each ember a sacred memory.

# CHAPTER 10
*"The Dawn of Vengeance"*

Dawn rose behind the mountains of Arvernia as Athanor rode into the village square atop his black steed, his gaze dark with pain and hatred. The morning light caught in his eyes, revealing the full depth of his torment. A harrowing sight, indeed, that—even amid turmoil—reminded us how sorrow could transform into unsuspected strength, awakening parts of ourselves we never knew existed. Grief is both our curse and our source of resilience.

He stopped apart from the warriors mounting their horses, ready to depart. Around thirty men stood gathered there, surrounded by loved ones who feared the worst—for their sons, cousins, uncles, brothers, fathers, or friends. Beyond the village, edged by forest, a morning mist clung to the trees, lending an otherworldly touch to the tension-heavy air. From the wooden palisades fortifying the village, sentinels kept watch from raised platforms.

Children dashed here and there, a flicker of life and

innocence in that grave moment. The scent of freshly baked bread mingled with the damp earth, creating a sharp contrast between daily life and the looming departure. The innocence of children, blind to the weight carried by their elders, offered a fleeting spark of normalcy. Their carefree joy—fragile though it was—reminded us of the world for which so many sacrifices are made.

Chief Aridix had just arrived on horseback, trotting slowly along the line of warriors preparing for the journey. From time to time, he nodded with approval as he met the gaze of those who would ride beside him into battle. He stopped before two young men, barely more than boys, already mounted and puffing out their chests like young cocks ready for their first fight.

"You're certain you wish to come? Most likely, death awaits you."

"Yes, Chief! That's what we want! Isn't that right, Paritos?"

"We're not afraid to die! And besides, an adventure like this may never come again," replied the second, eyes alight with excitement.

"Very well, as you wish. A true warrior must have a first battle," Aridix said as he moved on. "And if you return, you'll count among the greatest warriors in the region, lads!"

The two friends exchanged glances, nudging one another with glee, glowing with pride. Innocent, headstrong youths—they had no idea of the dangers that lay ahead. Lugotorix and Paritos were inseparable, just like Taranatos and the twins whom they so admired. From early childhood, they had been a pair of troublemakers with hearts of gold.

Paritos, quiet and clever, was smaller and wirier. His eyes, bright and mischievous, were always alert. His cropped brown hair added to his nimble, quick-footed appearance. For the occasion, he wore a supple leather tunic reinforced with light metal plates, perfect for close combat. A leather belt hung with a dagger adorned in Celtic patterns encircled his waist. He also wore leather greaves and sturdy boots, ready for the roughest paths. One could tell he'd chosen every part of his outfit with care, anticipating the adventures—and dangers—to come.

Lugotorix, on the other hand, was tall and broad, with a wild ponytail of fiery red hair. He wore a thicker leather tunic suited to his size—though a touch too snug—and a reinforced cuirass over it. A linen trouser bound at the ankles by leather thongs completed his garb. He bore a great sword strapped to his back, his weapon of choice.

Often clumsy, yet never ill-willed, Lugotorix's steadfast loyalty made him a precious companion. All the villagers loved him for his cheerful spirit and boundless energy.

Further off, still apart from the others, Athanor waited, his eyes locked on the gathering with a glacial intensity. Garedix and Alexix watched him from a distance, hesitating, before finally walking toward him. The silence between them was heavy, and each movement bore the weight of solemnity and sorrow.

"If he could speak," said Alexix, "Garedix would tell you how deeply he grieves for our sister, Athanor. We grieve with you… Her death will be avenged, you have our word."

Athanor nodded silently as an old woman slowly approached.

She was the mother of the twins—and of Anna. Her face

was etched with the lines of time, every wrinkle a tale of wisdom and pain. Her gray hair, braided with care, framed eyes dulled by a night of tears and grief.

She wore a thick woolen tunic, time-worn but clean, and a beige linen shawl draped over her shoulders.

Her hesitant gait betrayed her exhaustion, but her unwavering gaze radiated a quiet strength. She took the hands of her two sons and held them before her. Her look said what no words could. The two grown men clenched their jaws, heads bowed, eyes brimming.

Without a word, she turned her stern, yet compassionate gaze to Athanor. She stepped toward him and gently placed her hand upon his thigh, then turned away and walked off, her steps slow and unsteady.

The three men shared a brief nod, their expressions resolute. A silent pact had been sealed—one that nothing and no one would ever undo. Alexix, jaw tight, growled softly and walked off to rejoin the warriors, his brother following behind, leaving Athanor alone with his burning rage and the thirst for vengeance that gnawed at his soul.

I watched the scene with sorrow as Divinix stepped up beside me and held out a small leather pouch.

"His ship will be easy to find—it's the largest. Take these few gold coins, they'll be useful. Ah yes… take this as well."

He handed me a second pouch, smaller.

"In the darkest hour, this stone may be of great help to you. At least… I believe so. I've never used it myself, so I cannot say for certain that it works. Speak my name when the time comes—but only if there is no other choice. You'll know… when the moment arrives."

"Thank you," I said, accepting the objects with care. "I

won't forget. Take care of the eagles… and our village. I entrust you with my sweet girl," I added, glancing down at my faithful dog, who was sitting beside me, watching with steady eyes. "She is the light of my life. Be kind to her in my absence."

"Of course. Don't worry," Divinix replied. "Be cautious. Many dangers await you… I'll take shelter in the Guardians' hut while I await your return."

He mounted his horse and quickly rode away, leaving me in the fog of my doubts and darker thoughts. What a strange man! There's something about him… A shadow in his gaze, a burden in his step. I can't say what he hides, but hide something he does. Of that, I am certain.

Suddenly, a voice rang out—

"Look over there! It's Taranatos! He's coming back alone!"

Emerging from the mist on a staggering, exhausted horse, Taranatos approached slowly. His head hung low, his body caked in filth. His hair, matted with a thick black substance, clung to his face. As he drew nearer, it became clear—it was blood, mixed with sweat and mud.

The warriors' expressions hardened at the sight of his many wounds and the broken shaft of a lance still protruding from his horse's side. His eyes blazed with a wild, haunted gleam—half madness, half fury.

No one spoke as he stopped before us, slowly lifting his gaze. A woman and her young son ran toward him.

"What happened, husband? You're hurt? By the gods, all that blood!" cried the woman, panic in her voice.

"Don't worry… it's not mine," he murmured.

"Papa! What happened? Why are you alone?" asked the

boy, anxious.

"Yes, where are the others?" Alexix's voice was cold, stern. He remained mounted, his horse shifting restlessly beneath him.

"They're all dead," Taranatos answered, dazed, lowering his head once more.

His wife took his hand, but he pulled away, uneasy. Furious, Alexix rode forward, his expression blazing with barely-contained rage.

"Why are you the one still alive?" he hissed, as his horse reared slightly.

"Enough! Let him speak, Alexix," I interjected, my tone firm, seeking to defuse the spark.

"You ran! You abandoned them! I know you did—it wouldn't be the first time!" Alexix shouted, leaping from his saddle, sword drawn.

"Leave my father alone!" the child screamed, terrified.

Taranatos, suddenly inflamed, dismounted as well.

"No, it's not true! I didn't run! I… I don't understand what happened!" Taranatos yelled, madness widening his eyes.

The two men once again stood face to face, ready to clash.

"Alexix! I command you to stand down! Step away from him at once!" I ordered, my voice rising with authority.

Alexix hesitated, but obeyed at last, turning away in fury. He passed his brother Garedix, who looked at him disapprovingly.

"Speak, Taranatos! Tell us what happened—exactly!" I demanded.

Taranatos, his face a mask of terror and confusion, struggled to find the words.

"It wasn't my fault, High Druid. I don't know what happened! We were following the tracks when suddenly the horses froze. There was this stench—it might've been that. And then… wings! A thousand birds at once, it sounded like! And then madness! We turned on each other—we fought! I don't even know why! In the end… I was the only one left. I swear I didn't flee. I'm no coward!"

His horse collapsed then, spent and trembling, unable to rise. It lay there in the muddy earth, heaving. The warriors, dumbfounded and bewildered, looked to me for meaning. Even Divinix seemed perplexed.

"He's been touched by a madness-spell," I said, though my voice betrayed my uncertainty. "Bring him a fresh horse! We ride soon."

One of the warriors obeyed, yet worry hung heavy over the camp. A shroud of dread wrapped itself around us, and in each man's eyes, I saw the same reflection—a silent, unanswered question.

Taranatos stepped toward his wife and son, who looked up at him with anxious eyes.

"Don't worry. I'll come back. I always come back. And you, my son—take this time with Divinix to learn all you can!"

"Really, father? You mean it?"

"Yes, my son… Your path is yours to choose. Come here."

He took his boy in his arms and held him tightly. His wife joined them, embracing the two loves of her life. Then, suddenly, she pulled back with a grimace.

"Ugh… you stink, my love!"

Just then, a warrior stepped up with a fresh mount, and

Taranatos climbed into the saddle.

Watching his son—so eager to become a druid—I saw in him a reflection of my younger self, when I too burned with the desire for knowledge, with the mysteries of the world whispering to me through every tree and stone. I'd watched this boy grow, and early on, I saw that spark in him—that hunger to understand. No, he will never be a great warrior like you, Taranatos. But you… you've understood this. And for that, you have my deepest respect.

"So, what about us, eh? Do we get some of that potion too?" called out one of the warriors, waiting impatiently atop his horse.

"Of course I have a potion!" I snapped, my gaze sharp as flint. "Do you doubt the extent of my knowledge?"

Fixing my eyes on the warriors around me, I tugged on my reins and turned to the chief.

"Enough talking. Time is against us. Let us ride."

The small company moved out at a steady trot, Athanor taking the rear, his face dark and unreadable, like the shadow of a storm gathering behind us.

\*\*\*

High above, near the Guardians' hut, Divinix stood watching the village far below, his eyes fixed on the departing riders now dwindling into the valley. He followed their path in silence for a moment, then turned toward the hut.

Something near the entrance caught his attention—something motionless on the ground.

As he approached, he discovered the lifeless body of one of the eagles.

He bent down, gently lifted the fallen bird, and seated himself on a nearby rock. A shrill cry pierced the still air. He raised his eyes. The other eagle wheeled above him in slow, somber circles, cutting through the sky like a spirit in mourning.

Divinix looked back toward the horsemen disappearing into the mist. His face had grown grave as he ran his fingers across the noble feathers of the departed creature.

He gave a slow, solemn nod—he understood now the weight of what was to come. The path ahead would be steep. Their ordeal had only just begun.

In such troubled times, even the wisest and the bravest must face trials that seem insurmountable. But it is in those very moments that the true nature of a soul is revealed.

Ah, trials… cruel mirrors that show us nothing but what we truly are.

# CHAPTER 11
*"The Celts' Odyssey"*

The shifting shadows of the morning clouds stretched long across the Gaulish lands, guiding us southward, toward the shores of the great sea where the Ligurian fishing port awaited us. We rode on through plains and forests, and along the way, Celtic villages passed beneath my watchful gaze. I, Smérix—shaman, philosopher, stargazer, keeper of the earth's mysteries and the sky's riddles—was now accompanying my people on this fateful journey.

I could scarce believe the path I now walked. I was a man of thought, of ancient lore—not of battlefields and blades. And yet, something in my heart stirred with each step of this grand voyage. The promise of discovery, the hunger for knowledge yet unknown, beat like a joyous drum in my chest.

With quiet reverence, I murmured my thanks to the gods. This journey was more than flesh and stone—it was the soul's passage through the many veils of existence. Each step a lesson whispered by the Ancients, each gust of wind a divine breath reminding us of the unity of all things.

\*\*\*

Days passed, marked by encounters with tribes and ever-changing landscapes. Towering mountains gave way to gentle green hills, and winding rivers became wide-flowing streams guiding us into lands unfamiliar. The vegetation shifted as well—oak giving way to maritime pines and twisted olive trees.

We passed bustling villages, their markets brimming with vibrant life: fruits and fish, clay jars and handwoven cloths. The locals greeted us with curiosity and kindness, offering food for our long road ahead. Children ran to meet us, their wide eyes filled with wonder at our strange procession.

With the warm breath of the southern wind at our backs, we finally emerged onto the shores of the ancient Ligurian port. Before us stretched a living tapestry of color and motion: large merchant ships swayed gently on the deep blue waters, fishing boats with bright sails drew near the docks, and elegant skiffs skimmed along the coast. The village itself buzzed with activity—sailors unloading crates, merchants haggling, fishermen mending nets. The air was thick with salt, fish, and spices—a symphony of scent born of sea and trade.

As we dismounted and stepped onto this new land, I felt within me the solemn weight of our purpose. Every step now drew us not only closer to our destination, but deeper into the mystery we were bound to unravel. The gods had led us here—it was now up to us to uncover the hidden truths cradled by this land beneath the Mediterranean sun.

With the shadowed mountains behind us, our journey would now continue across the great sea, into realms no Celt had ever dared tread. Each day would bring new marvels, each lesson etched into our spirits by the unseen hands of the Ancients.

Upon a wooden pier stretching out over the bay—soon to become the famed Massilia, jewel of the Greeks—stood a man of the sea: Coléos of Samos, broad of shoulder, clad in a short tunic of finely woven linen. Leaning on the rail of his imposing ship, his muscular arms bore the story of many voyages, veins like rivers tracing years of oar and sail. His sun-darkened face, framed by carefully trimmed curls and a neatly kept beard, was marked with wisdom born of salt and stars. His eyes, sharp and gleaming, scanned our group with a keen curiosity softened by mirth.

"Ah, there you are! Divinix spoke of you!" he called out, his deep voice echoing across the salt-kissed air as we dismounted, our horses weary from the long road.

Despite his formidable presence, warmth radiated from his stance and smile. There was something noble in his bearing—an adventurer's soul, a merchant's wit, a storyteller's heart.

"Yes, he sent us," I replied, lifting my gaze to meet his.

As I stepped forward, Coléos descended the gangplank with long strides, his leather sandals tapping smartly against the dock's planks.

"Welcome, my friends! What can I do for you? But first, allow me to introduce myself—Coléos, explorer, navigator, trader... etcetera, etcetera, etcetera..." he said, his eyes glinting with mischief.

His voice rang out like a sea shanty among the sounds of the bustling port, captivating our ears with tales not yet told. His hands, wide and animated, moved with his speech, weaving images in the air.

"We hail from Arvernes. I am Smérix—shaman, philosopher in idle hours, herbalist, astronomer… etcetera, etcetera, etcetera…" I answered, eyes twinkling.

The jest drew a hearty laugh from Coléos, his laughter deep and full, rolling across the bay like distant thunder. It warmed the air between us.

"…And these are my companions: Alexix, Garedix, Taranatos, and Athanor, to name but a few!"

"Divinix spoke of your voyage to northern Thrace. A bold endeavor, my friends—and one that shall cost you a few clinking coins!" he said with theatrical flair, sweeping his arms wide as if to embrace us all.

Then, pausing, he frowned slightly. "You're many. And the horses—ah no! No horses aboard my ship!"

"No horses?" I echoed. "How then shall we complete our journey in Thrace?"

"Too risky," he said firmly. "My vessel would not withstand a stampede, and I do not fancy a storm of hooves at sea. Sell them here on the dock. You'll find new mounts in Thrace easily enough. There! That man over there—tell him I sent you, he'll offer a fair price!"

"Very well," I said with a sigh. "Alexix! Sell the horses to that Ligurian! Tell him Coléos vouches for us!"

Alexix obeyed without delay, his brother following close behind.

Hm… judging by the state of our beasts and the bartering skills of my companions, I feared those negotiations would be brief… I chuckled inwardly.

"Very well, very well! Now let's talk business, my friends!" Coléos exclaimed, cheerfully rubbing his hands together. "I am a very busy explorer, you see… and as such, I'm preparing my next expedition to the western edge of Africa, beyond the Pillars of Heracles. An endeavor of great ambition—requiring, above all… gold."

"Will this do?" I interrupted, drawing from my satchel the pouch Divinix had entrusted to me.

Coléos' eyes lit up as he caught the weighty purse and felt its heft with a knowing smile. The clink of gold rang sweetly in the salty air—an echo of promises, voyages yet to come, and dreams forged on the high seas.

"Divinix is a man of his word—and a good client, too! This shall more than suffice. On board, my friends! Gather your belongings from the horses—everything's ready for your stay!"

At that moment, the Ligurian man arrived in haste, shouting to his comrades for help handling the horses. The twin brothers returned, faces bright with success and steps full of resolve.

"The horses will be well cared for until we return!" said Alexix, grinning.

"I expected no less," I replied with a smile of my own.

Coléos extended his arm with theatrical flair, ushering us aboard with infectious energy. His movements bore the ease of a man long used to taming the sea.

"Let us hope Poseidon shows us mercy, and that Aeolus blows kindly upon our sails! A long voyage lies ahead! Come aboard, come aboard! The winds favor us today!"

As he spoke, my companions retrieved their belongings

and boarded the vessel, ready to face the adventure that awaited beyond the waters.

The ship—a sturdy trireme, its white sails gleaming and oars aligned like the teeth of a leviathan—was poised to ride the sea. The sailors, swift and disciplined, guided us with steady hands.

As I watched the preparations unfold, a thrill surged in my chest. This was to be my first journey upon the sea—and for most of my companions as well. To me, it was the threshold of infinite discovery. Each wave would be a question, each gust a whispered answer from the divine.

The Ligurian fishing port unfurled behind us, alive with the morning bustle, as our ship, propelled by oars, drifted slowly from the quay. The sails climbed high and caught the wind, swelling like the breath of the gods. Commands rang out, oars struck the water in rhythm, gulls cried above—a symphony of salt, wood, and will.

***

Days passed, and we sailed between islands and rocky headlands. The ship, proud against the blue horizon, charted its course between mighty Kyrnos—known in times to come as Corsica—and Sandalyon, today called Sardinia, cleaving the glistening waters of the Middle Sea. Jagged coasts and sheer cliffs gave way to secret coves and golden beaches. The sea air, tinged with salt, filled our lungs with strength.

As I gazed upon these changing lands, I pondered the beauty of creation. To me, each island was a pearl of wisdom, each crag a lesson in endurance. And the sea—ah, the sea! A reflection of the human soul, vast and unknowable, serene one moment, wrathful the next.

On a day that seemed calm, a darkness loomed far on the horizon. Heavy clouds gathered—the telltale sign of a coming storm. The gods had spared us thus far... I hoped they would turn their eyes elsewhere.

On deck, Coléos and Athanor studied the skies, their furrowed brows betraying concern.

"A storm's coming," muttered Coléos through his beard. "And from here, it looks like a bad dance with the gods."

"We Celts are terrible dancers," Athanor replied dryly. "Let's sit this one out."

\*\*\*

But far from our sight, at the edge of that brewing tempest, a towering figure rose from the sea. A giant formed of water alone emerged from the waves—his hair and beard flowing with the currents, his powerful limbs parting the surface with divine grace.

Around him, the sea churned and raged, clouds massing above his brow. Yet with but a glance, he stilled the waters. His arms moved, and the elements obeyed.

And then, above him, another figure took shape—a body of wind and cloud, shifting and vaporous. Barely human in form, it hovered silently. Facing the storm, it breathed deep... and exhaled gently.

The storm dissolved.

Clouds scattered. The sea calmed. A hush fell across the

world.

***

Aboard the ship, Coléos stood at the helm, eyes fixed on the horizon where chaos had loomed. Athanor stood beside him, both men silent, witnessing the impossible.

The storm had vanished, as if carried off by a mother's lullaby. The sea shimmered with peace once more.

The silence between them said everything. They had seen the hands of the divine.

"The gods watch over us, my friends," Coléos murmured at last. "The gods are with us."

***

Far off, as the waters stilled and the clouds cleared, the man of water smiled once, then sank beneath the waves. The figure of air dissolved into the sky, leaving only a whisper of peace and promise.

***

What I had seen from afar stirred something within me. The gods walked with us. I felt it in my bones, in my blood.

Our journey was blessed. Every trial would bring us closer to the divine. Every wind a lesson, every wave a whisper of the sacred.

Our ship pressed onward, skimming past Sikeliala—Sicily—and then between Hellas, the many city-states of ancient Greece, and Kriti, the fabled isle of Crete, before entering the dark waters of the Black Sea.

Each island, each promontory we passed bore the marks

of ancient peoples, of myth and memory etched into the very stone.

And at last, after long weeks at sea, we made landfall along the northern coast of Thrace, where our voyage across the waters came to an end.

We Celts, weary but undaunted, stepped ashore with the quiet strength of those who have looked the gods in the eyes… and survived.

Our odyssey had only just begun.

# CHAPTER 12

*"First Encounters"*

Night had long since fallen by the time we made landfall. The dark shoreline of the Black Sea stretched before us, framed by a dense forest where our group had made camp.

As often since our departure, Athanor kept to himself, seated cross-legged upon a great stone, his gaze fixed with fierce intensity on the darkened horizon. He looked as though he were searching the infinite, hoping to glean some answer whispered only by the silence of the night.

Around the fire, my companions and I had gathered to speak of what came next.

"How are we to find these strangers?" Aridix asked, frustration sharp in his voice. "We don't even know where to look!"

"The winds favored us," I replied calmly. "We gained time at sea. The strangers cannot be far ahead. Coléos assured me this is the most likely place for their landing."

"Perhaps," Alexix snapped, "but we have no more horses! There's nothing here! And no trace of the strangers either! I searched the moment we arrived. Finding the trail they took in this unknown land will be no easy task—especially on foot! Coléos has duped us!"

"We need only push northward," I answered. "Surely they don't expect us to pursue them this far. Divinix believes the Underworld lies to the north. And Coléos told me we would find horses once we emerged from this forest." I pointed to the vast expanse of trees stretching beyond the hills. "He spoke of a land where horses are kings—Cimmeria."

"Oh, perfect," Aridix muttered bitterly, "a land of horses now! What's next—the Kingdom of the Pretty Little Magical Bird?"

With a groan of exasperation, he rose and strode past Taranatos, whose face bore the twisted shadow of pure hatred. Every scar on his flesh seemed to tell a tale of vengeance still waiting to be fulfilled.

"I'll hunt them down even if it takes me years!" he snarled. "I'll find them—and I'll tear them apart with my bare hands… and devour them afterward!"

With a sudden movement, he stalked away into the shadows to lie down, Alexix casting him a disapproving glance.

Nearby, Paritos and Lugotorix were seated around a small campfire, eating as they listened to the older warriors speak.

Lugotorix, ever the glutton, devoured his meal with little grace, food dribbling down his chin. His friend, more composed, ate slowly, savoring the meal the gods had granted them. But worry darkened his young face.

"They don't seem to know what they're doing," Paritos muttered, glancing at us.

"Adults never seem to know what they're doing," Lugotorix replied with a snort. "Aside from shouting at me and giving me chores, they're not good for much else!"

"To be fair, you do get into quite a bit of trouble," his friend teased with a grin.

"Hey! You're always right behind me, don't forget that!"

Their laughter rang out, light and genuine, a welcome contrast to the weight that pressed upon the night.

"We're on guard duty tonight," said Paritos. "I don't want to disappoint the chief. You take first watch. Wake me when you start to drift off."

"Count on me!" said Lugotorix. "Though I might be waking you sooner than you think…"

"Hmm, I don't doubt it," Paritos grumbled, curling up beneath his cloak. "Just try not to chew so loudly. It's infuriating."

Sitting by the fire with my fellow warriors, I cast my gaze across the camp—the flickering flames painting shadows on the faces of the brave Celts who had followed me into this madness.

All were settling in for what rest they could find. It was humbling to witness such resolve. My people, ready to cross the ends of the world for faith, for vengeance, for each other… May it always be so, for we know not what awaits us on the path ahead.

My eyes found Athanor again—still unmoving atop his stone. I watched him in silence, pondering all he had endured.

"Taranatos is losing his mind," Alexix growled. He had

not taken his eyes off the man, who now lay apart, muttering to himself. "Madmen are dangerous—for all of us."

"He's suffered more than most," I replied. "And like Athanor, his thirst for vengeance is boundless. He'll find peace only when he's spilt the blood of our enemies."

"Yes… and so will we all."

No more was said. One by one, we lay down, grateful for the solidity of earth beneath us. Many had suffered during the voyage—myself included. We Celts were never meant for the sea… land was our realm, and now, finally, we were home—at least, in spirit.

\*\*\*

Yet even as we slept, far deeper in the forest's embrace, near the edge of the beach, something stirred.

Shadows slipped silently among the trees. Horses stamped the earth nervously—too far for us to hear or see.

Riders watched us from the dark—silent, motionless. They bore lances, and their faces were hidden beneath hoods. The night veiled their features… and their intentions.

"They are here… as the goddess promised," one of them murmured.

"Yes," another whispered. "Tonight, we feast. And we'll drink to her glory—drink the sacred brew she gave us, the drink of the gods."

\*\*\*

Later that night, as our camp lay cloaked in darkness, silence reigned, and most of the warriors, worn down by our journey, slept the deep sleep of exhaustion. Aridix and I were still awake, the flickering glow of the fire casting long shadows across our grave faces. Unbeknownst to us, our eyes had both settled on Athanor. It was Aridix who broke the silence, his voice tinged with frustration.

"Athanor has barely spoken since we left. He always keeps to himself. It's as if he never sleeps. If this continues, he'll drop from exhaustion… or go mad."

I studied Athanor in silence, my gaze soft with compassion.

"He is mad… mad with grief, Aridix," I answered quietly. "He loved Anna more than life itself. Whatever happened to her must have been unbearable. He won't speak of it, but I can feel it. Believe me, he won't fall from exhaustion—no, he'll only fall once his task is done, and his vengeance complete. He's an eagle. He thinks, sees, and acts like them. Only death will stop him."

The Chief fell silent, pondering my words. Slowly, I closed my eyes, seeking rest. Aridix soon followed, and one by one, the warriors drifted into slumber. Only Lugotorix remained awake, sitting near the fire, standing guard as best he could.

High upon his rock, Athanor sat unmoving, his eyes fixed upon the flames. In his mind, echoes of Anna's laughter still rang clear. Visions of her danced before his eyes: they were out hunting together, riding through the forest beneath a golden sun. They reached the summit of a mountain, dismounted, and gazed out over the valley from a high promontory. In one another's arms, they watched twin eagles wheel through the sky above. They laughed together over a meal by the hearth, seated on the ground.

Anna smiled at him, and they kissed, deeply, passionately. Her hands rested upon his cheeks, her gaze ablaze with love.

"You are me, and I am you. We are one, my love," she whispered tenderly.

But the memory was torn apart, ripped away by the sound of galloping hooves—distant at first, then thundering closer. A scream shattered the stillness of the night…

Athanor was jolted from his trance. Shadows burst forth, storming the camp with the roar of charging hooves. Spears hissed through the air, finding the bodies of sleeping warriors. Waterskins were hurled, dousing the fires one by one in a hiss of steam.

Awakened by the cries of pain and the sudden chaos, the men scrambled to their feet. Athanor drew his sword and rushed toward his companions.

"To arms! We are under attack!" he roared.

Weapons were seized, but many, still groggy and blinded by the dark, could barely see. Panic surged. Men screamed as they were skewered by unseen foes or dragged off into the night by mounted shadows. Garedix and Alexix stood guard over me, shielding me with their blades.

"What is this? I can't see a thing!" shouted a warrior.

"They're taking me! Help me—they're taking me! It's not—" another cried, before vanishing into the night.

Athanor fought like a wild beast, sword flashing in the darkness. Around him, his comrades swung blindly at enemies they could scarcely make out. Taranatos, laughing like a madman, spun his blade wildly.

"Come! Come die on my sword, you cowards!" he howled.

Suddenly, the shadows withdrew into the forest, dragging with them the stunned, the wounded, the unarmed. Six bodies were left behind, strewn upon the earth.

The Chief and the remaining warriors formed a circle around me, shields raised, weapons ready. Athanor, dark-eyed, surveyed the carnage. Silence fell, broken only by the moans of the wounded. I pushed past the warriors who shielded me and listened to the forest… but there was nothing. Not a sound.

"They're gone," I said softly, shaken by the speed and violence of the attack.

"Was it them? The strangers we're pursuing?" asked Paritos, waiting for my answer.

I was troubled, though I tried not to show it. My brow furrowed to mask my doubt. I let the silence hang before replying.

"I don't know, my good Paritos. I don't know. But whatever the case, if we mean to reach the Underworld, we'll need to stay vigilant—day and night."

The Chief, furious, looked upon the fallen, then turned toward a smoldering campfire.

"They… they crushed us like insects!" he stammered, aghast.

His words caught in his throat, for a strange sound interrupted him—a deep, steady snore.

All eyes turned toward its source.

Lugotorix was fast asleep by the fire, snoring peacefully. Something in the Chief snapped. He lunged toward the boy in a frenzy.

"By all the gods! I'll kill you, you wretched marmot!" he

roared.

But Athanor moved like lightning, intercepting Aridix's blow and catching his arm mid-air. The Chief's face was a mask of rage, eyes wild with fury.

"What are you doing?! He deserves to die!" he screamed.

"He'll die soon enough," Athanor replied coldly. "You said they swept through us like insects. You're right. But remember—the strength of insects lies in their numbers. Look around! We're barely twenty left."

I stepped in at once, my voice sharp as steel, as Lugotorix blinked awake, groggy and confused.

"Athanor is right. Even if Lugotorix is king of all fools, we need every pair of hands we've got. His included."

The young man sat up, dazed and unsure. The Chief, still shaking with fury, turned toward the bodies of our fallen.

"You'll dig," Aridix growled.

"Huh? What? Why?" stammered Lugotorix.

Still fuming, Aridix pointed toward the corpses.

"To bury them. They died because of you."

"Relight the fires—by all the gods, what are you waiting for?" he bellowed to the others. "Do you want to wait for the sun to rise?!"

Lugotorix… Always dwelling in some imagined realm, even when awake… He had always been that way—lost in the clouds, clumsy and distracted, utterly absent from the moment. I often wondered why Aridix insisted on bringing him along. Surely, Lugotorix was meant to be an artist, a bard, or a sculptor—not a warrior.

The men set to work. Wounds were bound, the fallen gathered, the fires rekindled, while Lugotorix began digging with a flat stone he had found, under the Chief's cold, watchful gaze. Paritos came over without a word, head bowed. He picked up another stone and began digging beside his friend. Aridix let him be and turned away.

"Thanks," whispered Lugotorix. "But you don't have to… This is my fault…"

"I should've taken first watch. Just dig."

We could not risk a funeral pyre—not here, not in this haunted forest, not with unseen enemies lurking in the shadows.

The camp slowly returned to a fragile calm, but a heavy tension hung in the air. The flickering flames cast long, dancing shadows across the tired faces of our warriors. Each man seemed adrift in thought, dwelling on the sudden violence of the attack and the perilous road ahead.

I approached Athanor, who had returned to his solitary perch atop the rock. He sat as still as ever, seemingly locked in silent communion with the night itself, searching the depths of the Black Sea's darkness for some elusive answer. He was an enigma—a young man burdened by grief, yet burning with unyielding strength.

"Athanor," I said softly, "though it may seem small comfort in the darkness you carry, know that the stars above and the spirits of our ancestors are watching over us. Never forget—you are not alone in this quest. The strength of our people lies in our unity, and in our faith in what lies beyond us."

Athanor slowly turned toward me. His eyes, glistening with a strange blue fire, shone with a force beyond understanding.

"Smérix," he replied, his voice heavy with sorrow and

resolve, "I feel a great trial awaits us, and many will die. But I will not falter. Let me see this through while there is still time."

"You cannot face this alone, Athanor," I said. "And know this: none of us will abandon you. Not even sweet, foolish Lugotorix. We will follow you—to the end."

I placed a reassuring hand upon his shoulder, sensing how deeply my words resonated in his soul, how heavy his burden already was. The night wrapped itself around us like a sacred veil, but in that silence shared, I knew Athanor's spirit had already begun its march—toward the fire and fury of what lay ahead.

And thus, beneath the cloak of darkness and the veil of uncertainty, a new oath was made. One that would guide our steps, bind our resolve, and steel us for the dangers yet to come. The fate of Athanor, and of us all, had begun to unfold… and we would face it together, until the very end of our sacred quest.

# CHAPTER 13
*"The Forest of Torments"*

At daybreak, we left the stony beach that bordered the Black Sea, our silhouettes outlined against the rising light. Step by step, we were drawn into the forest, our worries and fears swallowed by its looming shadows. Our hearts beat in unison, a deep ancestral rhythm echoing the living pulse of the land—as though the forest itself were summoning us to face its hidden mysteries.

Bit by bit, we ventured deeper into its dense and dark heart, where every rustle, every snapping branch stirred a fresh wave of dread. Ever the scout, Taranatos prowled a good twenty paces ahead, his senses sharpened, his movements fluid and feline. There was something about him that I could not help but admire—a devotion carved in iron, a courage no wound could break.

Chief Aridix moved along the line of warriors, his piercing gaze ever watchful. As he passed by Lugotorix, he muttered with undisguised scorn:

"You, brave soul, should stay in the rear—watching our backs. I'm sure your screams of terror will be the best warning we could hope for."

Aridix's words were harsh, yet they carried the raw truth of survival. Lugotorix needed to learn—and fast—that there was no room for dreams or childish fancy on this path. Here, only those who faced the void with open eyes would see the journey through.

Without protest, Lugotorix fell back and took his place beside Athanor. The forest was thick, its canopy blocking even the morning light. Birds scattered noisily before us, their cries adding to the weight that already hung in the air. It was as if nature herself, tormented and restless, mirrored our inner unrest, amplifying it with every step.

A distant cry pierced the hush—faint at first, but distinct enough to bring our march to a halt. We all turned our ears toward it, unsure of what we'd heard. Aridix looked toward me.

"Shaman! What was that?"

I shook my head, uncertain.

"I do not know. Keep moving!"

The forest whispered its own language—one older than any god, older than the stones. Its stories curled through every root and leaf, but even the wisest spirits might struggle to read their meaning.

The cries grew louder as we pressed on—long, anguished, echoing from tree to tree. The unease among us deepened. At my side, Alexix and Garedix exchanged dark glances.

"I don't like this…" muttered Alexix. "This forest reeks of death."

His words spoke a truth none could deny. This place

felt cursed, like a graveyard of forgotten gods.

"I thought our gods were fearsome," he added, grimly. "But the Greek ones… they're mad. How can they allow such horrors to exist? Those shadows that attacked us… that wasn't—"

"Our gods reflect the soul of nature and of men. The Greek gods… they mirror the full spectrum of human folly," I replied, my tone grave. "This forest is their mirror—twisted, tormented… and entirely too human."

A part of me, even in fear, felt the pull of fascination—at this alien faith, this world of capricious immortals. It was a reflection of all we are and all we dread.

At the rear of the line, Athanor walked beside Lugotorix, who made a clumsy attempt at conversation.

"Do you ever speak? I get it—you're grieving. You miss your wife. That's gotta be hard…"

The words were awkward, but not unkind. A flawed attempt at connection in a place where everything conspired to tear us apart. Athanor cast him a look of cold fire, then moved up the line to join Garedix and Alexix. Each man bears grief in his own way, and Athanor's silence was a storm unto itself.

"This forest is cursed!" Aridix spat.

Athanor halted and laid his palm against the bark of a nearby tree. His fingers brushed the rough surface with reverence. He closed his eyes a moment, then looked upward to the shadow-wrapped canopy—almost alive, writhing above our heads.

"All I feel here is pain and madness," he murmured. "Nature suffers in this place. She loathes those who dwell within her."

His words rang true. This forest was not simply dark—it was wounded, twisted, screaming beneath its skin.

Each shadow was a threat, each path a potential snare. And then, a shriek tore through the air—inhuman, agonizing.

"AAAAAHHH! Help me! Help!"

Paritos froze, eyes wide. He knew that voice.

"That's Artix! We have to help him!"

With a savage roar, Taranatos broke into a charge, sword gleaming, his battle cry shaking the leaves. We followed, hearts pounding with dread. Adrenaline seared through our veins—every breath, every step a dance on the edge of death.

"Damn fool's leading us straight into a trap!" Alexix growled behind me.

As we ran, breathless, the undergrowth closed in on us, as though the forest itself sought to bar our passage. There was something unnatural about it—almost alive. The very air felt thick and stifling, hard to draw into our lungs, as if the woods wished to drown our will.

A few hundred paces deeper, we reached the edge of the forest, where a small hill overlooked a deep ravine. The cries came from below, still hidden from view. We had to be cautious, remain unseen. We had learned the lesson well: our foes were merciless. Aridix gave a sharp nod and pointed to several warriors, ordering them to stay behind. Strategy—even amid chaos—was his second skin.

Atop the ridge, Taranatos lay prone at the brink of a precipice, eyes fixed on the depths below. Aridix, Alexix, Athanor, Garedix, and I joined him, crawling forward on elbows and knees. What we saw twisted our stomachs with revulsion. A gash in the earth, fifty meters deep, where hell itself had spilled its bile.

Down there, five of our comrades were impaled upon stakes. Two yet clung to life—barely. The others had been grotesquely mutilated, their bodies butchered, desecrated. Fury and horror rippled across every face.

"I was sure you'd get us spotted," Alexix growled at Taranatos.

"Did you see how high it is?" the latter snapped. "Even I can't jump that far. And I'll need you lot to take them all down. Look—they're ours. They're right there. What in the gods' name have those beasts done to them?!"

Another cry rang out, deeper into the canyon.

"We have to help them!" shouted Athanor, rising.

"No!" I cut him off. "It's far too risky. We don't know how many of those things are down there. Or where the accursed foreigners might be lurking. It's a trap, surely!"

Just then, Garedix, who'd crept a few steps away, motioned us over, his face twisted in disgust. I had never seen that look in his eyes before—horror carved deep. On hands and knees, we joined him… and I wished we hadn't.

Gods preserve us.

There, on the canyon floor, a dozen half-man, half-horse creatures tore at the remains of our warriors. Centaurs. But not like those of the tales—no noble heroes of marble and bronze. These were monsters, feral and frenzied, their equine bodies slick with blood, their humanoid faces warped by madness. They gorged on human flesh, fighting over bones, snarling like wolves. Blood soaked the rocky earth. Their blades hacked indiscriminately. Some drank from foul-smelling skins that released curling wisps of vapor—some potion or draught that made their eyes shine with lunacy.

I shall never forget those eyes. Nor the sound of bone splitting under their jaws.

"We're going down there!" Athanor raged, trembling with fury. "We won't leave our kin to be devoured!"

"No!" I snarled through clenched teeth. "It's too late! There's nothing left to save. We don't even know what we're dealing with—not truly. And we still have a mission to complete!"

Every part of my being cried out for vengeance. My heart beat like war drums, demanding blood for blood. But the mind—the mind must prevail over rage. The path of the wise is not always the path of the brave.

Below, the centaurs laughed—horrible, guttural sounds. Some poured more of their strange brew down their throats. Others licked blood from their arms or faces. Unaware of us. Unaware, perhaps, even of themselves.

"Enough!" I whispered hoarsely. "I can't watch this any longer. We must go."

"But they're feasting on our brothers!" Alexix cried, his voice cracking with fury.

"It's too late, Alexix! They're gone. You want me to bring them back from the dead? I cannot!" I snapped, rage and sorrow mingling in my chest like smoke and flame.

This was the weight of impotence. All the knowledge in the world could not save the lost. All the prayers I knew were no match for death and madness.

"I've changed my mind," Taranatos growled. "Forget capturing the bastards. I'm going to tear them to pieces and scatter them to the winds."

"Shut up, Taranatos," Alexix snarled, shooting him a murderous glare. Then he turned away and stalked back toward the warriors waiting in the shadows beyond the trees. One by one, we followed.

We left behind the laughter and the screams—those terrible echoes of inhuman glee that would haunt our dreams for many nights to come.

And that was when, of all people, Lugotorix spoke—cheerful as ever, clueless to the weight of what we had witnessed.

"So? When do we start bashing skulls?" he asked, bouncing slightly. "I'm bored! We never get to fight anything!"

Alexix spun and shoved him to the ground without a word, walking past him like he wasn't even worth a second glance.

Lugotorix scrambled up, confused, brushing dust from his tunic. He hadn't seen what we had. Hadn't felt it. But even so—he could've read the pain on our faces, if only he'd tried.

Paritos, ever loyal, came to his side, silent. The two friends rejoined the others, sobered by the cold air that clung to us like a shroud.

I fell in beside the rest, Aridix close behind. His eyes were as dark as the forest, and his silence weighed more than iron.

And so we walked—back into the suffocating shadow of the woods.

That forest, ancient and heavy with secrets, seemed to absorb our hope, dim our purpose. With every step, it reminded us of our fragility—how small we were before the unknowable powers that ruled these lands.

My thoughts wandered to our lost companions, and I

prayed to the Gods that their spirits might find peace in the land of our ancestors. I was certain—they would return to us one day. They had been good men, brave souls. The kind who never truly vanish.

Aridix, his steps weighed down by grief, stopped suddenly and turned toward me. His eyes burned with a mix of sorrow and rage.

"Smérix… you must find a way to protect our people!"

I nodded solemnly, fully aware of the burden he was placing upon my shoulders.

"I will do all that is within my power, Aridix. But the forces that surround us are ancient… and strong. We must remain vigilant, and more than that—united. If we fail to hold together, we shall never reach the end of our path."

At that moment, the forest seemed to respond to my words. A gentle breeze stirred the leaves overhead, whispering like a quiet breath of encouragement. It was a sign, subtle but undeniable, that we were not alone. The spirits of nature were listening—watching—ready to offer their protection to those who still remembered how to listen.

\*\*\*

We pressed on, step after heavy step. The hours wore on and led us deeper into the veil of night. Shadows danced around us, forming strange and shifting shapes. Fear still gnawed at our hearts, but something new stirred among us—a solidarity born of shared pain, a courage nurtured by purpose. Whatever horrors awaited us ahead, we would face them together. We had no choice. We were Celts.

Suddenly, a sharp cry tore through the air, followed by

the crashing of broken branches. Taranatos, ever at the vanguard, sprinted toward the sound, sword in hand and ready to strike. We followed at once, hearts pounding with dread. Another danger, I thought. Already.

But the sight that met us in the clearing was not what we expected.

A strange light bathed the space—a supernatural glow that seemed to rise from the earth itself. At the center, a creature writhed, grotesque and malformed, like a twisted child born from nightmare. Bat-like wings flailed helplessly as thick roots wound around its limbs, binding it fast to the earth. The roots… they were alive. The tree that held them pulsed with a will of its own.

Taranatos stepped forward, eyes locked on the creature.

"What in the name of the gods is that?" he muttered, more to himself than to any of us.

"I told you," Athanor said darkly. "This forest does not love the beings that dwell within it."

We stood motionless, weapons in hand but uncertain. The creature thrashed and shrieked, but the roots only tightened. The forest was judging, punishing. The land itself rejected the presence of this misshapen, foul intruder.

"The forest is showing us something," I said aloud, my voice cutting through the thick stillness. "It tells us that we are not alone. That it can fight… and that it loathes those who bring it harm. If we respect its laws—if we honor its spirit—it may yet stand by us."

Aridix gave a slow nod, and a flicker of hope glinted in his otherwise grim face.

"Very well, Smérix," he said, turning to address the others. "The forest is with us. And I swear, the first fool who breaks a branch or tears a leaf—I'll cut his head off myself. Do I make myself clear?"

The warriors nodded—some slowly, others with haste. None wished to test the wrath of Aridix, nor that of the forest. They understood, at last, that survival here would depend not only on courage, but on humility.

We pressed on, deeper into the woodland's heart, our steps quieter now, guided not just by need, but by a newfound reverence.

\*\*\*

Behind us, in the hush of the dying light, something stirred.

From the branches of the tree that had just crushed the foul beast, a radiant figure emerged. A creature of impossible grace—a Hamadryad, guardian spirit of the tree.

She appeared as a young maiden, her body lithe and delicate, her skin tinged with the gray of bark, ethereal and shifting like lichen under moonlight. Her presence was eerie, both beautiful and terrible. The bark of the tree seemed etched into her very being. Her eyes, twin pearls of pale fire, shone with fierce purpose. Her hair, long tendrils of ivy, floated gently as though caught in an unseen current.

She had lent her essence to the tree, gifting it strength. Her fingers pulsed with ancient energy, weaving it back into the wounded roots. Together, tree and spirit had crushed the blight that defiled the sacred land.

And as the twisted creature fell limp, crushed and still, the Hamadryad's form softened. Her skin brightened, her features eased. Her task was done. Slowly, almost imperceptibly, she faded into the foliage, returning to her silent watch, her eternal bond with the tree renewed.

The tree itself pulsed with life once more. Leaves flushed with color. Bark glistened with sap. A small triumph of balance reclaimed.

And we—we knew none of this.

But something had shifted within us. Though we had not seen the spirit, we felt her. A presence. A will. A warning.

We moved through the trees in silence now, torches held low, the firelight flickering across faces hardened by loss and lit by a quiet awe. We would not speak of it aloud—not yet. But the forest had become more than a place of danger.

It was now a presence. A force. An ally.

Each rustle in the underbrush, each flicker of shadow, was no longer just a threat. It was a message. A sign. Something to be read and honored.

And so we marched onward, hearts heavy with grief, but arms steadied by purpose. The forest had tested us—and perhaps, for now, accepted us.

We were no longer alone.

# CHAPTER 14
## *"The Throne of Shadows"*

Night cloaked the realm of shadows. At the heart of this sunless dominion, Hades, lord of the Underworld, sat upon his throne of obsidian and brimstone. The black, gleaming promontory overlooked an arena where his trembling subjects brought tidings from the world of the dead. The flickering torchlight cast restless shadows, heightening the sinister atmosphere of the place.

His figure, towering and ghostly pale, echoed that of his brother—but spectral, more ancient still. A long beard and hair streaked with silver drifted about him as if submerged in water. A halo of translucent, blue-gray flames emanated from his form, blurring his outline like heat rising from scorched earth.

Hades, king of shades, wore a mystery and authority that transcended the boundaries of the worlds. His presence was dreadful yet majestic—a silent force, inescapable, watching without judgment. His eyes, twin abysses of midnight, mirrored the eternity of his reign and the unfathomable depth of his thoughts.

At the center of the arena, a tall, athletic man paced with visible agitation. A radiant halo of white and gold shimmered around him, dancing with his movements.

It was Hermes, clad in his golden chlamys and winged sandals—a gleaming figure in this dismal court. His wavy blond hair framed a face of refined features and steady resolve, while his bright eyes sparkled with divine mischief, betraying his nature as a celestial envoy. Upon his brow rested his winged helmet, enhancing his quicksilver grace and elusive presence.

Beyond his role as the gods' messenger, Hermes held a sacred charge in the Underworld—he was the psychopomp, guide of souls to their destined rest. His task was to see that every spirit found its rightful place, whether in the Elysian Fields or in the depths of Tartarus.

A short distance away, three dreadful women beat the air with their vast black wings. Their hair writhed with blood-dripping serpents, creating a ghastly contrast against their moon-pale skin. Their eyes blazed with wrath and unwavering resolve, while their shredded, blood-stained robes and clawed hands proclaimed their merciless purpose.

The Erinyes—also known as the Furies—were the arbiters of infernal justice. Alecto, Megaera, and Tisiphone were charged with punishing the vilest transgressions, hunting guilty souls without mercy and ensuring the divine law remained unbroken.

Hermes halted his pacing, his voice ringing across the amphitheater:

"Hades! This cannot go on—the Elysian Fields are empty. Something is gravely wrong!"

Ah, what bitter irony, to see Hermes—messenger of the gods—tormented by the growing disorder in the land of the dead, a realm that ought to be steeped in eternal stillness and balance.

Hades raised a hand, weary, cutting him off.

"Hermes, Hermes, Hermes… Speak to Alecto and her sisters. I have other matters to attend to."

One of the winged women stepped forward. Her honeyed voice belied the horror of her appearance. Alecto's pallid skin and piercing gaze gave the impression she could see through the very marrow of the soul.

"We're not to blame if Tartarus is bursting with wicked souls," she said, breaking into a chilling laugh, promptly echoed by Megaera and Tisiphone.

Megaera, her immense wings tattered by centuries of torment, lingered in the shadows, her face hardened by endless vengeance. Tisiphone, youngest of the three, had emerald eyes and a voice as soft as a lullaby—haunting, almost sweet, at odds with her monstrous form.

"We labor day and night to make them repent," she added. "It takes time, you know—delicacy, patience. When their sins are finally confessed, we do as custom demands. We make them drink from the river Lethe… so they forget everything."

Hades' voice thundered suddenly, cutting through the chamber like a bolt from the void:

"Enough! Get to the point!"

Startled by his fury, the three sisters flinched and retreated into the shadows. Alecto bowed low, her wings folded like mourning veils.

"Forgive me, Master. But that is the very problem! They forget everything… and once they return to the land of the living, they sin again. It's a cycle without end."

Hades exhaled deeply, worn thin by the weight of eternity. With a silent wave of his hand, he dismissed them. The Furies vanished into a dark corridor that spiraled down into the bowels of the Underworld, where torment was meted with method and cruelty.

Hermes remained alone in the arena, waiting for his master's will.

"Hermes! Find a solution. Until then, give me news of my Thunder Eagle! Where are they now?"

"They're on the move," Hermes replied, bowing slightly. "All goes as you wished. They'll be here soon. Your faithful pawns are progressing well. I believe they'll have to slow down, though, if we want those foolish Celts to keep up the chase…"

"Good. Good. Then go to the Erinyes. You are the messenger, are you not? Work with them. Heal my kingdom."

"At once, Hades. I shall seek a cure for the sickness plaguing your realm."

He turned on his heel, then paused, visibly intrigued.

"Ah yes, your friend keeps her promises," he muttered. "Though I never took her for one to use such… radical means. I don't know how she's done it, but she has awakened the darkest instincts in the wild centaurs. I wonder what else she has in store for us," he added thoughtfully, before vanishing from the arena.

Hades watched him go in silence, a low growl rumbling in his throat. Where would all of this lead? Defying his brother had never been the wisest idea he'd had over the countless centuries. He knew his wrath—and he feared it. Had he not received the Underworld only by the will of that beloved brother?

The eternal darkness reigned over the realm of the dead, while the Lord of the Underworld, immersed in thought, brooded on the challenges ahead and the troubled state of things. What irony, what twisted complexity, in this domain where even gods must seek solutions to ceaseless suffering.

Hades, weary yet mighty, steeled himself for trials that touched not just the souls of the dead, but the very essence of the cycle of life and death. Hermes—so often the gods' carefree herald—now found himself burdened with the dilemmas of the Underworld. A heavy task for divine shoulders more used to flying than to bearing the weight of fate.

Was there truly a solution, Hades wondered? Could anything break the eternal loop of sin and redemption? The fatigue of millennia lined his face. Was he to repeat the same motions forevermore, or could a new path be carved into the bedrock of eternity?

From the far corners of his realm, the whispers of wandering souls echoed softly—murmurs of confusion, longing, and despair. Perhaps these aimless spirits were the true reflection of the infernal paradox. Even gods are not immune to the endless turning of the wheel.

As he stood lost in thought, a voice, soft and seductive, curled through the shadows and reached his ear. Feminine, smooth, alluring.

"I hope you haven't changed your mind about our

agreement, Lord of the Dead," it purred. "Your realm is steeped in sorrow… The light of the Thunder Eagle would do it much good."

Hades smiled faintly, then rose from his throne and stepped toward the balustrade overlooking the arena.

"I always honor the pacts I make. So long as no one tries to deceive me," he said, placing his pale hands upon the cold stone.

"I hear your warning," the voice replied sweetly. "Do not worry. You may keep him here in your realm. I only seek to weaken Zeus—and use the bird's power when the time comes. If all unfolds as we planned, together, we shall hold more sway over Olympus. Zeus will no longer be all-powerful."

"Then we are agreed. He'll serve me well. Now leave me be. We'll speak again in due time. Tend to those Celts."

With those words, he turned from the balcony and vanished into a corridor, deep and endless as the grave.

***

Far below, in the winding hollows of the Underworld, Hermes walked a narrow corridor lost in thought. He entered an oval chamber lit by torches sputtering in silence. The burden of the task given by Hades weighed heavily on him. To find a solution to this eternal impasse… not a simple matter.

He knew that consulting Alecto and her sisters, the Erinyes, would be inevitable. For all their dreadful appearance, their ancient wisdom was unmatched.

Alecto, Megaera, and Tisiphone—though tormentors by role—understood the soul more intimately than any.

They knew the human heart was a labyrinth of light and shadow, virtue and vice. Their duty was to hunt and judge the guilty, to uphold the divine sentence, and ensure that the justice of the dead was done.

Hermes approached them with gravity. The three sisters awaited him, wings folded, their eyes glinting with dark fire.

"Ladies," he began, bowing low, "Hades has tasked me with finding a solution to our plight. We must break this endless cycle of sin and rebirth. What do you propose?"

Alecto, the eldest, narrowed her eyes and spoke slowly, her voice dripping with arcane wisdom.

"Perhaps… it is time to consider a different approach," she said, her tone veiled with mystery.

"Speak. I'm listening," Hermes urged.

"For eons, we've followed the same protocol. Perhaps, when a soul returns to the living world, a sliver of memory must remain—just enough for it to learn. I would call it… déjà vu. From time to time, they will feel as though they've lived a moment before. A glimpse. Just enough to recall past errors… and maybe, choose differently."

Hermes nodded, contemplative.

"It is bold. Risky. But I'm not saying no."

Tisiphone, youngest of the trio, then spoke—her soft voice in sharp contrast to her ghastly visage.

"True change comes from within. If we are to awaken the conscience, perhaps we must sow seeds of wisdom… even if it means breaking old laws."

They spoke at length, weaving thoughts like the Fates spin their thread—debating, dreaming, daring. Hermes bore it all, knowing that when the time came to present their ideas, Hades might not welcome such upheaval. But maybe, just maybe, it was time for a silent revolution in the land of the dead—a reimagining of ancient tradition for a more balanced eternity.

And as I reflect on this tale, I wonder—can the very nature of the gods evolve? Perhaps, in the end, it is not only mortals who are shaped by time… but immortals too.

## CHAPTER 15
*"The Procession of Shadows"*

To the left stretched the edge of the dense Thracian forest; to the right, a barren slope, a deceptive plateau, then a gentle rise leading to naked hills, scattered with a few trees and shrubs. We had entered Cimmeria—a land of nomads from the wild steppes that spread as far as the eye could see, where only the strongest dared to survive.

Birds sang joyfully, and insects buzzed past in a gentle murmur. One of them, a large beetle, settled on a plant, adding a pulse of life to this tranquil landscape. Ah, what serenity! I, Smérix, silent witness to this natural symphony, marveled at how every creature held its rightful place.

The contrast between the sick, brooding forest behind us and these sunlit plains—symbols of space and freedom—was striking.

Suddenly, the peace was broken. Hoofbeats and the sound of wings disturbed the hush. Birds, the faithful watchers of this vast realm, burst from their perches in a flurry. Something was coming.

At ground level, a dung beetle was hauling its burden when the drumming of hooves shook the earth, shattering the delicate order of that microcosm. Startled, the insect took flight—only to fall abruptly, struck down mid-air by some invisible force. As if fate itself had chosen this moment to remind us of the fragility of life.

At the head of a procession of riders, carts, and foot soldiers, the massive dark figure of the leader of the foreigners took form. Cloaked in a long black mantle, his hood veiled his face. He halted his mount and turned, slowly riding back along the halted column. His warriors—twenty men, all rough, grim, and bristling with weapons—stood watchful and ready.

In the center of the convoy, a wagon bore a great cage, and within it, a smaller one. Inside, the Thunder Eagle lay on a bed of straw, wounded and silent. Such sorrow, to see a creature born of the skies, an emblem of liberty and might, reduced to this state of helplessness.

The Leader stopped beside the cart. He stretched out one powerful arm, seized a bar of the cage, and shook it violently. A deep, rasping breath escaped from within his hood.

As he moved, the fur covering his muscular forearm became visible—black and thick—and his clawed hand left no doubt: this being was not human. The Thunder Eagle remained motionless, unconscious, suffering. With a dissatisfied grunt, the beast released the cage and turned away. His ears had caught the beating of powerful wings near the forest's edge.

Two bird-women had appeared.

Harpies. Wretched, emaciated creatures—half-human,

half-bird—with skeletal limbs and wide black wings. They hovered just above the ground before landing. To cross paths with such beings could only herald omens dark and dire.

"Where are they?" barked the foreign leader.

"They've entered the forest," answered one of the harpies. The man shook his head, annoyed.

"So slow! I can't afford to wait! They must move faster—get them through the forest! Thin them out if you must! Kill a few! Perhaps their numbers are slowing them down. Go now, you stink like rot!"

The two harpies looked at each other, offended.

"It's her that reeks, not me! I swear it!" one of them protested.

With a sudden movement, the man lunged toward them, unleashing a roar so terrible that it made half the horses rear. His hood slipped, revealing a monstrous mouth and a snout like a bull's, lined with fangs dripping saliva. His eyes, glowing crimson, flickered with malevolent fire. The rest of his face remained hidden in shadow.

His men struggled to calm their steeds while their master advanced on the harpies, who shrank back in fear. This creature—part man, part beast—was the embodiment of dread itself. A reminder that evil does not always wear a human face.

"But, Master… how shall we do it?" one harpy dared ask, trembling.

"Figure it out!" he snapped.

Without another word, the harpies flew off, and the beast turned away.

"Is there a village nearby?" he asked one of his men.

"Yes, Master. Not far from here."

"Good. Let's leave some traces of our passing. Those Celtic fools might actually lose our trail!"

He burst into laughter, echoed by his men. But just as suddenly, his face turned to stone. With a sharp nudge of his heels, he urged his mount forward, and the entire column resumed its grim march…

# CHAPTER 16

## *"The Mysteries of the Canopy"*

For days we had walked, and the deeper we pressed into its heart, the more the forest thickened around us, closing in like the walls of an ancient dream. It mirrored the darkness within our souls, the pain each of us carried like a sacred burden. With every step, it felt as though the trees bent inwards, their leaves whispering at our passing, stirred by a wind no one could feel. Even Lugotorix—usually so lost in his own world—was beginning to sense the weight of something that pressed upon us from all directions.

This forest seemed… inhabited. Not merely alive, but possessed—by something far greater than itself. At times, I could swear I saw openings in the canopy above, like blinking eyes, opening and closing again in an instant—as if something immense were watching us.

Yes, something watched us. Of this I was certain. The very density of life here mirrored our own tormented spirits, an entity that read our fears like runes carved into bark. Others too had glimpsed these fleeting eyes in the treetops, though none dared speak of it aloud. "Let it remain in our imagination," they must have thought. For to give voice to such fear would be to summon it fully into the world.

But it was no illusion. If we had seen what loomed above us—had we but risen high into the air—what terror would have gripped our hearts! For from the sky, the leaves of the forest formed the unmistakable outline of a colossal woman in flowing robes. She lay above the trees like a living canopy, drifting slowly as if to follow our every move.

Had we witnessed that sight, I have no doubt it would have crushed our spirits and stripped away all illusion of control. We were mere mortals, wandering through a realm governed by forces we could neither name nor fathom. And as the day gave way to dusk, the night descended quickly, cloaking the forest in a darker shroud.

Taranatos, ever the scout, prowled ahead with narrowed eyes. He sniffed the air, glancing left and right with increasing unease. Every now and then he turned back to us, a strange smile playing on his lips—half warning, half invitation. As if he sensed something was about to unfold.

Some among us lit torches to pierce the growing gloom. Their flickering flames cast shifting shadows that seemed to dance of their own accord.

Aridix drew near to Alexix, who walked at my side.

"I don't like this," Alexix muttered, his voice strained. "I keep feeling like we're being watched."

"We are," I answered with quiet certainty. "We have been for quite some time now."

Aridix, ever pragmatic, grumbled:

"Maybe. But what bothers me is Taranatos. Look at him—he's got the stare of a madman. And that grin when he looks back at us? I don't like it. Not one bit."

And he was right. There was something unhinged about him now—a gleam in his eye that was not courage, but something darker. At that moment, Taranatos turned toward us.

"Can't you feel it?" he shouted. "The stench of death! It's coming for us! You'll soon know what it's like when it crawls through your veins and turns you into its puppet!"

Then, with a twisted laugh, he added:

"But not me. I'm no coward. I'm a Celt. I don't wait for death—we meet it head-on!"

His laughter echoed like a challenge hurled into the void. A defiant cry in the face of the inevitable. And in his eyes burned a fire that stood in stark contrast to the fear tightening the faces of his companions. With a final burst of maniacal laughter, he vanished into the trees.

We stood frozen. Was it courage that had driven him—or madness? Only time would tell.

Night fell fully now, and around us the forest stirred with strange noises. Leaves rustled with a windless breath. Distant calls of creatures—some familiar, some decidedly not—rose and fell. Each sound was sharper, deeper, more… meaningful in the dark. As if the forest were whispering to itself, plotting, deciding our fates.

"Taranatos is mad," Alexix declared. "And as I've said before, madmen are dangerous."

"He's right about one thing," added Aridix, sniffing the air. "There's something foul in the wind…"

Athanor had stopped walking. He studied the

movement of the trees, their branches swaying though no wind touched them. A look of dawning realization passed over his face. He saw something in that forest—something we could not.

"Something's coming," he murmured. "It's close. The forest… the forest is trying to warn us, Smérix."

"Enough!" I said, my voice firm. "We go no further tonight."

We had pushed to the edge of exhaustion. To press on now would be folly. We needed rest, even here.

But Athanor stepped forward, his voice low and urgent:

"No. We must keep moving. The less we stand still, the safer we are."

He paused, eyes sweeping the treetops. An eagle let out a cry from a nearby branch, watching Athanor as if it understood.

"Anna is near. I can feel her. We have to keep going."

His words struck like an arrow into the night— yearning, mournful, determined. Love and loss had become his compass. Aridix and I exchanged a look. Athanor was unraveling. Was he slipping, like Taranatos? The madness that hunted us in silence now crept into our hearts.

"That's it," Aridix growled. "He's cracking too. Just what we needed."

"I worry for him too," I confessed. "But he's right about one thing. We can't stay here."

We pressed forward. Taranatos would find his way back to us—or not. We couldn't linger. The torches flared and flickered as we moved, casting wild shapes in the dark, as though we ourselves were becoming shadows among shadows.

Wings beat above us. Cries—some of birds, some not—rose and fell. Truth be told, we no longer knew if they were natural. It didn't matter.

We moved deeper into the unknown. The darkness swallowed our trail, and only the dim flames of our torches bore witness to our passage through the realm of secrets.

Thus did we continue—like phantoms in the deep wood—our hearts pulsing with the rhythm of an endless night…

# CHAPTER 17
## *"The Camp of Shadows"*

In the steppes of Cimmeria, as the sun dipped behind the hills in a haze of crimson and gold, the strangers were finishing the preparations for their night camp. Around the rough bivouac, there was a frantic bustle—men hauling firewood, setting up tents, feeding and watering their steeds. In the twilight's warm glow, their silhouettes almost seemed dignified… Almost.

But it didn't take long for a darker truth to rise and choke the light.

A little off to the side, bound to a tree like wild animals, lay a group of captive women, huddled together in pain and exhaustion. Most were unconscious, sprawled atop one another in filthy, bloodied garments that bore grim witness to their brutal treatment.

These savage lands bore silent witness to the depths of the shadows that dwell in men's hearts. Was this what passed for strength in the world of mortals? To break the weak, to crush the sacred softness that still survives in this world?

Three warriors approached the prisoners, cruelty gleaming in their eyes. One crouched beside a young girl and tried to rouse her—unsuccessfully. With brutal indifference, he untied her, gripped her hair, and dragged her limp body behind him like a sack of refuse.

To witness life so casually reduced to nothing—it sickened me. These men, drunk on their own authority, had long forgotten that true power lies in compassion, not domination.

The third soldier lingered near another girl. He bent over her, lips curled in mockery.

"Look at this," he sneered, flipping over her lifeless body, blood soaking her belly. "Cimmerian girls—real tough ones, eh?"

Beneath her lay a hidden shard of metal. One of the other prisoners reached for it, but he struck her down with a brutal punch that left her slumped and motionless.

"Get rid of that one," he barked, eyes blazing with hatred. "Before her stinking guts foul the place!"

Despair, yes... but even despair has teeth. No one knows from which trembling hand hope might strike when the night seems most suffocating.

The other man hauled the body away, grumbling, while the third stood, staring at the surviving women with sadistic satisfaction.

"Where are your gods now, Cimmerians?" he mocked. "Seems they don't care what happens to you!"

"Yours must be real proud of you, coward!" one of the prisoners spat. "Untie me, and we'll see whose side the gods are really on!"

He laughed and seized her by the throat, leaning in to reply—but she lunged and sank her teeth into his forearm, biting down with all the fury of the hopeless.

He staggered back, howling in rage.

"Cursed Cimmerian whore!" he growled, retreating, blood dripping down his arm.

From nearby, others had witnessed the scene and now burst into mocking laughter.

"Shut your mouths!" he snarled as he stormed past them.

Farther away, the towering Chief approached the cart that carried the great cage. He halted before it, arms crossed, eyes narrowing as dusk bled across the sky.

The shadows gathered. The twilight deepened. Inside the cage, something stirred.

Slowly, the Chief pulled back his hood, revealing a monstrous head crowned with horns and the gaping maw of a bull. Great fangs glistened in the fading light, and his eyes—those cursed red eyes—blazed like coals in a pit of ash.

The Minotaur.

A creature of myth, yes—but more than that. He was the embodiment of the darkness we all carry within. Rage, hunger, obsession… All given form in this brute.

And then—light.

As the night descended, a glow began to bloom within the cage. Slowly, a figure took shape. Seated, legs crossed, arms resting on her knees, head bowed. Then, she raised her face—and looked straight at the Minotaur.

He stepped forward, his clawed hands gripping the bars as he leaned in.

"Good evening, Anna. Your darling is very close now. Don't worry—I'm doing everything I can to make sure he finds you…"

His laughter rumbled like thunder in a crypt. The foul stench of his breath made the air curdle.

Anna stared back, fire in her eyes, her face drawn with suffering but unbroken.

"You don't frighten me," she said through clenched teeth. "You can't touch me! Athanor will kill you. He'll gut you like the beast you are!"

The Minotaur bared his teeth in a jagged grin, his voice slick with venom.

"For now, you're right—I can't reach you. But where I'm taking you, that will change. You'll be mine… forever. Until then, remember: three things are real to you now— this cage, that Bird… and the love I have for you."

He gave a hideous grimace that may have been a smile, then turned away, his voice trailing behind him.

"Oh… and about the Bird… he's dying. Heal him!"

Anna's breath caught in her throat as he disappeared into the gloom.

What cruelty, what twisted irony, to force such a choice upon her. Yet in that moment, amidst chains and filth and torment, a light still burned. The light of love. Of hope. She clung to it fiercely.

She turned toward the Bird, crumpled and still upon the straw.

"Athanor will come for you, noble friend… And he will avenge me," she whispered, fury igniting in her eyes.

## CHAPTER 18
### *"Dwellers of the Forest"*

Later that night, as the forest wrapped itself in a cloak of thick darkness, we moved forward with caution. Every one of us was on edge, reacting to the faintest rustle of leaves or the strange cries echoing through the woods. At the rear of the line, Lugotorix and Paritos marched together, their eyes darting at every suspicious sound.

"This forest gives me the creeps... Sometimes I wonder what the hell we're doing here. Don't you?" Lugotorix broke the silence.

"It's not exactly what I imagined either..."

"And this whole story with the bird, the Greek god—come on, isn't it weird? We're Celts! What are we doing out here in the middle of who-knows-where?"

Paritos was starting to get annoyed. His friend wasn't wrong, but perhaps it was better not to ask too many questions.

"Look, all I know is those damned foreign bastards

sacked our sacred mountains and killed Anna! She was one of ours—and no one, no one does that without paying the price. Can you imagine what the Lemovices would say if they knew we just let it go?"

"Yeah, sure," Lugotorix replied pragmatically, "but in the meantime, we're not exactly protecting our village either, are we? And don't you think it's strange? No one talks about that Greek god who dragged us into this whole mess. And that Thunder-Bird—what's so special about it anyway?"

"That bird is special, no doubt about it. Otherwise, Smérix wouldn't be here just for revenge… And that Greek god? Word is he split a massive rock in two like it was nothing but bread. So yeah—I'm not keen on finding out what he'd do if we turned back…"

"You've got a point," Lugotorix admitted. "He must be something, that bird. And anyway, I'm all in for avenging Anna."

"By the gods, what's that stench?" Alexix suddenly complained, walking up toward the Chief and me.

For a while now, a vile stench had been clinging to the air—something acrid and foul, like decay mixed with damp earth. I couldn't help but grimace, and the Chief beside me did the same. Further ahead, Alexix was glancing around in disgust, trying to locate the source of the abomination.

"Shaman, can't you do something about this smell? I don't know—maybe a perfumed potion or something?" he pleaded desperately.

I raised my eyebrows and gave him a solemn look. The forest's odor, unpleasant as it might be, was part of its essence—its mystery.

"I do have a most effective remedy, Alexix," I said with

a satisfied smile. "Close your nose! It works wonders—wonders, I tell you!"

The Chief burst out laughing, and Alexix, grumbling, let us walk ahead. That laughter echoed through the heavy air, a rare flicker of warmth amid the looming shadows of night.

Unbeknownst to us, hidden in the underbrush, two Harpies slinked through the darkness, spying on our group. The laughter of Aridix and myself still danced through the forest—an echo of foolish lightness.

"Next time, try keeping your mouth shut!" snapped one of the Harpies. "You've given us away! Your breath's so foul there isn't a bug left alive within leagues!" she cackled.

These creatures—half-woman, half-bird—were a chilling sight, and their laughter pierced the silence like banshees.

The Chief and I fell silent at once, stopping our mounts. That shrill, mocking voice seemed to come from all directions. Athanor, too, had come to a halt, his gaze now fixed on something shifting in the brush alongside our line of riders. Shadows danced all around us, toying with our senses.

"Speaking of giving us away—you're not much better, you old bat!" came a second voice echoing through the trees.

Athanor turned back and moved toward the others, who were now drawing their weapons. The tension thickened. Everything around us seemed to tremble with unease. Instinctively, we shifted into a defensive stance. The trees, solemn witnesses to our plight, seemed to hold their breath in anticipation of what was to come.

In the undergrowth, the harpies, absorbed in their endless bickering, seemed to have momentarily forgotten their original mission. Their ridiculous quarrel added a bizarre note of absurdity to the night's growing tension.

"You're the fool, you mangy, molting shrew! You decrepit old carcass!" snapped the first harpy.

"How dare you speak to me like that, you…!"

All around us, the forest stirred. Sounds of struggle, flapping wings, and shrill, crone-like screeches rang out—then, suddenly, all movement ceased. All but the brawl between the two harpies.

The creatures clawed and flailed, rolling on the ground, crashing into a tree in a tangle of wings and talons. It would've been almost comical—had it not been so dangerously close.

Around them, small hunched creatures emerged from the shadows. Half-human, half-beast, they resembled the twisted thing the forest had swallowed earlier. These were Kobaloi—stunted, misshapen imps with hunched backs, tiny horns, and bat-like wings. They stared at the squabbling harpies with wide eyes, slowly twitching their scorpion-like tails tipped with wicked barbs.

Their appearance added a sinister weight to our already precarious situation.

"Who speaks?! Who's there?! Show yourselves!" I shouted, my voice slicing through the thick night like a blade.

Out of our sight, the harpies froze, their heads turning sharply in my direction. The Kobaloi around them watched in silence, flitting in and out of the foliage like mischievous shadows.

"What are you gawking at? Go on then, greet our guests!

Go on, don't be shy!" one of the harpies screeched.

Without delay, the little fiends darted into the underbrush and vanished with startling speed. They were quick—so quick they were nearly impossible to follow with the eye.

Meanwhile, we stood tense, bracing for the unknown. Whose dreadful voices were those? We all exchanged glances, uncertain. Then once again, the forest came alive. The bushes, the trees—the very air—quivered with motion. But just as suddenly, everything fell still.

Weapons and torches in hand, we held our ground. My warriors were ready, eyes wide with fear and defiance.

Then, from the darkness, a single Kobalos crept forward—smiling timidly, hesitating, then vanishing again.

Another appeared a few steps away, then more followed. Their timid, twitchy behavior made them seem almost harmless. Pitiful, even.

Lugotorix grinned. Strange as they looked, their size gave him confidence.

"They don't look dangerous! Seems like they're more scared of us than we are of them," he said softly, crouching and reaching out a hand to one of the little creatures. "Sorry, fella, I don't have any food for you."

"Leave it, Lugo! We don't know what it is!" Paritos said quietly, moving closer. "Come on now, leave it be."

"I think it's scared of us," Lugotorix replied, still calm.

The creature gave a shy little grin and edged closer. Its face—almost human—might even have been called cute… in a strange way.

Feeling safe, Lugotorix reached out again to touch the

creature.

Then suddenly—it opened its mouth wide, saliva dripping in thick strands, and let out a horrible, piercing screech. Inside its maw: hundreds of needle-sharp teeth.

Our companion froze—too stunned to react—as the creature clamped its jaws onto his hand.

Lugotorix's scream shattered the stillness—a cry of both pain and pure terror.

That scream was the signal. All around us, the grotesque kin of the Kobalos surged forward. With shrieks and wild eyes, they sprang from the darkness, gnashing, clawing, howling like demons unchained.

Paritos lunged to his friend, yanking him backward and slamming his torch into the creature. The flame's wild dance revealed the full horror of its face.

They swarmed us, howling like banshees. Their speed was impossible—blurring from one place to the next, then suddenly latching onto a warrior's throat, or tearing a sword-hand clean off.

They had no restraint. With their teeth they ripped flesh from bone, with their claws they flayed open skin like parchment.

Panic swept through our ranks. Some men broke formation, running and screaming—some with Kobaloi still clinging to them.

Very quickly, the dead piled up. Men bled out, throats torn open. Others were mutilated beyond recognition. The air was filled with blood and madness.

Paritos swung his torch in desperate arcs, shielding Lugotorix as best he could. The young fool clutched his wounded hand, writhing in pain. Finally, spurred by his friend's courage, he snapped out of his daze, drew his blade—and began to fight, bellowing with rage and fear.

Elsewhere, Athanor fought like a man possessed. Every creature that came within reach of his blade fell in two. His movements were sharp, precise, relentless.

Not far off, the twins—Garedix and Alexix—stood back to back, carving a bloody path through the monsters. Garedix's long spear spun like a windmill, while his brother's sword split the beasts with surgical ferocity.

Beside the Chief, who shielded me from the storm, I felt completely overwhelmed. Men were running in every direction.

"Stay close! Don't scatter! Get back here!" Athanor cried, his voice straining to restore a shred of order in the madness.

Torches fell to the ground, and each time one did, another warrior was swallowed by the creatures. Despite the chaos, those still standing—pushed by Athanor's will—rallied around me to aid Aridix.

My hands fumbled through my leather satchel. Panic made my fingers clumsy. But at last, I found it—a small ball of hide, smooth and knotted. I raised it above my head.

"I've got it! I've got it!" I shouted, a foolish smile on my lips despite the desperate situation.

I hurled it upward. It soared, then dropped like a stone. I frowned, disappointed. It hit the earth with a soft thud.

Nothing.

Then, with a hiss and a pop, it exploded into a dense white smoke that swallowed us whole in an opaque fog.

To my dismay, we were blind. Shapes dissolved into nothingness, companions blurred, and the creatures vanished into the smothering mist.

"What have you done?! We can't see a bloody thing!" Aridix shouted, his voice lost in the swirling fog.

"Agh—it itches! It itches like mad! What in the name of the gods is this, shaman?!" Paritos wailed, scratching furiously at his skin.

"Get us out of here, by Taranis! Now! Move!" Aridix bellowed, cutting through the confusion with his commander's voice.

"By the gods—I grabbed the wrong pouch!" I groaned. "Ésus forgive my foolish hands… It's a camouflage powder. Yes, it itches, but it works well! The creatures can't see us now!"

"But neither can we!" Athanor roared. "Out! We have to get out—now! This way, follow me!"

Athanor burst through the pale fog, dragging warriors behind him, all scratching themselves raw. The beasts lunged at us from the edges, but the mist hid us well, and many failed to find their mark.

From the thickets, the two harpies emerged, fuming at the sight of our retreat. They hovered just above the ground, their wings flapping in angry bursts.

"Enough! Stop them, you fools! Or… no—no, get out of my sight, the lot of you!" screeched the first, overcome with fury.

The little beasts halted, turning to her. One shrugged, then grabbed a dead Celt by the ankle and began dragging him away. Others joined in, snatching limbs and carcasses, disappearing into the shadows with their macabre trophies.

The harpies glared at each other.

"We didn't kill enough!" whined the second, her face contorted with frustration.

"The Master wanted them to move faster, didn't he?

Well—they're running now, aren't they?" said the first, grinning crookedly.

"Still not enough blood! That's your fault, you half-witted featherbag!"

"No, yours! You should've shut that rotting trap you call a mouth!" the other snapped, eyes blazing.

"WHAT?!" screeched the first, talons flashing.

And with that, they hurled themselves at one another once more, screeching and biting and rolling through the mud, wings flailing like battle flags in the wind.

As for us—we were fleeing through the forest, hearts pounding, putting as much distance as possible between us and the scene of the massacre. The eerie stillness that returned to the woods seemed almost comforting after the infernal storm we'd just escaped.

"By the gods, we need to get out of this cursed forest," Athanor gasped, catching his breath.

"If only I'd taken the right powder to begin with…" I muttered, more to myself than to anyone else.

"You did your best, Smérix. We're alive because of you," the Chief said, laying a firm, reassuring hand on my shoulder. "This forest must end somewhere, by Taranis! We'll find a way out."

So we pressed onward, the night as dark as the souls of those who hunted us. Each of us knew deep down that our greatest trial had yet to come. Only through unity, through steadfast will, could we hope to overcome what lay ahead.

Aridix and Athanor were right. We had lost too many. We had to leave this ancient and enigmatic forest—a place holding far too many secrets, secrets we could no longer afford to uncover…

# CHAPTER 19
*"A Glimmer of Hope"*

Far off, across the wind-swept steppes of Cimmeria, night had long since draped its veil over the camp of the strangers. And there, bathed in a faint glow, sat Anna in her prison, her face marked by both determination and sorrow. With infinite care, she had been trying for some time to feed the Thunder Eagle with strips of meat.

The majestic raptor, wings dulled by suffering, lay still, refusing the nourishment she offered. Patiently, she insisted, stroking his mottled feathers with the tenderness of a mother helpless before her child's pain.

"Come now… just a little. You must eat. You have to," she murmured, her voice barely more than a whisper, fragile as a dream against the vast hush of the night.

But the bird remained motionless, its eyes clouded with the fading light of life. With a resigned sigh, Anna set the bowl down beside him. She did not see the monstrous shadow lurking behind her in the dark—an immense silhouette, half-hidden in the gloom. The Minotaur stood there, his crimson eyes slicing through the darkness, watching her every move with grotesque hunger.

She kept her gaze fixed on the bars of the cage, testing their strength, calculating their limits. Above, the stars hung like distant sentinels, cold and silent witnesses to her torment.

"You must be wondering," came the Minotaur's voice, deep and jagged like stone cracking, "why these bars can hold you… Why you can even touch them—though you no longer belong to this world, yes?"

Anna turned, her eyes blazing with fury, defiance burning in their depths.

"These bars are forged from matter drawn from the Underworld," he continued, lips curling into a wicked grin. "And thanks to this cage, you are visible to the living during the night. A clever trick, don't you think?"

His laughter rang out, deep and echoing, like some abominable bell tolling in the dark.

Anna stepped toward him, her glare sharp as iron. One could almost see flames flickering in her eyes.

"And above all," he sneered, "the Thunder Eagle cannot escape. He must not die. If he does… my master would see you suffer torments the likes of which even the gods avert their eyes from. Believe me, it is better for you both that he lives."

Anna clenched her fists, trembling with rage.

"You cannot force him to live! His true nourishment is freedom! You've stripped that from him—of course he withers! And your wretched mission is doomed! Your master will thank you kindly for your incompetence!"

Her voice struck like a blade, each word carved with the

steel of defiance.

The Minotaur, goaded by her words, stepped closer, his breath turning thick and hoarse. His clawed hands grasped the bars, and the infernal stone cracked under his grip, fragments falling to the cage floor.

"Do not think yourself clever!" he growled. "When I hold Athanor in my hands—" He crushed the bars harder, splintering them like dry wood. "You'll find a way to keep that cursed bird alive. Or I'll feast on your lover's brain… starting with his eyes."

A mad howl escaped his mouth—a howl that could shatter the silence of the deepest Hell.

Anna lunged at him, fists flying, but her hands passed clean through his head. Laughing, the beast turned and walked away, leaving her to collapse against the cage, drained and furious.

She stared up at the night sky, at the stars cold and indifferent to her suffering. She searched them for a sign, a path, anything.

Then—a movement.

She turned her head, stunned. The Thunder Eagle was standing. On both legs. Its golden-silver wings half-unfurled.

Anna gasped.

"What…? You're not…?"

A soft, melodic voice, clear and feminine, drifted through the gloom like a forgotten song.

"My time is short, Anna. They must not take me to the Underworld. We must escape. You must help me. I can open the cage—but I cannot fly. I am dying, Anna. I must return to the sacred mountains. Athanor is the key. That is why the Minotaur lures your friends onward…"

"But… I no longer belong to the world of the living," she replied, voice shaking. "Outside this cage, I vanish."

"You saw the bar he damaged," the Thunder Eagle said gently. "Take a fragment of it. It will anchor you to the night. It will allow you to carry my cage. I belong to both realms now—you can touch me."

Anna rose, found the fractured stone, and tucked it into the straw bedding. The piece was cold. Heavy. As if a shard of the dark itself had fallen into her hands.

"Tomorrow night," the Thunder Eagle whispered. "We flee."

And so, beneath the distant stars, that dim celestial tapestry, a fragile ember began to glow in Anna's heart. A glimmer of hope—fragile, flickering, yet fierce enough to challenge the shadows. A vow of freedom, of love, of vengeance.

And above all… a promise.

# CHAPTER 20
## *"The Endless Forest"*

Night had fallen thick and silent upon the forest. Out of reach from our enemies, we had set up a meager camp around a flickering fire. The wounded lay by the flames, tended to by my hands—hands of a shaman now stained with blood and balm. The Chief, Aridix, the twins, and Athanor sat nearby, their faces etched with fatigue and tension.

Aridix scanned the surroundings with a grim expression. A few men kept watch, others ate in silence or tended to their weapons. All of them were worn thin, taut as bowstrings. Barely fifteen of us remained, halved by relentless combat.

It was Aridix who broke the silence, his voice heavy with bitterness.

"We've lost nearly half our men in just a few days in this cursed land! At this rate, none of us will live long enough to see the end of this."

His words were harsh, yet they rang true.

Alexix, his gaze shadowed with weariness, answered him with steel in his tone.

"What are you saying, Aridix? That we turn back?"

"I said no such thing!" snapped Aridix. "It's just—every step forward makes this whole business with the Bird feel more and more absurd. What do we even gain from this? We're dying for nothing! We're not fighting to claim lands, or to protect our kin! Earlier, it didn't feel like warriors dying an honorable death—it felt like we were fodder for beasts."

Athanor nodded slowly, torn between guilt and grim resolve.

"You're right, Aridix. All this… it's my burden. I've failed in my duty, and it's mine alone to set it right. The rest of you should return home."

I came to sit beside them, my voice solemn, resonating beneath the heavy canopy.

"And if you fail, what becomes of our people? The wrath of the gods will fall upon us like a storm, and wipe us from the earth! No—we must hold fast, together. We must find a way out of this forest, and quickly."

The forest felt eternal, like a sea of shadow and silent perils. The more we pressed on, the more the path ahead seemed like a fading dream. It gnawed at us like some creeping rot of the spirit.

But Athanor, still convinced he could carry the weight alone, protested.

"I can do this! Alone, I'd move faster. Quieter, too."

I shook my head.

"Once we're out of this forest, we'll be less exposed,

that's all. Divinix spoke of wide desert plains, where nomadic horse tribes roam. Coléos assured me we'd find mounts there with ease."

Alexix let out a long sigh.

"Fine! But does this forest ever end?"

"Divinix said it takes only a few days to cross. We must be close now. Beyond it lie the open steppes, and mountains."

Aridix sniffed the air, eyes narrowing.

"You smell that? By Taranis, not again…"

His blade sang from its sheath, his warriors following suit. Lugotorix, as ever, nearly cut one of our own in his clumsy panic. The undergrowth rustled—tension crackled like a drawn bowstring. Paritos moved to stand beside me.

Garedix hefted his great spear, ready to strike—when Taranatos's upper body rose above a bush, a wide grin on his face.

"I see you're all thrilled to have me back!"

He stepped out fully, dragging the corpses of two Harpies behind him, one in each hand. A wave of stench hit us all, and men clutched their noses, grimacing.

"By the gods, Taranatos! Get rid of that filth!" I exclaimed, appalled.

The grisly sight said much of the cruelty of our journey. Taranatos only laughed, defiant.

"Oh no, old man! I went to some trouble catching these two."

He sat by the fire, the others recoiling from the reek. There was madness dancing in his eyes, some fevered delight.

"No, I lie—I didn't go through any trouble. The fools

were clawing each other to shreds. Smashed themselves against a tree. I just slit their throats… Come on, sit! You'll get used to the smell."

"Enough of this!" Athanor said, rising with sudden resolve. "We move now. We must leave this forest."

One by one, we followed his lead. Even I, though weariness clung to my bones. Taranatos hesitated, then sighed and abandoned his prizes. Perhaps he'd meant to keep their heads as trophies. Perhaps we were better off not knowing. He fell in behind us.

And so, under the dark boughs of the endless trees, we pressed forward—our band of battered warriors, clinging to one another, driven by purpose.

Our will was our only fire, and in the suffocating dark, it shone like a beacon of hope.

# CHAPTER 21
*"The Cry of Warriors"*

At dawn, we finally emerged from the forest that divided the land of Thrace from the territories of the Cimmerians. That endless, gloomy woodland, steeped in shadow and whispering secrets, was now behind us.

At last, before us stretched arid plains and hills scattered with brambles. Now we had to find horses—quickly.

Heartened by our release, my companions stepped forward with renewed purpose into this new, unexplored land. I could feel the dry earth crunch beneath my feet—a sharp contrast to the sodden softness of the forest soil. The wind stirred gently, sweeping the sun's first rays across our weary but resolute faces. The air was dry, almost biting, a promise of trials to come—a rite of passage for battle-worn souls.

I stood at the forest's edge with Athanor, watching our group resume their march, a quiet unease blooming in my chest. The murmur of their footsteps mingled with the rustle of the brush, weaving a melody both stark and determined. The metallic taste of fresh blood still clung to my tongue—a bitter echo of the ordeals we had survived.

Before stepping away, I cast one last glance at the woods behind us. That brooding expanse still seemed to watch us, its earthy scent clinging like a final embrace. Yet the crushing weight we had felt within was gone. In truth, I was convinced now that the forest had never meant us harm… Something far greater, far darker had disturbed its balance, and we were not the intruders. I believe it had sensed the reverence for nature that lives within us—and it had shown mercy.

"This forest is terribly sad," Athanor murmured.

"Yes… I feel the same. Look at its colors. Dull. Faded. There's a sickness in its roots…"

No sooner had I spoken than cries of beasts rang out from within the forest. The trees began to tremble wildly, and suddenly bodies were flung high above the canopy.

Kobaloi.

They shrieked in terror and pain as they were hurled skyward like broken dolls. The forest was purging them, one by one. No longer would it tolerate their corruption. The sound of cracking branches and the howls of dying creatures filled the air—a cacophony of brutal cleansing.

"It waited until we were gone," I said, awestruck. "And now it's ridding itself of those things…"

The sight was astonishing. All of us turned to witness the power unfurling behind us. Paritos approached, his eyes wide with disbelief.

"I told you," Athanor said, a hint of a smile on his lips. "She never liked her inhabitants. Now she's cleaning house."

"Yes," I replied, my heart swelling. "Nature always reclaims what is hers."

Above the forest, heavy clouds began to gather. Then came the rain—gentle, steady, soaking the earth. The howls fell silent. And as the forest cast off its invaders, color returned to its leaves, and life to its soil. The clouds drifted toward us, and the first raindrops kissed our skin.

"The gods are displeased," Paritos muttered.

"No, my good Paritos," I said. "This is not wrath. This is renewal. A gift to the wounded land… this is the breath of life."

The leaves shimmered with sunlight once more, glistening with droplets as green returned to their veins. A soft fragrance of resin and wildflowers rose from the earth—a sign that darkness had been vanquished, and peace restored.

Revived by this vision, we pressed on, leaving behind that ancient witness of resilience. We moved forward with renewed courage, across dusty plains and windswept hills. Dust rose around our boots, wrapping us in a veil of mystery and silence.

The sun climbed higher, casting its relentless heat across that stark landscape. The scent of sun-warmed earth filled our lungs, searing and alive.

After several hours, we stumbled upon the ruins of a nomadic camp—strewn with bodies. Scorched tents stood like ghosts in the morning light. Smoke still rose, curling skyward, heavy with the acrid stench of death. A vision of apocalypse that etched itself into the soul.

"Well, they're not exactly hard to follow," Alexix muttered, his tone biting.

No one replied. The truth needed no echo. Perhaps the marauders had meant to leave a trail. Perhaps they wanted us to follow them into madness… all the way to the Underworld.

We moved on without lingering, crossing plains where the silhouettes of Cimmerian nomads drifted like spirits. Their appearances were fleeting, their gazes wary. Words were scarce. In these lands, trust was thin as air, and silence safer than friendship.

We walked, eyes fixed on the distant horizon, where an uncertain future waited to unfold.

The plains of Cimmeria stretched vast and merciless before us.

Our journey had barely begun—and already, the shadows of coming trials rose like distant banners…

…heralding wars to come, and glories yet unclaimed.

# CHAPTER 22
*"Lygdamis"*

Several days later, across the vast Cimmerian plains bathed in the harsh light of the noonday sun, a dozen riders thundered through the arid land.

Their steeds—powerful, unrelenting—galloped at full speed, as though fleeing the very breath of death. Muscles slick with sweat, their dark-coated mounts seemed born of this hostile land, molded for its cruel trials.

Among the riders, many bore the scars of recent battle: arrows still lodged in flesh, sword gashes hastily wrapped in blood-soaked cloth. At the head of this desperate charge rode two men supporting a grievously wounded warrior, a titan of fifty winters whose body bore the map of a life spent in war.

Arrows pierced his right shoulder and his left thigh; blood mingled with sweat upon his sinewed frame. This man was a colossus—even weakened, he towered over his peers. His thick mane, wild and dark as the storm, was matted with blood, and his face—half-shrouded by a bristling beard—was a mask of grim resolve. Deep brown eyes, sharp and unyielding, burned with defiance despite the agony.

Each jolt of the horse beneath him was a trial, yet his arms—scarred, bulging with strength—held fast to the reins. His breastplate bore tribal carvings; his weapons, ornate and well-worn, told of status. But more than armor or blades, it was the countless scars etched upon his skin that proclaimed who he was: a warrior whose endurance defied fate itself. He was their chief—of that, there was no doubt.

The two men struggling to bear his weight rode with teeth clenched, fear and effort carved into their faces. The group surged onward at a reckless pace, the heat shimmering across the plains like the breath of some ancient beast. Each hoofbeat echoed like a drumbeat of survival, while the chief, despite the blood soaking his wounds, never took his eyes from the horizon.

This Cimmerian king, wounded and swaying in the saddle, still embodied the raw power of his people—a living symbol of ancestral fury and defiance.

Behind them, not far now, came their hunters: a horde of some forty Scythian riders, howling like wolves on the wind, their war cries rending the air. Some were wounded, wrapped in stained cloth, but still they pressed on with savage determination.

These Scythians, clad in hardened leather embossed with beasts and feathers, rode nervous horses of varied coats. At their sides hung short, deadly bows—tools of precision and slaughter.

At their head was a giant with a shaven scalp and a torso

laid bare, scrawled with menacing tattoos. His cries were maddened, his horse slick with lather. Bloodlust danced in his eyes, mirrored by the feral gleam in those of his kin. This brute—muscle-bound, commanding—was a force unto himself. The ink on his flesh told tales of conquest and carnage, and his voice, guttural and thunderous, swallowed the tumult behind him.

The gap between predator and prey shrank with every heartbeat. Ahead, a slope appeared—a steep incline followed by a rise. From its summit, perhaps, a chance to rally. Perhaps.

The Cimmerians pushed forward, rallying what strength they had. As they reached the crest, the Scythian leader raised a single hand—and his men reined in.

"We're not letting them escape! We slaughter them now!" one of his warriors spat, rage twisting his features.

But the leader only smiled—a cruel, deliberate grin. His gaze fixed on the distant figures like a hawk watching prey too weak to run.

"They'll stop. They'll fight. They are not running," he said coldly, as if speaking fate itself.

Atop the opposite hill, the Cimmerians reached the summit, breath ragged, horses steaming.

"They've given up! We're saved, my king!" cried one of the warriors holding their chief, his voice thick with hope.

But the chief pulled his horse to a halt, his face twisted not with relief—but fury. His men, startled, turned back and gathered around him, their loyalty as firm as the earth beneath their feet.

Drawing his sword with a grunt, he ignored the blood that flowed anew. A wild light burned in his eyes.

"I thought I heard the voice of some trembling maid relieved to be spared," the chief growled, his voice like flint on steel.

"We only sought to protect our king. You must live—for our people," replied the warrior, torn between duty and despair.

"I am Lygdamis," he roared, "a Cimmerian—King of Cimmeria—and never have I fled from my foes!"

He raised his sword high, its blade catching the sun, his voice rising like a war drum against the wind.

"My blade thirsts for Scythian blood! Or else I'll snap it in shame!

To arms! Death to them!"

His war cry echoed across the steppes, mingling with the morning breeze… and the warriors of Cimmeria answered.

As he bellowed his order, Lygdamis spurred his steed and charged the Scythians. His warriors followed without hesitation, their loyalty unshakable. From the other side, the Scythians answered with howls of war, their eyes gleaming with rage and madness.

The two forces thundered toward one another at full gallop, weapons raised, screaming like the damned. The space between them vanished with each heartbeat, every hoofbeat drawing them nearer to a bloody reckoning. Arrows whistled through the air—Scythian shafts that struck down two Cimmerians, their cries of pain swallowed by the storm of onrushing steel. Ten remained to face the onslaught, their voices drowned in the din of war.

And then—impact.

The clash was cataclysmic. Steel shattered bone, flesh tore, horses screamed in agony. Scythian heads fell like ripe fruit, steeds collapsed in shrieks of pain, and eight

Cimmerians cut deep into the enemy line. Two more fell, their bodies crashing into the blood-soaked earth.

Without hesitation, the survivors wheeled around, ready for another charge. They would not die without carving their names into the bones of the earth.

The Scythians, though more numerous, slowed their mounts, breath heaving, bodies slick with sweat and gore. They stared across the field at the battered Cimmerians, minds fogged by the reek of blood and the taste of fear.

Lygdamis, jaw clenched, his sword a weight of fire in his grip, glanced toward his men. They were as spent as he— but still standing. Still breathing.

Then, from the depths of exhaustion, a smile crept across his face. And Lygdamis laughed—a deep, defiant laugh that rolled like thunder across the plains.

"What is it, my King?" asked one of the Cimmerians, baffled by his joy amid the carnage.

Lygdamis turned to him, lifting his sword in a fist of iron, energy surging anew in his limbs.

"If only you could see your faces!" he cried. "Smile, my brothers! Today is a glorious day! You'll die as warriors, blades in hand!"

His laughter turned to a battle cry, fierce and exultant.

The Scythians, startled, exchanged wary glances. Their chieftain, enraged, brandished his own blade and bellowed the order to charge, his eyes ablaze with fury.

Lygdamis answered in kind, roaring into the wind, and hurled himself once more toward the enemy. His men followed, loyal to the end, bound by blood and honor.

It was in that very moment that my companions and I heard the cries—raw, terrible cries of rage and pain. Their echoes rode the wind like ghosts of war, clawing at the silence of the plains. Hooves hammered the earth with such force the ground seemed to tremble beneath our feet. The noise came from just beyond the hill ahead of us.

The air was thick with the stench of sweat and blood, stirred by dust rising into a shroud that choked the sky. Our hearts beat faster, pounding in time with the hoofbeats below. Our tunics clung to our backs, damp with tension and heat.

Without a word, we rushed to the summit, the whole company scrambling up the rise, eager and apprehensive. And then—we saw it. The chaos, the fury, the noble carnage below.

Aridix turned to me, his face grim.

"What do we do?" he asked, uncertainty thick in his voice.

I weighed our choices, the wind carrying the scent of death into my nostrils.

"There's nothing for us down there. This battle does not concern us, Aridix. Let's move on," I replied, turning away.

His warriors, overhearing, looked to him—disappointed. But it was Taranatos who broke the silence with his usual irreverence.

"So, who are the good guys?" he asked, his tone almost childlike.

Before Alexix could answer, Athanor drew his blade, eyes blazing.

"The outnumbered ones, Taranatos. The outnumbered," he declared.

With that, he charged down the hill, sword high, his voice rising in a wild war cry. Without hesitation, the others followed, blood singing in their veins—except for

Taranatos and Alexix, who glanced at Aridix and me in confusion.

I was aghast, caught between pride and panic.

"Come back! By the gods—come back here!" I shouted.

"If we join them, doesn't that make us the more numerous? Which would mean… we're the bad guys?" Taranatos muttered, head tilted in thought.

"You're an idiot," Alexix snapped, and sprinted after the others, his grin savage.

"At least I think before I swing…" Taranatos chuckled, then looked to Aridix and me before shrugging and racing off with his usual crooked smile.

Aridix watched them go, his eyes lit with fire.

"Let them fight," he said. "For once, a true battle. No monsters, no shadows—just warriors, steel against steel. We're Celts. Born to war. And who knows—maybe we'll leave with a few new horses."

I sighed, raising my hands in exasperation.

"They listen to me less and less," I murmured.

Aridix only grinned, then bellowed as he descended toward the clash.

"We are Celts!"

I watched him vanish into the storm of blades and blood.

"What did I just say?" I muttered, shaking my head.

The wide plains of Cimmeria roared with the cries of war, hooves thundering, swords clashing, and hearts breaking in a storm of steel and fury. There, amid the dust and death, warriors gave their breath for glory.

It was then that my companions arrived—like a storm unchained, a wrathful wind sweeping across the steppe, leaving ruin in its wake. The Cimmerians, spent and bloodied, looked up and saw us strike at their foes with savage resolve. That unexpected reinforcement rekindled their flame. Their blades once more carved through the air, severing Scythian limbs and skulls, spreading confusion and dread through enemy ranks.

Aridix, the last to join the fray, let out a cry of pure rage, his eyes alight with the joy of battle. Yet he had no time to wield his sword. A whistle—a Scythian arrow pierced his mouth, exiting through his neck with fatal precision. Before his body hit the ground, a mounted Scythian galloped past and beheaded him in a single, brutal stroke. His corpse crumpled, while his head rolled into the bloodied dust.

One of the Scythians grabbed it, letting out a frenzied scream of triumph, then hurled it back into the fray. To Lugotorix's horror, it landed in his arms. He stood frozen, staring at the twisted grimace of pain still etched on his father's lifeless face.

"Papa...? What are you doing with that thing in your mouth...?" he murmured, numb, lifting Aridix's head by the hair.

Then rage ignited within him—pure, blinding fury. Screaming vengeance, he searched for the killer. He spotted the Scythian, dismounted now and grappling with Paritos. Lugotorix walked toward him, blade in one hand, his father's head in the other, raised like a standard of wrath.

"You killed my father! I'll eat your heart!" he howled, his eyes aflame with unfiltered hate.

As Paritos fought desperately for his life, Lugotorix placed his father's head gently on a nearby stone, a strange mix of reverence and fury burning within him. Then, possessed by vengeance, he seized the Scythian by the hair and slit his throat in a feral act of justice.

The man collapsed, blood spraying in a grotesque arc. Without a word, Lugotorix drove his blade into the chest of the corpse, tore out the still-beating heart, and sat beside his father's head. He began to devour the organ raw, his face and hands drenched in blood, his eyes vacant.

Paritos, shaken by the scene, turned away, a shadow of disgust flickering across his face. But he had no time to dwell—he plunged once more into the fight.

Taranatos and Athanor, blood-drenched and wild-eyed, fought like madmen, slicing through the enemy ranks with grim joy. Lugotorix, still seated, watched them with hollow eyes, his mouth stained red.

"I protect you, father… I carry your spirit… You will find your place among the Ancestors. I'm here. I'm here…" he murmured, the words lost in the whispering winds.

A Scythian crept toward him, a vulture scenting easy prey—but Paritos saw, and would not let it pass. He flung himself between them, hacking the warrior through the belly with a roar.

"Get up, Lugo! Fight! Avenge your father, damn it, don't sit there and die!"

Lugotorix looked at him, blank. His mind was fog, time crawling, sounds distorted. But then, a stinging slap from Paritos broke the trance.

"Move! Or we both die here!" Paritos shouted, soaked in blood, his voice like thunder.

Lugotorix blinked. Awareness rushed back into him. He looked at his father's face—and something shattered inside him.

While Paritos fended off a new assailant, Lugotorix rose, picked up his blade, and let loose a scream that tore through the sky. Hatred twisted his face as he dove into the fray, a hurricane of steel and fury. The dreamer was no more. The man who rose was forged in grief and fire.

Elsewhere, Lygdamis, though gravely wounded, fought with infernal resolve, each blow a testament to his iron will. Alexix and Garedix, deadly and precise, moved through the enemy like blades through grass. One by one, the Scythians fell before the wrath of Celt and Cimmerian alike, their courage crumbling beneath the ferocity of our assault. None fled. They chose to die on their feet.

When the last foe fell, Lygdamis dropped to one knee, breath ragged, wounds weeping. Only five Cimmerians remained—including their king.

Lugotorix, panting, finished his final enemy with a growl, driving his sword deep into the Scythian's chest. Then, wordless, he returned to his father's head. He sat in the dirt, cradling it once more, a solemn sentinel beside the lifeless gaze of Aridix.

Athanor passed him in silence, grim-faced. He dragged his long blade behind him, his body caked in gore. Weariness hung heavy on his shoulders. Around him lay a field of torn flesh and shattered dreams, a sea of crimson ruin.

He paused, surveyed the slaughter—and grimaced. The trance of battle fading, he spat into the dust, mounted a riderless horse, and rode away from the charnel field, his heart heavy, yet proud of the valiant fury that burned within us all.

# CHAPTER 23
*"The Invisible Bonds"*

Night had fallen upon our camp, laying its velvet shroud over the land. Around several fires, we tended to our wounds and those of the surviving Cimmerians, wrapped in a silence so solemn it felt carved in stone. The flickering flames cast restless shadows across the faces of the weary, each one etched with the memory of recent battle.

At one of these fires sat Athanor, Taranatos, Garedix, Alexix, a handful of Cimmerians—and myself. I was applying a salve of crushed herbs to a wound in Lygdamis's chest, the kind of remedy passed down from hands long gone, yet never forgotten. The silence weighed heavy, like a stone altar over our souls.

Lugotorix and Paritos kept their usual distance, yet tonight there was no laughter between them, no murmured jests. The firelight revealed two young men who had crossed the threshold into manhood—violently, irrevocably.

Paritos watched his friend. Lugotorix's eyes were locked on the fire, brimming with grief and rage. When we returned home, it would fall to him to lead. His father was gone, and now that heavy mantle would rest on his shoulders. Paritos, I believe, knew it. He would stay by his side, as he always had—but nothing would ever be the same again.

Not far from us, warriors dragged the corpses of the Scythians into a heap for burning. Other pyres had been prepared for each fallen Celt and Cimmerian. Lygdamis stood still, his face grim, watching the grim procession.

"These men are mad," he said at last, "but they are brave. They don't deserve to rot under the sun, torn apart by carrion beasts."

I had just finished tending his wound. I sat beside the Cimmerian king.

"Why this battle?" I asked him, my voice low. "They seemed possessed… like rabid beasts lost to madness."

Lygdamis fixed his gaze on the fire, thoughtful. All eyes were on him now, waiting for his words like some forgotten oracle.

"Something has risen from the bowels of the earth to the north," he said at last. "They say it's demons, from the Greek underworld. They say a Greek god lives beneath that place—a god of darkness and death. They flee it like madmen. Death and chaos pour from that wound in the world, and nothing seems able to stop it."

"The gates of the Underworld…" I murmured, recalling Divinix's tales. A chill ran down my spine.

"You're Greeks?" Lygdamis asked, his brow furrowed in confusion.

"No," I answered, "we are Celts. We've come from far

beyond these lands—and it is to those very gates of the Underworld that we now march."

At this, Lygdamis burst out laughing.

"Madmen," he said with a grin. "I knew you had to be mad."

My friends didn't take kindly to his laughter. Athanor stood abruptly, eyes burning.

"You have no idea what you're talking about!" he growled, his voice tight with fury.

Alexix reached out, placing a firm hand on his arm.

"Sit down, my friend. He meant no harm. It's a long story, Lygdamis. The creatures you speak of… they killed his wife—my sister. We will have vengeance for her."

Lygdamis paused, then gave a solemn nod.

"If you've the courage to face such monsters for vengeance… then I am glad I do not stand against you. Enough talk—let us drink to the fallen, Celts. Tonight, we mourn. And then—we drink until the silence leaves us."

He seized a leather flask filled with honey-wine, lifted it high.

"To our brothers in arms!" he cried, and drank deeply, the golden liquid running freely across his chest and into the wound still burning there.

He passed the flask on, and one by one, we all drank in turn. When it was done, we rose and made our way to the pyres. There were no rites, no words. Just flame. Dry timber caught quickly, and the night became a cathedral of fire.

The survivors stood in grim silence, faces bathed in orange glow. Among the Cimmerians and Scythians alike, death was no end—but a journey to a parallel world, where the soul wandered, armed, fed, and adorned. Normally, the dead would be sent off with gifts, steeds, and slaves—but not tonight. This was war. And fire was quicker.

Athanor stood apart, staring into the flames. His jaw was set. In his eyes, the rage returned. Visions struck him—Anna's funeral pyre, the moment he'd driven his blade into her heart, the endless cycle of grief.

He staggered back, haunted. Then he turned and fled the firelight, climbing a small hill, his body trembling.

I watched him go, my heart heavy with the weight of what he bore.

He crested the hill and vanished on the other side. The slope was steep. He slipped, fell, tumbled to the base—and let out a cry of rage.

Then, rising to his feet, he drew his sword and tore into the saplings around him, hacking without restraint. In seconds, the grove was shattered.

At last, exhausted, he collapsed to his knees. His blade stood planted in the soil. Breath ragged, his forehead rested upon the pommel, seeking something between madness and mercy.

Further across the vast plains of Cimmeria, as night enveloped the camp of the strangers, Anna remained inside her cage, eyes scanning the horizon. All was still. A short distance away, most of the warriors lay asleep on the bare ground. One man kept watch by a dying fire, his head nodding, nearly asleep.

"This is the moment. But how are we supposed to get out of this cage?" Anna whispered, a flicker of hope glowing in her eyes.

Within the small prison beside her, the Thunder Bird stood on its feet.

"Come closer. Take one of my feathers," the creature said calmly.

It spread one of its wings and, with a swift snap of its beak, plucked a single plume. It shimmered, shedding flecks of gold and silver that floated gently down. Anna crouched, reverent, and reached out to take the feather, her fingers trembling slightly.

"A feather? That's your great escape plan?" she asked, incredulous at the simplicity.

"The bars bind me. But not metal. Lay the feather on the chain," the Thunder Bird instructed.

Anna stepped to the cage's barred door, glanced around one last time, then obeyed. As soon as the feather touched the chain, a crackle erupted—soft, yet bright—and with a sudden jolt, the chain snapped. The door creaked open.

"Let's go. Quickly. No sound," urged the bird, its voice taut with urgency.

Without hesitation, Anna seized the small cage and crept from the prison, moving like a shadow toward the brush at the edge of the camp. She darted into the darkness, keeping low, clutching the cage close to her chest.

Ahead rose a broad hill, looming like a silent sentinel. She hurried toward it and began to climb. It was steep, and she was soon on all fours, dragging her burden behind her. Then—an inhuman howl split the night.

Her torturer had awoken.

The Minotaur stood upright outside his tent, a beast wrenched from nightmare, howling with hellish fury. His eyes landed on the empty wagon nearby.

With a guttural snarl, he stomped toward the firepit. As he passed, his clawed hand lashed out and struck the sleeping guard. The blow was so powerful that the man's head tore from his body, which fell lifeless into the coals.

"You useless worms! Find her! Bring her back!" he roared, his voice echoing like a storm across the plains.

From the slope, Anna could see the camp stirred to chaos. Yet on the hillside, a faint light now glimmered—like a star, guiding the lost homeward.

"There! She's climbing the hill!" he bellowed, his hooves pounding the earth as he began the chase, his soldiers scrambling to follow.

Higher up, Anna gasped for air. Every step became an ordeal. The hill grew steeper, crueler, as if conspiring to stop her ascent. She was close to the summit, yet each motion felt like lifting a mountain.

"Call him, Anna," said the Thunder Bird gently. "Call him. Athanor is near. You are free of the cage. He will hear you—wherever he is."

"Why is this cage so heavy?" she muttered in desperation. "The farther I go, the heavier it gets…"

"It is bound to the Minotaur. And to the Underworld," the bird replied. "Just reach the top. Athanor will see us. Trust me. Just a little further."

Anna looked at him, her eyes clouded with exhaustion, yet burning with love. She closed them tightly.

"Athanor… my love," she whispered, drawing in one last deep breath.

With a trembling grip, she clutched the rocks and pulled herself onward, dragging the cage behind her as though it weighed the world itself.

"You can do it, Anna," urged the Thunder Bird, eyes glowing. "He is close. I know it."

"Athanor! Athanor, I'm here! Hear me, my love!

Please—Athanor!" she cried, her voice piercing the night with its desperation and hope.

Far away, Athanor sat slumped against a splintered tree, its trunk cleaved clean through. Slowly, he raised his head. Above him, the moon emerged from behind a thick bank of clouds, casting its glow over the endless hills and valleys of the steppes.

In the distance, one hill rose higher than the rest.

He blinked. Something stirred within him.

A whisper reached his ears, faint, as if on the wind. He tilted his head, listening—uncertain whether it was memory, madness… or something more. The whisper grew, turning to a cry—a voice calling him, from beyond pain, beyond death.

And then, at the crest of the hill near the enemy camp, a hand appeared above the ridge. Then Anna's face—worn, streaked with tears, but unbroken.

"We're here," said the Thunder Bird, calm and urgent. "Pull me to the top. They're coming. We won't get another chance."

With a final burst of strength, Anna lifted the cage and set it atop the hill. On her knees, hands pressed to the ground, she gasped for breath. From up there, the view stretched on forever—rolling hills, smoke rising on the horizon like thin grey fingers.

She raised her head.

"Athanor! Athanor, my love!" she cried once more, her voice breaking like a wave of longing.

"That's him," said the Thunder Bird. "Close your eyes. I'll send the signal."

Anna obeyed. The Thunder Bird spread its wings.

And a blinding light—pure, brilliant white—burst forth, slicing the night open like a blade of dawn.

Back near the Celtic camp, Athanor narrowed his eyes. On a distant hill, a sudden light flared—brief and radiant. He leapt to his feet.

But just as quickly, the light vanished.

At the summit of the hill where Anna knelt, a large black hand, covered in matted fur, suddenly snatched the cage and yanked it down with brute force.

It was the Minotaur.

His warriors were fast behind him. The Thunder Bird flapped its wings with furious defiance as the beast passed the cage to one of his men.

"You won't keep them apart for long, Minotaur! Their bond is too strong. Even for you. Even for the Underworld," cried the Thunder Bird.

"Do not underestimate me, bird," the Minotaur snarled in reply.

He turned his horned head back toward the summit, where Anna still fought against the pull of the curse. His men were already descending, the Thunder Bird secured once again.

"Return it to the cage. We move at once! Anna, your struggle is meaningless! Your Athanor will not come," he called out, his voice like thunder rolling across the plain.

"It is useless to resist. You are bound to the Thunder Bird. Wherever it goes, you will follow," he added with a voice born from caverns older than memory.

At the top of the hill, Anna strained, her whole being resisting an invisible force dragging her backward. She stared out at the flickering fires in the distance, her cheeks wet with silent tears. She leaned forward, clutching the earth with both hands, her fingernails clawing at the stones.

"Athanor!" she screamed, a final cry torn from the depths of despair.

But it was no use. Inch by inch, she was drawn down the slope, pulled toward the cage, toward the beast, toward the waiting jaws of fate.

\*\*\*

Far away, Athanor stood motionless, staring into the horizon as the last trace of light faded. The moon slowly disappeared behind a heavy cloud. His eyes remained fixed.

"Anna…" he whispered, his voice trembling.

"Athanor! Come, we must return to the camp. We will find her, my friend… wherever she may be…"

It was I, Smérix, calling to him from the dark.

I reached out a hand. He seemed lost, shaken by the vision he had just received.

"She's here, Smérix. Anna is near. She's calling me—I know it. I… I don't know how. But I feel it."

His voice was shaken, but his certainty rang deep and true. A certainty older than language. Older than doubt.

"Your souls are bound, Athanor. They are part of this vast tapestry that surrounds us. You think the gods are cruel. You believe they toy with you. But listen well… nothing happens without reason. Even the pain that sears your heart has its place."

I placed a hand upon his shoulder, hoping to still the storm within him.

"Too many of our brothers have died because I failed, Smérix. I'm just a man. How can I fight the will of gods?"

he said, and in each word, I heard the weight of grief, the ache of guilt, the anguish of love.

"You carry no blame. This is the path written in the stars. All of this—every death, every tear—has meaning, Athanor. And one day, you will understand. But for now, you must rest, my friend. Greater dangers still lie ahead."

He stepped toward me, shoulders sagging beneath a burden no man should bear. But I knew the truth. I could see it in him, in the way he stood against the wind, in the way his soul refused to break.

"At the end of this road, you will find the answers," I said softly, letting my voice be the thread that held him.

And so, slowly, he followed me back toward the camp.

Behind us, the night deepened. The cries had faded. But in Athanor's heart, a storm still raged. A storm of love and vengeance, loss and hope. He carried it all. And he would carry it still.

For love, I knew, would guide his steps beyond the reach of fear, beyond the grasp of the gods.

I knew it in my bones.

# CHAPTER 24
## *"Cimmerians: Dawn of a Battle"*

Dawn unfurled its colors over the horizon—golden hues brushed with rose, painting the sky with the promise of another uncertain day. From the dying embers of last night's fires, thin trails of smoke still curled skyward, lazy whispers in the morning chill. After the battle, we had seized the Scythians' horses—at last, we could travel with greater speed!

We were making ready to depart. Around me, my companions busied themselves with saddles and bridles, the muffled clatter of hooves and leather echoing softly in the hush of dawn.

Lygdamis, already mounted, loomed like a figure carved from granite against the glowing sky. One of his men approached him in silence. The Cimmerian king gave him a wry smile and nodded once.

"Go. Find Bartatua and Ardamu. Tell them to meet me at the women's place. They'll understand," he said, the corner of his mouth curling into mischief. "Now ride. I'm counting on you."

The man thumped his fist to his chest and galloped away, a plume of dust rising in his wake. Lygdamis watched him disappear before turning toward Athanor, who was tightening his saddle straps with quiet focus.

"We'll ride with you a while. Our paths lead in the same direction," he said, his tone grave but open.

A pause, as he studied Athanor's features—then, lowering his voice, he added:

"Don't take to heart the words I spoke last night. The blood was still hot in me. My tongue runs faster than my thoughts after a fight."

Athanor looked up, his face unreadable, and gave a silent nod as he swung into the saddle.

"It's forgotten. And more blades on the road are never unwelcome," he answered, curt, but sincere.

"I owe you that much," said Lygdamis, and there was weight in those words.

I rode up alongside them, flanked by Alexix, Garedix, and Taranatos. Each wore the look of hardened resolve and silent brotherhood.

"Then let's be off," I said, my voice firm and ready.

And with that, our column set out toward the plains of Scythia. Riding beside Lygdamis, I turned to him with curiosity burning behind my calm.

"What awaits us in these lands?" I asked.

A grin tugged at his lips, and mischief sparkled in his eyes.

"We're headed into Arimaspian territory—those one-eyed devils," he said with mock solemnity.

He circled his finger around one eye and furrowed his

brow in exaggerated fashion, drawing laughter from our riders.

"They've only one eye, right in the middle of their skulls. Hard to tell what they're thinking. And impossible to meet their gaze for long."

He laughed—a deep, rumbling sound that rang out among the horses—and his mirth was infectious. Even Athanor, burdened though he was, cracked the faintest smile.

"How do they shoot a bow with one eye?" Taranatos asked, miming a clumsy archer with a childlike glint in his gaze.

"They throw the whole thing at you," Alexix quipped, and laughter erupted once more.

"Enough chatter—let's see if we can reach the mountains before nightfall," I urged, letting the wind carry our resolve forward.

Our pace quickened, the rhythm of hooves stirring the dust of the steppes as we pressed toward the distant peaks, jagged shapes carved into the far horizon.

\*\*\*

Elsewhere across the Cimmerian steppes, as was custom whenever his clan paused in one place, a boy named Darios prepared to lead the herds to pasture. Son of a warrior, Darios bore his task with pride. His eyes, keen and focused, reflected both youth and a burgeoning sense of duty.

Clad in a woolen tunic and sandals of rough leather, he guided the goats and sheep alongside his faithful dog, Kora.

"Come on, Kora. Toward the valley," he called,

pointing toward the lowlands.

The sleek black dog barked with bright energy and sprang into motion, circling the herd with instinctive grace. Darios followed, gripping a herdsman's staff adorned with carved Cimmerian sigils—symbols of his role and lineage.

When they reached the green pastures, where the wind played over the swaying grass like a whisper from the ancestors, he sat down upon a stone. He pulled a piece of bread and a sliver of cheese from his satchel and shared it with Kora. As they ate, the boy hummed an old tune—his mother's song—of spirits, guardians, and sacred fields.

Too young to grasp the shadows gathering on the plains, Darios did not yet know that danger stalked the steppes. His people, the children of the wind, were coveted by a ravenous warlord—Madyes, king of the Scythians. His greed for land and blood knew no bounds.

Lygdamis, king of all Cimmerians and lord of Darios' clan, knew this truth well. It was to rally the scattered tribes that he had ridden out… and into ambush. The tale of his escape was now ours to tell.

In his absence, leadership fell to his son, Taloros. Steadfast and capable, Taloros had sent out emissaries, carrying secret instructions from his father—words meant for the ears of war chiefs only. For the storm was coming, and soon the plains would echo with hoofbeats and steel once more.

The Cimmerians were a nomadic people—herders and warriors—akin in many ways to their enemies, yet different in others. Like us Celts, and like the Scythians they fought, they lived in reverence of the spirits and the dead, bound to their land by a sacred respect.

Their camps, formed of beast-hide tents, often circled

large communal fires. They honored the spirits of nature and the souls of their ancestors. Their beliefs infused every act of daily life—ritual songs, dances by the flames, and ceremonies meant to invoke divine protection were woven into their way of being, forging an unshakable tie between the seen and the unseen.

Back at their encampment, after a long ride across the steppes to still his mind, Taloros walked among the tents, pausing to speak to the warriors and encourage their readiness for the war to come. Around him, the tension was a living thing. Each man, each woman, could feel the storm rising in their bones.

At the heart of the camp, by a great fire still crackling with embers of the night, Taloros addressed his gathered advisors.

"Our envoys will return soon," he declared, his eyes sweeping over the faces around him. "We must be ready at a moment's notice. Skoithos and his warband will grant us no mercy."

Murmurs of assent rippled through the circle. Taloros raised a hand for silence.

"You all know it. Dark hours approach… We must steel ourselves for battle! And in the coming days, we must remain united and strong—just as our people have always stood! We are Cimmerians! Never forget—the Ancestors are watching! We cannot fail them! Prepare yourselves, and be ready to defend our lands! A great battle draws near…"

The Cimmerian warriors, clad in hide tunics and cloaks of thick wool, bore tattoos of their lineage and exploits etched into their skin. As they listened, they sharpened their blades and spears, honing them with care. Nearby, the women prepared remedies and meals, working ceaselessly to ensure the wellbeing of the clan. Their hands shaped cheeses and dried meats—vital provisions for travel and for war. With nimble fingers, they spun wool and tooled leather, crafting garments and gear sturdy enough for the harshest trial.

An elder, his hands trembling but his gaze unshaken, stepped forward.

"Our ways, our beliefs… they are our strength," he said. "We must remember who we are and why we fight. If we forget… then our people will vanish from these lands, and none shall speak our names again."

The hours passed. As night fell once more, the camp stirred with a solemn rhythm. Ritual chants rose into the air—blends of prayer and preparation. Children played nearby, mimicking the battle-stances of their elders, their wooden figurines of warriors and beasts acting out the old stories, the values they would one day bear.

With his heart full of pride and love for his people, Taloros climbed atop a stone and raised his voice to all who would hear:

"Cimmerian blood! Soon we shall fight—not only for our survival, but for our freedom! For our children! For the honor of our forebears! Let our enemies know we are ready! We shall never bow! Our king, Lygdamis, will return and lead us to victory! Of this, I am certain!"

A cry rose up from the gathered warriors, a single voice forged from many throats—a cry of defiance, of unity. The dancing shadows cast by the firelight fell across their faces, fierce and unwavering. A vision of resistance, ready to meet the storm.

They knew the battle was near. Their nomadic life,

shaped by ritual and ancient lore, had forged them into survivors. Did they not wrestle with the sky and the seasons each day, challenge the winds and the whims of the earth?

Each soul had a place. Each spirit, a thread in the great tapestry. And beneath the vast star-crowned sky of Cimmeria, this people, bound by courage and ancient memory, steeled themselves to meet the dawn of war.

The next morning, as daylight unfurled over the Cimmerian steppes in a grand spectacle of color and light, a horse pawed nervously at the ground, steam rising from its nostrils in the chill of dawn.

A lone rider, seen from behind, stood poised atop a hill, her gaze sweeping across a vast plain where a plume of dust trailed swiftly toward a low mountain range and a wooded valley beyond. It was us—Celts and surviving Cimmerians—riding fast, chasing shade and hope alike.

Her black hair, tied back in a warrior's tail, danced in the morning breeze, cascading over her broad, sun-warmed shoulders. She wore a light linen tunic edged with intricate tribal motifs, colors alive in the breeze, revealing now and then the supple power of her bare legs. Her arms, too, were bare—cords of trained muscle rippling beneath skin of ochre-brown, glowing in the early sun.

Around her waist, a thick leather belt bound the tunic close, adorned with bronze medallions etched with delicate patterns. Each of her movements sent a soft clinking of metal into the air—a silent rhythm that hinted at her deadly precision. Her gaze was locked onto the plain below, cutting through the dust with predatory calm, calculating our numbers, seeking the perfect place to intercept us. She was all tension and poise, like a falcon seconds before the dive.

Her almond-shaped eyes, pale green and luminous as mountain glass, fixed on our galloping band with sharp intent. In the heavens above, a great eagle cried out, its wide wings slicing the sky in lazy circles. The woman raised her head to it for the briefest of moments, then turned again to follow our trail, vanishing into the dust with the quiet menace of a shadow.

At last, we neared the wooded valley that marked the edge of the low mountain chain. We could finally ease our horses, and our own aching bones, after the grueling gallop through that sun-seared expanse.

With relief, we rode at a walk into the greener lands ahead, sparse trees dotting the path like sentinels of a new realm. Our weary company entered this Scythian domain cautiously, where the land breathed a heavier air, strange and waiting. The horses, drenched in sweat and breathing hard, clopped forward, while their riders slumped in the saddle, cloaked in dust and weariness.

"The horses are parched. Let's find water," said Athanor, his voice hoarse from heat and silence. "Paritos—ride ahead. There must be a stream or river nearby."

Paritos broke rank, spurring his mount forward with a grin.

"On it! Been dreaming of fresh water for hours. First puddle I find, I'm diving in head first," he called, already trotting off, dust swirling behind him.

Lygdamis rode up beside Athanor and me at the head of the column, his grim expression shaded beneath a battered helm.

"We're entering Arimaspian land now… Scythian soil," he warned, his voice low, heavy with the weight of myth and danger.

# CHAPTER 25
*"The City Hidden in the Mountain"*

Somewhere deep in the mountains of that Scythian valley, there stood the hidden city of the Arimaspians. It had been built within an immense cavern, vast as a celestial amphitheater, encircling a wide central plaza beneath the earth.

Rising tiers of stone dwellings formed the city's concentric levels, each riddled with cavern entrances that tunneled deeper into the mountain—an intricate and mysterious labyrinth. Wooden bridges stretched from ledge to ledge, crude shortcuts that defied reason or symmetry, swaying slightly as if suspended between chaos and order. They seemed to hang in midair, forming a tangled dance of paths—an apt metaphor, perhaps, for the unpredictable course of one's life.

The uppermost levels were home to the dwellings, save for the very highest, where natural fissures and underground springs fed into a great cistern. Suspended above it, two enormous barrels—capped and sealed—loomed impossibly, testament to the odd ingenuity of these one-eyed folk.

Water poured from sluices carved into stone and channels lined in wood, descending from level to level, flowing like a sacred lifeblood to each tier, before pooling at last in the very heart of the plaza.

There, carved from the rock itself, stood a statue of a squat, stocky figure, his wild hair untamed, one foot planted proudly upon a wooden chest. A wide grin stretched beneath the single eye set above his nose. Though he was hewn of stone, the statue wore real garments—furs stitched together, and a cape made of bird feathers, vivid and multicolored. This figure was a symbol, plain yet noble—a tribute to the strength and stubborn pride of his people.

Throughout the massive cavern, torches flickered and crackled, casting trembling halos of light upon a city brimming with life. The lower tiers housed merchants, blacksmiths, carpenters, fishmongers, cooks, tiny theaters—and more still. A ceaseless bustle, as if the mountain itself had a pulse. The shifting glow of flame played upon the faces of the inhabitants, all of them like their statue—short, wide-bodied, with a single eye in the center of their brow. Some were bearded, some bald, some both. The women wore their hair long, adorned with polished stone necklaces, their clothing—like the men's—made from animal hides, more or less fine depending on status.

Atop a high ledge overlooking the amphitheater, a small orchestra played—flutes, drums, lyres, cymbals—their music drifting through the cavern, lending rhythm to the chaos. It was not music meant to dazzle, but music meant to live, pulsing in harmony with the life of the people.

From a stone house on one of the upper tiers, a child darted out at full speed. Elbows flying, he pushed through a crowd of passersby, racing down narrow steps. He tripped often, nearly bowling over several elders, but pressed on. Judging by the number of folk stumbling about or knocking into walls, it seemed clumsiness was a shared trait among these folk—almost sacred.

The boy slowed briefly as he entered a market alley, pausing at an archery contest.

"Missed again! Hah! You shoot like a Cyclops who's lost his eye!" jeered a bystander as another arrow flew wide of the mark. The ground around the target was littered with arrows like fallen hopes. The crowd jeered and booed in good cheer.

"Hooooooo!" the child chimed in, grinning, then darted off once more.

He passed a smith who roared an oath after smashing his thumb with a hammer, eliciting laughter from those nearby. Chaos, it seemed, had taken up permanent residence here.

At last, the boy reached the central plaza—the base of this subterranean hive—where the morning market was alive with voices, smells, and motion. He paused just long enough to catch his breath, glancing toward the massive mouth of the cave, where carts entered and exited in a steady stream, bearing goods and noise from the outside world.

The air was thick with scents—grilled meats, tanned

hides, herbs, oil—and alive with the clamor of deals, debates, and greetings. Then, a voice called out.

"Hurry up, boy. We've got work today!"

An old man in a simple wool tunic sat at the reins of a rickety cart, pulled by a wheezing horse. His face was lined, but his eye gleamed with mischief.

"I'm coming, Grandfather! I'm coming!" the boy answered, tripping again before scrambling onto the bench beside the old man.

"The gods must be laughing at us. Why'd they make us all so clumsy?" the boy muttered.

"Because the gods love to laugh, lad," replied the elder with a hoarse chuckle as he flicked the reins. The cart creaked into motion, parting the crowd like an old sea vessel through thick fog. And all the while, the old man's laughter echoed through the vast cavern—carefree, absurd, and oddly divine.

# CHAPTER 26
*"The Invitation…"*

The Scythian forest stretched before us, dense and enigmatic, as we made our way forward at a measured pace. The trees formed a thick vaulted canopy overhead, filtering the daylight into a soft, shadowed gloom. We advanced in silence, the faint clop of hooves lost amidst the blanket of fallen leaves and tangled roots. At the front of our column, Athanor, Lygdamis, and I rode side by side, each of us heavy with thought and memory.

"You haven't spoken of your kingdom yet, Lygdamis," Athanor said, his voice breaking the hush like a stone cast into a still pond.

Lygdamis turned toward him, one brow raised, then spread his arms wide as though to embrace the very horizon—though none could be seen in this wooded world. A gentle breeze stirred his hair, adding drama to the theatrical grandeur of his gesture.

"My kingdom?" he repeated with a grin. "My kingdom

is wherever I stand! There! Beneath my feet! That is where my realm begins!"

I couldn't help but smile at such a declaration. It echoed the claims of every tribe under the sun. Yet what creature can truly claim ownership of the land it treads? We humans all stake our flags in earth we believe ours, yet we are but fleeting shadows upon it—caught in the eternal cycle of life feeding on death, and death giving purpose to life. The earth belongs to nature, and to nature alone. Without understanding our place within the grand weave, we are nothing more than lice squabbling on the back of a slumbering hound…

"Many a proud nation would beg to differ, my friend," I said with gentle irony, amused by the boldness of his claim.

Lygdamis replied with a roguish gleam in his eye. "That's what keeps things lively, isn't it? There's always a battle brewing when the land's at stake!"

"You're not exactly marching with legions anymore," Athanor noted dryly.

But Lygdamis straightened his back, the fire of pride burning still in his voice. "Worry not! My people await me—not far from here. Plenty of good fights ahead! But first, we'll see to these wretched Scythians. The bastards lust after our lands… Their king, Madyes, has sent his son to crush me!" He scoffed. "Let's see who does the crushing."

"You ought to be with your people," I offered.

He waved the thought away with a grin. "Bah! I've ladies to visit first! My son can manage without me for a while. I trust he'll do what must be done."

"Your strength is welcome. Since setting foot in this

cursed land, too many of our kin have fallen, and our path is yet long," I said, my tone heavy.

"As I told Athanor—I owe you that much," he replied.

"I hope your people prevail. There's honor among them—and I admire that," Athanor said.

"Oh, I've got a little surprise planned for those dogs," Lygdamis answered with a sly smile. "They'll return home in fewer numbers… if at all. Depends on my mood, really."

Suddenly, the beat of hooves drew our attention. Paritos came galloping up, slowing his mount as he approached.

"There's a river a few leagues ahead," he said, catching his breath. "We can camp there for the night."

I nodded, relieved at the promise of fresh water and rest.

"Well done, Paritos. Lead the way."

We followed him, the promise of a safe camp breathing new life into our weary horses. Soon, the quiet gurgle of water reached our ears—a gentle song of refuge and renewal.

At the riverbank, we came upon an unexpected scene. An old one-eyed man and a young Arimaspian boy sat by the water, fishing in peace. The boy giggled as the elder pulled slowly on his line.

Startled by our approach, they turned. For a moment, tension hung between us, as wary glances were exchanged. Then, the old man took a step forward and raised a hand in greeting.

"Well met, strangers. What brings you here? I take it you're no fishermen," he said with a twinkle in his single eye.

My companions eyed them curiously. Taranatos's jaw dropped slightly, while the twins, Garedix and Alexix, frowned in confusion at the cyclopean figures. The Cimmerians, as ever, remained impassive, faces as unreadable as stone.

"Greetings, elder. We're merely passing through. Seeking a safe place to rest. Our horses are parched," I replied calmly, hoping to ease any suspicion.

The old Arimaspian gestured toward a nearby clearing.

"There's that spot over yonder… Hmmm… Though the nights get cold by the water. And… well… not always safe. Bloody griffons like to swoop in on travelers, snatch 'em right out of sleep. Not safe. No, no, not safe at all…"

He scratched his chin, deep in thought. Then the boy, his eyes bright with excitement, chimed in.

"They could come to the city! There's a festival tonight!"

The old man's face lit up. Reaching into a basin beside his cart, he pulled out a magnificent pike nearly a meter long, his smile broad with pride.

"Yes, yes, that's a fine idea, lad! It's been a bountiful catch today. There's more like this one. Fine meat, and tonight—plenty of mead flowing!"

He chuckled and began clumsily gathering his things, fumbling with the grace of a life spent delightfully off-balance.

"Mead, you say?" Lygdamis exclaimed, his eyes gleaming.

"You sure we wouldn't be imposing?" I asked warily. "My companions… they drink deep. You could say they fall into the cask rather easily…"

The old man waved a dismissive hand.

"No, no, no. Worry not! It's a feast night! The stores are endless. Trust me. Come, boy—help me now. Your idea was a fine one indeed."

As they hoisted the basin of fish into the cart, spilling water and flailing fish in all directions, we couldn't help but laugh. It was like watching chaos rehearsed, and somehow choreographed.

Then, the old man paused, fixing us with a serious gaze.

"You're not some sort of brigands, are you? Killers? Thieves prowling for helpless souls and forgotten treasure?"

"Nothing of the sort," Athanor answered, his voice steady and resolute. "We are no raiders, old one."

The man stared at us a moment longer, then returned to his packing.

"Good, good, good. Then it's settled. Come now—join the merriment. But you'll have to share your tales. We're starving for stories here."

"With pleasure, friend," said Lygdamis, his grin broad. "Fish and mead on the table—just what we needed."

"Especially the mead!" added Taranatos with a wink.

We all laughed heartily. The old man and the boy clambered aboard their cart, tugging the reins to set off. We followed, spirits lightened, thoughts of war and death momentarily silenced by the simple promise of firelight, music, and stories shared over cups brimming with golden drink.

# CHAPTER 27
## *"Skoithos, the Scythian Tyrant"*

In the arid steppes of Scythia, not far from the lands of the Cimmerians, the troops of the Scythian king's son were advancing across the vast plains. Beneath a blistering sun, the horsemen rode in single file, raising whirling clouds of dust in their wake. The procession passed by a towering tomb—a monumental tumulus, bearing witness to the stature of the soul laid beneath.

This nomadic warrior people held deep beliefs concerning life and death. When a Scythian king died, an immense burial mound was raised in his honor. His body was embalmed, clothed in his finest garments, adorned with golden jewelry and ornate weapons. He was buried with his favorite horses, and at times even with sacrificial servants meant to accompany him into the afterlife.

Around the mound stood stone statues of warriors—the balbals—guardians of the king's soul, meant to shield him from malevolent spirits and ensure a peaceful passage to the next world. Offerings of food and drink were regularly laid at the foot of the tumulus to honor the dead and appease the gods.

At the head of the column rode Skoithos, son of King Madyes—a dreaded tyrant, as hideous as he was cruel. He was the embodiment of terror. His hulking form loomed over his men, every motion heavy and menacing.

Grotesquely massive, his head seemed ridiculously small atop his broad frame, and his rotting teeth made his presence even more revolting. A scar slashed across his brow and cheek, lending his brutish face a look of perpetual wrath. His small, piercing eyes, sunk deep into that grim visage, glimmered with a cold, ruthless cunning.

His skull was shaved on the sides, with a greasy tuft of hair tied into a ponytail adorned with animal bones—trophies from conquests, or charms for his twisted superstitions. For every battle, Skoithos wore leather armor reinforced with iron plates, each studded with spikes and tribal markings, bearing the imprint of his rank and savagery.

Spiked pauldrons exaggerated his already monstrous frame. A thick leather belt, hung with trophies plucked from fallen foes, supported a war skirt of raw hides, the hem lined with nails and rusted blades. He never parted with his weapon—a massive club of wood and iron, its head bristling with spikes and jagged edges, forged to crush and cleave in a single stroke.

His arms, sinewy and inked with war-tattoos, clutched his weapon like talons. He sat astride a hapless steppe pony, far too small for such a beast of a man. The creature wheezed, its flanks trembling under the weight of its monstrous rider.

Everything about Skoithos—his war cries, his staggering gait—reeked of violence and domination. He was the perfect tyrant: ruthless, gluttonous for power, and blind in his own belief of invincibility. His men followed him more out of fear than loyalty, knowing full well that Skoithos's fury could be as deadly as the blades of his enemies.

He halted before the ancient king's mound, lifting his gaze to the summit.

"May this dead king grant me his strength and cunning, so I may crush all who stand before me," he muttered hoarsely.

Beside him rode a black-clad seeress—a wizened woman with braided hair and eyes that pierced like obsidian. Draped in pelts and feathers, she wore a necklace of bones and animal fangs. This was Zerna, a name whispered with equal reverence and dread. She was the tribe's oracle, and her visions carried the weight of the gods.

"Victory shall be yours, Skoithos," she intoned, staring at the tumulus. "The gods are with you—but tread carefully."

At that moment, a rider approached at a gallop, interrupting the solemn exchange.

"My lord Skoithos, we've found a water source where we can set camp for the night," the scout reported, breathless.

Skoithos gave a curt nod and motioned for his men to prepare the encampment.

Scythian warriors were seasoned and efficient. Arriving at the site, they swiftly pitched their leather tents near the water. Fires sprang to life, and soon the scent of roasting meat drifted through the evening air.

This people held to strict and sacred customs. Before every meal, a portion of food and drink was offered to the spirits and the gods—a rite of respect and protection. Ritual songs and dances circled the flames each night, strengthening the unity of the clan and honoring the ancestral dead.

As night fell, the camp glowed beneath the stars. Skoithos sat beside the largest fire, watching his men with a silent, brooding gaze.

Around him, war-chiefs gathered, and Zerna prepared herself for the council. A lavish feast had been laid out—sacrificed beasts, roasted meats, exotic fruits and vegetables arranged across low tables. Skoithos bit greedily into a mutton shank, juices dripping down his chin.

Nearby, his trained hunting falcon sat perched. He tossed it a scrap of meat, which the bird snapped up. A twisted grin curled his lips.

"My scouts bring curious news," he declared, eyes glittering with glee. "Lygdamis is in for a surprise."

Zerna, seated cross-legged by the flames, stretched her hands toward the fire and chanted softly. Suddenly, her eyes shot open.

"I see blood. Much blood," she said in a voice woven of smoke and vision. "But it is not ours. The gods have written your triumph in the stars, Skoithos. You shall prevail—but you must strike without mercy. Beware the stone, say the voices of the dead."

Skoithos let out a guttural laugh, a sound that rumbled like distant thunder.

"The gods are wise, Zerna. And I am their blade. We shall crush them, and their blood shall feed the steppes. As for their stones, let them tremble—I fear no rock," he jeered, nearly choking on a mouthful of meat.

One of the war-chiefs, a broad-shouldered man named Mardok, raised his cup of wine.

"To Skoithos! To Scythia's glory!" he shouted.

All around the fire, warriors lifted their cups and roared their approval. Skoithos, drunk on wine and visions of conquest, stood tall and bellowed:

"Ready yourselves, brothers! Tomorrow, we march on the Cimmerians—and take what is rightfully ours. Let the weak perish beneath our blades!"

At once, their weapons struck the ground in a pulsing war-rhythm. Chants rose once more into the night sky, mingling with cries of fury and bloodlust. Beneath the stars of the Scythian steppes, the tyrant's camp prepared for war—bound by tradition, by fear, and by loyalty to their savage lord.

# CHAPTER 28
*"The Feast of the Arimaspians"*

Night had settled over the Scythian mountain, and at the heart of the Arimaspian cavern, the feast was in full swing across the city's main square. As was customary, the orchestra on the promontory above played a powerful, rhythmic tune that echoed through the stone like the very heartbeat of this people. The air itself pulsed with revelry—a celebration of life nestled deep within the rugged bones of the mountain.

A massive U-shaped banquet table had been set up before the statue of the Arimaspian king, which stood proudly in the middle of a central basin. The table overflowed with a bounty of foods, wooden cups and platters, and more drink than any man could count. Within the curve of the U, the locals danced with wild abandon, joined by a few of our own companions—stumbling and awkward, trying their best to follow the crowd of weaving, wobbling feet. Laughter burst all around, tankards raised high, as dancers did their best to avoid the ever-present Arimaspian clumsiness.

Around the feast, stalls of wine, roasted meats, pastries, cured game, fish, artworks (some truly appalling), pelts, pottery, weapons, and other wares beckoned the passersby. The market shimmered with life and color—each stand a tale waiting to be told.

At one end of the table sat a crowned figure, garbed in the finest furs the Arimaspians could offer. Beside him, a woman of rare beauty, her face delicate and serene, also bore a crown. Those seated nearby were clearly of noble blood—likely kin to the royal pair.

Just beside them, the Celts and the surviving Cimmerians had been given honored seats at the curve of the great table. The Arimaspian king, beaming with joy, raised his goblet in time with the music. His queen watched it all with quiet delight, a glint of pride in her eyes, as if she beheld in this celebration the soul of her people. Behind her, a small troop of servants stood straight as spears, ready to spring to their sovereigns' every whim.

Everyone laughed and sang, some joining in the song echoing through the cave. My companions drank and feasted with unhidden pleasure—just as promised, the mead flowed like a golden river. In that moment, despite all the miles between our lands, there was a strange and sacred harmony between us.

Then came the sound of a great gong, loud and resonant. The music ceased in an instant. Silence fell like snow. All eyes turned toward the topmost level of the cavern. There, by the reservoir and the two suspended barrels, stood a priest near a massive cymbal. In one hand, he held a staff; in the other, an instrument shaped like a strange, twisted horn.

Beside him, two men stood at the ready near the basin's great wooden sluices. The priest raised his arms and cried out:

"Mead! Glorious mead! Nectar of the Gods! On this day, you shall feed the lifeblood of our city!"

A wave of jubilation rippled through the cavern. The two men shut the valves—the flow of water through the channels ceased, draining swiftly. Even the central fountain ran dry, revealing several confused frogs flopping about.

The king rose, his goblet high above his head.

"Let the nectar of the Gods flow!" he thundered.

The priest pressed his horn to his lips, and out came the soft hum of a bee. At once, the entire crowd joined in, buzzing in unison—the Celts included, somewhat bemused. Near the reservoir, the two men pivoted the hanging pipes and aligned them with the barrel stoppers.

With a sharp blow from a mallet, the stoppers flew free, and a thick, amber liquid began to pour into the channels carved into the stone. The bee-buzzing swelled to a fever pitch, rising with the gurgling flow until, at the very moment the basin filled with golden mead, the sound ceased.

The crowd erupted in cheers. The music resumed in a whirlwind of pipes and drums. Dancers swayed and staggered, dunking their cups into the basin, scooping up the sacred brew.

Paritos, Lugotorix, and several of our lot dove right in. Lugotorix, drunk and laughing, slipped and landed backside-first into the basin, soaking himself to the bone and drawing uproarious laughter from the crowd. It warmed our hearts to see him smile again. The mead dulled his grief for a while.

All throughout the city, people pounded their fists in rhythm on the tables, or used jugs, spoons, and anything else within reach to join the thunder. The king, watching the foreign warriors revel alongside his people, seemed well pleased.

The evening blurred in a haze of dancing, singing, Arimaspian clumsiness, and a feast fit for a hundred kings. Bit by bit, the music softened, and the crowd did too. Bellies full and heads light, many slumped with dreamy smiles on their faces.

My companions slouched beside me, flushed and full, laughter bubbling between sips. For once, they seemed content, exchanging coarse jests and stories with gleeful abandon. Taranatos was in rare form, bragging of past exploits—but he faced stiff competition from Lygdamis, whose life, thus far, had been one long saga of madness and glory. Perhaps, if my scribe permits, I shall recount it for you one day.

"Why don't you like these folk?" Taranatos asked Lygdamis, curiosity slurring his words. "They're funny, warm… I find them endearing."

"When I look at them," Lygdamis muttered, narrowing his eyes, "I see sly marmots. Cute, yes. Charming, perhaps. But deceitful. They live half their lives burrowed in the earth like cowards. I've no taste for that. Always sniffing out how to steal what others earned in blood… No, I trust them as far as I can throw their fat king."

"I get that," nodded Alexix, his voice thick with drink, "but hey, they don't seem so fearsome. And I do like their ale… or mead… whatever. Come, drink up!"

"Aye, drink!" Taranatos echoed, raising his tankard.

Athanor smiled and raised his own in kind. It warmed my soul to see him like that—if only for a time, lightness had returned to his heart.

"To the Arimaspians," he said.

Taranatos covered one eye dramatically, lifting his mug high.

"To the A-ri-maspians!" he slurred—then froze as he caught Garedix's eye. The table fell quiet. Taranatos lowered his hand, awkward.

Garedix, stone-faced, stared him down… and then burst out laughing.

All at once, the table followed suit. Garedix had worn a patch for as long as any of us could remember, and not once had he ever given a damn.

"To Taranatos, the blind fool!" Alexix bellowed, howling with mirth.

"To fools!" cried Lygdamis and Athanor in unison.

And once again, our cups clashed in joy, and the mountain rang with laughter.

A little further down the long table, the king set down his goblet and let out a thunderous belch. At once, his queen elbowed him sharply in the ribs.

"Really, my husband! That's no way to behave in front of guests!"

Clearly, the king was quite drunk. He tried, with great effort, to hold back the gurgling roars rising from his belly. The queen turned to us, her expression one of regal warmth.

"I hope our little celebration pleases you. We're but a small folk!"

I replied with a sincere smile:

"It is absolutely wonderful, my lady! Truly! You cannot imagine the joy and honor you've given us tonight."

The king, ever curious, leaned forward.

"What brings you to our lands, then? Very few strangers pass through here! Bloody griffins! They make life hell for us!"

Athanor raised an eyebrow, intrigued.

"Griffins? We've never seen one."

Taranatos, clearly well past sober, bellowed:

"Surely fearsome beasts, from the sound of it! I love fearsome beasts—in stew! In broth!" He leapt to his feet, drawing his sword with a flourish. "Especially skewered!"

The Arimaspians recoiled at the sight of the blade. I quickly placed a firm hand on his arm.

"The only thing you're likely to skewer tonight is yourself, you drunken fool! Put that away! Forgive him, friends—he's deep in his cups."

The king laughed and raised his tankard, draining it in a single gulp before refilling it again.

"Who isn't, tonight?!"

Just then, one of the handmaidens approached the queen and whispered something in her ear. She frowned, then gave a satisfied nod.

"You've changed handmaidens again?" the king asked, eyeing the young girl. "I don't recognize this one."

"She's filling in for sweet Irna. The poor thing is ill," she replied softly, leaning in close to whisper something in return.

At her words, the king's face grew more serious. His eyes gleamed with a knowing look.

"The griffins," he declared suddenly, "oh yes, dreadful

beasts indeed. Lion's body, vast wings, and an eagle's face dripping with the blood of their prey! Talons sharp as knives, always caked with flesh and gore. They terrorize us! We are no warriors! But tell me—where are you truly from? What are you seeking in these lands?"

"We're only passing through," I answered calmly. "Our journey brought us here. Nothing more."

The queen leaned in, curiosity lighting her gaze.

"What kind of journey? Are you looking for treasure?"

At those words, the entire cavern fell silent. Even the music ceased. All eyes turned to us.

The king's brow furrowed as he scanned the table. Sensing the shift, I raised my voice.

"No treasure! Our quest is of another kind entirely. We seek the Gates of the Underworld. Something of immense importance was stolen from us. Loved ones were taken. We are driven not by greed—but by vengeance. That is our only truth."

The Arimaspians watched, waiting on their king's reaction. The old man from the river and the boy had crept closer, silent.

The king let out a short laugh and waved his hand, prompting the music to resume and the crowd to breathe again.

"Only madmen would venture there," he said with a chuckle.

"I told them as much," Lygdamis added with a smirk, "but they don't listen."

The king leaned forward, more solemn now.

"You're but two or three days' march from what you seek. But be warned—those gates lead deep into the earth, where creatures far worse than griffins dwell. Cerberus guards the entrance—yes, that hound of the Underworld, thrice-headed and monstrous! No one defeats it. No one returns. And the Minotaur—ha! That beast is even worse. I tell you, friends, you're walking straight to your doom."

"Anything that bleeds can die," Athanor said calmly, his voice unshaken.

The king regarded him, and a hint of admiration glinted in his eyes.

"Your courage is remarkable. But to make such beasts bleed, you'll need a special weapon. Only with such a blade could you hope to slay one of Hell's own."

He paused, thoughtful. The old man and boy stepped closer again.

"My king," the elder offered cautiously, "there's the old madman in the high mountains. He could make such a weapon."

"Steropes?" the king scoffed. "That foul-tempered hermit? You'll never win him over. He hates people. All people. A savage."

"Where can we find him?" asked Alexix, sharp-eyed as ever.

"He lives—" the old man began, but the king cut him off with a bark.

"Silence! And what would I gain, hmm? We've given you hospitality, filled your bellies and your cups. A little compensation wouldn't be unwelcome, don't you think?"

"Of course," I replied, though my tone was tighter now. "What do you ask in return?"

The king thought a moment, then grinned.

"Hmm… I see now—you carry only your thirst for vengeance… and for mead!" he laughed. "No, no. Do this instead: rid us of that blasted griffin who's haunted us for years. Slay it, and I'll tell you where to find Steropes!"

"A trickster's bargain," Lygdamis muttered near my ear. "I told you—these Arimaspians always have schemes behind their smiles."

"Perhaps," I replied under my breath, "but we need that weapon, Lygdamis. My people's survival depends on it."

I glanced at my companions and met Athanor's gaze. In his eyes burned a silent, steady flame. I nodded.

"I'll go," he said. "I'll bring you the griffin's head. Then you'll tell us where to find the blacksmith."

"Agreed!" the king declared. "So be it! Now drink, drink! It's dry as dust in here!"

He cast a look to his queen, who turned to her handmaid. They both wore pleased, knowing smiles.

The king drained his goblet once more—and, as if by magic, the music surged back to life. The revelry resumed. Yet though we laughed, our smiles were strained, brittle as dry bark. And still, we drank.

I trusted Athanor. I knew he would make the right choices, whatever trial awaited him. And Lygdamis was right—I too distrusted these Arimaspians. I've never had faith in people who smile too easily. They're either fools… or liars.

The feast raged on deep into the night. But our hearts were already far away, drawn toward the task that awaited us at dawn…

## CHAPTER 29
*"The Call of the Mountain"*

The first light of day barely pierced the heavy clouds, casting over the Scythian mountain a veil both majestic and foreboding. Before the entrance to the Arimaspian city, we readied ourselves for departure, while the townsfolk had gathered to witness our leaving. A solemn hush hung in the air, thick with unspoken fears and hopes.

Among them stood the old man and the boy, watching intently. The child's eyes sparkled with wonder, unable to contain his excitement. He stared at Athanor with near-reverent fascination, as if the warrior's courage alone could shape his future.

"When I grow up, I want to be a great warrior like Athanor," he whispered, his voice trembling with hope.

The grandfather gave a gentle laugh, full of tenderness and time-worn wisdom.

"They all are, little one. But great dangers lie ahead. Now go, let me rest a while. We'll go back to fishing soon.

Got a few nasty fish to wrestle with," he added with a wink.

He tousled the boy's hair, laughing softly as he walked away, leaving the child spellbound, still staring as we mounted our horses.

Not far off, the king and queen approached. The king, with a gravity befitting his station, addressed us.

"Bring me the head of that wretched griffin. I'm counting on you. It nests up there—just above us, at the peak of this cursed mountain. It watches us, mocks us, spies on our every move. A foul, conniving monster. Take this—it may help you find it more easily."

He handed Athanor a small hand-drawn map, a triangle for the mountain, childlike sketches of Arimaspians, and at the summit, a simple black cross. Athanor frowned at it.

"I don't think I'll need this," he replied flatly. "If I've understood you correctly, the beast lives above your heads. No worries. I'll return before nightfall—with its head."

The king nodded, satisfied, a glint of hope in his weary gaze.

"Good. Very good. You'll be bringing peace to an entire people with that single act of valor. I admire your courage. Just beware—don't listen to a word that creature says. It's sly, deceptive, a master of lies!"

Lygdamis couldn't help but scoff, a crooked grin stretching across his face.

"Sly, he says. That affliction seems to run rampant in this region."

I turned to my companions, my voice firm but quiet.

"Let's move out."

Already astride his mount, Athanor spoke over his shoulder with calm resolve:

"I'll catch up with you."

He spurred his horse and galloped toward the mountain, disappearing into the gloom beneath the trees as we rode on beneath the murmured farewells of the Arimaspians.

We entered the forest slowly, the shadows swallowing us one by one. Behind us, Athanor was alone, ascending the steep paths, his figure soon lost to the forest's dim embrace.

At the rear of our line, Lugotorix and Paritos rode hunched in their saddles, their faces ashen and gray—a sight that had the rest of us chuckling quietly.

I nudged my horse closer to Lygdamis and murmured low so only he could hear.

"Athanor will return. I'm sure of it."

He grunted, skeptical.

"Hm. Knowing those blasted Arimaspians, I wonder what trick they've got waiting for him."

"I admit," I sighed, "I have doubts about their real motives in all this."

We rode in silence a while, each lost in thought. The trail felt heavy with riddles yet unsolved, and dangers crouching just ahead.

Then Taranatos spoke, his voice taut with frustration.

"I could follow him, if you want."

I shook my head, sensing what Athanor needed.

"No. Let him unleash his fury on the beast. He needs this."

Just then, a cart creaked into view along the forest path, coming toward us.

Taranatos grumbled, still searching for a target for his restlessness.

"I need something to unleash my fury on too."

Alexix, ever the sharp tongue, offered with a smirk:

"Go piss on a tree. That ought to do it."

Laughter burst from the group, even Taranatos cracked a crooked smile.

"Very funny. Very funny."

As the cart passed, I eyed the old man at the reins. He raised a hand in greeting. Oddly, he looked almost exactly like the elder who had guided us to the Arimaspian city.

I frowned, unsettled.

"These folk… they all look the same to me," I muttered aloud.

"Yeah," Alexix chimed in, "I think there's only one mold for all of them."

We pressed on, our small band leaving behind the cave city and all its strange revelries. Paritos and Lugotorix swayed in their saddles, still nursing the mead of the previous night.

The hush of the forest was broken only by hoofbeats and the heavy breaths of the horses. The shadows among the trees felt thick with secrets, both ancient and new. Uncertainty walked beside us now, silent and invisible— but our resolve held firm. Something sacred bound us together—an oath not spoken, but lived.

And far behind us, climbing higher with each breath, Athanor carried our hope.

# CHAPTER 30
## *"Preparations for War"*

Later that morning, within a large tent of hide and leather, the Cimmerian war council had gathered. The pale light of dawn filtered through the seams, casting soft streaks of gold across the interior.

Woolen rugs covered the ground, and cushions made of animal pelts offered a semblance of comfort to the war chiefs seated in a circle. At the center, a low wooden table lay strewn with maps and parchments. Modest provisions were set out: hunks of bread, strips of dried meat, and clay bowls filled with goat's milk and hot broth.

Taloros, son of Lygdamis, stood tall amidst them, his features drawn with worry. Lean and athletic, with tousled black hair and piercing blue eyes, he searched the faces around him, trying to mask the storm of anxiety that churned beneath his resolve.

"We can't wait any longer," Taloros said, locking eyes with the elders surrounding him. "My father laid the groundwork. It's time we set his plan into motion. Each of you was given specific instructions, meant for you alone."

Murmurs passed through the circle. Some nodded in grim approval. Others exchanged doubtful glances. Brogar, a massive man with a braided beard and tattooed arms, finally spoke.

"Taloros, we understand the gravity of this moment. The Scythians draw near—but we are too few. And we must safeguard our people."

Taloros clenched his fists, trying to master the roiling within him. Every heartbeat felt like the countdown to disaster.

"You're right, Brogar. If we fail to rally more clans, we will be crushed. And yet some still hide like cowards in the depths of their tents. I'll dispatch the final envoys—those who bear my father's words—to the last clans we've yet to sway. But for now, we must follow the instructions we've received. And yes, we must shield our people even as we ready for war. I believe my father will return in time, with reinforcements. He's never failed us."

A heavy silence followed, the weight of his words pressing upon every warrior present. Then came a voice—steady and strong—breaking the hush. It was Kallian, a clan leader long respected for her wisdom and valor. Petite, lithe, with grey braids and keen eyes, she wore silver bangles that chimed softly as she moved.

"Taloros speaks true. We must act now. Let every clan set aside its fears and petty ambitions. If we fall, so too does our people. Unity is our only chance."

A murmur of assent rippled through the circle. A flicker of hope stirred in Taloros' chest. He raised a hand.

"Thank you, Kallian. And thank you all. Ready your

warriors. Follow the instructions entrusted to you. Move the women and children to safety. I will send the final messengers immediately. May the gods watch over us."

"But why all the secrecy?" Brogar interjected, frustration rising in his tone. "Your father made us swear silence on our roles—and we still don't know where the battle will even take place. It's… strange. As if he suspects betrayal among us."

The tent erupted with voices.

"What are you saying?" someone growled.

"Lygdamis must have his reasons!" another affirmed.

Taloros, teeth clenched, slammed his fist onto the wooden table, toppling bowls and parchments.

"Enough!" he roared. "Yes—perhaps there are traitors among us! You all know it's possible! And so does my father. If we broadcast our plan to the whole steppe, it'll be our ruin. He's protecting the greater design. The messengers I send tonight know only what they must. If captured, they cannot jeopardize the battle."

Silence returned. A heavy calm settled. These men and women were warriors—Taloros knew this. He saw it in their eyes.

One by one, they rose to their feet. The doubts and heat of debate had passed. What remained was purpose: the defense of a people.

Soon after, the final envoys readied themselves. Each bore instructions for a specific clan. Taloros watched them ride out into the breaking dawn, a silent prayer rising from his heart.

While the riders vanished into the haze, Taloros and the war leaders began the long labor of preparation. It was one of his father's strictest orders: every chief must ready his warriors apart from the others, ensuring that no single betrayal could unravel the whole.

Women and children were quietly moved to safe places, guarded by seasoned warriors. Cimmerian war songs rose on the wind, their rhythm stoking the hearts of fighters like the beating of war drums from the gods.

Before departure, the war council gathered one last time at the heart of the camp. Their faces were harder now, forged in the fire of unity. Taloros, standing tall before his tent, met the gaze of each one.

"We have little time—but we have will. And we have strength. The Scythians are near, but we are ready. For our people. For our ancestors. And for the honor of Cimmeria."

A cry of war rose in unison, fierce and unyielding. In every voice echoed a fire older than kings and deeper than steel.

And thus, within that Cimmerian camp, a people readied itself for a storm. Bound by their rituals, their blood, and the courage carved into them by wind and war, they stood at the threshold of a battle that would etch its name into the memory of the earth.

# CHAPTER 31
## *"Athanor's Trial"*

High upon the mountain that loomed above the Arimaspean city, Athanor urged his horse up a narrow, treacherous path. The incline was steep, the stones slick beneath the hooves, but the fire in his eyes did not falter.

He came to a narrow ledge that clung to the mountain's edge. From there, he could glimpse the little forest they had crossed, and the river winding through it like a silver thread. Beyond, his companions were leaving the woods, entering the wide, undulating steppes that stretched to the horizon. A pang of frustration stirred in his chest, and a wave of worry washed over him—not for himself, but for them.

He dismounted cautiously, unsheathed his sword, and moved forward, every step weighted with resolve. A little farther on, the mouth of a cave glowed with a strange light, as though it awaited him—silent, enigmatic... and threatening. The wind howled, tugging at his hair and cloak, lending a spectral voice to the mountain's breath. As he neared the entrance, shadows danced on the jagged stone walls—shadows that seemed alive.

"So, you've come. I was expecting you. You were quick. That proves your resolve. Come in."

The voice reverberated through the rocks as if it were the mountain itself that spoke—ancient, patient, and terrible.

Athanor took an instinctive step back, then clenched his jaw and pressed forward into the darkness. The cave was damp and narrow. Each droplet falling from the stone above echoed like a heartbeat, as if time itself were trickling down the walls.

"You've come for my head. Then come. I await you at the end."

The voice echoed again, commanding, unrelenting. It seemed to judge him with every word.

As Athanor advanced toward the source of the growing light, the voice resumed:

"Foolish notion, don't you think? Do you know what it costs to defy a Griffin? Why risk your life for creatures steeped in deceit and greed? They covet what I guard."

The words rang heavy, woven with old pain and deeper truths.

The tunnel opened into a wide chamber of shimmering white stone. There, sprawled atop a mound of gold coins, gemstones, and ancient jewelry, lay the Griffin. A creature both majestic and terrible—lion's body, black wings folded tight, and a raptor's head gleaming with an intelligence that pierced the soul. Its talons played idly with coins, the air around it thick with power and mystery.

"Do you believe you've chosen well, siding with these

vermin?" it asked, fixing him with eyes like burnished steel.

"I know nothing of the Arimaspes, nor what they truly seek," Athanor replied firmly. "They hold knowledge I need. I have a purpose. And if your death is the price to reach it… so be it."

The Griffin let out a roar, shaking the walls.

"My head. This little man wants my head. You fool. Do you think this cave will protect you from my wrath?"

Athanor glanced around. The chamber was tight—too tight for a fair fight. The Griffin rose, slow and menacing, forcing Athanor to step back.

"You're lucky. I restrain my fury. I heed the will of the gods. Listen… listen to your new friends plotting against me."

He gestured with a wing toward a small crevice in the stone.

"Put your ear there. Go on. They love to talk."

Athanor hesitated, then approached the hole. Voices filtered through: laughter, footsteps, the hum of life. But then—words that chilled him.

"…at last, the great day is here! We shall finally rid ourselves of that wretched Griffin! Rejoice, people! His treasure will be ours!"

Cheers rose, followed by drunken exclamations.

"We've run out of mead! But worry not—we'll buy millions of barrels with what we claim tonight! Enough to last us for generations!"

Athanor drew away, stunned. He turned to the Griffin, whose eyes were full of quiet, bitter understanding.

"You see? They care not for justice. Only for their thirst and their revelry. They want my head… for drink."

"I need what they promised," Athanor growled.

"You seek Steropes. I know where he dwells. You don't have to kill me to find him."

"And how do I know you speak true?"

The Griffin stilled. His breath came heavy. His eyes bore into Athanor's soul. Then slowly, he lowered his head, exposing his neck.

"I believe in the truth of your quest. The gods brought you here for more than blood. But if your path still demands my death… strike."

Athanor clenched his jaw. His hand trembled. He raised the blade—but could not bring it down. He drove it into the ground instead, the steel ringing on stone.

"My heart guides my hand. And it tells me: your death is not part of this."

The Griffin rose slowly, a softness in his gaze.

"Your heart is noble, Athanor. And your quest—righteous. You must save the Thunder Eagle. At all costs. Your fate lies at the end of the road. It waits for you."

Tears welled in Athanor's eyes.

"Then tell me. Tell me what you know."

"Your path is yours alone. But follow your heart, and you'll find all the answers. Come. I'll show you."

He led Athanor back to the cave mouth. The wind had ceased. Below, the plains shimmered. A cloud of dust marked the path of his companions.

"Hurry. They race toward danger. But this is not their burden. It is yours."

"I'm just a man. How can I protect them all?"

"They must not pass beyond the gates guarded by Cerberus. Or none shall return."

Athanor nodded.

"We're far from home. They do not deserve to die in that darkness. If death must come, let it be in the land of our forebears."

The Griffin lifted his gaze to a distant chain of mountains.

"There. You see that canyon? That is where you'll find the blacksmith. Go now. Fulfill your destiny."

"Thank you," Athanor whispered.

The Griffin bowed his head.

"Go. Time slips away."

Without another word, Athanor turned to retrieve his horse. The Griffin watched him vanish into the wind… then returned to the warmth of his cave. Down below, the Arimaspean celebration echoed faintly.

The Griffin shook his head, annoyed.

"Fools. Drunken, noisy fools. Will they ever hush?"

He paused.

"…Ah. But of course. They have no more mead."

And with a dry chuckle, he disappeared into the shadows once more.

# CHAPTER 32

*"The Tyrant's Games"*

The Scythians had halted their march. They awaited the arrival of reinforcements—a delay that gnawed at their leader, Skoithos, making him increasingly agitated.

To pass the time and still his nerves, Skoithos indulged in a cruel diversion of his own invention, a twisted amusement he called "the knife run." The rules, if they could be called such, were simple: he would hurl blades near the feet of a moving soldier, forcing the poor soul to jump and dance in a desperate attempt to avoid being skewered.

Sprawled atop a heap of cushions beneath a canopy held by crude wooden poles, Skoithos loosed guttural bursts of laughter each time a blade narrowly missed its mark.

"Faster, wretch! Or the next one lands in your leg!" he bellowed, raising a rusted dagger high.

With the sadistic glee of a cruel child tormenting insects, he plucked knives from a small table and flung them one by one. The soldier—trembling, soaked in sweat—shuffled and stumbled back and forth in a pitiful dance, until at last a misstep sealed his fate. The next knife sank deep into his calf, and his scream echoed through the entire camp.

"Poor sport," hissed Skoithos, his eyes gleaming with venom. "You did that on purpose, didn't you? Just to make it stop. Go, patch that up before your leg rots off."

He turned his gaze toward one of his nearby guards, staring intently. The man, already sporting a fresh bandage on his thigh, blanched under the weight of that gaze. Beads of sweat rolled down his temples—fear had found him too.

"Bring me food. I'm hungry," Skoithos growled at last. "I'm done with games… for now."

The man bowed and hurried away, relief flooding his limbs. He knew well: when his master feasted, peace followed—at least for a time. The brute was so gluttonous he could devour meat for hours on end. Afterward, bloated and sated, he'd collapse into a slumber so thunderous it rumbled through the whole encampment. His men rejoiced in those moments—finally free from his gaze, from his cruelty. If only for a while.

The Scythian war camp was a strange fusion of strict discipline and primal savagery. Leather tents arranged in rings marked the hierarchy—larger ones near the center were reserved for the war chiefs, and for Skoithos himself. Around each tent, fires burned ceaselessly, casting flickering light and the sharp scent of smoke and roasting meat.

The Scythians were also famed for their mastery of goldsmithing. And this day, an allied clan had brought new offerings: ornate gold jewelry, weapons adorned with precious metals, and ancient coins bearing forgotten symbols.

A knot of warriors clustered around the central table, marveling at the latest treasures laid before their monstrous leader. The torchlight danced on each piece—bracelets etched with intricate patterns, necklaces studded with jewels, and war axes engraved in gold and silver. They were not mere trophies, but heirlooms of a people both fierce and refined.

"These are remarkable," said a soldier, tracing the delicate curve of a golden bracelet. "Even in war, we remain a people of beauty and craft."

"Aye, perhaps," Skoithos muttered with disinterest. "But there's not enough. Is Rigdar being stingy?"

He waved a hand dismissively. "No matter. Leave me now—I eat. And you know how I despise being disturbed when I eat."

His men needed no further urging. They scattered at once, glad to be away, returning to their circles and laughter. The camp buzzed with life—clashes of voices, bursts of argument, crackling fire.

Near one such fire, a group of soldiers spoke in low tones, their faces half-lit by flame.

"This tyrant of ours… he'll lead us all to ruin," muttered one, clenching his jaw. "His cruelty knows no end."

"Hush!" said another, his eyes darting. "Speak like that and you'll end up like the poor bastard earlier. Best to follow him than feel his wrath. Or worse—his father's."

A third, older man spoke, voice low and tired.

"What we think doesn't matter. So long as he leads us to victory, we march. But mark my words—his hunger for power will drown us all."

Their words dissolved into whispers, each man casting nervous glances, ever wary of spies loyal to Skoithos. The air in the camp was thick—not just with smoke and the stink of sweat and leather, but with the tension of men who feared the very silence.

Not far from the main encampment, in a more secluded tent, Zerna the black seer sat cross-legged before a small fire. The bitter perfume of burning herbs filled the space, a pungent veil of smoke twisting upward. Her eyes were closed, her hands hovering over the flames as she chanted incantations in a forgotten tongue.

Crackling wood answered her murmurs, and the air seemed to tighten with every syllable. Then, without warning, her eyes flew open—white and wide—and she fell back as if struck by an unseen blow.

"The gods speak, Skoithos," she rasped, rising from the vision. "The blood of the Cimmerians shall water the steppes. But beware… betrayal stirs among us. Your enemies are not all beyond the camp."

Skoithos had entered the tent just in time to hear her. A grin spread across his face, revealing his yellowed, rotting teeth.

"Let them come," he whispered. "I am ready. They will all perish beneath my blade."

The rest of the camp buzzed with activity. All around, warriors sharpened their blades and strung their bows—the favored weapon of the Scythians. Others adjusted their armor, trading strips of dried meat and coarse black bread in preparation for the coming trial. The mingled scents of food, leather, and sweat hung heavy in the air—acrid, familiar, and strangely comforting.

By the fires, men swapped tales of past battles, their

deep, rhythmic voices weaving through the crackling of the flames. Laughter would burst forth now and then, but tension lingered always beneath the mirth—each unexpected sound sent a nervous jolt through the more anxious among them.

Debate flared here and there. A young warrior, his cheeks still pockmarked with the final traces of youth, burst out:

"How can we follow a man like him? He doesn't even respect his own soldiers."

An older veteran, his face weathered by time and war, shook his head grimly.

"Fear. Fear is his sharpest weapon. So long as he sows terror, he holds the reins. But you're not wrong, lad. One day, that terror will turn on him."

A third soldier, seated just outside the circle, listened in silence. His dark, piercing eyes swept the shadows with caution, as if he expected the very night to betray them.

"Watch your tongues," he whispered. "These tents have ears. And the tongue of a traitor cuts deeper than steel."

The tension in the Scythian camp was thick, nearly visible in the cold evening air. Some hated their commander, others feared him too much to speak freely. And Skoithos—drunk on power and cruelty—ruled through dread and violence. While outside the fire pits crackled and smoke spiraled into the darkening sky, inside her solitary tent, Zerna, the black seeress, continued her chants, whispering to the gods with incense and blood to ensure her master's triumph.

As the sun dipped behind the hills, the camp took on the flickering glow of countless fires. The scent of roasted meat drifted on the breeze, mingling with the cold that crept in from the steppes. Warriors huddled around the flames, seeking warmth and fellowship to soothe their war-weary minds.

Inside the largest tent, Skoithos feasted like a beast. Roasted animals had been laid out in excess—platters of charred meat, roasted vegetables, and exotic fruits lined the low tables. He tore into a leg of mutton with ravenous delight, the juices staining his thick beard. Grease slicked his fingers and chin. He ate as though war itself were an appetizer.

Suddenly, a figure pushed through the flap of the tent—a dust-covered rider, drenched in sweat and urgency. Clearly, he had ridden far. He leaned down and whispered something into Skoithos's ear, his words lost to the others in the tent.

Whatever the message, it pleased the tyrant.

A twisted smile crept across his bloated face.

"My scouts bring… promising news," he said, raising his eyes to his gathered warlords. "Our reinforcements will arrive at dawn—bringing with them a few surprises."

The war chiefs raised their cups in silent salute. The tension eased just enough for some to breathe again, but the specter of treachery still loomed, unspoken yet present.

Zerna, seated by the fire, her voice low and laden with prophecy, spoke:

"Victory shall be yours, Skoithos. The gods have written it in the stars. The Cimmerian blood will feed the earth. But beware… the knife that kills you may not come from your enemy."

A war cry rose into the night, fierce and unified. Warriors pounded their shields, their cries echoing through the steppes. The leaping firelight played across their grim faces, etching visions of fury and fate into the darkness.

Thus, beneath the starlit sky of the Scythian steppes, the camp of Skoithos prepared for war. Bound by custom, by blood, and by their ruthless commander, they stood ready to crush the Cimmerians—ready to defend their honor… or fall into ruin with their tyrant.

# CHAPTER 33
## *"The Warrior Women of the Steppes"*

Dawn was breaking when the strangers caught sight of the vast, dense cloud looming on the horizon—black as soot and veined with static lightning, slithering like luminous serpents.

Not a soul stirred in that barren expanse. A silence hung so heavy that even the land itself seemed to have fled. The column advanced slowly toward the darkness. Only a few hours remained before they would reach it.

A grim procession wound its way across the dry plain—carts creaking, riders cloaked in black, warriors on foot. They moved with purpose, like shadows summoned by an ancient curse.

At their head marched the Minotaur, flanked by warriors grim and silent. Behind him, a cage swayed gently with the motion of the convoy. Within it, barely visible behind layers of leather bindings, was the Thunder Bird—

and beside it, Anna, though hidden from sight, her spirit pressing like a heartbeat against the woven walls of her prison.

Step by step, the cortege crept closer to the suffocating gloom that marked the threshold of Hades.

Later that day, under a pitiless sun, we Celts rode alongside our Cimmerian allies. The heat drained us, sweat dripping from our brows, soaking our tunics and cloaks as we crossed the undulating hills of Scythia. The land shimmered with illusion, the horizon wavering like water in a stone bowl.

Those who had indulged too freely in the Arimaspes' honeyed drink were now paying the price. Paritos and Lugotorix, our merry fools, looked less like warriors than haggard ghosts. It had been their first true night of revelry—and if the gods were kind, it would be their last for some time.

A lesson learned the hard way, vomiting up every scrap of pride and fermented mead…

"You said the Scythians are preparing to strike at your people," I asked Lygdamis, curiosity lacing my voice. "Why are you not with them? Don't they need you now more than ever?"

He smiled knowingly and turned toward me, the glint in his eye betraying both wisdom and mischief.

"They do," he replied. "They need a leader to hold them together, to guide them through what is to come. But I won't live forever, Smérix. I must see with my own eyes what becomes of my people when I am no longer there to lead them."

"A test," I said, nodding.

"Exactly. A test of spirit and unity. We are fewer than

those who covet our land. If we are to survive, we must be smarter, more bound to one another than ever before."

"It's a bold gamble. But do they not feel abandoned? Some must see this as betrayal."

He laughed, hearty and unrestrained, and clapped me on the back. The gesture startled me—for few are so familiar with a druid of my station—but somewhere within, it warmed me. I felt more man than sage, and it pleased me.

"You're absolutely right, my friend. That's the very point!" he exclaimed. "When men believe they've been betrayed, the truth of their hearts is laid bare."

I smiled, pensive. This man—this king—was like no other. His people were fortunate to have such a mind watching over them, even from afar.

Not far behind, Alexix was riding up the line, his eyes sharp and alert. He slowed as he reached us.

"We're being watched," he said, his tone tight as a bowstring. "There's a rider on the hills. Hasn't taken their eyes off us."

Sure enough, silhouetted against the blazing sky, a lone figure on horseback loomed atop a ridge—too distant to see clearly, but positioned with uncanny precision, always hiding behind the sun.

"Yes… it's been some time now," Lygdamis murmured. "An Amazon. Best we avoid them. They've no love for men. To them, males are but seed-bearers—nothing more."

His voice held both bitterness and a strange reverence.

"I know a few who'd gladly volunteer for such a duty," quipped Alexix with a crooked grin.

"I second that," added Taranatos, ever the optimist, his naive cheer cutting through the tension.

"Yes, well… until they cut off your manhood and eat it before your eyes," Lygdamis chuckled darkly.

That wiped the smiles clean off my companions' faces.

Behind us, Paritos and Lugotorix, still reeling from their hangovers, paled visibly.

Whatever imaginative torment Lygdamis had conjured in their young minds, it had clearly jolted them from their haze.

"Is the Gate of the Underworld still far?" I asked, my voice taut.

"You'll reach it soon," Lygdamis replied, eyes fixed on the ridgelines ahead.

At that moment, another rider appeared—on a hill across from the first. Then another. And another. One by one, they emerged, spreading out across the hills, circling us like wolves stalking prey.

"We should try to avoid them," I said warily.

"Best to ignore them and press on," Lygdamis agreed, though his tone lacked conviction.

The horsewomen grew in number, their presence now impossible to overlook.

"I don't think we have that option anymore," Lygdamis muttered, pointing toward a line of fifty riders now blocking the path ahead.

We reined in our horses. The Amazons advanced slowly, their mounts stamping the dry earth with unnerving rhythm. Dust clung to the air, mingling with the scents of leather, sweat, and sun-scorched metal.

Our horses, too, were restless, sensing the imminent threat. They tossed their heads, snorted loudly, warm steam curling from their nostrils. Every creak of leather, every clink of metal from our belts seemed louder than usual—each sound magnified by the rising tension.

The Amazons were now fully within view, and each of them bore a presence that set her apart.

One of them was the rider who had been shadowing us across the steppe. Tall and statuesque, she sat proud atop her steed, head high, her black hair tightly braided beneath a helmet adorned with crimson feathers. Her eyes gleamed with a cold, almost inhuman intensity as she scanned our ranks, gauging, weighing—measuring us like a hunter eyeing prey. Her bow hung ready by her side, fingers idly caressing the string, poised to strike at a moment's notice.

Beside her, a smaller warrior adjusted the leather straps of her helm with swift, practiced movements. Her eyes, piercing green, carried the same patient hunger I had seen in wolves. Her armor, snug and dark, framed her lean muscles like a second skin. She plucked a feather-painted arrow from her quiver and let it roll between her fingers, lips curled in a half-smile—as if she already tasted the pleasure of battle.

A third figure stood out by sheer presence alone—broad-shouldered and muscular, with arms inked in winding tattoos of serpents and mythic beasts. Her flaxen hair was braided into dozens of fine plaits that clinked against her metal adornments with each motion. She leaned over her mount, whispering in a tongue unknown to us, calming her nervous beast with strokes as gentle as they were firm. Her bow rested across her back; in her hand she held a long spear, its point gleaming like a shard of sunlight sharpened to a deadly edge.

Off to the side, a younger warrior bore a hardened expression marred by a scar running across her cheek. No helmet covered her fiery red hair, which whipped wildly in the breeze. Her gaze locked on ours with defiant focus. She tightened the strap on her worn leather shield, claw-marked from old battles, and held a short sword already unsheathed. Her breath was steady—controlled. She was ready.

They formed a fearsome line before us—different in posture, in bearing, in gaze—but united in purpose. Their horses, varied in color from jet-black to speckled chestnut, stamped and snorted, tails swishing, muscles tense. Their manes were braided with feathers and talismans, charms clinking softly in the quiet morning air.

And the silence between us—by the gods, that silence!—was drawn taut as a bowstring, begging to snap.

A faint breeze stirred. Hair shifted. Something, perhaps a distant chant or warning, floated on the wind—too soft to grasp, too ancient to ignore.

We watched. We waited. Our breath visible in the cold air.

Then, of course—Lugotorix.

"Wow… they're beautiful," he murmured, awe-struck.

Paritos elbowed him hard.

"Shut it, you idiot! Do they look like they want to meet you?" he hissed.

"No, you're right… Now that I think of it… I'd rather keep my parts attached," Lugotorix muttered with a gulp.

"Battle? Against women?" asked Taranatos, incredulous, his voice betraying a nervous ripple that swept through us all.

"Bad idea," Lygdamis said calmly, eyes fixed on the

riders ahead, wary as a wolf watching its equals.

The tallest rider broke formation and advanced. First at a gallop, then slowing to a measured pace. She rode a black stallion, proud and powerful, its mane whipping like silk. She moved as one with the beast, every step a drumbeat of suspense echoing through our bones.

It was her. The one who had followed us since we left the Arimaspes. Her beauty was unsettling. Distracting. Even among hardened men and Cimmerian warriors, she stirred unease—and something more.

Her emerald eyes seemed to peer straight into our souls.

"Hello... We... I..." I stammered, trying to mask my nervousness.

"What are you doing here?" she snapped, her voice as sharp as her gaze.

"Well, we...," I began.

"We're just passing through, Amage. Just passing through," Lygdamis interrupted.

"I see you remember me," she replied coolly. "A detour would've been wiser, Lygdamis."

"I take it you know each other?" I tried to continue, but she cut me off again.

"Oh, we know each other. This so-called king is condemned by my people."

A heavy silence fell like a sword between us.

Hands reached for hilts. Shields rose. The black stallion reared, hooves cutting the air. Tension crackled like lightning.

Then... she laughed.

"Lygdamis! You old bastard! What are you doing out here? It's been an age since you last came to visit us!"

Her laughter burst the tension like a wine skin pricked with a blade.

Lygdamis chuckled, turning to his men.

"You should've seen your faces! Come on, smile a little! She's an old friend. I knew her when she was just a pup. How's your mother?"

"She's waiting to throw something heavy at your head," she replied with a grin.

"I thought Amazons were—" Taranatos began.

"Later, Taranatos," Lygdamis cut in.

"Come to our camp!" Amage called over her shoulder. "Your horses look half dead, you savages!"

She spurred her mount and returned to her warriors.

"She's stunning! Absolutely stunning," Taranatos sighed dreamily.

"Bit like your wife, don't you think?" Alexix teased.

"You really think so?" Taranatos beamed.

"No," Alexix answered flatly, smirking.

"That could've gone very badly," I muttered, still shaken. "One wrong move from our men and—"

"Oh, Smérix," Lygdamis interrupted, shaking his head. "Relax. Death's waiting for us just up the road. Might as well laugh before she takes us."

He kicked his horse forward, and we Celts followed the Amazon as she rejoined her sisters.

An uneasy truce settled over the path, and together, we rode onward—into mystery.

## CHAPTER 34
*"Toward Darkness and War"*

Night was falling over the plains of Cimmeria, cloaking the land in a hush of solemn shadow.

Upon a low hill stood Taloros, son of Lygdamis, surrounded by his scouts. The air was brisk, and the moon, partially veiled by scattered clouds, cast a silver light across the rolling landscape.

With sharp, watchful eyes, Taloros surveyed the Scythian host encamped farther out in the desolate plains. From where he stood, he could barely make out their forms. Their campfires flickered dimly at the edge of the darkening horizon.

He glanced toward his men—faces tense and silent, awaiting his word. Determination lined his features, but fatigue clung to him like a second skin. Taloros knew that every move, every command, had to be weighed with the utmost precision.

"As our king predicted, Skoithos is arrogant," Taloros

murmured, eyes fixed on the distant lights. "They march straight into our trap. This terrain is perfect for a strike from the shadows. A wiser leader would've avoided it entirely… taken a longer road."

The scouts nodded in silence.

Lygdamis's strategy was taking shape within his son's mind—each piece clicking into place like a sacred design. Taloros could almost hear his father's voice, guiding him through the stillness of this fateful night.

"We strike at dawn," he said at last, his voice low but resolute. "With or without my father."

The men exchanged looks of grim resolve. They knew the hour approached, and with it, the test of their courage and cunning.

Taloros drew a long breath, filling his lungs with the cool night air. The scent of damp earth and crushed grass rose to meet him—a grounding reminder of the land they were sworn to protect.

"Gather the war chiefs," he commanded. "We must ready the men and sharpen the plan. No one sleeps tonight. Every heartbeat counts."

The scouts obeyed at once, disappearing like ghosts into the darkness.

Taloros remained behind, watching the enemy. He inhaled deeply, as if hoping the gods themselves might answer his silent pleas.

He knew the hours to come would be decisive. And in his heart, he also knew some clans would not come, clinging to their petty interests, blind to the weight of the moment. The fate of his people would once again be decided here, in the steppe—just as it always had.

He stood there for a long time, eyes fixed on the moonlit

plain, the sky slowly thickening with stars—searching, perhaps, for a sign.

Later, back in the camp, Taloros entered the command tent.

In its center lay a rolled map, bound in leather, resting on a low wooden table. Around it burned oil lamps, casting wavering shadows across the canvas walls. The clan leaders were already present, their faces solemn, lit by the trembling flames. All eyes were on the map, awaiting, at last, the unveiling of Lygdamis's plan.

"Taloros, what news?" asked Brogar, the burly chieftain with a beard braided like battle ropes.

"The Scythians are moving directly into the kill zone," Taloros replied, unrolling the map and pointing to a marked area. "We strike here, where the ground favors us. Their pride will be their undoing."

The assembled chieftains leaned in, seeing for the first time the chosen battlefield—until now kept secret by Lygdamis himself.

Their faces lit up with understanding. The terrain was perfect for an ambush.

Kallian, wise and revered among them, nodded her approval.

"It's a dangerous move, but the best one we've got," she said calmly. "We'll need to strike hard and fast, before they realize their blunder."

"Everything Lygdamis asked of us is in place," added Brogar. "I don't know what orders the others received, but we're ready. My warriors know what must be done."

Taloros traced the map with his finger, outlining hills and valleys.

"This is the plan," he said. "Each colored mark represents a clan. I don't know who holds which position, and I won't ask. My father must have his reasons. I'll lead the attack here, force them into the canyon. The rest of you—you know your roles. May your warriors be ready."

The war chiefs nodded, murmuring strategies and adjustments. Taloros listened, weighing each suggestion, every risk.

"We strike the moment they are deep enough in the pass.

Speed and silence will be our greatest allies.

Let each man know his part.

And be ready to die for our people."

One by one, the leaders left the tent to deliver orders to their warriors.

Taloros lingered behind, eyes resting on the map. His thoughts ran deep.

Would Lygdamis return in time, with reinforcements? It no longer mattered. The burden now was his.

Outside, the night thickened, each minute tightening the noose.

Cimmerian warriors prepared in silence, adjusting their weapons and armor. The air reeked of cold iron, sweat, and old leather. Low voices rose in whispered prayers and ancient battle songs.

Taloros stepped out beneath the stars.

The weight upon his shoulders pressed hard—but with it came clarity.

He was ready. His people were ready. Together, they would meet the enemy. And fight—for land, for freedom, for honor.

"May the gods stand with us," he whispered, before

returning to his task.

Thus, under the darkened skies of Cimmeria, the clans stood united, awaiting the dawn of war. Bound by courage, custom, and a cause greater than any single life, they prepared to rise and face the tide of Scythian steel.

A few moments earlier, farther out on the plains of Scythia, as night began to descend upon the battlefield that lay before the entrance to the Underworld, the procession of the outsiders moved slowly through the desert, nearing their destination at last.

That immense black mass still veiled the mouth of the Earth's bowels, brooding and dense with the crackle of static lightning. A vast battlefield stretched before it, littered with lifeless bodies—silent witnesses to the fury of past clashes. And yet, standing unscathed amidst the death and madness, a single mighty oak rose from the desolation.

As if shielded by the Earth herself, or perhaps by the spirits of these ancient lands, its proud limbs bore a thousand leaves defying the winds of lunacy that howled around them. Life clung there still, stubborn and noble, in a place ruled now by death. Each corpse on the ground whispered a tale—of courage, of terror, of desperate resistance. The air reeked with the sour stench of blood and suffering, pressing upon the soul like a leaden shroud.

The caravan advanced in single file, threading its way among the fallen.

In the cage that held the Thunder Eagle—now lying motionless upon a bed of straw—the specter of Anna had begun to appear beside him, faint and flickering like a dream that refused to fade.

At the head of the procession walked the Minotaur, his

monstrous silhouette carving a dark shape through the gloom, like a cursed sentinel guarding the gates of dread.

As the convoy approached the threshold of the black cloud, the cloud itself seemed to shift in response, parting slowly—opening like a wound to receive them. It swirled and expanded, a living shadow that curled hungrily around the travelers, swallowing them one by one in its gaping maw.

It was a scene born of the darkest tales, a vision of fate made manifest: a force that calls all mortals toward the depths of their destiny, whether by duty, or by doom.

Then the Minotaur lowered his hood. And there, before our very eyes, his monstrous head began to change. The horns receded. The blunt snout shrank and vanished. The beast faded—and the man emerged.

No longer a creature, but a man in his forties now stood in his place.

His skull was shaven smooth, his features angular and cold as iron. His eyes, though—those eyes—still glowed red, burning like twin coals in the shadows. His frame remained the same: towering, muscular, forged in the shape of unrelenting power.

Behind him, inside the cage, Anna stood upright, hands gripping the bars. Her gaze was fixed upon the swirling cloud that now swallowed them whole.

A fierce resolve lit her face. Though a prisoner, her spirit had not broken. The fire within her remained unextinguished.

Silence reigned.

Only the snorts of horses and the groan of cart wheels dared pierce the hush.

It was the silence before a storm—the stillness of fate

tightening its grip.

A moment suspended, where even time itself seemed to hold its breath.

And I, Smérix, watching from afar in the weave of visions, knew this truth:

The dark had opened its gate. And war would follow close behind.

# CHAPTER 35
## *"The Tarasque"*

Night had fallen over the Amazons' camp, pitched some three hundred paces from our own. Their scattered tents flickered with the wavering glow of torches. A deep stillness reigned, most of the warriors already wrapped in sleep, their shapes barely discernible beneath their hides. The contrast between the apparent calm of that camp and the gnawing unease within some of my companions set the scene ablaze with uneasy omens.

A little further off, Paritos and Lugotorix slumbered in deep, raucous sleep. Their bodies were still recovering from the frenzied dances at the Arimaspe feast—and from the rivers of mead they had so cheerfully swallowed…

Around a modest fire, Alexix, Garedix, and Taranatos lay on their cloaks. Taranatos was restless, his nerves refusing the solace of slumber.

"Hundreds of women—more beautiful than the moon

itself—and here we are, sleeping on the dirt like stray dogs," he grumbled, his voice steeped in frustration that reached far beyond mere physical discomfort.

"Shut up and sleep," snapped Alexix, already irritated.

"How can you sleep with the intoxicating perfume of those fine women brushing your cheeks and—"

"Shut it," growled Alexix, sharper this time. He sighed, pausing before adding, "Tomorrow we'll face those beasts and you'll finally die. And then—at long last—I'll never again have to suffer your whining and your endless foolishness."

"We'll probably die together," chuckled Taranatos.

"No. No way I end up in the Land of Ancestors with you," Alexix muttered darkly.

"What if we both survive?" Taranatos asked, his grin audible in the gloom.

"I'll kill you myself. And if I die first, I'll beg the gods to keep you alive just to be rid of you. At last, peace."

"And what if—" Taranatos began again, but was drowned out by a chorus of voices.

"SHUT UP!" they barked.

Taranatos grumbled and rolled onto his side, sulking. Silence returned, thick and heavy, each man lost in the shadow of his own thoughts. The weight of what lay ahead pressed down on us all like a slow, silent stormcloud. Taranatos tossed and turned, plagued by restlessness. At last, he lay on his back, arms crossed beneath his head.

Dark thoughts crept into him, old memories stirring like ghosts in the still night. He turned his gaze toward his two companions. Garedix snored, his face softened in sleep. Alexix, even in dreams, wore a mask of severity and iron.

Regret welled within him like a bitter spring. He

thought back to the day their bond had shifted—when something fragile had cracked between them, forever altering the balance of their brotherhood…

\*\*\*

It had been a long-awaited morning. He and Garedix were still young then—impulsive, burning with the fires of youth. A plan long whispered and cherished between them was finally within reach.

Alexix wasn't there to watch over them as he so often did. He had gone hunting with their father for several days. Garedix and Taranatos, feigning illness, had stayed behind, too ill—so they claimed—to join. In truth, they had no intention of hunting boar or stag that morning. No. They were chasing something else entirely.

At dawn, they met at the edge of the village with their horses, hearts pounding with excitement. Today, they would discover the truth behind the old tale—a tale etched into their childhood like the lines of a sacred runestone.

It was said that a monstrous creature haunted the Duranius River, deep in the lands of the Lémovices—their belligerent neighbors, with whom border skirmishes were a tradition older than memory. For years, stories had circled the hearths: of a beast none dared name, save the old and reckless. The Tarasque.

Most who had ventured into that cursed forest never returned. And those who did spoke only in fragments, with eyes too wide and voices too low.

But Garedix and Taranatos, still untouched by failure or fear, had prepared their expedition in secret. At last, their adventure could begin. Perhaps they would bring back the beast's severed head. Perhaps songs would be sung of them across all the clans. Perhaps even the druids would remember their names…

"Are you ready?" asked Garedix, his voice thrumming with eagerness.

"More than ever," replied Taranatos, chest tight with anticipation.

He was nothing then like the warrior he would one day become. Only fifteen winters had passed over his head, while Garedix had seen twenty. The difference was made starker by Garedix's already formidable frame—he looked twice his age and fought like it too. But none of it mattered. They believed, as all young fools do, that the world was theirs for the taking.

And so, two friends set out on what they believed was destiny's road. They crossed hill and wood, river and ridge, until they reached the dark, silent forest where the Lémovices whispered of monsters.

It was said that somewhere along this river, hidden within its meanders and shadows, the creature made its lair. They had never laid eyes on it, of course—but they had a fair idea of what to expect. According to the half-mad survivors who had crossed its path, the Tarasque was a monstrous serpent, crossed with a dragon, bristling with colossal fangs and eyes so fearsome they pierced the heart with dread.

Excited, the two friends scoffed at such tales. They were exactly where they wanted to be, eager for the encounter.

Garedix, as ever, brimmed with confidence. Even then, he had earned his place among the warriors of his clan—unlike Taranatos, smaller, leaner, and far from the hardened fighter he would one day become through sweat and steel. His courage, still nascent, fluttered weakly against the storm of Garedix's reckless resolve.

They tethered their horses to a tree and began to make their way upstream on foot. Stealth was essential in such a hunt, so they waded through the river itself, hoping the water would mask their scent and noise once the creature was near.

Hours passed, their steps slow and cautious, ears straining for the slightest sound. But there was nothing—only the babble of water and the sigh of wind. Garedix began to simmer with frustration. Perhaps it had all been tales told by cowards frightened by their own shadows. Taranatos, though he didn't say it aloud, felt a surge of relief. No infernal monster meant they would return home alive.

"Let's head back," he dared to whisper.

"Damn stories… all nonsense," Garedix grumbled. "We'll go as far as that bend ahead. If there's still nothing, we turn back."

"Alright! But this time, we take the dry path home! I can't feel my legs. This damned river's freezing!"

Garedix chuckled. "You're right! Our… little warriors must be no thicker than worms by now!"

"Yeah, not the best shape to meet a lovely maiden," Taranatos muttered seriously.

They looked at each other and burst into laughter.

"If anyone saw us now—wading through a river, weapons drawn, faces grim—we'd look like a pair of absolute fools!" Taranatos added between fits of laughter.

"No doubt about it," Garedix agreed, howling even

louder.

But then—a low, guttural rumble echoed from around the bend. It stopped their laughter cold, freezing the blood in their veins. Something was there. Something unseen.

"By Taranis… we've found it," Garedix whispered, heart thundering. "It's the beast. Come—let's take a look!"

They crept toward the bank, crouching low, hiding among the foliage.

And there it was.

Beneath a waterfall, basking like a monstrous god, lay the Tarasque. It stretched in the water, luxuriating under the cascade as if savoring the caress of every drop. Its scaled hide glistened as rivulets coursed down its massive flanks. For a fleeting moment, it looked almost serene—less like a terror of legend and more like some slumbering titan at peace.

But that illusion shattered in an instant.

Without warning, the beast let out a deafening screech—a sound so sharp, so violent, it shattered the air and sent tremors through the earth. Its eyes snapped open, blazing with hatred. It reared up, water exploding outward in waves as it stomped forward, its flanks heaving, its nostrils flaring as it turned its snout in search of the scent or sound that had disturbed it.

The Tarasque was far worse than any tale had told.

Its dark green scales, streaked with brown, reflected the sunlight like burnished armor. Its skin was coarse, plated like roof tiles, and from its head down to the tip of its sinuous tail, a ridge of jagged spines gleamed menacingly. Its limbs ended in claws thick as scythe-blades, and its tail whipped the river into a frenzy.

Standing on its hind legs, it must have reached five

meters high, towering like a creature born from the fury of the gods. Its draconic head, massive jaws lined with razors, opened in a thunderous roar. Its eyes—those cruel, slitted eyes—glowed with a predatory fire, as if daring any soul to meet their gaze and live. A sickly stench clung to the beast: damp earth, rot, and the metallic tang of old blood.

"I'll climb that ledge," said Garedix, pointing to a huge rock overlooking the beast's path. "If she moves forward just a bit more, she'll be right beneath me."

He didn't wait for an answer. Like a mountain cat, he vanished into the undergrowth, scaling the height in silence.

"Wait—are you sure...?" Taranatos murmured, voice barely audible.

But Garedix was gone, already reaching the promontory. The Tarasque had stopped moving. It was tense now, its snout twitching. The scent of the boys—once masked by the cold river—was beginning to rise.

Taranatos was petrified. He glanced at Garedix, now crouched above the beast, signaling frantically for him to draw the creature forward.

His hands trembled. He wasn't the warrior his friend was. Not yet. But somewhere within, a seed of courage sparked.

He stepped into the open, sword clutched in both hands, and waded into the water toward the monster.

"Come on then! Come closer, you foul thing! You don't scare me!" he shouted—unconvincingly. "Come! Come on!"

The Tarasque froze.

Its snout lifted. Slowly, its head turned, and its eyes—

those cruel, ancient eyes—locked onto Taranatos.

Garedix smiled. Victory danced before him.

"So what now? Are you scared? Come on, you filthy beast! Come at me!" Taranatos shouted, his voice cracking.

The creature finally moved.

With a roar even more ferocious than before, it surged forward, sending ripples across the river's surface. Garedix didn't hesitate. As his friend faltered in terror, backing away step by step, Garedix sprang from the ledge like a raptor in flight, descending in a blur of motion. It was a dazzling leap—bold and graceful—and Taranatos, struck dumb, could only whisper:

"He's... he's mad. He's completely insane."

As he stumbled backward, Garedix completed his descent and, with all his might, drove his spear straight into the Tarasque's skull. The weapon pierced the monster clean through. Its jaw fell slack, frozen in astonishment. Death came instantly.

With a thunderous crash, the beast collapsed into the river, sending a massive wave that swept Taranatos off his feet.

Silence followed.

Taranatos resurfaced moments later, coughing, dazed. There stood Garedix, astride the fallen Tarasque's head, spear still clenched in hand—an image of triumph and ferocity. The sight etched itself into Taranatos' soul. In that instant, he vowed he would become like Garedix—strong, brave, revered. One day, he too would be a great warrior. Together, they would carve their legend across Gaul. And in silence, he swore it.

"Come, brother!" Garedix called, beaming. "Let's take its head and carry it home! We'll be legends, you and I!"

As ever, Garedix refused to bask in the glory alone. He loved his friend—this triumph was theirs to share. Taranatos grinned and waded forward. They had done it. They were alive.

Garedix leapt down, and the two embraced, laughing like the boys they still were.

And that's when fate broke them.

A thunder of hooves. Twenty horsemen emerged from the treeline. Silence fell like a blade. Taranatos and Garedix froze, joy evaporated. The newcomers were Lémovices—old enemies of the Arverni, ruthless and bitter.

They had witnessed everything. And they intended to steal the glory.

It was a gift from the gods, in their eyes—a chance to parade the Tarasque's head through their lands, to assert dominion over their ancient rivals. Who would the world believe? Two lads barely out of boyhood? Or a clan bearing the monster's head on their spears?

Without a word, the Lémovices approached. Garedix jumped back atop the beast and wrenched his spear free, defiant.

"This beast is ours! You'll not take it!" he shouted, teeth bared, standing with Taranatos at his side.

The fight that followed was brutal—and hopeless.

Taranatos, barely trained, lost his sword almost immediately. A warrior laughed in his face as he struck him with a mace, and the world vanished into black.

His limp body drifted downstream, unseen and forgotten, while Garedix, stronger and already a warrior, fought like a beast possessed. He wounded several before a blade drove into his left flank—not fatal, but enough to weaken him.

Then came the storm of blows.

He collapsed, unconscious. A Lémovice raised his sword to end him, but a commanding voice rang out:

"Don't kill him! Not that one. I'll deal with him myself. Take him!"

The chieftain stepped forward. "Cut the beast's head. We're taking it home. Tonight, we feast in our glory. And remember—I killed it. Agreed?"

Every man nodded. None dared say otherwise.

The head was hacked off, hoisted with ropes, dragged behind a horse. Garedix, unconscious, was slung across another. The column turned back toward their village.

What fate awaited him? Nothing good, that much was clear.

Farther downstream, Taranatos awoke.

His face was battered, his skull pounding. Drenched and dazed, he clawed his way from a tangle of branches. Through blurred vision, he saw them—Lémovices, carrying Garedix, still and slumped. The Tarasque's severed head trailed behind them.

He was alive.

A surge of dread and clarity hit Taranatos like a slap. If Garedix lived, it meant they had something worse than death planned for him.

He had to act. Now.

Stumbling, half-blind, he set off to find their horses—still tied downstream. Every step was agony, his thoughts thick with pain and fear. But he had to warn the village. He had to save his friend.

And yet… already, questions churned in his broken mind.

What would he tell them? How would he explain coming back alone? Would they believe him? Would Alexix?

No. Of course not.

And indeed, the future would prove him right.

Only Garedix could have defended him—and the Lémovices had torn out his tongue and gouged one of his eyes, as punishment for trespassing too far into their lands. He would never speak again.

And even when he tried, his brother would not listen.

For Alexix, Taranatos was a coward. And worse—guilty.

Taranatos did not argue. Perhaps, in his heart, he agreed. Garedix had dragged him into that madness—but he had been his friend, his brother-in-arms. He owed him everything. Perhaps silence was his way of atonement. His own share of suffering.

You know the rest.

Aridix and the warriors of the village launched a raid to rescue Garedix and punish the Lémovices. What followed was carnage—many lives lost.

Among them, the father of Athanor.

I believe Taranatos and Garedix still carry the weight of that day—and Alexix, in his brooding silence, still tortures himself, convinced he should have been there. But the past is the past. May those three fools one day tear out the rot from their hearts… and let it breathe.

\*\*\*

Let us return to that curious night among the Amazons. While most of my companions lingered around our modest camp, Lygdamis and I were seated near a large tent, sharing a rather delicious meal with Amage and several high-ranking Amazons. A fire crackled before us, casting warm shadows on our faces. The quiet intimacy of the moment contrasted sharply with the tension we knew awaited us at dawn.

Beside Lygdamis sat a striking Amazon in her sixties, still noble in bearing, her eyes sharp with mischief. A thin cut adorned Lygdamis's scalp—barely a scratch, really—and as a few beads of blood trickled down, she dabbed them away with a forearm, then poured him another cup of wine from a wooden carafe. Amusement danced in her eyes whenever they met his.

"You didn't have to go so hard on me," Lygdamis muttered, laughing.

"Next time, try saying goodbye before slipping away like a thief," she teased, her smile sly.

"I promise I won't forget again," he replied with a wink.

Amage, observing the scene, burst out laughing.

"Never provoke an Amazon's wrath, Lygdamis!"

The meal drew to a close. One by one, the other Amazons rose and slipped away into the night, bowing respectfully to Amage before vanishing into the dark. Even in armor, their poise and beauty were unmistakable—fierce, yet graceful. Around the tents, I caught glimpses of women preparing for rest, hugging their daughters or undressing with a kind of solemn elegance. I confess, the sight stirred something in me—not lust, but reverence.

"But tell me," I asked, still a little enchanted, "how is it that your people are made up only of women?"

The elder Amazon answered gently, yet firmly.

"We give birth only to girls. It's been that way for

generations. A curse, perhaps."

"Or a blessing," laughed Amage.

"Yes, the gods must have had their hand in it. Only daughters—beautiful daughters—and men, well… men tend to want us for only one thing. Isn't that right, Lygdamis? Women who birth only women—can you imagine the horror for all those proud warriors who only dream of war? So, we built a life of our own. We learned to fight, to fend for ourselves. And now men fear us. As they should."

She smiled proudly, her voice laced with fire.

"Men and women were never meant to live together. We're cleverer than they are," added Amage, with a conspiratorial grin.

She rose then and approached Lygdamis, pulling a gleaming blade from her belt.

"We—the poor, helpless little creatures you all feel so compelled to protect. So fragile, aren't we? But it's we who walk in the shadows… guiding your every step."

She dragged the blade lightly along Lygdamis's cheek, letting it trail down toward his throat.

"We, so delicate, so sweet… are in truth fearsome warriors. And one day, we will rule this world."

With a flick, she pressed the blade to his neck. Lygdamis only smiled and gently pushed it aside. Amage backed away, grinning, and returned to her seat.

"Oh, it will happen," she said, laughing with her mother. "Men are too weak at heart. Too easily manipulated."

"What won't a man do for a woman?" Lygdamis scoffed, laughing in return. "Enchantresses, all of you!"

The elder Amazon rose and grabbed Lygdamis by the arm.

"Come pay your tribute, fragile little man. Your debt is immense."

She cackled as she dragged him into the tent.

I stood and made to leave, still holding the vivid scene in my mind—strength wrapped in silk, fire hidden behind laughter. The Amazons: an untamed force, neither to be pitied nor trifled with.

Amage remained seated, her eyes now fixed on the distant darkness.

"I will join you at the gates of the Underworld," she said suddenly. "Your stories don't concern me. I care nothing for Zeus's Thunder Eagle. But a friend of mine went there—alone—and never returned. This is personal. My people won't come with me. Our seer warned against it. She says we must flee these cursed lands to protect our clan."

There was steel in her voice. Beneath her fierce exterior, this woman bore the unshakable weight of loyalty and fire. Her resolve stirred something in me.

"A seer, you say?" I asked, intrigued.

Amage gestured toward a wooden cart, covered by a draped cloth, standing at the edge of the camp. Inside, faint flames flickered. Two women sat within. Smoke curled into the night, the scent of sacred herbs drifting on the air. One of the figures moved her arms in slow, deliberate gestures—an ancient rite of the wild steppes.

"She's also a healer," Amage added. "She lives in that cart."

"In a cart?"

"Yes. She travels from clan to clan. Never stays long. She

prefers solitude. Says it brings her closer to the Ancestors."

"I understand. Nature is still the surest way to commune with the old spirits. Good night, Amage. We leave at dawn."

As I walked away from the fire, shadows gathered close, and I was reminded that the darkness of the Underworld was not only a place, but a truth. The night wrapped the camp like a whispering veil, and the moon above watched us silently, bearing witness to the fate that loomed ever closer.

From afar, I cast one last glance toward the seer's cart—just as the two silhouettes began to move. One Amazon climbed down and vanished quickly into the night. And then she appeared.

The white shaman.

Bathed in the firelight from a nearby brazier, she stood there in silence.

She was mesmerizing.

Clad in a robe of immaculate white, she seemed to float, more spirit than woman. Her presence drew breath and thought alike into stillness. Every movement she made was woven with elegance and an air of ancient power.

Her hair—white as snow, gleaming like silver—fell in waves to her waist, catching the moonlight like strands of starlight. It shimmered, unreal, celestial.

She turned to me.

Her gaze pierced the gloom like lightning. Eyes radiant and unearthly, glowing with knowing.

She said nothing.

And I—foolish, fascinated, spellbound—could not look away.

With a slow turn, she vanished once more into her cart, as though she'd dissolved into the night itself.

I stood frozen.

It lasted only moments… yet her presence burned into me, a brand I would carry always.

Still shaken, I made my way back to our camp. A smile tugged at my lips.

A shame, truly… that I would likely never speak with her. At least—not to exchange wisdom.

In all good faith, of course… I thought to myself with a quiet laugh.

# CHAPTER 36
## *"The Dawn of Partings"*

Later that night, beneath a sky heavy with revelations, our camp—with its scattered tents and flickering torches—looked like a fleeting constellation, doomed to vanish with the coming dawn. I was already awake, perhaps still troubled by the ethereal vision of the white-haired shaman. I lay beside a fire dwindling into embers, lost in thought. The thought of crossing the threshold of the Underworld, of facing unspeakable horrors and unveiling secrets buried in darkness, weighed heavily upon my heart. And yet, there was a strange thrill in it, a pull toward the unknown that urged me forward.

In this moment of calm before the storm, I allowed myself to reflect on the nature of our quest. We were walking toward the void, toward mortal danger—and yet, there was a tragic beauty in our resolve. Each step brought us closer to fate, to the inevitable confrontation with shadow and death.

The night was slowly yielding. Dawn began to paint the horizon with soft golds and tender greys, bathing our camp in a warm, tentative light. Around me, the first signs of life stirred. I rose and began to ready myself. The warriors, groggy but dutiful, emerged from their slumber in silence, preparing for the day.

The Amazons, graceful and resolute as ever, moved with quiet precision, their preparations as swift as they were efficient. The healer's cart, I noted with a pang of regret, had already vanished. A pity, I mused…

The sun had not yet broken the horizon, and already we were in the saddle, determination carved into our expressions.

Up on a nearby ridge, the man Lygdamis had sent to gather aid stood watch with two clan chiefs and their warriors—a good fifty brave Cimmerians awaiting their king. The battle against the Scythians was near, and a tense eagerness hung in the air like a blade unsheathed.

Lygdamis rode up to me, his face alight with satisfaction, a quiet confidence radiating from his bearing despite the looming storm.

"Did you sleep well?" I asked, curious how he'd fared after such a night.

"You have no idea," he replied with a mischievous wink, as if the question itself stirred pleasant memories.

Taranatos, clearly in a foul mood, mounted his horse with a huff of impatience.

"Let's ride. Can't sleep worth a damn around here," he muttered, his tone thick with irritation.

Garedix snorted out a strange sound, and Alexix mimicked him, their banter—a thread of lightness—cutting through the dawn's tension.

Then Lygdamis spoke again, and this time his voice bore the weight of farewell, laced with the gravity of what was to come.

"Our paths part here, friends. I must return to my people. Too many days have passed... and there's a bastard king's son I still need to kill."

"This is no longer your fight. Thank you for everything, my friend," I said, deeply grateful for his strength, his cunning, and his company.

"Perhaps we'll meet again in the afterlife," he answered, a dark glint of philosophy in his voice.

"The later, the better, my friend," I smiled.

"In the meantime, do me the favour of severing as many heads as you can before you take down that Minotaur," he grinned.

"Do the same with yours," I replied.

He spurred his horse into a rear, the beast rising on powerful legs, a vision of Cimmerian pride and ferocity. Then he turned, and with three warriors still at his side, galloped away toward the waiting clans. Their silhouettes soon vanished behind a hill.

And so, we turned once more toward our own path, leaving behind the Amazons' camp. Tents were being swiftly taken down, their women preparing for departure with fierce precision. Amage's mother, regal and commanding, oversaw it all. Around her bustled women and young girls, and though she bore herself with steel, her eyes betrayed both pride and fear as she watched her daughter mount up.

"Be careful, my child. Do not forget—you are our queen now. You bear great responsibility," she warned, her voice full of maternal gravity.

"I must know what became of her, mother. Do not worry—I will return," replied Amage, her voice steady as iron.

"Their war is not our war, daughter. We must flee these cursed lands. We cannot help them… The priestess has spoken, and she is rarely wrong!"

There was ancient wisdom in the elder's voice, a keen understanding of the madness awakening in these lands.

"I know, Mother. Watch over our people. I will come back to you."

She spurred her horse and rode toward us, her mind set on uncovering the fate of her friend, her spirit torn between duty to her people and the call of something more personal—and perhaps more sacred.

# CHAPTER 37
## *"The Forge of Fates"*

The canyon Athanor entered was flanked by steep, jagged mountains, their silence so profound it seemed to smother the very breath of the land. Drenched in sweat, Athanor rode on slowly, his steed's hooves grinding the rocky ground beneath. The air was motionless. The heat, oppressive. The silence, absolute.

Then, suddenly, he halted.

Before him, at a bend in the path, stood a lone wolf. The creature stared at him with piercing eyes, unmoving. For a brief moment, man and beast locked gazes—then, as swiftly as it had appeared, the wolf vanished.

Athanor exhaled, his voice low.

"A wolf… If you're seeking a meal, you'll find only my blade to chew on."

He pressed on, rounding the curve. There, once more, stood the wolf—still, waiting—at a fork in the path.

As Athanor approached, the beast bolted down the right-hand path, which curved sharply to the left not far ahead. The wolf vanished again. Athanor paused at the crossroads, hesitating only a breath.

"You're no accident. Show me the way, Wolf."

He spurred his mount, trotting into the new turn. The air began to tremble with a distant, metallic rhythm—a sound faint at first, but growing clearer. Hammer on metal. Sharp. Relentless. Echoing off the canyon walls like a heartbeat forged in iron.

Then, ahead, a gaping hole opened in the canyon wall.

Athanor dismounted, cautious, drawing his sword. He approached the opening, where firelight danced against the rock. Inside, a vast cavern yawned into the mountain. Torches lined the stone walls, casting long shadows over a sight that stilled the breath in his lungs.

At the heart of the forge, a roaring fire blazed within a massive stone basin. Before it stood a man—or rather, a giant of a man—nearly eight feet tall, hammering a blade of glowing steel against a blackened anvil.

This was Steropes, the Cyclops—titanic blacksmith of old. His broad, sinewed frame gleamed with sweat, his greying beard matted to his chest. His furs were torn and weatherworn, revealing tattooed limbs laced with scars. Wild, tangled hair framed a face carved by time and sorrow. Each blow of his hammer came with a guttural snarl, as though his agony echoed through every stroke.

Still hidden in the shadows of the pass, Athanor stood in awe. But then, the Cyclops let out a bellow—raw and heart-wrung—a cry of torment, not fury.

Athanor stepped down, sword still in hand, approaching the threshold of the cave. The wolf sat by the entrance, calm, unblinking. A sentinel of fate.

"How much longer?" the Cyclops howled. "How much

more? I've had enough!"

Inside the forge, Steropes plunged the glowing blade into a vat of water. Steam exploded around him, veiling his shape in mist. He lifted the sword, inspecting it through the haze.

"Not enough fire. Not enough heart. No hope. This blade has no purpose. It is unworthy," he muttered, voice low and bitter.

Slowly, he turned his head toward Athanor, revealing a face drawn by grief and solitude. His single eye—sky-blue, immense—gleamed beneath a heavy brow, filled with weariness.

"You've come. The gods told me you would. But your weapon is not ready. My heart is too dark. Too weary. I cannot forge it. I'm done."

He let the sword fall with a clang to the stone floor and slumped onto a boulder, shoulders sagging.

"I can't help you. Not anymore. My kind is gone. My brothers are dead. I am the last. And such a blade... it cannot be born from despair."

"I need that weapon," Athanor insisted. "It's just metal. Perhaps a clever alloy—but still, just metal."

"No, little man," the giant rumbled. "It's far more. Yes, it's forged from a secret blend of metals—but the most vital element is something no forge alone can provide: the strength of a heart driven by purpose. You do not fight darkness with more darkness. You fight it with light. And my soul is too shadowed. I cannot give you this blade."

Ah, how many times have we, fragile mortals, tried to overcome our own ruin through sheer will? Steropes, this giant of old, was no different than the rest of us—shattered beings in search of a reason to rise again.

But Athanor had not come to bow before despair.

He stepped toward the forge and seized the handle of the bellows.

"I didn't cross half the damned world to watch a weeping giant mope in his cave," he barked.

With all his strength, he worked the bellows. The forge roared to life, embers swirling, flames surging brighter. The cavern was cast in crimson and gold.

"Come now, giant! Show me what you can do. If it's death you crave, you're welcome to follow me—she'll take you gladly. But first, forge what I need. I must find the Thunder-Bird. I must find Anna. Rise. Strike. Let your hammer thunder. Let the world hear us, even down in Hell."

What strength of spirit, what fire in that call! In Athanor's voice rang the echo of every soul that still dared to hope. Through his sheer resolve, he became the very light Steropes had long believed lost. Perhaps this light—unbending, untarnished—might offer the old Cyclops a path back to purpose. Perhaps not. But one thing was certain: after so many years spent in silence and solitude, even the presence of a single soul was a balm.

The colossus let out a long sigh, rising slowly, the weight of the years heavy on his shoulders. His gaze lingered on Athanor, reading the storm in his eyes—defiance, urgency, hope. And at last, with a solemn nod, he yielded.

Together, they set to work.

Their movements were first hesitant, then gained in strength and rhythm, the clang of steel becoming a kind of chant. Sparks flew, the forge flared, and their shadows danced in the flickering glow. Sweat streamed down their faces as the heat rose, but their resolve did not waver.

A wild, primal music seemed to rise from the flames themselves—like drums echoing from the depths of the mountain, urging them on with each thunderous beat.

"Come now, blacksmith," Athanor shouted above the roar, "One last battle, and you'll be free of your burden."

Ah… And at that moment, I remembered the old wisdom: True strength lies not in brute force, but in the spirit's resilience—its will to rise again after every fall.

Steropes bent down, lifted the half-formed blade, and plunged it into the heart of the blaze. The steel screamed as the fire embraced it, turning it molten, malleable. The two men, eyes blazing, hearts aflame, hammered as one.

Blow after blow, their hammers rang like war cries, echoing off the stone. The blade pulsed with life—red, gold, then white-hot—as if the very forge had birthed a sliver of lightning.

And it was there—in that shared fury, that relentless rhythm—that the true magic took root. Not in the alloy, nor in the ancient technique, but in the union of two wills: one burdened by sorrow, the other fueled by purpose.

Yes… if only the world understood: light is not the absence of darkness. It is born from it, like a blade from the forge.

And in that cave, where sweat met flame and despair met defiance, a sword was born—one not forged by steel alone, but by destiny.

# CHAPTER 38
*"The Entrance to the Underworld"*

Beneath a heavy and brooding sky, as twilight crept ever closer, we finally drew near the source of all our woes. I could feel it in the depths of my bones, and I knew my companions did too. The gates of the Underworld were close, and my heart pounded in time with the war drums thundering inside my head. I heard them—booming, relentless—as if echoing from distant lands, urging me to press on.

We, the Celtic riders, accompanied by Amage the Amazon, moved with purpose across the steppe. Our swift advance tore through the stillness of that desolate land. The weight of the coming storm pressed heavy on our souls, every beat of the drum reverberating like a reflection of our dread.

At last, we reached the base of a great hill. Driven by the urgency that gripped our hearts, we began to climb, the rhythm of the drums inside me growing louder and more frantic. When we finally reached the summit—silence.

Utter, dreadful silence.

Our horses, breathless and slick with sweat, pawed at the earth, whinnying and rearing. That sudden hush—that moment suspended in time when every creature, man or beast, seemed to hold its breath before the unknown—was terrifying in its own right.

Before us stretched a barren plain. This place, drenched in the silence of death, was disturbed only by the restless movements of our mounts. Strangely, their hooves made no sound against the earth. It was noticed, but no one dared speak of it.

From every direction, insects crawled toward a massive black cloud—a living, breathing thing, swelling and contracting with bursts of lightning. It pulsed like a monstrous heart, a few hundred paces away, hiding something grim and unknowable within. The quiet—the absence of sound in a world that should be full of life—spoke of ill omens, of forces beyond our grasp."

Something was stirring inside that cloud. We all felt it. The very air was suffocating, as if the storm were pressing its weight upon our chests. Horses quivered with unease, drenched in sweat, just as we were. The silence was laden with invisible menace, that old terror buried deep within us—the fear of the unknown, of chaos unbound.

Come now—courage! We are here. There is no turning back now, I thought, trying to quiet the storm of doubt and fear within me.

Just before the great dark mass, a battlefield stretched wide. The bodies of Scythians, Cimmerians, and horses lay in tangled ruin. Dismembered, impaled, their faces frozen in agony—they told the tale of a slaughter too brutal to be forgotten.

Only the great oak still stood, proud and defiant amidst the desolation. What a vision of horror! These warrior souls, torn so brutally from life, had become silent sentinels of their executioner.

"We're not enough," Taranatos muttered, defeated.

"Athanor will come. He'll bring weapons capable of slaying those things that dragged the Thunder Eagle into the Underworld. He must," I replied, though I wasn't sure I believed it myself.

"Yes. He must. Or we are lost," Alexix added grimly.

"Myrina! No, no, no…" Amage whispered, her voice shaking.

She spurred her horse, ready to descend the hill, but I caught her reins before she could.

The anguish in Amage's eyes… May none ever know the agony of sensing a loved one lost in darkness, clinging to only the faintest hope of return.

"No, Amage. Night falls. We must wait for Athanor. To approach now would be madness. All these warriors—" I gestured toward the open-air grave before us, "—they paid the price."

"Myrina is there. I must find her—I must bring her back to our people!" she cried, struggling against my grasp, tears streaming down her cheeks.

"We will find her. At dawn, we will search the field. And you shall take her home. But not tonight. Come—let us leave this place."

In such moments, bravery must yield to wisdom. The loss of one soul does not justify the ruin of all. I turned my mount, drawing Amage with me, and wordlessly, the others followed.

Night crept in, heavy with grim promises and the scent of war. The silence atop the hill was unbearable as we pulled away from that haunted plain.

Our hopes clung to the return of Athanor—and the weapons forged in secret by a smith we had never seen, whose very name carried mystery.

A strange act of faith, was it not?

And yet… I could not afford to doubt. I had to believe our cause had meaning, even if that meaning had yet to reveal itself to me.

# CHAPTER 39
*"The Battle of Lygdamis"*

Earlier that day, in the arid steppes of Cimmeria, Lygdamis finally arrived with reinforcements at the site where his son, Taloros, was already poised for the coming battle. Just before joining him, the group of riders had split in two, and Lygdamis, leading one half of his men, climbed a hill overlooking the canyon where the clash with the Scythians would unfold.

He dismounted and approached his son, while the rest of his men held back, hidden from the enemy's sight. Everything was in place for the battle ahead.

Taloros, upon seeing his father arrive, felt a mixture of relief and admiration. The two men exchanged a knowing glance, fully aware of the gravity of the coming fight.

"Father, all is ready," murmured Taloros, pointing to the canyon below. "The Scythians approach, just as we expected. But there is something important I must tell you."

Lygdamis nodded, his sharp gaze fixed on the horizon.

"Perfect," he replied calmly. "What is it, Taloros?"

Taloros clenched his fists, rage simmering within him.

"Our scouts report that some clans have betrayed us. They've joined the Scythian host. No doubt hoping to usurp our kingdom."

Lygdamis gave a cold smile, a flicker of anticipation in his eyes.

"Do not worry, my son. Treachery is a blade that cuts both ways."

Taloros looked at his father, unease gnawing at him. His father seemed far too confident—and that unsettled him.

"The son of the Scythian king is a fool," Lygdamis added. "They outnumber us, yes—but we have the terrain. The battle will be over before nightfall. The canyon is short, and there is water beyond it… His arrogance will drive him to cross, thinking to make camp there."

I could not help but feel a deep awe for how Lygdamis had foreseen every move of his enemies. His strategies revealed a rare tactical mind, and I knew Taloros would learn much by his side…

The Cimmerians took their positions, just as planned. Some hid among the rocks and underbrush, invisible to the Scythians drawing near. Lygdamis knew each man was where he needed to be, ready to strike at the opportune moment.

The Scythians, smug in their superior numbers, entered the canyon without caution. At the front of the march was Skoithos, the Scythian king's son, utterly unaware of the looming danger.

Not all shared his hubris—Pergatos, in particular, had

advised against entering the pass. But just as Lygdamis had predicted, Skoithos, proud and impulsive, refused to listen. He had made his decision, and besides, he was hungry. He would not delay his meal for a detour.

The Cimmerians, hidden on the cliffs, waited with deadly patience—and when the Scythians were deep within the gorge, Lygdamis gave the signal. A storm of arrows rained down upon the rear guard, sowing panic and chaos.

Horses screamed in terror, some collapsing beneath their pierced riders. Skoithos, caught off guard, roared confused orders, trying desperately to reestablish his ranks.

"Retaliate, you useless curs!" he bellowed. "Form up!"

"Form up against what?" Pergatos shouted. "We can't even see them!" he added, realizing too late there was no way to create a proper formation.

That's when Taloros struck, leading his riders down upon the Scythian rear. A titanic battle ignited, war cries echoing across the canyon walls. Taloros raised his blade high, his commands cutting through the din.

"Charge! Hit them hard and fast! Show no mercy!"

The Cimmerians, skilled in mounted archery, struck swiftly and vanished into the shadows. Chaos reigned. Pain and fury filled the air.

Then, at the heart of the carnage, the clans who had seemingly betrayed Lygdamis turned against the Scythians.

"Traitors!" howled a Scythian chieftain. "We've been betrayed!"

The Scythians tried to retreat—but it was too late. Taloros and his men had sealed the exit, striking with a ferocity that shattered any attempt at order. Driven back, harried by arrows, the Scythians plunged deeper into the tightening canyon.

Blades clashed, the stench of sweat and blood thickened the air. Cimmerian horsemen swooped like falcons, their blades finding flesh without hesitation. Though greater in number, the Scythians were disorganized, every formation shattered by the lightning attacks.

"Stay together!" Skoithos screamed, his face twisted in fear and fury. "Don't let them divide us!" But his commands were lost in the chaos.

High above, Lygdamis moved along the ridge, tracking the battle's slow drift.

From below, he seemed like a god—colossal, calm, and commanding. His people drew strength from the sight of him standing tall among the stones.

He knew the moment of reckoning was near. The Scythians, driven by panic, were entering the narrowest part of the canyon—a natural bottleneck. Lygdamis signaled a warrior stationed farther up the cliff. Moments later, boulders tumbled from the heights, crashing down with merciless force. Screams mingled with the thunder of stone, a terrible music of despair and death.

The Cimmerians, using surprise and terrain, held the upper hand.

Yet the battle was far from won. A contingent of Scythians, more disciplined than the rest, managed to regroup and mount a counterattack. Pergatos, a seasoned veteran, led them with grim resolve.

"Hold your ground! For the glory of Scythia!" he roared.

He was tall and strong as a bull. His coarse, savage features only amplified the aura of brute strength he exuded. His men respected him—far more than they ever had that fool Skoithos, whom they saw as nothing more than a vain tyrant.

The Scythians locked their shields, forming a human wall, advancing steadily, pushing back the Cimmerians. Their archers, wielding powerful composite bows, began to regain accuracy, their shafts cutting down Cimmerian horsemen one by one.

"Father! They're regrouping!" Taloros cried, a flicker of concern in his eyes.

Lygdamis heard his son's warning. He gritted his teeth, assessing the tide of the fight with a warrior's instinct.

"Hold the line! Don't let them close ranks!" he commanded.

Then, without hesitation, Lygdamis spurred his horse and charged alone down the slope. He hurled himself into the fray like a thunderbolt, carving a path through the enemy lines with deadly precision. His blade sang its crimson song, felling warrior after warrior and shattering the Scythian formation. Taloros and the other clan leaders followed, unleashing a storm of steel upon the enemy.

"For Cimmeria!" bellowed Lygdamis, his voice booming like thunder across the battlefield.

I watched in awe. The raw fury and perfect execution of the Cimmerian assault were astonishing. They struck like a tempest—quick, calculated, and unstoppable. But it was the mind behind the tactics, the iron will of Lygdamis, that commanded my deepest respect.

He had but one goal now: the death of Skoithos, the Scythian prince. Amid the chaos, he spotted his quarry—trying to flee, of course. Skoithos, who liked to pretend at courage, revealed his true self when gripped by fear: a coward with the grace of a panicked doe.

"Come here, you coward!" Lygdamis growled, his blade glinting with cruel promise.

Skoithos, wild with panic, tried to lift his massive mace, but his movements were clumsy, his terror all too visible.

"You think you can defeat us?" he hissed, his voice shaking.

"I don't think—I know," Lygdamis replied, cold as the steel in his hand.

With a few swift blows, he disarmed his foe—and with one clean, decisive stroke, he severed Skoithos's head. Hate burning in his gaze, he picked it up with disdain. His chest rose and fell like a bellows, and as he raised the bloodied head high, he let out a terrible war cry, tongue lashing out like a demon's. Time itself seemed to freeze. All turned to look.

Skoithos was dead.

Seeing their leader slain and their defeat sealed, the remaining Scythians dropped their weapons. There had been no love lost for Skoithos, and now, without his lash or his threats, no man felt compelled to fight.

For a leader they respected, they would have fought to the last breath—Lygdamis knew this.

"We surrender," declared Pergatos.

He tossed his sword at Lygdamis's feet.

"We are leaderless. You have won."

Lygdamis regarded them with cold indifference.

"Gather your dead. Burn or bury them—I care not. They fought well. They deserve a warrior's rest, even if they served a fool."

The Scythians, grateful not to be slaughtered, began tending to their wounded and retrieving their dead. Some had to end the suffering of their dying horses. Among the steppe peoples, horses were sacred—revered like gods. To a nomad, putting down a dying steed was a sacred duty.

It was a grim scene. The moans of the wounded, the last gasps of the dying, and the shrill cries of injured mounts filled the air.

The Cimmerian chieftains gathered around Lygdamis and Taloros, offering words of thanks and praise.

"That was no easy fight, but we proved our mettle," said Brogar, the massive, braided-beard chief.

"Your strategy was masterful, Lygdamis," added Kallian, the wise and respected matriarch. "Without your cunning, we'd have been overwhelmed."

Lygdamis gave a slight nod, accepting the praise, though his eyes were already fixed on the survivors.

"We must stay vigilant. They'll return—with new leaders, new pacts. This is just one victory in a war that has barely begun."

Taloros, watching his father converse with the other leaders, felt a deep swell of admiration. Every word, every gesture, revealed the wisdom and gravitas of a true ruler.

I, too, could not help but feel a deep respect for these warriors. Their grit, their strategic mastery, and their resilience marked them as a formidable people. I was honored to bear witness to their valor.

As the sun began to set, casting golden light upon the canyon soaked in blood and honor, the Cimmerians began to recover their fallen. They tended to the wounded, applying herbs and rough bandages. The scent of earth, blood, and crushed greenery hung in the air. Soft chants of mourning rose among them, solemn and sacred, turning the ravaged battlefield into a place of remembrance.

Lygdamis stood apart, his gaze lingering on his people. Taloros came to join him, his eyes drifting toward the distant horizon.

"Father… I've learned so much today," said Taloros softly. "Not just about battle, but about cunning and strategy. You are a master of war."

Lygdamis gave a faint, knowing smile.

"And one day, you will be a master too, my son. Remember always—war is not only brute strength. It is patience, foresight, and the art of turning the enemy's own blade against him."

"We must honor our dead," said Taloros. "They gave their lives for our freedom."

"Yes," Lygdamis replied. "And we must prepare for what lies ahead. This battle is done, but more will follow. We must be ready."

As the Cimmerians tended to their wounded and recovered their fallen, Lygdamis watched in silence—a blend of pride and solemn determination etched upon his weathered features. The setting sun bathed the canyon in molten gold, transforming the battlefield into a painting of sacrifice and glory.

Sensing the moment, Lygdamis stepped forward and climbed atop a rocky outcrop. Taloros, seeing his father ready to speak, motioned for the warriors to gather. Murmurs died down. One by one, the Cimmerians assembled, their eyes fixed upon the man who had led them to victory.

Lygdamis raised the severed head of Skoithos high into the air, drawing every gaze like a lodestone.

"Warriors of Cimmeria! Today we have proven our worth—our strength! This head is our trophy, yes—but more than that, it is a warning! Let it be known to all who would challenge us: they shall perish!"

A war cry erupted from the ranks, echoing through the canyon like the roar of a thunder god. Weapons rose skyward, gleaming with the light of dying day, as faces lit with pride and fervor.

"We have won this battle—but the war is far from over," Lygdamis continued, his voice steady, imbued with ancient wisdom. "Stay vigilant. Stay ready. And remember—our true strength lies in our unity… and our cunning."

He descended from the rocks and laid the head of Skoithos upon a stone, a grim offering to the gods of war. His warriors returned to their tasks, hearts burning with renewed purpose and belief in their future.

He approached his son and laid a strong hand upon his shoulder, shaking him firmly.

"You must believe, my son. We are a great people."

"I do believe, Father. With you leading us… nothing can break us."

"Yes. So long as we remain united… But the Assyrians are at our door as well. We must be ready," he added, his tone turning grave once more. "Go now. Return to our clan. Bring them word of our victory—and begin preparations. We must move."

"You'll join us soon?"

"Yes. Soon. I'll stay behind just a little while, to ensure those damned Scythians truly leave our lands. We wouldn't want them following us."

Taloros nodded, mounted his horse, and rode off, his father's proud gaze following him into the twilight.

And so, beneath the broad sky of Cimmeria, another

chapter of their story was etched in blood and defiance. A tale of valor and strategy, where the mind of Lygdamis and the fire of his warriors turned the tide of fate. And as Taloros learned by his side, the forge of war shaped him—day by day—into a leader worthy of the name he bore, one destined to carry the mantle of his father.

# CHAPTER 40
## *"A Glimmer in the Darkness"*

A few hours' ride from the clash between the Cimmerians and the Scythians, as the night deepened into a pitch-black void devoid of stars, we made camp, waiting for Athanor's return. Several campfires flickered faintly around us. Everyone was tense, alert to the slightest sound. But there was none. A deathly silence reigned in the damp, heavy air of the Scythian steppes. The very world seemed to hold its breath.

Seated near a fire, Alexix, Garedix, Taranatos and I stared into the flames, the crackling of logs barely breaking the oppressive stillness of the night.

"Not a single insect. Not a sound," murmured Alexix.

"It's too quiet. Much too quiet. Life has abandoned this land. I don't like it," I said gravely. But then, with a wry smile, I added, "Though we've seen worse."

My words echoed our shared thoughts, capturing the

anxiety that gripped each of us.

"We're too close. Maybe we should've kept farther back," said Taranatos, uneasy, watching the faint flickers of light that sometimes danced above the hill.

His eyes scanned the dark for an unseen threat, darting with nervous energy. Everyone had noticed the strange lights—but none dared speak of them. Paritos and Lugotorix joined us, tense and alert.

"For once, I agree with Taranatos," Alexix chimed in. "This whole thing is madness. What can we possibly do against that black mass down there? We're not strong enough. Look at us—we're just a handful," he said, gesturing to the few companions we had left.

He jabbed at the ground with the stick he'd been using to stoke the fire, frustration radiating from his every move. He was right—but retreat was no longer an option. To turn back now would make all our fallen comrades' sacrifices meaningless. I placed a reassuring hand on his shoulder, trying to lend him some of the calm I barely held onto myself.

"You'll avenge your sister, Alexix. Trust in our gods. Taranis would never have let us come this far if our quest were hopeless."

My voice aimed to soothe—but the weight of uncertainty pressed on me like a storm gathering at sea.

"Athanor is coming… but he's just a man," muttered Taranatos, dejected. "What can one man do against the gods' monsters? Thousands of warriors fell before that thing…"

Feeling my patience crack, I snapped:

"Enough! Wallowing in despair serves no purpose. Trust! All of this has meaning—even if it ends with our deaths."

My tone, sharp as flint, betrayed the tension coiling within me. Silence fell again, heavy with the weight of unspoken fears. I looked at them, compassion and doubt stirring inside me—but I dared not let it show.

Suddenly, something felt off.

"Where is Amage?" I asked, frowning.

"She said she'd keep watch atop the hill," Alexix replied, hesitant.

"What?" I exclaimed, springing to my feet, exasperated. "And you let her?"

"But… she was calm, she…"

"She tricked you, you fool!"

"Hey! I wasn't the one who said it, you fool," retorted Taranatos, grinning mockingly.

"Silence! To arms! She's going to get us all killed!"

I stormed up the hill, my companions right behind me, blades drawn, a fierce determination pounding in my chest.

When we reached the crest, a strange and chilling sight awaited us. The immense black cloud had spread even wider, pulsing like a great, monstrous breath. In the night, the lightning that laced through it burned brighter and more violent than ever. Always silent, the flashes lit the horror sprawled at its feet.

Across the battlefield below, ghostly lights flickered—drifting above the corpses. Others wandered slowly in all directions, their wavering movements adding to the surreal atmosphere. We stood there, stunned by the uncanny vision.

"Spectres…" I whispered, horrified.

These things were nothing less than the souls of the

dead, trapped where they had fallen. But to what end? Perhaps this black mass was using them—raising an army for some unspeakable purpose. They hovered above the earth like hunters in search of prey to unleash their wrath upon. I could feel their rage and torment—a vortex of violence, hate, and despair. Perhaps they'd been promised deliverance in exchange for a new soul… I could not say, but I sensed something infernal at work.

As we scanned the darkness for Amage, a foul stench rose suddenly into the air—a mixture of rusted iron, damp earth, and the sickly sweetness of burnt flesh. It coiled into our lungs like a living thing, choking me with a despair I could not name. The cold intensified, seeping deep into my bones, as if each spectre drained the warmth from the very air. My skin shivered beneath an invisible breath that whispered unintelligible words in my ears—a tangled chorus of wails and desperate cries.

The spectres, both luminous and translucent, moved in silence, yet the air throbbed with their presence, vibrating like the hum of a thousand insects. But these vibrations were not mere sound—they were palpable, like a pressure weighing down on my chest, stealing the air from my lungs with each breath.

Tears burned my eyes—not from sorrow, but from an acid sting, as though these tormented souls shed a dust invisible to the eye, a residue of old breaths, of pain, and lamentation. I tasted blood in my mouth, metallic and bitter, though no wound marked my flesh. Just gazing upon them felt like drinking in their anguish, swallowing their despair whole.

At the foot of the hill, one of the spectres drew near— and I saw its face. Or rather, the lack thereof. It bore no features, just a gaping hollow, from which two glowing orbs burned with spectral fire. Their light pierced into me, and a voiceless wail echoed through my skull. I felt as though my bones might shatter under the weight of that oppressive energy, heavy as lead. There was a pounding in my head—was it my own heart, or the pulse of that tormented thing? A deep panic gripped me, an instinct to run, to break free of its grip before my soul was swallowed by the maelstrom.

These weren't mere lost souls—they were present, tangible, marked by the tragedy of their deaths. Their nearness made the very air thick and poisonous. I knew we had little time before their curse began to claim us.

Caught between dread and fascination, I stood frozen, until Lugotorix broke the spell. He pointed toward a figure weaving carefully among the corpses. It was Amage, moving through the shadows, searching for her friend.

"She's going to get us all killed," I muttered. "We have to pull her out of there."

Suddenly, a sharp clink of metal shattered the stillness. Amage had stumbled against the rusted armor of a long-dead warrior. At once, every ghost-light froze in place—and then, like arrows loosed from every direction, they rushed toward her.

"By Taranis, they've seen her!" shouted Alexix.

"Gods, we've got to do something!" cried Lugotorix, panic rising.

"With what? Blades and arrows won't stop that!" barked Alexix, exasperated.

"Light!" I shouted, the thought surging into me like a divine whisper. "They don't show themselves by day! Light torches—now! Fire the arrows!"

"You heard him!" roared Alexix. "Move!"

Paritos and the others scrambled to the campfires, seizing torches and sparking them into life, while others quickly wrapped cloth around their arrows. We had only moments. The spectres were closing in, surrounding Amage like wolves around a deer.

"Hurry!" bellowed Alexix from the hilltop.

Warriors came running with oil jars and lit arrows. Amage was now fully encircled.

"Shoot! Shoot all around her!" I commanded.

The archers dipped their arrows, lit them, and let fly. A rain of fire fell around Amage as she readied her bow, teeth clenched in fierce defiance. The flames hissed against the damp earth, rising like a shield.

"It's working!" cried Alexix. "Keep the circle tight!"

He grabbed a bow and loosed arrow after arrow. Around Amage, a ring of fire was forming. Spectral wails echoed across the hillside as the phantoms recoiled from the flames.

"We'll run out of arrows soon!" Lugotorix warned.

"Then we go. Now! Grab torches!" Alexix barked.

We descended the hill in a rush, torches blazing. Reaching Amage, we closed ranks in a circle of fire. The ghosts writhed and screamed, unable to breach our fiery bulwark.

"Come on then, damn you!" roared Taranatos, brandishing his torch like a mad prophet.

Alexix's voice cut through the chaos, taut as a drawn bow.

"Move! These flames won't last forever!"

Garedix thrust his spear futilely into the air, trying to

hit shadows, while I grasped Amage's arm.

"You were told to wait! Are you trying to get us all killed? Come, now—back to camp!"

"I didn't find her. I didn't find her," she repeated, broken.

"We will. Just not tonight."

Then, the cries ceased. The spectres stopped their charge. A thick, heavy silence returned.

"They're leaving?" murmured Taranatos.

"No…" I whispered, my voice dark with foreboding.

A terrible laugh rang out, sharp and female. Then another. And a third. The air filled with the beating of wings.

Through the flickering torchlight and the lightning-streaked gloom, they appeared—winged women, terrible and beautiful, their hair a nest of living serpents, their eyes glowing with blood-red fire.

"The Erinyes… cursed witches," Amage hissed, her voice raw with dread. "We have to flee!"

One of them laughed louder, sweeping her great black wings.

"Flee?" said Alecto. "You want to flee, little fools?"

"We don't flee," added Tisiphone, her voice like broken glass.

"Not from this place," finished Megaera.

Alecto exhaled—and several of our torches died in an instant, plunging our circle into dangerous shadow. We huddled closer, the darkness pressing in like a tide.

"Smérix," whimpered Paritos, eyes wide. "Do something…"

Their sisters followed suit, extinguishing the flames one

by one. Panic seized us. Our weapons were useless against these creatures. Arrows loosed at the Erinyes were swatted away like bothersome flies. Soon, only a few torches remained. Escape was impossible.

Another flame died—and with it, a warrior, snatched screaming into the dark. Then another, and another still.

"Druid—now! Use your magic, or gods help us—anything!" Alexix cried, his voice a strangled thread of despair.

"I'm no magician!" I shouted back, fury and fear battling in my throat.

"Then we're dead," said Lugotorix grimly.

The spectres and the Erinyes closed in, their shadows falling heavy on the scorched earth.

"Smérix!" bellowed Taranatos.

Garedix lashed out with his spear, desperate. I ransacked my thoughts—my bag—my very soul, seeking a thread of salvation. And then, a flicker of memory: Divinix.

"He gave me something…" I muttered, tearing open my satchel with trembling hands.

There it was—a small pouch, and within it, a crystal-like stone, pale as frost. Clutching it, I breathed deep and summoned every ounce of hope I had left.

You will know when the moment has come, Divinix had said.

"Smérix!" Taranatos again, closer this time, his voice taut with panic.

If this was not the moment, there would be no other.

I raised the stone high above me, then hurled it skyward with all my strength. Closing my eyes, I whispered his name, barely a breath:

"Divinix…"

The stone climbed, slow and sure, then reached its apex—and exploded in a brilliant, blinding flash. A shockwave radiated outward, slamming us to the ground and ripping through the spectres like a divine scythe. The Erinyes were hurled back, shrieking in agony as the holy light scorched them.

Chaos. Screams. Then—silence.

The spectres were gone. All that remained were the corpses, heaped and broken upon the field. We staggered to our feet, dazed and bloodied, some lying atop half-rotted dead. The stench was unbearable.

Paritos, his hand sunk deep in a decomposing chest, vomited violently. Lugotorix, pale and shivering, helped him up, his face twisted in horror.

Above us, a sphere of pure light now hovered, illuminating the field with a cold, celestial brilliance. For a moment, our disgust gave way to wonder.

And then—triumph.

Cries of joy rose, weapons brandished high… but that moment did not last.

One of the Erinyes—Alecto—pointed a clawed finger at the glowing sphere and laughed.

"Fool," she spat. "Do you think your little light can stop us?"

"Megaera! Tisiphone! Let us show them."

With slow, sinister grace, the three sisters rose into the air. Their vast black wings cast monstrous shadows over us, and their wicked smiles chilled the marrow.

"Children," Alecto hissed, "wake up…"

"Rise," commanded Tisiphone.

"Let the slaughter begin," crooned Megaera.

Then they screamed—a sound that shattered the world. The ground trembled, the sky twisted, and all around us... the dead began to stir.

One by one, bodies twitched. Corpses rose—skeletons in rusted armor, warriors with rotting flesh and hollow gazes. A macabre host lumbered toward us, drawn by the voice of their foul mistresses.

The smell of death surged—wet rot, burnt hair, blood long dried into rust. The rattle of bone and the clang of armor echoed across the field.

"There's too many, Smérix! We're finished!" Alexix shouted, fear etched deep in his face.

"I have nothing left," I growled. "Then give me a damned sword. I won't die like cattle."

Alexix tossed me a dagger—a pitiful weapon—and I caught it with a snarl.

"You mock me?" I spat.

Garedix, wordless, offered his sword. It felt right in my hand. Heavy. Final.

"Thank you, brother."

Armed now, blade and dagger in hand, I faced the coming tide. The dead rose even beneath our feet—we struck them down as they reached up for us.

"Druid! We can't hold them!" cried Paritos, his voice cracking.

"Athanor will come. He must. This cannot end here, Paritos. It cannot!"

But the dead were too many. We were fifteen—no more—surrounded by hundreds, perhaps thousands. Their empty sockets stared, jaws agape, as if laughing at our folly.

"If I must die here," growled Taranatos, "then I'll do it taking heads. By Taranis!"

And then he charged, sword high.

We all did. Even I—Smérix—cried out a war-shout that clawed up from my soul like fire.

The battle was a storm of horror and iron. The stench of rot and blood was thick as fog. Blades flashed like lightning in the gloom. Garedix spun his spear in deadly arcs, splitting skulls and spines. Our weapons sang, and the dead fell.

But not fast enough.

Their numbers swallowed ours like the sea over rocks. Men screamed, fell, were drowned beneath the tide. Each cut seemed pointless. For every corpse we felled, two more rose.

The dark mass at the heart of it all pulsed and throbbed, swelling with power. Bolts of black lightning crackled across the field. The ground grew slick with blood, our boots slipping, weapons wet and red.

And above it all, the Erinyes circled, shrieking with cruel joy.

We were dying.

And still—no sign of Athanor.

Garedix, consumed by rage, had strayed too far. A swarm of skeletal warriors and rotting corpses closed in around him like wolves on a stag. Taranatos saw it—too late.

"Garedix!" he cried, desperate.

But the warning came a heartbeat too late. A spear pierced Garedix's side, and the great warrior collapsed, his blood darkening the already crimson earth. Taranatos leapt toward him, striking wildly to shield his fallen brother-in-arms—but he too was overwhelmed. Blows rained down like a tempest, steel cracking against bone and flesh.

"Garedix, no!" Alexix roared, grief and rage tearing from his throat.

He fought with fury, carving a path toward his brother, but a brutal blow knocked him off his feet. The world spun. Through blurred vision, he watched helplessly as Garedix was torn apart by skeletal claws.

Taranatos gasped for air, his sword strokes growing desperate. The dead pressed in, orbits of hollow bone fixed on him like predators savoring their kill.

And we fared no better.

Paritos and Lugotorix fought like devils, their blades shining with blood and fire. But for every one we felled, ten rose in their place. It was like drowning in a tide of death.

Paritos, gasping, plunged his blade into a skull—only to be tackled by another corpse and thrown to the ground. Lugotorix, his body soaked in sweat and blood, shielded him with relentless strikes, muscles taut, eyes wild.

Despite the slaughter, I could not help but admire the warrior Lugotorix had become. A leader in the making, he had proven me wrong—again and again.

At the heart of the fray, I fought with a frenzy born of fear and fire. My blows rang out like smith's hammers against the bones of the dead. For once, my bulk—so often a subject of jest for a druid—served me well. I struck with force I did not know I had… but even that was not enough. We were drowning in numbers.

High above, the Erinyes floated, cruel and mocking. Their shrieks cut through the clamor of steel and screams like razors, stirring terror in the hearts of the bravest.

And then—a thunderous rumble shook the ground.

From the crest of the hill, Cimmerian cavalry came crashing down like a storm. Torches flared, blades gleamed, and Lygdamis rode at their head, his war cry splitting the night.

Among them—Scythians. I blinked. Allies? But there was no time to question it.

The dead turned to face the new assault, and for a precious moment—we breathed. We struck back, renewed by the promise of survival.

Lugotorix, Paritos, and I fought shoulder to shoulder, our strikes a rhythm of desperation and wrath. The stench of death hung heavy, but we held.

Then—more salvation.

From every hilltop, Amazons emerged, raining flaming arrows upon the battlefield. And there she stood, Amage's mother, her hair whipping in the wind like a war-banner.

Hope surged.

The Erinyes shrieked in fury, driven back by fire and steel. Screaming, they were forced toward the black stormcloud that now raged and spat lightning in fits of madness.

And then—he came.

Athanor.

Silhouetted against the storm, he stood atop the hill, holding aloft a glimmering blue sword. It shimmered like moonlight on sacred water.

Beside him, a colossus—Stéropès, the cyclopean smith. Somehow, Athanor had convinced him to join our cause.

With a roar, they charged.

The giant's warcry was thunder incarnate. His massive hammer smashed through the undead like clay, scattering bones and gore. He strode among them like a god of ruin, his blows shaking the earth.

He reached us and threw down a great sack—a gift of arms. Out spilled blades, glinting blue like Athanor's, forged from the same enchanted fire. We seized them with no hesitation.

Revived by the weapons, by their light, by hope itself, we charged once more. The dead faltered before us. Slow and stiff, they could not withstand the fury we unleashed.

The Amazons, precise and pitiless, focused their fire on the Erinyes, whose shrieks turned from laughter to rage, then to fear. They were being driven back, toward the Gate of the Underworld—the pulsing, seething heart of all this darkness.

Lightning flashed. Arrows fell like rain. The sky itself seemed to burn with our defiance.

The three sisters—Alecto, Tisiphone, Megaera—retreated, howling in fury, wings black against the firelight.

The tide was turning.

And perhaps… perhaps the gods still watched.

Garedix, swept up by his fury, strayed too far. In moments, he was surrounded by a horde of skeletal warriors and rotting corpses. Taranatos saw it—and immediately charged to his aid.

"Garedix!" he shouted, desperate.

But he was too late. A spear pierced Garedix, who collapsed, his blood spilling in a dark torrent, soaking the earth already drenched in crimson. Taranatos leapt to shield him, but he too was overwhelmed by the sheer number of foes. Blows rained down around him, each impact echoing through his bones.

"Garedix, no!" Alexix cried out in rage, witnessing the

scene.

He struck wildly, furiously, trying to reach his brother. But a crushing blow threw him to the ground. His vision blurred as he watched Garedix being slaughtered, the blurred images of the skeletal blows searing into his eyes.

Taranatos was overwhelmed. His breath came in ragged gasps, each swing of his blade more desperate than the last. The skeletons and withered warriors circled in on him, their empty sockets fixed mercilessly on their prey.

And we fared no better.

Lugotorix and Paritos fought like madmen, possessed by the need to survive. Their weapons flashed beneath the blinding light of the storm, but for every monster brought down, ten more surged forth—like endless waves. The screams of the dead echoed across the field.

Paritos, panting, drove his sword into a skeleton's skull, only to be struck and thrown to the blood-slicked ground. Lugotorix, covered in sweat and gore, stepped in to shield him, striking without pause, every muscle taut with effort. Yet each motion grew slower, each strike more labored.

And amidst the horror, I could not help but see the warrior he had become. Should he survive this wretched night, there is no doubt he would rise as a great chieftain. Strange to think I once doubted him…

At the center of the melee, I fought with everything I had, beating back the dead with a fury I didn't know I possessed. My blows rang out like smith's hammers upon the forge. At last, this bulk of mine—so often mocked for a druid's frame—served me well. But even my strength waned under the endless tide of enemies.

Above us, the Erinyes hovered, smiling cruelly. Their

piercing laughter cut through the clash of weapons and the screams of men, a note of madness in the orchestra of our despair.

Then—a low rumble, deep and ominous, rolled through the ground beneath our feet.

Cimmerian riders surged over the ridge, torches raised, weapons gleaming, storming down the slope like an avalanche of fury. At their head, Lygdamis, his war cry thundering alongside the pounding hooves. The storm had brought salvation.

To my astonishment, there were Scythians among them. I blinked, surprised—but this was no time for questions. Lygdamis surely had his reasons.

The skeletons and revenants turned to meet this new force, giving us a fleeting moment of respite. Without hesitation, we threw ourselves back into the fray, hacking through bone and rotted flesh.

Lugotorix, Paritos, and I fought side by side, our blows striking in rhythm like a deadly dance. Blood and sweat flowed freely, but we stood firm, driven by desperation and sheer will to live.

Then—another miracle.

From every ridge surrounding the battlefield, hundreds of Amazons appeared, loosing volley after volley of flaming arrows upon the dead and the Erinyes. Among them was Amage's mother, her hair whipping in the wind like a war banner.

The battle still raged, but for the first time, a flicker of hope burned in the darkness.

The Erinyes screeched in fury, driven back by fire and steel. Their howls mingled with the roar of weapons as they retreated, unwillingly, toward the writhing black cloud.

Lightning struck the earth before them, as if the Underworld itself roared in anger.

And then—at last—Athanor appeared.

He stood atop a hill, holding high a magnificent sword, shimmering with a bluish light that cut through the gloom. At his side towered a colossus—Stéropès, the cyclopean smith. I do not know how Athanor persuaded him to come… but here he was.

Together, they charged.

The forge-giant bellowed and plunged into the melee, his massive war maul swinging wide. Each blow thundered like a tempest, scattering enemies like dry leaves, smashing bone and rotted sinew with terrifying ease. Blood splashed across his face with every strike.

He reached us, hurled a large sack from his back, then turned and dove once more into the fight.

The sack burst open with the clatter of steel—weapons, dozens of them, glimmering like Athanor's own blade. A gift of salvation. Without hesitation, we seized them, their bluish glow lighting our eyes with new fire.

Rearmed and rekindled, we charged again.

The dead, once so unstoppable, now faltered. They were many—but slow. And we were swift, and furious, and filled with the fire of the living.

The Amazons pressed their assault, loosing precise volleys at the Erinyes. The air was thick with flame and fury. The demon-sisters shrieked and reeled under the hail of fire. Slowly, steadily, they were forced back—toward the Gate of the Underworld, where black lightning struck the ground with violent force.

Projectiles rained around them, relentless.

And they had no choice.

They retreated.

A short distance away, Amage fought with unrelenting fury—when suddenly she came face to face with an Amazon: Myrina, her friend, disfigured, her gaze vacant and drenched in shadow. Myrina charged blindly, her face an impassive mask of death. Amage parried the blows, their weapons clashing in the heavy, storm-choked air, and with a desperate motion, she slipped behind her friend and pinned her to the ground.

"Myrina! Myrina!" she cried, pleading to bring her back to herself.

But Myrina was no longer there. She was only a hollow shade—lost, entranced in a deathlike trance.

Meanwhile, Lygdamis, striking like a war machine, reined in his mount. Amidst the roar of battle and the ferocious clash of his warriors, he raised his ebony-black steed, sword high above his head.

"Now!" he bellowed, his voice booming over the din of combat.

It was the signal.

He had split his army in two. The second force, lying in wait, had been poised for this very moment—to charge and deliver the final blow. And so they did, without hesitation.

Once more the earth trembled. War cries rang out. A hundred riders thundered down a nearby hill in an unstoppable avalanche of hooves and steel. Their mounts, armored with bladed barding, plowed through the ranks of the dead. Skulls flew. Limbs were severed. The charge was a relentless engine of destruction—compact, brutal, and merciless.

At that moment, under a storm of Amazonian arrows,

the Erinyes were finally forced to retreat. Caught between the fury of the archers and the surging riders, they vanished into the black cloud, their screams of rage and defeat echoing into the night. With their departure, their power unraveled.

And so it happened—their army, already shattered, collapsed all at once.

The thundering fall of thousands of undead bodies crashing to the ground was nearly deafening.

Myrina crumpled into Amage's arms, her final breath gone, whatever life had lingered now extinguished. Amage wept in silence, her face streaked with tears, sweat, and blood, cradling her fallen friend to her chest.

The dead crumbled around us, their vacant eyes returning to the nothingness from whence they'd come. And just like that, the battle ceased. The silence that followed was eerie, oppressive.

Above, Divinix's light still shone—suspended in the heavens like a beacon of hope, piercing the veil of darkness. We stood there, stunned, broken. Our bodies battered, our minds haunted by the horrors we had endured.

Lugotorix and Paritos, bloodied and dust-covered, leaned back-to-back and collapsed to the ground, panting. I remained upright, though dazed, my heart pounding, my eyes scanning the battlefield with a wary dread, muscles clenched, ready to strike at the next threat.

Athanor and Stéropès stood side by side, their weapons still dripping with blood. The giant blacksmith, breathing hard, cast his gaze across the field with a mixture of triumph and sorrow. He knew the battle was won—but at what cost?

Lygdamis, at the head of the Cimmerian cavalry, turned to us with a weary smile of victory. His men, and the Scythians among them, were exhausted, yet a deep satisfaction lit their faces—they had overcome.

The battlefield lay strewn with corpses, both ours and theirs. The undead, now freed from their unholy bonds, returned to rest. Those warriors—slain long ago in other battles—could finally know peace. The air still reeked of death, smoke, and blood… yet for the first time in what felt like ages, there was calm. Even the black mass, still pulsing and spitting bolts of lightning, seemed to rage in frustration.

We knew this was but one battle—many more would come. But here and now, we could taste the bitterness of triumph.

Divinix's light continued to blaze overhead, a radiant reminder that even in the deepest dark, hope endures. The gods were watching. The spirits whispered. Life—woven from shadow and light—marched ever on.

Lygdamis, Athanor, and the great smith came to meet us.

"Athanor… praise the gods—you made it," I said, the relief in my voice heavy.

He raised his sword before me. It was a thing of beauty, and its bluish gleam seemed to challenge the very shadows.

"These blades were made to kill what walks in the Underworld," he said, eyes burning with hatred and resolve. "This one… is for the murderer of Anna."

I turned my gaze toward the giant, Stéropès, his massive frame illuminated by the wavering torchlight.

"Thank you, Stéropès," I said, inclining my head with true reverence.

The colossus gave a silent nod.

Then my eyes found Lygdamis, and I was still taken aback by his presence.

"Lygdamis! I never thought I'd see you again," I said, emotion welling in my chest.

He grinned, that grin of his—etched with a thousand battles.

"I told you—war is my thing. No way I was missing this one," he replied with a laugh.

"I didn't think I'd ever see you again either, Lygdamis," rumbled Stéropès, his voice like cracking granite.

The two men locked eyes. For a long moment, there was silence—then a grin crept across the Cimmerian king's face again.

"You know me. I always bring surprises."

Stéropès grunted and turned away, clearly displeased. He walked off in silence.

Still too many secrets, I thought. But some truths, perhaps, are not meant for my ears…

I stared at him for a moment as he walked away, my thoughts drifting back to the battlefield, when I noticed the surviving Scythians in the distance. There were about a hundred of them, scattered a little further down the slope. Some were gathering the bodies of their fallen comrades, while others were watching us with strange intensity—though it was clear they weren't looking at us, but at Lygdamis.

"How is it that Scythians followed you into this battle? Aren't they your enemies?"

"Oh, those ones! I almost forgot about them," he replied with a mischievous grin.

He turned his horse and beckoned to one of them.

Clearly impatient and visibly angry, a warrior rode up swiftly. Judging by his armor, he was likely their leader.

"I keep my word, Pergatos!" Lygdamis said, smug and sharp. "Here, take the head of Skoithos."

He leaned down and grabbed a severed head tied to his saddle.

"Now you can return the full body to his father."

He fixed Pergatos with a cold stare, locking eyes.

"Be sure to tell him this—from Lygdamis, King of Cimmeria: I'm coming for him, and he'll meet the same end. By my hand."

Then, with a contemptuous flick, he tossed the head to the ground. The Scythian's fury was barely restrained. Without a word, he dismounted, retrieved the head, and galloped back toward his men.

We watched as the Scythians retreated, until Pergatos paused atop a ridge.

"We will meet again, Lygdamis! And I'll be the one to take your head! You have my word!" he shouted before vanishing into the night.

None of us had noticed the grim trophy Lygdamis had been carrying in the chaos of battle. But now, everything made sense. Like us, the people of the steppe held deep reverence for their dead—and believed, as we did, that the soul resided in the head of a man. To lose it, to have it stolen, was the worst of sacrileges.

"No Scythian can ever seem to keep his head," Lygdamis quipped, laughing aloud.

"They're furious with you now," Athanor observed.

"Good. The angrier they are, the more mistakes they'll make."

As we spoke, I noticed Amage had been joined by her mother. The presence of the Amazons had been just as crucial as that of the Cimmerians, I thought.

"They came too," I murmured. "Didn't listen to their oh-so-wise priestess…"

I couldn't help but smile, remembering the beauty of that mysterious woman.

Lygdamis grinned back, the mischief lighting up his weathered face.

"Yeah… now I owe a heavy debt."

"An enormous one, I imagine," I replied, feigning a grave tone.

"You have no idea, my friend! But it was a pleasure to fight at your side. Now I must go. We'll recover our dead and return to our people. My debt to you is paid. Other adventures await me, my friend. Farewell."

"And I thank you for that. Farewell, my friend."

Lygdamis rode off to rejoin his warriors, who were already preparing to depart. As the Cimmerians disappeared beyond the horizon, I couldn't help but admire them—a people of honor, brave and selfless.

I know now that this man lived a life unlike any other. Very few mortals can boast such a fate… But that, dear listener, is another tale I shall tell you—should my humble scribe permit me. Now, let us return to our story…

Lygdamis gone, my gaze turned toward Taranatos, who was kneeling nearby. He cradled Garedix's head in his hands, tears streaking his face. Alexix, wounded and staggering, had just joined them.

"Forgive me, my friend… Forgive me," Taranatos whispered, broken. "I went for help. I didn't abandon you.

I swear, I never would have. I was just a kid… I did everything I could… but they were too many… too strong… and I didn't know how to fight…"

Garedix, terribly weak, gave him a faint, painful smile. A single tear rolled from his eye as he gripped Taranatos' hand.

Alexix, jaw clenched, knelt beside them.

"He knows," he murmured. "You were a boy… and my brother, just a reckless fool. I should have been there."

"They tortured him! Those bastards… they cut out his tongue!" Taranatos cried, burning with rage and sorrow.

Garedix's breathing slowed, became ragged. Then it stopped.

Without a twitch, without a sound, he simply let go, his spirit returning to the Land of the Ancestors. Peaceful. Ready.

Alexix, his voice shattered by grief, whispered:

"All these years… he never blamed you. I was wrong, Taranatos. You've proved yourself—since the very beginning of this damned journey. I was blind. I should've seen why my brother never held a grudge. He knew… you weren't to blame."

"I'll kill them all," Taranatos swore, his voice trembling with rage. "I'll gut every last one. You have my word, Alexix."

Devastated, he remained there, on his knees, while Alexix gently lifted his brother's body and walked away. The weight of that loss pressed heavily on his shoulders, and his heart screamed within his chest. A pain too deep for sound, too vast for tears, swallowed him whole.

Taranatos could only watch as Alexix carried Garedix away from that cursed battlefield.

Alexix gave one final order, voice rough:

"Get up. Find the bodies of our brothers. They must not remain here."

I was crushed by that scene—and so was Athanor. We exchanged a long look, heavy with sorrow. No words were needed.

Garedix had been dear to us all. Loyal. Selfless.

He would be missed. Long and deeply.

Athanor, grim and silent, walked off to join Alexix.

We had lost many that night.

Now it was time to bury our dead before we carried on.

Once more, funeral pyres would blaze through the night…

Stéropès, ever silent and resolute, had already taken the lead. A towering stack of wood balanced effortlessly on his shoulder, he walked alone toward the place where the bodies of our fallen companions were being gathered. Others soon followed his example, each carrying logs, preparing the ground for the sacred flames.

I looked down at my arms, bloodied and torn, my hands trembling with exhaustion.

I'll have many wounds to tend tonight, I told myself. And the same could be said for the others.

As I made my way toward Lugotorix and Paritos, we prepared to rejoin the rest of our group. Not far from there, Amage's mother helped her daughter to her feet. Around them, the other Amazons began to gather their fallen with solemn grace—every movement slow, deliberate, full of reverence and grief.

Amage's eyes were filled with tears as she stared at the lifeless body of Myrina, her pain etched into every line of her face. Her mother, proud and strong, stood by her in silence—a pillar of unwavering support. At her signal, several Amazons stepped forward and carried Myrina's body away. And just like that, the warrior women slipped back into the shadows, their departure marked by a sacred stillness.

And I, Smérix, shaman and witness to this nightmare of a night, watched our allies of fate disappear into the darkness, carrying with them fragments of this brutal clash.

Strange are the weavings of fate, I mused.

Indeed, the encounters that shape our lives are never random. Each has a purpose, each a hidden thread in the great tapestry of existence. Perhaps She—who is everything and in everything—is merely playing with the strands of destiny, braiding them into paths unknown. What remains to be seen… is where She will lead us next.

Amage, the magnificent Amazon… Yet another tale worth telling—one day. As great and wild as that of Lygdamis. My poor scribe will have much work ahead of him…

Lost in these thoughts, I reached my companions alongside Paritos and Lugotorix. The battlefield, strewn with corpses and memories, was quiet beneath the shimmering light of Divinix. That celestial flame still hovered above us, casting its pale glow over the bloodied earth—a symbol of hope and rebirth in the face of ruin.

Athanor and Stéropès were already preparing the next step. Athanor, with that sharp, ever-searching gaze, seemed to see far beyond the horizon, already weighing the trials ahead. The giant blacksmith, his back broad and sturdy, murmured silent prayers for the fallen. His massive hands, now so gentle, moved with unexpected tenderness as he set the wood in place.

Our companions, worn but alive, began to gather around the campfires. Paritos and Lugotorix, though battered, walked among them with renewed purpose, checking on the survivors. Their eyes, once clouded by fear, now held only defiance.

The brotherhood that bound us—Celts, Amazons, Cimmerians—was stronger than ever. Each face reflected the same resolve: we would carry on, not in spite of the dead, but because of them.

Alexix, having returned after laying his brother to rest, took a deep breath and addressed us all:

"Brothers. We survived this night… but the war is not over. Tomorrow, we avenge our friends. We avenge our kin!"

His words rang out with gravity and fire. They reminded us why we fought, and why we had to go on.

We knew worse awaited us.

But the light of Divinix, ever-burning above us, was a silent promise: the gods were watching, and so long as we stood together, we would endure.

I stepped forward and spoke, my voice ragged from battle and grief:

"Let us be brave. The light of Divinix shall guide us. But it is our unity that will give us strength. Together, we can face the dark. We've done it before—we'll do it again."

Their eyes turned to me. And in every one, a spark.

We were ready.

To face the unknown.

To fight the monsters of the gods.

To keep marching on.

This night would be forever burned into our memories—a night of courage, of sacrifice, and of unbreakable bonds. And though the road ahead would be darker still… we would walk it.

Together.

# CHAPTER 41
*"At the Threshold of the Unknown"*

Dawn was rising behind the distant mountains, painting the sky in hues of rose and gold. The battlefield, still scarred by the night's horrors, lay in an oppressive silence, as if nature itself held its breath after the carnage. Smoldering corpses littered the earth, silent witnesses to the violence now past, and the metallic scent of blood and burnt flesh still lingered, mingled with the acrid sting of smoke.

Not far from there, the funeral pyres of the night before were dying down, sending thin trails of smoke into the crisp morning air. Alexix and Taranatos, their faces dark with grief and resolve, stared wordlessly at the solemn scene, their eyes reflecting both sorrow and unbreakable will. The crackle of dying embers and the occasional snap of charred branches broke the heavy stillness.

A little further off, we were drawing near to the menacing black mass that loomed in the sky. The light of Divinix—lower now than during the battle—hovered above our heads like a silent guardian. Its gentle glow seemed to whisper promises of protection and hope, warming our hearts despite the heavy atmosphere of loss.

"We'll destroy them," Alexix said through clenched teeth, his voice carrying the weight of buried fury.

Taranatos gave a silent nod, and the two of them made their way toward us. At my side stood Athanor, Paritos, Lugotorix, Stéropès, and the other surviving warriors—grave-faced, jaws tight, all watching the opaque black mass before us. The ground beneath our feet was damp and sticky—a grim mixture of blood and mud.

There were no longer any lightning flashes or thunder, but the cloud still pulsed, disturbed now by the presence of Divinix's sphere of light. A tension hung in the air, thick and suffocating, as fear mingled with wrath upon our faces. Athanor drew his new sword, its bluish blade glinting with an almost otherworldly light. He turned toward us, his gaze hard, his jaw set.

Alexix and Taranatos joined us, drawing their own weapons—those gifted blades forged by Stéropès. They gleamed with purpose, forged with vengeance in mind. The reassuring weight of steel in our hands, the cold texture of the metal against our skin—these things anchored us to our resolve.

"Let's go find the Thunder Eagle. Let's find Anna. Let's avenge our brothers," declared Athanor, his voice echoing with our own burning rage.

A single cry rose from our ranks, fierce and defiant:

"TARANIS!"

That name, shouted with such intensity, seemed to resonate in the very air, infusing our souls with a new, electric energy. The cry echoed off the mountainsides, a symphony of fury and defiance.

Determined, Athanor stepped forward into the shadow of the black cloud, and we followed him, that same fire blazing in our chests. The sphere of Divinix moved with us, unsettling the dark mass, which writhed and shrank from its touch, as though repelled by its sacred light. The air grew colder, denser, as though the darkness itself sought to swallow us whole.

With each step, we sank deeper into the gloom, swallowed by the opaque blackness. The sky above vanished completely, leaving only the guiding glow of the divine stone to light our path. No sound but the wet suction of our boots in the mud accompanied us as we moved among the dead.

Before us yawned an enormous pit, descending deep into the bowels of the Earth—a colossal funnel, wide at first, then narrowing into a jagged tunnel carved into stone, like the gaping maw of some ravenous beast waiting to devour us. A stench of mold and damp earth assaulted our senses, anchoring us further in the notion that we were crossing into another world entirely.

The light of Divinix entered the tunnel before us, clearing the path. We followed, descending cautiously down the steep slope. Step by step, we moved further into the deep, our hearts pounding in rhythm with our purpose. The rock walls closed in tighter, the passage becoming more narrow with each meter, but still we pressed on, driven by a blend of determination and desperation. Our breath echoed against the stone, amplifying the suffocating weight of our descent.

We were standing at the very threshold between two realms—the comforting light of the surface world and the suffocating darkness of Hades. The air grew wetter, thicker, harder to breathe. Our clothes clung to our bodies, damp with sweat and condensation.

Each step brought us closer to our fate, to the end of our journey. We had come a long way, survived countless dangers, but it would be here, in the shadowed tunnels of the underworld, that everything would be decided.

The answers we sought, the truths we'd chased—they all lay at the end of this path. Every drop of sweat, every scar, every life lost had led us to this moment. At the end of these tunnels lay the resolution of our tale—the purpose of our struggle.

The darkness was almost tangible now, like a living force pressing in on all sides. But the light of Divinix was with us—our beacon, our hope.

I felt the weight of it all pressing on my shoulders. This crossing from light into dark was more than just a physical one. It was symbolic. The passage from innocence to knowledge, from life to death, from despair to hope. I knew this moment was pivotal—not just for our mission, but for each of our souls.

The underworld of Hades, with its secrets and horrors, would soon unveil itself. And we had to be ready to face it.

All of it.

# CHAPTER 42
*"The Gates of the Underworld"*

Deep within the tunnels of the Underworld, beneath the flickering light of the magical stone, we moved forward in silence. The rough rock walls closed in around us, forging an oppressive and unsettling atmosphere. The stone sweated with glacial dampness, each droplet falling like the beat of a lugubrious heart.

The stone's glow cast shifting shadows, breathing a strange, flickering life into this mineral labyrinth. Every sound was amplified by the stone, creating endless echoes. Our fingers, when brushing against the walls, felt their jagged, almost cutting texture.

The stench of sulfur and mold clung to us—soaking into our clothes, invading our lungs, making each breath a labor. Our footsteps echoed in the absolute stillness, reinforcing the feeling of desperate isolation.

"I hate this place," muttered Taranatos, covering his

face with a strip of cloth in a futile attempt to filter the poisonous air. "Feels like Hell itself is trying to choke us."

"We're getting close, Taranatos," Athanor replied, his voice steady and assured. "They're near. I can feel it."

From time to time, Stéropès had to stoop low to avoid smashing his head on the uneven ceiling. In some chambers, great cauldrons filled with burning pitch lit our path with a grim glow. The warmth of these flames clashed against the ambient chill, creating gusts of warm and cold air that sent shivers down our spines. The acrid smoke of burning oil mixed with the sulfur, stinging our nostrils.

We passed through massive caverns where towering stalactites and stalagmites formed forests of stone. The metallic taste of fear lingered on our lips—a bitter reminder of the peril we faced.

Suddenly, a deep rumble broke the silence, like a tremor rolling through the earth. Chunks of stone fell from the ceiling, forcing us to halt.

"What was that?" Paritos asked, his eyes wide with alarm.

"Probably just another trick of this damned place, trying to scare us off," grunted Stéropès, tightening his grip on his weapon.

We struggled onward through a narrow passage. The crushing silence was broken again, this time by Taranatos' voice, tense with frustration.

"Will this ever end? We've been walking for hours. At this rate, we'll starve or die of thirst before we ever swing our blades."

No one answered. But every one of us felt the same gnawing doubts. Still, we pressed on, descending deeper and deeper into that endless dark.

Eventually—though I cannot say how long it took—our path led us to a vast cavern, stretching beyond sight like a starless night sky above us.

At the center of what appeared to be our final destination, the orb of light flickered, then slowly dimmed... until it fell silent into my hand. We now stood on a narrow shore, at the edge of a mist-choked, wretched marsh.

Boulders jutted from stagnant waters, and dead trees loomed here and there. The water bubbled as if disturbed from below, adding to the unease that hung thick in the air. The sickening stench of decay wafted up from the bog, turning our stomachs.

"It reeks. Not this again..." groaned Taranatos, eyeing the expanse of water warily.

"No, Taranatos. And no, I don't have a potion for foul smells," I replied with a dry smile.

On the far bank, a massive fortress loomed, lit by torches and burning cauldrons. A colossal gate, made of two immense doors, marked the entrance. Below, a line of people shuffled forward in silence, watched over by warriors dressed in black. The sound of their footsteps on the slick stone echoed eerily, adding a new weight to the already stifling air.

Suddenly, a deep horn blew across the marsh, announcing the approach of a boat emerging from the mist. The ferryman's vessel. A tall, thin figure, robed in grey and hidden beneath a deep hood, guided the craft with eerie grace.

His bony hands, with long blackened nails, clutched a dark pole, steering the vessel with unearthly precision. At the front and rear, two lanterns cast a dim glow across the bog, their light trembling, painting twisted reflections on the foul waters.

The gate began to open, slowly, with a groan like a mountain yawning. The long, grim vessel drew up to the far shore, and strange glimmers stirred within it—too solid to be ghosts.

As it neared, we saw them for what they were: men and women, not specters, their faces marked with suffering and resignation.

"The ferryman," murmured Stéropès. "He carries the dead across the Styx."

"They're going to Hell?" I asked, unsettled.

"Some, yes. Others, no. Beyond that gate lie two paths: one to the Underworld, the other to the Elysian Fields. They'll be judged—and sent where their past deeds have earned them."

"Well then," said Taranatos grimly, "I'd rather go to the Land of the Ancestors. These damned Greek underworlds don't sit right with me… It's cold, it stinks, it's black as pitch—and even the place for the good souls doesn't sound any better… What sort of gods lock away the dead like prisoners? Not for me…"

"Yeah," quipped Alexix. "And we all know where you'd end up."

As the procession of the dead and their black-clad escorts drew closer, the massive gate finally creaked open—revealing a colossal beast: the famed Cerberus, hound of the Underworld. Towering, monstrous, its three heads loomed like nightmares wrought in obsidian. Its red eyes glowed like coals pulled from a divine forge. Each maw, lined with venom-dripping fangs, snarled with infernal rage. Its pitch-black fur seemed to devour the very light around it. And its tail—no mere appendage, but a forked blade—lashed the air with lethal intent.

Stéropès growled between clenched teeth.

"That thing… guards the gates of Hell."

"By the gods… It's massive," Alexix gasped in disbelief. "That's Cerberus?"

Stéropès nodded grimly, black fire burning in his gaze. Even for a giant such as he, this beast was a terrifying foe.

Cerberus's throaty growls thundered through our bones, forcing the last of the dead to press forward beneath its shadow. Its howls echoed through our very souls—a chilling reminder of our own mortality.

"How do you kill something like that?" Paritos whispered, terrified.

"I'll handle it," said Stéropès, his voice low, resolute. "The rest of you—deal with the Black Guards."

Without waiting, he stepped into the foul waters, which quickly rose to his waist. We followed, more reluctant, but no less determined. The swamp water, viscous and ice-cold, clung to our skin like coagulated blood.

Amid the hellish gloom of the marsh, we moved with caution. Ahead, the last of the dead vanished into the yawning gates, herded by the silent, faceless Black Guards—those stoic sentinels of the Underworld, cloaked in deep hoods and clad in black iron, their obsidian swords catching the firelight like whispers of death. Each step they took seemed calculated to inspire dread.

Cerberus, majestic and monstrous, was the last to enter. Its three heads turned, scanning the murky shore before slipping into the shadows. The gates groaned shut behind it with a finality that sounded like a funeral toll.

"So… how do we open that?" Taranatos muttered. "Do we just knock?"

"Exactly," said Stéropès with a crooked grin. "Knock. Knock. Knock."

When we reached the shore, even we were struck silent by the sheer size of the door. Alexix looked up and whispered:

"They must've chopped down an entire forest for this thing…"

"Hide along the walls," Stéropès ordered. Then, with that same glint of mischief, he added, "Taranatos, knock."

Taranatos blinked, looked at the gate, then back at Stéropès.

"I feel like a bloody worm wriggling on a hook… And with a monster like that behind the door, we're gonna need a much bigger worm…"

"Enough talk, Taranatos," I growled. "Do as you're told."

Grumbling, he stepped forward, muttering curses all the way.

"This is a joke!" he cried, standing before the towering gate. "Look at the size of this thing! I look like a ridiculous ant begging to be stepped on—"

"Knock on the damn door, by Taranis!" Athanor barked, his patience fraying.

Finally, Taranatos raised his fist and knocked. Three pitiful taps followed, nearly lost in the dead air. Trying to knock louder, he only managed to hurt his hand.

I couldn't lie—he did look like a miserable insect before that titanic gate.

Stéropès had had enough. With a grunt, he strode

forward.

"TOC. TOC. TOC."

Each word punctuated by a tremendous blow, echoing like thunder through the thick wood. Taranatos shuffled back, defeated.

"Toc-toc… toc…" he grumbled.

A tense silence fell. Then came the growls—deep, guttural. Snorting breaths followed. One of Cerberus's massive heads shoved through the gap, snarling violently. Slobber flew from its fangs as it barked with earthshaking rage. The stench of its breath hit us like a wave of rot and bile.

Then, the door crashed open. Cerberus lunged at Stéropès, who met the charge without flinching. With a mighty swing of his war maul, he struck the beast and knocked it sideways. They collided with thunderous force, grappling, biting, striking.

At the same moment, from either side of the great hound, two dozen Black Guards emerged.

No hesitation. We Celts surged forward, blades raised, screaming like madmen.

"Athanor!" I shouted. "This isn't your fight. Go! Find the Thunder Bird!"

He hesitated—then nodded once and sprinted through the gate, vanishing from view.

The rest of us held our ground, hacking into the black-armored foes with fury sharpened by grief and vengeance. Stéropès and Cerberus rolled into the water, thrashing like gods of war. He seized one head by the throat while smashing the others with hammer-blows. One skull cracked beneath the weight of his rage.

Cerberus, wounded, leapt away, panting, blood dripping from its mouths. Both combatants stood opposite, bloodied, wild-eyed, unyielding.

Meanwhile, we cut down the last of the first wave of guards.

"Come on, then!" shouted Taranatos, his eyes blazing. "Who else wants a taste of my blade?!"

But even as he roared, another wave of black-cloaked warriors appeared—twice as many, perhaps more hidden in the shadows.

The brief flame of victory flickered.

Our companions, thinking it was over, had lowered their swords in relief—only to be met by a tidal wave of new death.

"Do not falter!" bellowed Stéropès from across the battlefield, still locked in savage combat. "Fight! FIGHT!"

Had we been able to rise above that cursed scene, we would've seen it clearly: the hopelessness, the sheer imbalance. Another hundred enemies poured forth. More still came behind.

But we would not fall without a fight.

Not while breath still filled our lungs.

Not while steel remained in our hands.

Not while the memory of our dead burned in our hearts.

The clash of blades, the cries of the dying, and the stench of blood and terror filled the air once more.

And thus, beneath the gaze of the gods, we charged—into the jaws of Hell.

# CHAPTER 43
*"The Inevitable Confrontation"*

At the end of a long and stifling tunnel, Athanor stepped into a vast circular chamber—gloomy, oppressive, and shaped like a titanic arena: the arena of Hades. Torches flickered along the walls, casting deep shadows that seemed to watch in silence. The shifting flames danced across the stone, giving life to shapes that ought never to stir. The air was thick, laced with the acrid scent of soot and blood—a suffocating blend that gripped the lungs and stung the throat.

At the far end of the arena, he saw it—a massive cage. His heart leapt as he recognized the Thunder Bird. And beside it… a slumped figure. Anna. His lost love, the one he had thought never to see again in this life.

The great bird lay on its belly, wings spread, head bowed. Where once its plumage had blazed like living fire, now it lay dulled by exhaustion and suffering. The fierce light of its gaze was veiled by pain and weariness.

"Anna…" whispered Athanor, his voice a fragile thread of hope and joy.

The cage was bathed in a spectral glow that filtered from the abyssal ceiling above—a ghostly light that clung to Anna's drawn features, to the hollowness of her gaze. And looming higher still, set upon a balcony of obsidian, was the empty throne of Hades—an ever-present shadow, a monument to unyielding dominion.

At the center of the arena stood the Minotaur.

Still. Immense. One hand resting on the pommel of a gigantic blade—its dark metal veined with silver. He had assumed a human form, but the monstrousness of his being radiated from every fiber of his towering body. A smile twisted across his face, feral and mocking, revealing sharp, animal teeth. Beneath heavy brows, his eyes gleamed with malevolent purpose. Each ripple of his muscles bore the promise of destruction.

Around the arena, the Érinyes had gathered once more. Recovered from their earlier defeat, they loomed in the shadows, wings half-spread. Their eyes gleamed with cruel delight, and the whisper of their feathers filled the air like the rustle of death itself. Scarred and monstrous, they watched, their laughter rising like the jeers of ancient spirits.

Unseen for now, down a dim corridor lit only by distant flame, Hades strode forth with unhurried steps. His long hair, streaked with grey, flowed behind him like smoke, and the folds of his black cloak whispered against the stone. Harsh features carved from stone, his gaze held the cold severity of judgment. A shadow before the shadow.

Back in the arena, Athanor, motionless for a heartbeat

more, took a step forward. The ring of his boots echoed like a bell of fate upon the stone.

"Anna!" he called, his voice trembling with emotion, with defiance, with love.

She stirred.

Curled in despair only moments before, Anna lifted her head. Her eyes found him. And for one fleeting breath, her soul lit with joy.

But that joy faded fast.

He was alone.

And she knew—the Minotaur could not be beaten by strength alone. Not by one man. Not in this cursed place.

In her heart, even now that he stood before her, she knew she was dead. Truly dead. Nothing would change that. He could not save her. All that mattered now... was the Thunder Bird.

And even for that, hope had grown cold.

Yet, as if summoned by Athanor's voice, the great bird rose. Slowly, shakily. Its talons gripped the earth, its wings trembled, its eyes once more sparked with fading fire. A weak rustle of feathers, a dying echo of ancient storms.

Anna stood as well, hands clutching the bars of the cage. Her smile flickered and died.

"Athanor... Run! Don't give him what he wants! You can't save us!" she shouted, her voice torn between terror and love.

The Minotaur moved.

His steps fell like drums of doom. With each stride, the point of his massive sword scraped the stone, trailing sparks, howling as it dragged—a sound like iron wailing in grief.

"How touching…" he said. "Reunited at last. It took long enough to lure you here. You let her suffer. So long. So sweetly."

Athanor's fury lit his eyes like twin fires. He advanced.

"I had to work hard, you know," the Minotaur purred. "To make this moment happen. So many hints. So many screams. I thought her cries when I took her would be enough to stir you…"

He laughed. Cruel. Mocking. His laughter echoed like blades on stone, slicing the silence.

Athanor's jaw clenched. His hand tightened on the hilt of his sword. His muscles coiled like springs.

They circled.

The Minotaur still dragged his blade, drawing a ring of sparks between them.

A dance of death had begun.

"You're angry. Understandable," said the Minotaur, voice dripping with disdain. "But you will die. Even with that pretty sword."

"We'll see," Athanor spat, rage in his voice.

"Alecto! Tisiphone! Megæra!" the Minotaur bellowed, summoning his demonic allies.

"I'm already dead, Athanor! Dead!" Anna cried. "You must leave! You can't save the Thunder Bird!"

Her voice rang through the arena—a plea of despair and love. The Érinyes beat their wings and drifted toward the cage. Long spears in hand—forged from the same cursed metal as the Minotaur's blade.

Anna backed away, heart pounding, while the Thunder Bird shrieked in feeble protest.

"She is your weakness," sneered the Minotaur. "What drives you forward, what keeps you alive… is her. And she will destroy you."

Athanor roared and swung.

The Minotaur evaded, laughing. He tossed a glance at the Érinyes, then lunged toward them. Athanor slashed wildly, trying to reach them, to protect Anna. But the sisters laughed, their wings beating louder, their mockery slicing through the air.

"Fight me!" Athanor cried. "Let's end this!"

"You still don't understand," said the Minotaur. "Your path ends here. This is what the gods have ordained. Your death will free me from this monstrous form. That is the promise they gave me!"

And then he struck.

A great downward arc.

Athanor barely parried, knees buckling beneath the blow.

Sparks exploded where their blades met, streaking across the arena like shooting stars.

Again and again, the Minotaur struck, a storm of fury incarnate. Athanor staggered under each blow, teeth gritted, breath ragged—but he did not yield. He fought like a man possessed. A man with nothing to lose but everything to protect.

This was not a battle of warriors.

It was a reckoning of souls.

And it had only just begun.

# CHAPTER 44
## *"The Battle of the Giant"*

We were besieged on all sides, my companions and I, still fighting with a fierce determination before the Gates of the Underworld. But the fight, for us too, was unequal.

The clash of weapons and the war cries echoed through the oppressive night like a dark funeral orchestra. The air was thick with the metallic scent of blood and sweat, each breath steeped in despair. The ground trembled beneath the weight of the fallen, and the bitter taste of defeat clung to the air, as Paritos collapsed to the ground, struck by a violent blow to the shoulder.

For every Black Guard we felled, another emerged from the shadows to take his place—tireless, relentless. Death itself seemed to rise from the gloom. Every vanquished foe was but a drop in an ocean of darkness, and their ceaseless tide suggested infinity. Their eyes, glowing with malevolence, pierced the gloom, their sinister forms melting into the shadows.

Lugotorix, fighting with the fury of a demon, carved his way through enemy ranks with unmatched ferocity. His sword traced arcs of light through the dark, cleaving flesh and bone with deadly precision. Each strike was followed by a spurt of blood, and the cries of dying foes added a grim note to the cacophony of war. When he saw Paritos on the ground, surrounded, he let out a roar of rage and plowed toward him. With superhuman strength, he struck down the attackers, driving them back one by one.

Pushed back, we began to retreat toward the marshes. The situation was dire. Our feet sank into the wet earth—a tangible symbol of our despair—dragging us toward an inevitable end. The mud clung to our legs, slowing our every movement, while the shadows seemed to draw us deeper into their bottomless void. Each step grew heavier, each breath more labored.

Stéropès, despite his courage, was struggling. His arms and legs were torn by the monstrous fangs of Cerberus. The creature's jaws sank into his flesh with merciless cruelty, every bite a promise of death.

The beast, with its two remaining heads, snarled viciously, offering the giant no respite. He fought with all his strength, his body bloodied, his breath ragged. The smell of blood and sweat mingled with the stagnant air, turning the battlefield into a theatre of agony.

Terror was etched on our faces. We fought with desperate fury, but the enemy swarmed us relentlessly, overwhelming us by sheer numbers. Each face bore the mark of exhaustion and despair, eyes wide with fear, features frozen in resignation. Our battle cries had turned to lamentations, merging with the clash of steel and the beasts' growls. Every movement slowed, every strike grew weaker, as exhaustion and injury took their toll.

The swamp behind us offered a final escape—but to retreat was to abandon our divine quest. And that… was unthinkable. No, we had to fight to the bitter end. All the suffering, the sacrifices, the lives lost to bring us here—it could not end without answers. It must mean something. We believed in our cause, in the values of our quest. We had to press forward, finish this dark odyssey, and uncover the truths that would give meaning to it all. It must be so.

To retreat into those marshes would be to drown both our bodies and our spirits in a destiny void of hope… void of light.

Stéropès, still wielding his massive hammer, struck with supernatural strength, but even his titanic efforts seemed to falter before the fury of Cerberus. The ground quaked beneath each blow of his weapon, yet the beast, tireless, continued its merciless assault. Blood poured from the giant's wounds, each bite tearing a fresh cry of pain from his throat, his howls lost in the chaos of battle—a constant reminder of life's fragility before war's brutality.

"Do not falter!" roared Stéropès, his voice blazing with resolve. "Fight! Fight to your last breath!"

His words rang out like a final prayer, a call to resist the inevitable. Despite the pain, despite the fear, despite death itself pressing in around us, we gritted our teeth and fought on, refusing to yield. We knew defeat was nearly certain—but as long as we had strength left, as long as a single drop of blood ran through our veins, we would not stop. For beyond those gates of Hell, Athanor too was fighting, and our fates were bound to his.

Our sacrifice was not in vain. It was an offering to hope—a flickering flame in the darkness of our fate.

Lugotorix guarded the grievously wounded Paritos, fighting with the burning desperation of a man who would not lose another friend. His blows, precise and powerful, struck down the foes who tried to finish Paritos off. He cleared a path and dragged him to safety, heart pounding, breath ragged.

"Hold on, Paritos! We won't die here!" he cried, his voice fierce with conviction and rage.

The two friends, bound in battle, found the strength to go on despite the odds. The flickering torchlight illuminated their bloodied faces, etched with pain and unwavering resolve, as they fought for their lives and for ours.

Hell itself seemed to close in around us—but we refused to give in. Our spirits blazed like stars defying the void.

# CHAPTER 45
## *"The Final Trial"*

Athanor was at his limit. The Minotaur towered over him, every devastating strike of his blade seeming to slow time itself. The dull thud of impact echoed across the arena, mingling with the distant flicker of torches. The air was thick with the acrid scent of metal and sweat. Each breath became a torment, as Athanor fought off suffocation.

He staggered backward, trying to counterattack—but his opponent caught his wrist, blocking the blow, and struck him mercilessly with the hilt of his sword. The blows rained down like a storm, and Athanor buckled under the savage assault. His face and scalp were bleeding in streams. A particularly vicious strike hurled him several paces away, his body landing like a broken puppet.

"Athanor... No...!" cried Anna, her voice tearing through the arena like a blade.

Bruised and bloodied, he lifted his eyes toward Anna, then toward the Minotaur, trying to rise despite the agony. The sight of Anna behind the cage bars—desperate, pleading—rekindled a flicker of resolve in his gaze.

"Go, Athanor… I beg you… I don't want to lose you too," she pleaded, her voice shaking.

On all fours, panting, Athanor clenched his teeth in fury. The taste of blood flooded his mouth; pain pulsed through every limb. The Minotaur approached, ready to strike again—but in a final burst of strength, Athanor ducked, then drove his blade into the beast's chest. The Minotaur grunted, stunned, and stumbled back, hatred twisting his face. Blood spilled from the wound in his torso, his red eyes burning with fury. With a deafening roar, he swelled with rage.

As he bellowed like a savage beast, his form began to shift—slowly reverting to that monstrous horned bull. Froth dripped from his maw as his scream rang like thunder, shaking the stone walls of the arena.

"I've had enough fun… Let's end this!" he roared.

He lunged at Athanor, unleashing his fury. Pressed by the onslaught, Athanor could only try to parry the blows. The battle was desperate. The Minotaur's rage was unrelenting, his massive body a storm of horns and steel. Athanor faltered. He cast one glance toward Anna, still crying out in her cage, and another toward the Minotaur, snarling with bared fangs, his face mere inches away.

Then, in a final act of desperation, Athanor summoned what strength he had left. Fueled by raw adrenaline, he hurled the Minotaur away in a titanic shove. The beast was lifted from the ground, crashing hard onto its back.

Exhausted by the feat, Athanor froze. His mind blurred.

Time seemed to slow around him. Anna's voice—warped and distant—still called out to him, begging him to flee. Short of breath, his jaw clenched, he looked to his beloved… and to the Erinyes now stirring around her. A faint smile touched his lips. He had made his decision. He knew what had to be done…

Athanor ran. Every step felt eternal. Then, gathering his remaining strength, he leapt—an immense and magnificent arc through the air. With his sword angled downward, he descended upon his foe to deliver the final blow.

But just as the blade neared the Minotaur's throat… it stopped.

Silence.

Blood burst from Athanor's mouth. Eyes wide with shock, his face contorted in pain, he looked upon the Minotaur, whose mouth twisted in a smug, satisfied grin. The beast's own blade had pierced him to the hilt.

With a slow gesture, the Minotaur let Athanor's body slide to the side, withdrawing the weapon and rising to his feet. Athanor lay bleeding on the ground, convulsing, his vision fading. He saw Anna. The Thunder Bird. The Minotaur.

And then… voices echoed within him.

Smérix's words, from after the battle with the Scythians:

"Your souls are bound, Athanor. They are part of the great whole that surrounds us."

"You see the gods as cruel. You may think they toy with you. But know this—everything has purpose. Even the pain you feel serves a greater design. That is the will of the gods."

Those words, turning and turning in his mind, ignited one final ember. With great effort, he pushed against the earth, lifting himself to one knee.

He looked to Anna, weeping in anguish—and in his heart, he heard her voice:

"I am you. And you are me, my love…"

The Minotaur's mocking tone shattered the moment as he took back his human form.

"See? I told you. You die here. Your quest was meaningless. You understood nothing," he sneered. "You'll give me back my true form. So die, and let this end."

Then came Smérix's voice once more, deeper, clearer:

"All of this was meant to be, Athanor. I tell you again—there is an explanation. Even if you cannot yet see it. At the end of the path, you will find your answers."

Athanor reached for his sword. With a fierce cry, he plunged the blade into the ground and, leaning on it, pulled himself to his feet, swaying.

At that precise moment, a voice from deep within roared louder than all:

"Every move must have a reason, a purpose to fulfill!"

"Only then shall it be perfect!"

Taranatos's words.

"No… It is you who understand nothing," he gasped.

Drawing upon the last embers of his strength, Athanor hurled his sword toward the cage. Once again, time itself seemed to slow… The blade spun through the air, a whisper of steel slicing the silence. It passed just beside the Minotaur—who dodged, startled—and kept flying, as though guided by Athanor's very will. It cut through the air with a faint hiss, heading straight for its true mark.

The sword struck true—severing the bindings that

locked the cage holding Anna and the Thunder Bird. It clattered to the floor with a metallic chime. That blade—forged by nobility, by courage, and by the reborn hope of Stéropès—had now fulfilled its destined purpose.

The Minotaur stood frozen, disbelieving, as the Erinyes backed away in alarm. Then, as if the very cage had taken breath, its door flung open with a jolt.

Anna sprang forward, reaching Athanor just as his body gave way, collapsing to the ground. She dropped beside him, tears streaming down her cheeks.

"We're free, my love… We're free," Athanor murmured.

"Yes, my love. We're free," Anna whispered through her tears, smiling despite her grief.

The Minotaur was seething, pacing beneath the throne of Hades. He suddenly threw his arms up in twisted triumph.

"Free? Free? You're dead! You're mine—for eternity!" he bellowed.

He calmed, smiling with a wicked gleam, pointing to his own face.

"Oh, and thank you for this! Now I no longer have to transform into that abomination. You cannot imagine the agony I endured each time that beast returned…"

Then, high above, the great doors behind Hades' throne slammed open. The god himself appeared, stepping to the edge of the balcony to survey the scene below, his face unreadable. All around, his minions turned toward him, proud of their grim task fulfilled.

In the center of the arena, dying, Athanor reached out and gently caressed the face of Anna's spirit—tangible here, in this realm of suffering. His life slipped away slowly, as memories of their shared moments passed through them both like drifting petals.

"You are me… and I am you…" he whispered in his final breath.

He died without another word. Anna held him close, sobbing, her tears soaking the bloodstained earth. And in her mind's eye, a vision appeared—an eagle soaring, wings beating against a twilight sky painted in gold and crimson. She heard its cry, and saw it joined by another. Together, they wheeled and danced, unchained and eternal, bound by a love that defied even death.

"You are me… I am you…" she murmured through her sobs.

At that very instant, in the cage, the Thunder Bird collapsed as well—its great body trembling, as if in death. The Minotaur froze.

"Alecto! What's happening? What's wrong with the Thunder Bird?" he screamed.

Alecto and her sisters stepped closer to the cage.

"I don't know, master. It looks like… it's dying."

"What?!" roared the Minotaur, stricken with fury.

He rushed to the cage, grabbing the bars, shaking them violently. Hades, still standing on his throne's balcony, did not move.

"Don't die! You cursed bird—don't die on me!"

And then, from Athanor's body, a light emerged. Crimson at first, it flared outward like a radiant tide. Next to him, Anna's spirit began to dissolve, her own violet aura rising and mingling with his.

All eyes were fixed on the scene, stunned. Then, in a burst of brilliance, their two souls fused—Athanor's body and Anna's shade vanishing in a shimmer of light.

"What... what is this...?" the Minotaur stammered.

A single halo of purplish light took shape, hovering above the arena. Such beauty, such divine presence—it radiated majesty and sacred strength. Slowly, it glided toward the cage, the Minotaur and the Erinyes staring in silent disbelief.

"What's happening?!" the Minotaur shrieked. "Alecto, do something!"

"What do you want me to do?" she snapped. "You can't fight a halo."

"I think it's... beautiful..." Mégaera whispered, unable to hide her awe.

The halo drifted gently to the lifeless form of the Thunder Bird... and slowly, began to sink into its body. Then—nothing.

The Minotaur, enraged, slammed the cage shut and clutched the bars, his face twisted in fury.

"What is—?"

He never finished the sentence.

A blinding explosion of pure white light burst forth from the bird, dazzling the Minotaur and throwing the Erinyes backward. They stumbled, the rough stone and scattered debris scraping their skin as they fell.

And then... like a miracle...

The Thunder Bird returned to life.

A tremor passed through its ethereal feathers, releasing a warm and radiant energy into the air. It rose to its feet, glowing with golden and silvery light. Sparks danced in the air around it, forming a halo of sacred brilliance.

The scent of ozone—sharp, electric—filled the arena.

Suddenly, it unfurled its massive wings in a single, powerful motion, unleashing a shockwave of searing light that shattered the cage into a thousand shards.

The Minotaur and the Erinyes were thrown to the ground, overwhelmed. The roar of splintering metal, the blinding glow—it was a storm of glory.

The Thunder Bird, resplendent in divine light, rose into the sky. With every wingbeat, golden dust cascaded around it like falling stars. Its flight was silent, majestic, untouchable.

It circled once, then fixed its gaze on Hades—who watched it from his throne, a faint smile playing on his lips. A distant rumble echoed through the stone, like thunder rolling across the heavens.

Then the bird vanished, lightning trailing in its wake.

Still on the ground, the Minotaur howled, his screams of rage reverberating through the coliseum.

"This cage! He wasn't supposed to escape! Hades, you lied to me!"

From his balcony, Hades watched the Thunder Bird soar away, amusement dancing in his eyes as the echo of his laughter mingled with the distant rumble of storm clouds.

"No, Minotaur! It is Zeus—my ever-devious brother—who's fooled me once again…" he declared with a grin. "This was all a trial for the Guardians. Their souls, through their purity, have magnified the Thunder Bird's power… and Zeus knew it would happen! At least this whole story has had the merit of entertaining me! This was their last journey among men," he concluded, still smiling, as he turned and began to walk away from the arena.

Suddenly, a female voice rang out, sharp as lightning through the silence that had returned.

"You knew! You knew, Hades! You suspected your brother was plotting something—again!" the voice cried, livid. "Then why? Why did you let it happen? You deceived me too! You played along with his game! Tell me why!" she screamed.

Hades paused. A sardonic smile curled his lips.

"Because I was bored! Quite simply," he said, erupting into laughter that echoed through the stone. "The Underworld is murderously dull! My brother has far more imagination when it comes to passing the time… And his endless games of deceit amuse me greatly! That's all! Tell him of your displeasure if you must. I, frankly, couldn't care less."

With those words, he vanished into the shadows of his corridor, the sound of his boots on the cold stone fading. His laughter continued to bounce off the walls, a ghostly echo that refused to die. The voice said no more. She, too, fell silent.

Down in the arena, the Minotaur collapsed to his knees. Mad with rage, he slammed his fists into the ground again and again, each strike shattering the stone beneath him.

"No, no, no, NO!" he screamed, his voice monstrous. "Zeus! I curse you! I curse you!"

As he raged, his features twisted in unbearable agony. Slowly, he reverted to the monstrous form he was doomed to inhabit for all eternity.

The Erinyes, terrified by the scene, slinked back into the growing darkness. One by one, the torches sputtered out, until the arena lay in utter blackness. Only the Minotaur's hellfire eyes remained—twin coals glowing with hatred in the night.

\*\*\*

Far from the arena and the depths of the Underworld, in Arvernian lands near the hut of the Guardians, a great eagle dropped from the sky, its lifeless body landing heavily in the grass. The surrounding forest whispered with birdsong and the rustle of leaves in the wind. A gloved hand reached down and gently gathered the fallen bird. Divinix, his gaze sharp as ever, studied the creature with a quiet smile. Without a word, he stepped into the dense forest, the rustling of foliage and snapping of branches marking his departure.

\*\*\*

Meanwhile, before the Gates of the Underworld, the darkness thickened, wrapping the shore in a suffocating shroud. My companions and I were spent—our backs to the fetid swamp, our strength all but gone. The stench of stagnant water and sulfur clung to the air. Only I, Smérix, remained standing with Alexix, Taranatos, Paritos, and Lugotorix. All the others had fallen, their lifeless bodies strewn across the blood-soaked mud. We were surrounded, escape a fading dream.

Stéropès, in one final act of heroism, wrestled with the last head of the Cerberus. With all the might in his colossal frame, he clenched the monstrous neck, resisting its snapping jaws.

The beast's jawbones cracked under his grip, emitting a grotesque, grinding wail. But then—the third head awoke. Despair struck deeper than any wound. Roars and screams filled the air, mingling with the hot scent of blood and sweat.

As we braced for the end, a blinding light burst forth from the Gates of Hell. Thunder rolled, lightning tore the sky apart, and bolts of pure wrath struck our enemies with devastating force. The brightness cut through the gloom, casting wild shadows. Our enemies reeled—shrieking, disoriented—as a path to freedom tore open.

Stéropès, still locked in battle with the beast, screamed with pain and fury, the monster's fangs now buried in his throat.

"GO! Run!" he bellowed, his voice a thunderclap of sacrifice.

We hesitated. The sight of him broke our hearts, but I spoke, my voice trembling with grief.

"We must go. There's nothing more we can do for him. The Thunder Bird is free. Athanor has fulfilled his destiny," I said, my throat tight.

Taranatos's face was twisted in anguish.

"Where is he? We must wait for him!"

"No. He won't return, my friend. Let's flee this cursed place," I answered firmly.

Lugotorix slipped Paritos's arm over his shoulders, supporting him as he staggered forward.

"Come, my friend. You will live. I swear it," he vowed, his voice fierce with loyalty.

Without another word—but with hearts leaden—we threw ourselves into the foul waters of the Styx, wading through its freezing blackness to escape that accursed land. Alexix and Taranatos led the way. The water bit into our skin like ice, every step a trial.

For the rest of our days, we would be haunted by the

image of Stéropès… torn apart before our eyes.

Even as the beast devoured him, he never let go. Not until the last.

In his final breath, he saw us vanish beyond the threshold, protected by the light of the Thunder Bird. A smile touched his bloodied lips.

"I'm coming… my brothers. At last…" he murmured before dying with a smile.

We ran breathlessly, the fury of the Underworld clawing at our heels. Above us, the Thunder Bird soared through the air, its golden feathers shimmering with every crack of lightning. Each beat of its wings seemed to summon the very elements, sweeping away our pursuers in a whirlwind of wind and brilliance.

At that moment, the sheer majesty and might of the Thunder Bird struck me more deeply than anything before. It was as if all the grandeur of the ancient gods had been distilled into this mythical creature, reminding us, humble mortals, that hope can still blaze even in the blackest of shadows. In a deafening roar of thunder and light, the Thunder Bird brought the tunnel behind us crashing down. The enemy could no longer reach us. Gasping, spent, we finally slowed our pace, beginning the long ascent that would lead us back into the light of day.

Later, as we trudged through the darkness of the immense underground passages, a thought pierced my weary mind: Athanor and Anna had given their lives for this moment. Their love and their courage had transcended death, granting the Thunder Bird a second chance…

A long climb awaited us. Every step through those steep, oppressive tunnels was a torment. Our legs felt like lead, our wounds screamed, but each footfall was charged with hope—the very essence of survival. The yearning to reach the world above lent strength to limbs near breaking.

After long, endless hours, we finally emerged from the darkness, breathing the open air with a renewed, desperate intensity. Before us, the steppes stretched out, calm and welcoming, a jarring contrast to the horror we had just left behind. The scent of wildflowers and the rich earth caressed our senses, soothing our bruised spirits.

No more battlefield. No more corpses. No more swarms of death. It had all vanished, swept away by the triumph of light over shadow. Perhaps the gods themselves had chosen to erase every trace of the horror that had unfolded here.

And there he was—the Thunder Bird—awaiting us. He wheeled high above the plains, crying out his joy and his victory. His battle—our battle—was over. The light had prevailed. The darkness would return to its place, buried deep in the bowels of the Earth.

Proud and radiant, wings spread wide, he rose higher still into the heavens, unleashing a triumphant cry that rang out like a hymn of glory. Thunder boomed, lightning crackled. But there was no menace in these celestial sounds—only celebration. This was not destruction—it was the sky's rejoicing, the echo of our wrath transformed into victory… through our friend. Or should I say, our friends.

We had faced the trials. We had stared down death. And love had triumphed. What more powerful image could there be to testify to the beauty and might of love than the very soul of Athanor and Anna reborn in this sacred creature: the Thunder Bird.

Now, my friends live on—forever—in our hearts and in

our legends. They will watch over my people always. Whatever may come, they shall remain the living symbol of love victorious over adversity, of resilience, of unbreakable hope. Two souls, bound by eternal love, will journey through the ages as an enduring example—for all who seek meaning in their brief, flickering lives.

Yes, my friends… there is always hope. Even in trial. Even in grief. Even when all seems lost, the answer lies somewhere—if we only believe.

Taranatos, breathless but unshaken, approached and placed a hand on my shoulder.

"Let's go home," he said. "Let's tell our people what happened here."

I nodded, a new resolve burning within me.

"Yes. And we will honor the memory of our friends. Their sacrifice will not be in vain. We shall sing this tale for generations, so it will never be forgotten."

Alexix, silent until now, finally spoke, his voice heavy with an emotion I had never seen in him.

"They shall be sung of in our legends. Athanor and Anna—the heroes who freed the Thunder Bird. Their story will inspire the generations to come. And our fallen brothers shall be honored with them. No one must ever forget!"

He turned toward the two inseparable friends, Lugotorix and Paritos, who stood with tears brimming in their eyes, shaken by the weight of the moment.

"You two—never forget the bond that unites you. Your friendship is precious," he continued, casting a glance at Taranatos, whose eyes too shimmered with emotion. "It is a sacred bond, not to be broken. And you, Lugotorix… I am proud of you. You'll be a great chief to our clan, and

Paritos will be your wisest counsel. Now come—we have a long road ahead."

With hearts full of pride and emotion, we began our long journey home, under the gaze and protection of our two friends above, who now were one and the same.

As we walked, heading for our Arvernian homeland, I couldn't help but glance back… toward the dark gate to the Underworld, now slowly closing behind us. A thought crossed my mind, a silent tribute:

Even amidst the deepest shadow, light always finds a way.

The tale of Athanor and Anna was shining proof of that truth.

And so, guided by their sacrifice and courage, we moved forward—carrying a new legend. We would keep their memory alive in every word we spoke, in every choice we made. Their heroism would dwell in our deeds.

My friends… let us always remember: courage and love are the true weapons against darkness. And even through the gravest trials, the light of hope and freedom can rise again—illuminated by the sacrifice of those with pure hearts.

# CHAPTER 46
*"The Return of the Heroes"*

Beneath a clear sky, the Arvernian valley stretched out in all its splendor, ringed by towering mountains and split by a glittering river. The mighty beat of an eagle's wings echoed through the crisp morning air, like a symphony composed by nature itself.

The piercing cry of the raptor was soon joined by that of another, and together the two birds wheeled and danced in the azure sky, scattered with white clouds.

Below, the Celtic village stirred in quiet harmony, witness to the eternal rhythms of life. The people—tanners, blacksmiths, merchants, builders—went about their morning tasks with palpable devotion.

As a child dashed across the central square, he suddenly froze and pointed toward the village gates.

"They're here! They're back! Smérix! Our shaman has returned!" he cried out, his voice brimming with excitement.

At the entrance to the village, I appeared, flanked by Alexix, Taranatos, Lugotorix and Paritos. Our faces and clothes bore the scars of battle—filthy, torn, covered in wounds and dust. The trials we had endured seemed etched into our skin and burned into our spirits, the indelible marks of destiny.

The villagers halted their tasks and rushed to meet us. My beloved was there too—she ran toward us, releasing a mix of barks and strange, elated cries, swept up in emotion. I dismounted, every muscle aching, but grateful—grateful to be home at last. I could not help but embrace her. She had so much love to give… and after so much madness, it healed more than I can say.

But the villagers' joy quickly gave way to a quiet unease as they saw we were only five returning. A heavy silence settled over the crowd as we walked through the village, leading our horses.

Above us, the eagles still circled, their cries echoing like a hymn to our fallen brothers. I lifted my gaze, a wistful smile on my lips, thinking of life's fleeting breath and the eternity of memory.

"Work awaits us, my friends," I said, my voice steady, marked with a new sense of purpose.

A voice rose from the crowd, trembling with grief and hope.

"Where are the others?"

We stopped, our mounts growing still. The crowd pressed close around us. Every face reflected the same dread—an aching need to know.

"Our friends have joined the land of our Ancestors," I declared solemnly. "They fought with honor, and because of them, we have triumphed! We saved the Thunder Bird! And tonight, we shall honor their bravery as it deserves to be honored! Tonight, the ale must flow freely!"

Even as I spoke those final words, a smile tugged at my lips. It reminded me that even in death, life must be celebrated.

"Ah… it brings back memories," I added with a nostalgic chuckle, thinking of our dear, ridiculous Arimaspean friends.

My companions shared a knowing grin. They too were recalling that strange, raucous night with those merry, clumsy revelers…

The crowd erupted in cheers, waving whatever they held in their hands as the news spread like wildfire through the village, warming every heart with immeasurable pride. A wave of euphoria pulsed through the gathering, filling the air with newfound energy.

\*\*\*

That night, atop the sacred mountains, Divinix watched the Celtic village below, aglow with the fires of celebration. Beside him, the Thunder Bird stood in majesty upon a great stone, its wings casting off showers of gold and silver into the starlit night, like a divine benediction. Divinix smiled as he watched the flickering lights below, a glint of mischief in his eyes.

"What a wondrous madness it is, this human urge to live so fully, even after so much loss," he thought, deeply moved by the resilience of such fragile beings.

\*\*\*

In the heart of the village, the square pulsed with life. Everywhere, people danced and sang with wild abandon. Flutes, drums, cymbals, and lutes rang through the night, while ale flowed as if from a sacred spring.

The mood was joy, unfiltered and raw—a rebirth after the storm. Laughter rang out as Taranatos recounted his tales. Though half his words were lost in the din, his audience hung on every one. Alexix, ever the curmudgeon, shook his head… but in time, even he was smiling and laughing, caught in the tide of celebration.

Elsewhere, surrounded by flirtatious maidens and cheerful villagers, Lugotorix and Paritos were similarly swept up in the moment, soon dragged into a mad round dance of song and feet.

I had climbed up onto a small dais and looked out over the crowd, a smile of rediscovered joy on my face. I loved this people with all my heart, and to be among them again filled me with a joy beyond words. Who else, I thought with an admittedly overblown pride—who but the Celts could have achieved such feats?

Lost in reverie, my gaze landed on two young adolescents flirting shyly in the midst of the merriment.

"Perhaps the next Guardians…" I murmured to myself, pondering the future generations who would carry on our sacred legacy.

Yes, the task would live on. The tradition must endure. We would continue to bear the duty of guarding the sacred mountains, as long as the Greek god deemed us worthy… Though to my people, it would always be Alisanos, god of the mountain, who required our devotion. And in the end—what does it matter, if the task is just and the heart pure?

A sudden sense of peace swept through me, as though a wave of serenity had spread deep within. Something wondrous was unfolding far from here, in the verdant lands of the Elysian Fields. A vision took shape in my mind with astonishing clarity.

I saw Steropês, our old friend. Beneath a radiant blue sky, he walked slowly through undulating meadows, his face aglow as I had never seen it before. The tall grass brushed gently against his calloused hands as he passed, and the warm breeze tossed his tangled grey mane, carrying with it the delicate scent of poppies and lavender. From the trees nearby came the melodious song of birds, adding a harmony of life to that peaceful scene.

As he neared a solitary cabin in the distance, the clear, rhythmic sound of metal striking metal rang out through the air—coming from a wooden shelter beside the home. There, two giant Cyclopes labored tirelessly—one hammering an anvil, the other pumping an enormous bellows.

Sparks burst with every blow, briefly lighting the shadows of the forge. They looked much like Steropês, save for their distinct hairstyles, each bearing its own soul, its own tale.

One of them spotted Steropês, and with a gesture full of recognition, placed a heavy hand on his brother's shoulder, pointing to the path.

At once, the two giants rushed forward, their thunderous steps shaking the earth beneath them. The joy they radiated was palpable, like a warmth that filled the air. In a burst of laughter and unrestrained delight, the three brothers embraced, their laughter ringing out like a hymn of reunion, illuminating their faces and warming the heart of any who might have witnessed that moment.

What a beautiful vision I had just received! I emerged from what felt like a dream, my heart swelling with joy for our friend. Those images had soothed my soul, gently washing away the painful memories I still carried of him. And now, my spirit was at peace. I was grateful for the ending his story had found…

\*\*\*

At that very moment, atop the sacred mountains that towered over our valley, Divinix smiled, his mischievous gaze turned toward the village below. A cool breeze passed over the summit, carrying the earthy scent of pine and the soft whisper of rustling leaves.

He stood still for a while, breathing in the wild herbs, feeling the chill of stone beneath his bare feet, until slowly, his form began to change.

His face shimmered, shifting shape—first becoming Coléos of Santos, then the old Arimaspe, then the ancient Griffon, then a wolf's head… before finally revealing his true form: the majestic visage of Zeus. His long grey beard and flowing hair streamed in the wind, glowing with such brilliance that the very air around him seemed to warm in response.

Zeus smiled and turned to the Thunder Bird, now perched proudly on his arm, its feathers crackling with soft, static energy.

"It is good to see you again, old friend. Go now—let thunder roll! Let lightning dance and split the skies! But please," he added with a hearty laugh, "try not to soak our dear Celtic friends."

The Thunder Bird took flight under Zeus's watchful eye, his wings beating with the sound of power, rhythm and command.

In that instant, a radiant light appeared beside Zeus. The goddess Hera materialized, wrapped in a jasmine-scented breeze. She did not look pleased—on the contrary, she seemed vexed, annoyed, perhaps furious.

"You tricked us, husband. Clever, as always," she said coldly, her voice sharp as an arrowhead.

"Oh come now, my beloved," Zeus replied with playful delight, "if I didn't love you so much, I wouldn't know you so well. You and my brother—so very predictable… Come, let's return to Olympus."

"And the bird?" Hera asked, her gaze narrowing.

"Look at him—he is freedom incarnate. He'll return when he chooses. It is not for us to command him, my dear—it's he who chooses. Not even I can claim ownership. Do you truly believe I entrusted him with that power without purpose?" he said, smiling broadly, his eyes twinkling with mischief. "Come now. Let the Celts celebrate the legend of the Thunder Bird."

He held out a hand, and she took it with a smile.

"One day," she said, "I shall have my revenge. I'll be the one to trick you."

She began to transform before his amused gaze—first into a shrieking, grimacing Kobalos, then into the handmaiden of the Arimaspean queen, bowing low before Zeus. At last, she assumed the form of the beautiful White Shamaness of the Scythian plains.

Zeus burst into laughter as Hera returned to her true shape.

"You forgot the Centaurs…"

"I didn't need to shapeshift for them. They're mad about me!" she grinned. "All I had to do was make them drink… just a little."

"You went a bit far with those poor fools," Zeus chuckled, taking her hand once more.

"Come, let's go home. You can tell me all your heroic tales… in bed, my love."

They laughed heartily, and together vanished into the starlit sky, while above the village, the Thunder Bird circled wide and proud.

\*\*\*

At first, the villagers watched with awe, uncertain, their revelry halted by the sight. The music fell silent. The moment belonged to the magic.

The Thunder Bird traced glowing patterns in the heavens, dazzling all below. Lightning lit the sky in bursts of brilliance, the scent of ozone thick in the air. Thunder rolled, vibrating through every chest, and clouds churned like sleeping giants. The first drops of rain brushed their skin—but true to promise, the storm never fell. Above them, the stars shone brightly, unmarred.

"The gods thank you, my friends," I cried with joy. "Drink! Dance! And most of all—make babies tonight! Our fallen must be reborn!"

My words, full of wisdom and jest, echoed through the square like a vibrant hymn of life and renewal. The villagers raised their mugs, cheering wildly. The music resumed, and the feast came back to life, while the Thunder Bird soared above, painting the sky with light. Rain fell all around the village—but not within. As though heaven itself wished to bless, but not disturb, their celebration.

The Thunder Bird vanished into the clouds, thunder rumbling after him, lightning flashing like celestial fire.

And the revelry continued, alight with a newfound energy, as the village rejoiced in life, in love, and in the eternal journey of souls.

And so, my friends… thus ends this incredible tale. I hope it stirred your hearts, and spoke to your spirit.

Never forget: close your eyes now and then—open your mind. Perhaps the encounters along your path are no mere coincidence. Perhaps the world around you still speaks—perhaps it guides you to your destiny.

We are all part of something far greater than ourselves. Even the gods in this story, reflections of our fears and hopes, are but echoes of "She who is all and in all."

And above all, remember this:

"All that is… All that surrounds us… has meaning. It is yours to discover."


THE END.

# SMÉRIX'S CONCLUSION

My dear fellow travelers, it is with a heart full of gratitude that I invite you to close this book—not as an ending, but as a beginning anew.

The story I have told you is not only that of Athanor and Anna, nor solely that of proud Celts and mighty gods. Above all, it is the tale of our world—its mysteries, and the forces that shape us, often unseen, but always present. Every breath of wind, every crack of thunder, every birdsong carries within it a story—an ancient truth that humankind has sometimes forgotten.

Our heroes have walked a path strewn with trials, doubts, and dangers, but they have also discovered that the truest quest for meaning lies deep within ourselves. They have learned that love, friendship, and sacrifice can overcome even the darkest of nights. That the light of hope may shine, even in the deepest shadows. Their brave souls show us that true strength is not only in the battles we fight against visible foes, but in the silent struggles we endure against our own fears and uncertainties.

This tale, my friends, is but the first step on a far greater journey—a quest that will carry us deeper still, into the lands of our ancestors, where the breath of life and the echoes of the gods entwine. What you have seen and heard here are only fragments of a greater whole. A whole that, perhaps, you may begin to glimpse in the stories yet to come.

Remember, Nature in her boundless wisdom never reveals all her secrets at once. She prefers to whisper them to those who listen with the heart, not with the ears. She leaves behind traces, signs, and omens for those who are ready to read them—and to understand. For, my friends, every stone, every leaf, every star holds within it a truth— an ancient murmur waiting to be heard.

I am but a humble messenger, a storyteller lending my voice to the tales that have marked my path and those entrusted to me by the spirits of earth and sky. I invite you to keep your mind open, and your soul ready, for what lies ahead. For the tale of Athanor and Anna is but a single thread in the great tapestry of our existence—one echo among many in the eternal song of life.

May these stories live on in you—nourishing your thoughts and rekindling the flame of curiosity and courage within your hearts. We are one with the world that surrounds us, and every encounter, every challenge, every dream is a part of our great quest for meaning.

As you close this book, remember that your own story is still being written. Be strong. Be brave. And never forget to listen to the whispers of the wind and the tales the world yearns to share with you. For in the end, it is not the destination that matters, but the journey itself.

Until we meet again for another tale, may you walk in peace along the path that is yours.

I leave you now—but always remember: the whispers of the ancients still live within you. Hold this story in your heart, share it, and let it guide you in your own quests for meaning, resilience, and love.

For in the end… is that not the very essence of our existence?

# ABOUT THE AUTHOR

First of all, allow me to thank you for journeying through these pages to the very end. I hope this story has moved you, and that—even if only for a short time—it transported you into my world. Let me introduce myself: I am a humble, self-taught scribe, deeply passionate about history and the wisdom it has to offer.

I believe that sometimes, we must look to the past in order to better understand our present—and our place in the vastness of the universe. Through this novel, my intention was to draw from the deep well of ancient beliefs and traditions, and to bring forth a message that is both timeless and universal.

The peoples you met along the way—Celts, Greeks, Cimmerians, Scythians—all shared an intimate connection with the forces of nature. Their gods, myths, and legends were manifestations of this sacred bond with the world around them. Their beliefs were not merely superstition, but a quest for meaning—a way to find one's rightful place within the great web of life.

To them, nature was not a resource to be used, but a living presence—omnipresent and powerful—a force with which they communicated through the elements and their deities. "She who is all and in all," whatever name they gave her, was the ever-present sacred energy honored in myriad forms.

Today, in our modern world, that sacred bond has faded. We often sense nature's presence only when it disrupts us or frightens us. The old voices that once helped us understand her have grown silent. And so nature, neglected and misunderstood, now speaks through violent signs—storms, earthquakes, climate shifts… cries of distress we can no longer ignore.

Athanor: The Legend of the Thunder Eagle is an invitation to reconnect with that lost link, to relearn how to listen to the murmurs of nature. It is the very heart of this story—a living force we must learn once more to honor and respect.

I hope this tale has touched you. I hope it inspires you to return for the next stories told by Smérix, the old shaman, who—through me—will continue to share tales from another time.

The next adventure will delve into the extraordinary life of Lygdamis, one of the last kings of Cimmeria, and his fierce struggle to save his people. Then will come the unforgettable saga of Amage, the Amazon queen, whose story brings this series to a close by exploring deeper realms of Greek mythology—and the fading connection between humankind and the natural world.

If this journey stirred something within you, don't hesitate to share it, and please consider leaving a review on Amazon. Your feedback means everything. Every comment is precious—and it encourages both Smérix and me to keep offering you a unique perspective on this world of ours.

To follow the next chapters and discover exclusive content, you can also find me on Instagram and YouTube under the name @ThierryJoubertAuteur, or on Facebook at Thierry Joubert Auteur.

To leave a comment or connect more directly, simply scan this QR code:

A heartfelt thank you—and I hope to meet you again soon for new adventures

Printed in Dunstable, United Kingdom